FLIGHT TO FACILIS

Flight to Facilis

The Waiz Chronicles
Book Two

Mikelyn H. Bolden

Solletico Books

Flight To Facilis
Copyright © 2014 by Mikelyn Bolden. All rights reserved.

This book is available in hardback, paperback and ebook formats. For more information visit **www.mikelynbolden.com**

Bolden, Mikelyn H.
The Waiz Chronicles Book Two: Flight To Facilis

Cover design by Blair Thompson

ISBN 13: 978-0-9909993-0-0
ISBN 10: 0-9909993-0-0

To my beloved Miss Josephine.
Thank you for choosing to share your light with me.

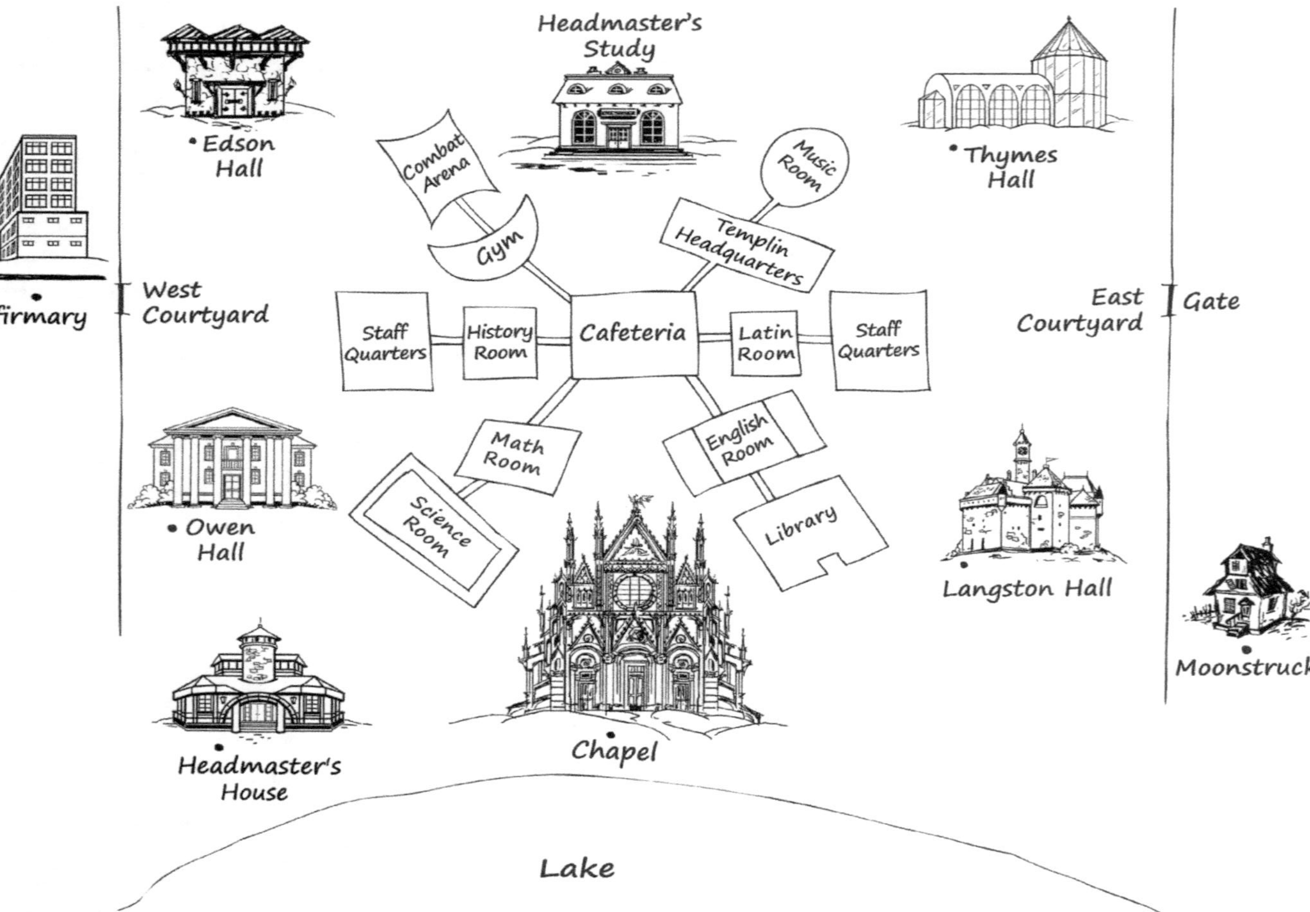

Infirmary
West Courtyard
Edson Hall
Headmaster's Study
Combat Arena
Gym
Music Room
Templin Headquarters
Thymes Hall
East Courtyard
Gate
Staff Quarters
History Room
Cafeteria
Latin Room
Staff Quarters
Owen Hall
Math Room
Science Room
English Room
Library
Langston Hall
Moonstruck
Headmaster's House
Chapel
Lake

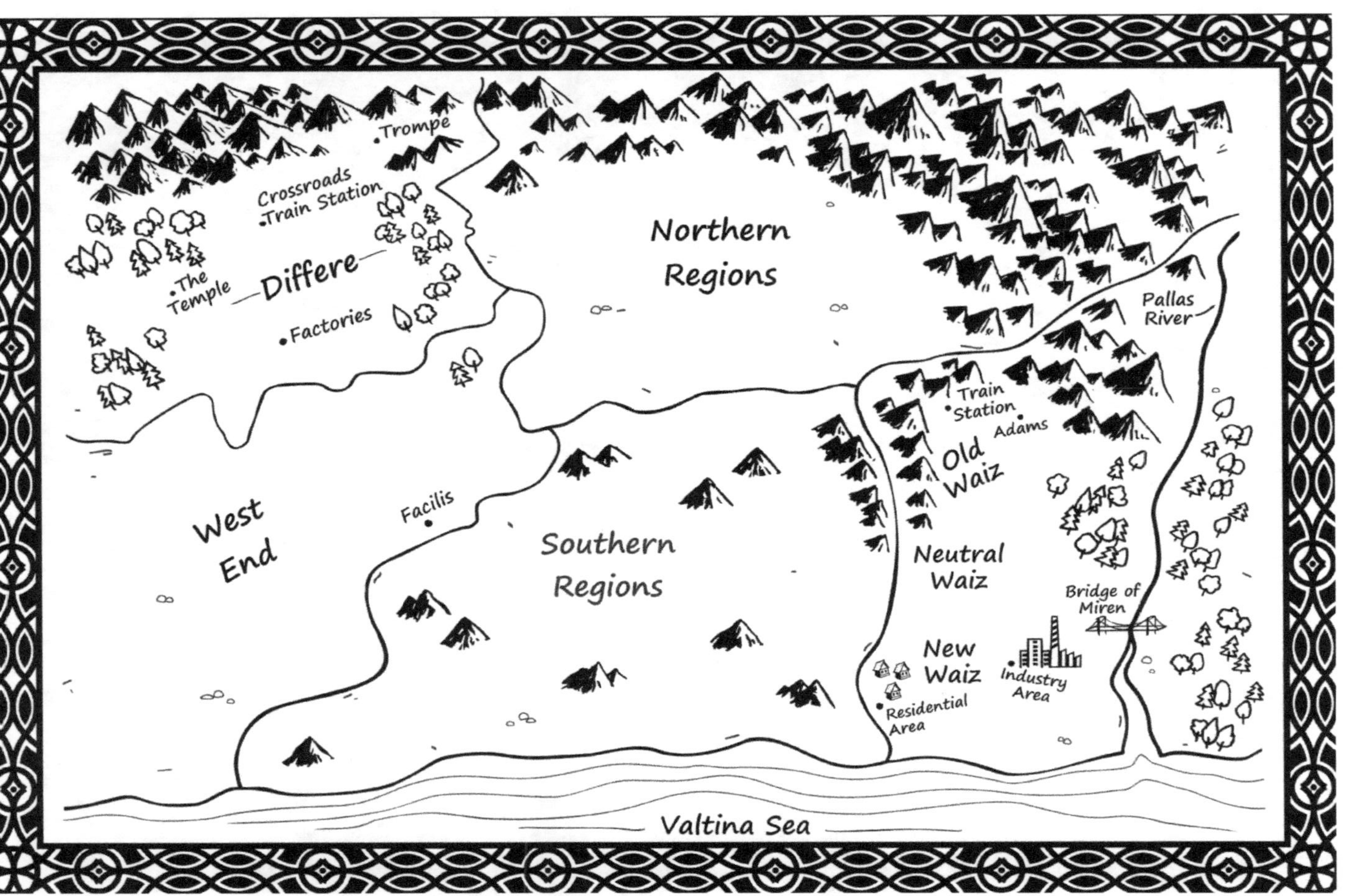

Trompe
Crossroads
Train Station
Northern Regions
The Temple
Differe
Factories
Pallas River
Train Station
Adams
Old Waiz
West End
Facilis
Southern Regions
Neutral Waiz
Bridge of Miren
New Waiz
Industry Area
Residential Area
Valtina Sea

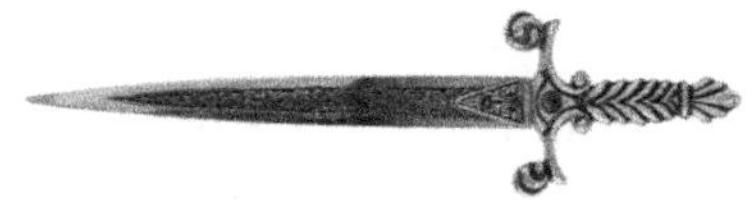

Pronunciation and Terms Guide

Barique: (Ba-reek) Weapon used by those following the Majestic.

Bridge of Miren: (Mer – in) Waiz landmark serving as the dividing line between Old and New Waiz.

Caychura: (Cay – chur – uh) Legendary places used to connect with the Majestic's presence and power.

Differe: (Di – fear) Region of indifference containing The Temple of Differe School, Trompè, city of Differe, and factories. It is snowy, dark and resistant to change.

Facilis: (Fuh – sil – lus) Politically neutral city located in the West End.

Ferox: (Fair – ox) A new task force in New Waiz.

Galanne: (Guh – lan) Area in the Northern Regions meaning "frozen."

Kalona: (Kuh – lone – uh) Village communities located throughout Old Waiz.

Majestic: Old Waiz's Deity.

Moonstruck: Old building on the temple grounds with its original purpose being to house unruly students.

Norrac: (Nore – rack) Vehicle used in Old Waiz made from part-wagon and part-carriage.

The Temple of Differe School: Most prestigious facility in all Differe with its reformatory principles holding immeasurable power over students and Differe's politics.

Templins: Differe's elite regiment in control of security and the Diffierian Army.

Teneh: (Tin – ay) Object used to pay homage to the Majestic.

Trompè: (Trom – pay) Medical facility in Northern Differe.

Rhydid: (Rye – did) Weapon used by those following the Majestic.

Waiz: (Wise) Region of wisdom containing traditional Old Waiz in the north and progressive New Waiz in the south. It is warm, colorful and political.

Watchmen: The Patrolling officers in New Waiz.

CHAPTER 1

PAUL AWAKENED TO the sound of a man's screams. By the time he reached his master's room Philip was already inside with his weapon drawn. He nodded to Paul, indicating he saw nothing. Paul rushed to his master's side. The middle-aged man sat on the edge of the bed, his clothes soaked through with sweat.

"Master, some water." Paul grabbed the water pitcher and gently handed the man his glass.

The man drank the full cup before he spoke. "Thank you, Paul." He handed the glass back to him then turned to Philip. "I'm sorry I disturbed you both." He gripped his mostly gray hair and shook his head in frustration.

Paul patted the man's shoulder reassuringly. "It's no bother, Master. It's almost time to rise. Listen." The three paused to hear the roosters crowing.

"Would you like some more rest, Master?" Philip gestured to the easy chair.

The man waved his sun-kissed hands. "No. Please, help me get dressed. Some breakfast please." He nodded to Paul.

Paul shot Philip a tentative glance, then walked into the hallway in search of breakfast. As he wandered through the halls and down the stairs of Reagan Manor, he worried for his master. He and Philip had begun serving the man at the manor nearly ten years ago. At that time Master Reagan had been younger, good-humored, and appeared to have the strength of an ox. He and

Philip even had difficulty keeping pace with the man once they started working in the fields alongside him. The manor and its surrounding lands, Paul's favorite in all the Southern Regions, were renowned for their abundant harvest and overall beauty. His master had made a good life for himself, and yet . . . each servant knew the man held a deep and quiet sadness inside him. For though it seemed none matched him in wealth, he had no one to share his good fortune with. *Maybe it's the loneliness that's done him in.* Paul realized it was the third time this week his master had encountered something foul in the night. Two years prior to this harvest season something dark and oppressive had settled on the man. He seemed to age overnight—his wrinkles deeper, hair grayer, eyes droopier. Paul and Philip had tried to cheer him; they saw him not only as their master but a father figure as well. The cousins had dedicated their lives in grateful service to this man who had taken them in as orphans.

As Paul set up the breakfast tray he wished there was something he could do to make his master feel more at ease. The maids had not set up the dining room yet, so he hurried inside before his master arrived to draw back the thick, floral drapes and set out the breakfast silver. The sun was just beginning to rise over the mountains. *Good. He needs to see the light.*

Paul soon heard his master's sighs and shuffling feet. "Come, Master, see the fields this morning." Paul led him to the window. "Look, you have fields of gold." He was delighted to see the man smile as he took in the wheat fields glowing in the sun's morning light.

He squinted at the view. "Yes, I see."

The two gazed across the vast fields in front of the manor ready for harvest. The orchards and vineyards stood behind the manor, so they were able to observe the wheat, cotton, and sugarcane fields with an unobstructed view. The fields stretched out for miles until met by the green mountain hills in the distance.

"And look at your wildflowers over here—they're saying 'good morning, Sir.'" Paul walked to the opposite window.

The man inhaled deeply as his brown eyes surveyed the brightly colored knee-high blooms surrounding the front of the manor. "And what do my trees say today, Paul?" He pointed to the rows of cypress trees that lined the private drive.

"That all will be well." Paul hoped in his heart these words were true.

The man nodded and pursed his chapped lips. "Yes, they would say that for they are pointed west, but look behind them."

Paul saw a host of dark clouds forming near the mountain range. "Rain's no harm, Master." *Focus on the light. We must get your eyes off the darkness.*

"Rain, no, but a storm, yes." The man slouched forward as his face began clouding over.

"Master, breakfast." Paul pulled on his burly arm in an attempt to distract him, but the man didn't budge.

Philip cleared his throat from across the room and shot his cousin a forceful look.

I'm trying, okay? What do you want me to do? Paul grabbed a spoon from the table and placed it in his master's hand.

"Oh, yes, yes." Master Reagan nodded then murmured on under his breath.

Paul hated the fog he saw in the man's eyes. The twinkle he had known for years was now gone. "Master? Are you trying to tell me something?"

"Fields of gold you say? I am a rich man."

Paul heard the sadness in his voice and quickly tried to bring his master back to reality. "Indeed, and you need not worry about your trees. They have withstood storms and can do so again."

The man nodded to Paul then turned toward the green pillars again as if to check on them one more time before heading to the table.

As Paul lightly tugged at the man's arm again, Master Reagan jerked upright. He thrust his hand across Paul's chest, knocking him against the window.

Paul searched his face. "What is it, Master?"

"A message . . . a messenger!" The man rushed through the dining room into the nearest hallway.

"Master!" Paul panicked as he ran after the man. *He's finally lost it.* He raced through the manor after him until the man broke into a full sprint out the door. Paul stopped to catch his breath at the bottom of the stone steps that led onto the sandy drive. He felt something wet drop on his head; the rain was beginning to fall. "Master!" Paul started the chase again, now accompanied by Philip.

Philip held the man's shoes in his hands. "Your feet are bare! And, it's raining! Come back, Master! You—Paul, look!" Philip slammed his hand into Paul's chest.

Both stopped, as Paul rubbed the tender spot. "Did you *have* to do that? What is it?"

"Master was right. Look! There's a rider." Philip gestured to a figure barreling down the drive. "Come on! And . . . man up." He pounded Paul's chest again then rushed past him.

"Ow! Really? Again?" Paul hurried behind him, the rain now misting. Though Master Reagan was well ahead of the cousins, Paul made out the rider's signal to his horse, "Whoa!"

"News! You have news!" His master yell as the rider jumped down from the horse and ran toward the man.

"Yes, Sir!" the rider gasped as he held out a satchel. "I have news about your son."

Joel's heart pounded as Augustine's eyes fluttered, and he gently shook her awake. "Wake up!"

"Wha-what's going on?"

He looked over at the window again. "The train's stopped."

"Is that all?" She started to roll back over.

"Augustine, wake up! We've been stopped for nearly an hour."

She sat up quickly. "What's wrong?"

"I don't know. I just have a bad feeling." He carefully lifted the window shade for the tenth time in the past hour. "They've been unloading and reloading the same stuff—like they're searching for something."

Augustine moved next to him at the window. "I-I don't think we have anything Waiz would want. Do you think it's the Green Cloaks?"

Joel ran his fingers through his auburn hair and noticed Augustine studying his face. He knew it was still pretty bruised up from the night before— the night he escaped from Differe . . . again. "Any better?"

"Some." She reached out toward one of his cuts then jumped as a loud horn blew outside their window. The two covered their ears as the train's PA system started up with a screech.

"All passengers off! All passengers are commanded off this train for inspection by order of His Majesty, Master Dark!"

"His Majesty? Who does he think—"

"Joel, what are we going to do? It's the Templins! Why are they involved with a Waiz train?" Augustine grabbed his wool cap and started piling her hair on top of her head to disguise herself as a boy for the second time in twenty-four hours.

Joel clenched his fists in anger and frustration as he heard compartment doors open and shut around them. He wondered why the Templins, the headmaster's elite followers, were hunting a Waiz train. *We can't get off but we can't stay on . . . or, at least I can't.* He looked over at Augustine and knew what he had to do. "Augustine, you can get off." His words were so quiet he wasn't sure if she heard him at first. "Augustine, you're a boy they're not looking for—they think it's me and a girl. The guy you chained to the wall in Moonstruck will have told them that."

Her face crumpled in dismay. "No! I'm not leaving you!"

He knew her tone wasn't defiant—it was fearful. He took her hands. "This is where you keep your promise. Remember? You promised to get away even if I couldn't . . . I'm sorry. You've got to take your rhydid to Sebastian . . . I'll be fine. Anyway, one of us has a much better chance of not getting caught versus two of us." He shrugged nonchalantly attempting to hide the explosive pressure he felt in his heart. "Come on, hide your rhydid under your clothes. Get your backpack. Is there anything in there we need to get rid of . . . anything that would be suspicious?"

Augustine trembled as she lifted the backpack, knowing Joel's temple file was stashed inside. She had stolen it from Moonstruck the night before. *What should I do?* Sebastian lay heavy on her mind, but she hated the thought of leaving Joel, the one who had led her every step of this journey. She hated the thought of leading herself and being alone even more. She told herself not to cry as Joel straightened the cap on her head.

"Do I look like a boy?" She looked intently into his face as she hid the rhydid dagger under her top layer of clothing.

His eyes darted toward the door. "A pretty one, so keep your head down."

The horn blew again. The blaring reminder let her know it was time to leave the train . . . *without him.* "What will you do?"

"Try to stay free."

Something in his voice made her turn back and hug him. "Thank you. Thank you for everything. I don't deserve it."

He quickly pushed her away. "Don't worry about it, and don't worry about me."

She nodded but knew inside that she would worry about him until he was safely back in Waiz with her. She felt him grab her fingers after she opened the door and smiled as he swung their hands back and forth just as he had in the dungeon of Moonstruck.

"Go show 'em what you're made of."

The stunning brunette cautiously marched through the train corridor and made her way to the exit. She kept her head low and tugged her cap even lower to cover her eyes. Her heart raced as she neared the exit, the image of Joel hiding back in the compartment haunting her thoughts. She was surprised at his terse response to her hug and wondered if she shouldn't have let her guard down in that way. Uncertainty mixed with jealousy crept in as she thought about how he had looked at Isabelle and reached out for her the night before.

The blonde was small, graceful, and beautiful beyond words . . . *And, she can sing.* Of course Joel would want her. She couldn't blame him or any other boy for being enchanted by the striking songbird. Augustine knew comparing herself to another rarely brought peace of mind, but she hadn't been able to forget what the burly boy she'd imprisoned in Moonstruck had said to Joel. It had something to do with Joel writing about Isabelle in his journal. Why had Isabelle been "bait?" Had Joel loved her? Did he still love her? And, if he still loved her, why did he leave her there?

"I can answer that," Augustine whispered as she opened the door to step off the train. *Me. It was my fault.* She knew after her outburst on the trail—

attacking Isabelle—that Joel had lost all confidence in her. Though her head was already low, her countenance fell as she recalled the moment.

A loud speaker interrupted her thoughts. "This train will be delayed indefinitely. If you have any information regarding two teenage boys traveling alone, you are to report to the Temple Guard immediately. Please escort your belongings to the nearest train station in order to secure a connecting train to Waiz."

Two boys? Augustine paused on the last step as she pondered the announcement. *Two boys!* She hastily retreated up the steps back into the train. She pushed into the next train car, leading her further from Joel, and searched frantically among the empty compartments for a place to hide. The dining car looked promising so she ducked into the small pantry. She quickly removed her hat, loosened the hair piled on top of her head, and studied her reflection in front of a pot hanging on the wall. She fiddled with her thick, wavy locks then froze. From somewhere in the room, a man cleared his throat.

"So, you're a girl."

CHAPTER 2

AUGUSTINE KNOCKED DOWN a rack of spices as she struggled against her attacker. The large hands released her after she landed on the floor amidst the tin containers. She brushed off the tiny specks now covering her clothing and hair and scrambled to her feet. "Ah-choo!"

"Bless you, Dear."

Augustine looked up at the voice in shock.

"Yes, it's just me." The ticket master, the man who had given her and Joel their rhydid sheaths, held out his hand in response to her stare. "Sorry, I didn't mean to scare you."

Augustine couldn't help thinking of Mr. Rutherford when the man called her "dear" and wondered if this man would be as helpful as the shopkeeper. He was even short and round like Mr. Rutherford, yet had a head full of brown hair. She cautiously stared at his trim goatee then focused on the black glasses framing his dark eyes.

He broke the silence after she had been on her feet a few moments. "What's your plan?"

Augustine shrugged, still too frightened to speak.

"Where's the other young man? Or is *he* a 'he'?"

She wrung her hands nervously. "*He's* back in our compartment. He . . . we thought the Templins were looking for a boy and a girl. He sent me off the train in disguise to keep me safe."

"Well, considering the announcement, you're not safe as a boy anymore. Hmm . . . ."

Augustine shuddered as the man paused to look her over then moved forward to unbutton her coat.

"It's all right. Just seeing if you hid the dagger."

"Why do they want me, Sir?"

"Because you took something from them, or more importantly, from the headmaster. To keep you safe, I have to get you off this train. Do you trust me?"

Augustine looked into his eyes and bit her lip. She thought about how she and Joel had followed the man through the woods to find this train. He had given them rhydid sheaths, commended them for their efforts, and had yet to give them up to the Templins. She nodded in confidence. "Yes."

"All right, hurry and put this on. Leave your coat in the closet."

Augustine obediently changed into a waitressing uniform, yet hoped she wouldn't leave the train in such a thin garment. After she was dressed the man shoved a grocery bag against her chest and slid a cloth bag onto his shoulder.

"Keep your head down and follow me. We'll stop at your compartment to see if your friend is still inside."

The two moved quickly through the corridor and into the next train car. Augustine tried not to shiver as the cold air from outside poured in from the open exits. Her heart throbbed when she saw the Templins roughly rummaging through the compartments in front of her. She sucked in her breath when two guards stopped them.

"Ho! All passengers have been ordered off the train." The sturdy Templin blocked their path.

"We are not passengers. We serve in the dining car. We were instructed to retrieve goods from the supply car in order to prepare lunch for your troop."

Augustine hid her face behind the grocery bag as they awaited the Templin's response.

"Ah, very good. Continue on."

When they reached the last compartment, the two paused and Augustine gasped. The seats were shredded, the overhead bins torn open, and even the shades had been ripped down. *Oh, what happened? Is he okay? Did they get him?*

She trembled at the thought of Joel being caught. He had been free and, if not for her, would have stayed free. He had risked his freedom, and after seeing him get physically beaten in Moonstruck she was convinced he had also risked his life. She held back tears. "Oh, please be okay. Please be okay, Joel."

The man stopped at the end of the last passenger car to unlock the door that led to the supply cars. She was surprised when he rushed her through the food car and into the luggage car. He looked over the trunk labels carefully, then focused on one that had the initials "N.W." Augustine soon saw the owner's name.

"Madame Bontecou!" She squatted down near the enormous piece of luggage as the man pulled a crow bar loose from behind a stack of trunks.

"You know the woman?"

"Yes. She gave us a tour of the Old Waiz Museum. I—" Augustine stopped when she noticed he was about to open the trunk. "Wait, uh . . . I'm— I'm pretty sure I won't be able to fit into any of her clothes." She didn't want to be rude, but the lady was the biggest person she'd ever seen.

The man laughed as he pried open the trunk. "Don't worry, these aren't her personal trunks. She has a clothing store in New Waiz."

Augustine was delighted to find the trunk full of colorful items in her size.

"Here, change into one of these and pack this rolling bag with extra clothes. And listen, you can't just wear the clothes, Dear . . . you must also play the part. No woman wearing these kinds of clothes would depart a train—or anywhere else for that matter—without any luggage. Wouldn't you agree?" He smirked when she didn't seem to understand.

Augustine had never had more than a few things in her wardrobe. She had always wanted more, of course, but the cost made the desire impossible. As she dug deeper into the trunk, finding frivolous item after item, she eventually understood the man. "It's Augustine, Sir. And, yes, I would imagine not."

"Remember—think disguise. I'll leave you to change. I need to get a few things from the food car."

Augustine couldn't believe her eyes. The items ranged from soft and silky, to woven and taut. She ran her fingers over the bright fabrics then hurried to change. Much to her chagrin, there weren't any pants among the clothes, so she settled on an orange lambskin coat and matching skirt. She tucked a tightly knit navy crewneck underneath and tugged a pair of tall black boots over her tights. Without glancing at the other clothes, she stuffed a wad of them into the luggage bag.

The ticket master soon returned and nodded at her in approval. "Very good, but I think we should top it off." He touched her head then pulled a brown hat with a burnt orange feather from the trunk.

"Brown, black, navy, orange . . . I don't really match, Sir."

"That's exactly the point. And here are two more bags. You'll need to empty your backpack in here. It doesn't match your attire." He stroked his chin as he pointed to her new bag. "You trade out while I paint your face."

"The women in New Waiz aren't painted." She was already dressed outside of her comfort zone; makeup seemed a bit too far.

"Not exactly, no. But we need you in disguise. The makeup will help you look older."

"Oh." Augustine settled back down and emptied the backpack. She slid Joel's file inside the bag while the man rummaged through the makeup kit.

"Open," he commanded as he ran a mascara wand over her eyelashes. "Augustine, listen carefully. You are from New Waiz. You are a fashion scout for Madame Bontecou. You travel the regions in search of fresh ideas and future models. Your personality is arrogant, inconsiderate, girly, whiny, and, well, you're pretty much dumber than dirt."

She pulled away from him in disgust and even opened her mouth to refuse, but the man stopped her.

"Uh-uh. This is to keep you safe, and your rhydid." He pulled her back and brushed her cheeks with something.

"What's my name?" She sighed, knowing it would be as terrible as the persona.

"Honey Paisley . . . like it?" He winked at her before stuffing some paper sacks of food into the other tweed bag.

"It's worse than I thought." She pursed her lips, wondering if she had any choice in the matter. "How old am I?"

"That *you* can choose."

"Twenty-one."

"Sounds perfect. Now, think like Honey and tell me why you are just getting off this train."

Augustine shoved her pride and mustered her best doe-eyed expression. "But, officer, I couldn't leave such high-end items in the luggage car. The train's been stopped for over an hour, which means my fabrics were being exposed to the ungodly frozen temperatures of this region. Who knows how long you would've let them sit here before they got to Waiz?"

Her new ally grinned. "That'll do just fine."

Chapter 3

AUGUSTINE FOUND HER fabricated high-pitched tone almost as irritating as the Templins seemed to.

"Miss, you can't just disobey orders!" The young Templin rubbed his head in frustration.

"I got off the train didn't I?" She stopped to bat her eyes in annoyance. "And, no thanks to you. All those strong hands and I had to lug these bags all by myself. What am I to do now? Hike to the nearest station? Have you even found the boys you were looking for?" Judging by their expressions, she was certain the Templins didn't quite know what to do with her. *I'm starting to enjoy this.*

"Well, the station is not that far away. You could walk—"

"I refuse to leave my bags."

An older guard made a firm move toward her. "Let's see your ticket, then we'll see about transportation."

"Take a good look at this bag." Augustine shoved the enormous tweed purse in his direction. "Do you honestly want me to search for my ticket in this abyss?"

The Templin sighed and stepped back. "I can't help you, Miss. Just follow that trail to the road and maybe you'll be lucky enough to be picked up on your walk to the station."

"Well," Augustine huffed for effect. "Well, I never . . . ." She turned her nose to the air and gathered her bags. "You there, at least help me up the trail."

Her accomplice soon rose up behind her.

"How was that?" She grinned back at him.

"Finest acting I've seen in a while." He grabbed all the bags from her hands.

"Funny, I wasn't even afraid . . . well, until he asked about the ticket. Joel has mine."

"You'll just have to buy another at the station. You can do the same as you did in Differe. Just buy a ticket to Facilis."

His words reassured her as they reached the road. "Right. Well, thank you. I guess this is goodbye . . . Mister . . .?"

"Hubert. Hubert Denby." He bent down and took her hand. "And I should be thanking you. I haven't had the opportunity to help someone in a long time."

She marveled at his words, and he immediately bounded back down the trail.

She hoisted a tweed bag onto each shoulder then began dragging the wheeled luggage bag down the road. She stopped to switch hands then looked around and wondered where she was. *I should've asked Hubert.* The area was cold but not covered in snow like Differe. She looked down to where the train track had to be. *Can't see a thing through these woods. It's—it's just like the others . . . why does every place want to conceal Waiz?*

As Augustine pondered this question she heard a vehicle approaching. She looked down, suddenly feeling embarrassed at how ridiculous she must look—out in the freezing cold, dressed to the nines, and walking down the road with three enormous bags. A shiver went up her spine when an official looking motorcar drove up. The car slowed, and as it came to a stop one of the dark windows rolled down.

"May I be of any help?"

Augustine had expected to see an old Black Cloak, but to her surprise green eyes, a handsome face, and wavy brown locks met her gaze. The face even caused "Honey" to falter in her guise. "Uh, I—yes, please. I'd be so grateful."

"Driver, put her things in the back."

Once inside the plush automobile, Augustine removed her gloves and smoothed her hair, all the while reminding herself that she was Honey Paisley.

"Where are you headed?" The man was old enough to be her father, yet handsome enough to make her heart skip a beat.

"Just to the train station. I, uh, had some transportation difficulties."

"Well, I'm glad to be of service. A pretty little thing like you doesn't need to be walking these roads alone, especially this time of year. The area is populated with bears."

Augustine gasped, and it seemed the man enjoyed her girlish reaction.

"Yes, and well, there are other things out there . . . but, you're safe now. Where will you go once you reach the train station? Would you care for some water?" He offered her a bottle from the container next to his seat.

"Yes, please." She fidgeted trying to remember everything Hubert had told her. "Well, I'm headed to Facilis for research purposes."

"Scientific?"

Augustine blushed underneath all the paint on her face. "No, fashion."

He winked and cast her a grin. "I never would've guessed. What's your name?"

"Honey Paisley."

He stroked his chin before handing her the water. "Hm. Honey, you aren't trying to hide anything beneath all those colors and feathers are you?"

Her stomach churned as she felt the leather strap from the rhydid sheath around her waist. *Is he baiting me?*

His piercing stare commanded the truth for a moment until he broke into laughter, flicking the feather on her hat with his fingers. "I mean, you're such a pretty young lady already, why do you need all this fuss?"

Augustine breathed a sigh of relief. "That's the price of fashion, Sir."

"Oh, call me Talan."

"Talan, where are you headed if I might ask?" Augustine hoped she could change the subject. She was afraid his eyes would tempt her again to share her secrets.

"Oh, well, it's top secret." He motioned to the car and his dark suit. "This official getup is actually legit. I always wanted a job that held some excitement. So, let's just say I help folks get a fair trial in Facilis . . . or, I smuggle them to safety. What is it you want to do? And don't tell me fashion, Honey. I sense you have another dream."

The way her name rolled off his lips gave her both a thrill and scare. "I, well, I suppose if I could do anything I'd like to be a musician . . . maybe teach. I play piano."

"Fine instrument. My son sings in his school choir. He's about your age. How old are you?"

"Twenty-one."

"Oh, you're a bit older than him then. Well, look, here we are." He gestured to the window, and the two were soon saying goodbye.

"Glad to have found you, Honey. Here's my card if you ever need a knight in shining armor again." He turned to leave then leaned back towards her. "Just one more question. The far east side . . . the Waiz Region—it's one of my 'safe' places. Most of the folks I help are desperately trying to get there, and, well, most would prefer never to leave after arriving. I, so . . . I'm curious as to the nature of your 'fashion' research . . . are you perhaps Waizen?"

She clenched her jaw shut.

"I mean, your dark features would lead me to believe you are, but your mannerisms . . . your blue eyes . . . that's Differian." He didn't wait for her to answer before getting back into his car.

As the motorcar rode away she felt remorse about Joel and muddled about the man she'd just encountered. She read his card. "Talan Holt Langston, Head Counselor and Diplomat to the West End." *Hmm, might be nice to have someone like that in your favor.* She slid the card into her bag.

Chapter 4

DURING JOEL'S SECOND flight from The Temple of Differe School, Sarah was forced to help hunt for the "fugitives." Naturally she was sent to search Moonstruck as most of the other professors had rarely set foot in the place where she had once cared for Joel and Isabelle. She hid the sword she'd retrieved from the attic under her cloak then headed down the snowy path. Enough time had passed that she was confident Joel and his new friend would be rounding the frozen lake by now. Night was fading by the time she reached the old house, and a frown spread across her face when she discovered the front entrance appeared dismantled. She had hoped the two wouldn't leave a trail of clues for the temple. "Oh, what have you done?"

The sound of chains rattling and a voice from inside the house soon distracted her. "Hello! Someone there?"

Sarah rushed into the house with a hand on her sword, but quickly shoved the weapon back into its place. "Holt! What happened? What are you doing here?"

Holt Langston, the headmaster's lead junior Templin, was bound by handcuffs and chained to the wall.

She looked through the mess of tools on the floor. "Where's the key?"

"It's gone."

She heard the defeat in his voice and knelt down next to him. "Tell me what happened."

"Isn't it obvious? I came here after the alarm sounded. The intruders attacked me and chained me to the wall."

Sarah thought very carefully about her next question. "Intruders? There was more than one?"

"Yes, two men."

She cocked an eyebrow at him. "Really? Two *men* you say?"

Holt nodded, yet his eyes avoided hers.

"Hm. Well, did they say anything—tell you why they were here?"

"Didn't speak Differian. I couldn't understand them."

She was surprised at how quickly he was coming up with the lies. "Oh, right. Well, I suppose I should look for something to help set you free. Perhaps there's another key downstairs. A spare's—"

"No! I mean, it's no use. Just go get one of the officers."

She shrugged and made for the stairs. "Well, I'll at least try. It would take some time before I could get anyone here anyway."

"No, Miss Harte, wait! Don't leave me up here."

"I'll just be a minute."

"No! Please, there's nothing down there. Wait!"

"It's all right, Holt. Just let me check—"

"No! The key's gone—Joel took it with him!"

Sarah leaned halfway back into the doorway.

Holt put a hand over his mouth, shocked at his carelessness.

"Uh-oh. Didn't mean for that to slip out, did you?" She marched back over to him. "Speak up, and be honest this time."

He turned his head away.

"Holt, everyone has secrets. I'll keep this one, but I want the truth."

His jaw tightened, but when his eyes met hers again she knew the truth was forthcoming. She had kept too many of his and Isabelle's secrets for him not to trust her.

After he finished rehashing his meeting with Joel and Augustine, she pressed him about the one who had been left behind. "Will you keep your promise to Isabelle—to help her escape?"

"The terms were *if* I caught Joel."

Sarah crossed her arms and moved toward him. "I see. Well, maybe . . . you could convince her to stay."

"You know I can't do that. My status—"

"Holt, you have a choice! She can even offer you something in return, yet you threw her away without a care."

"That's not true! I-I thought about it. I mean, she and I . . . I even tried to think of a way—" He shook his head. "You don't understand. Mixing my work with her, my future—being with her complicates my work."

"Oh, I understand. I just don't agree. Many men are remarkable in what they do because of the strong females in their lives."

"That's not what my father says."

Her eyes narrowed in anger. "I'm well aware what your father thinks."

"What do you know of my father? He loves my mother. It's dangerous business disrespecting a Differian general, Miss Harte." He struggled to get to his feet.

"Oh, I don't question his love for your mother. "

"Your tone clearly communicates disapproval."

"And so does your father's toward Isabelle. Isn't that right?"

He instantly fell sullen and silent.

"Holt, I want you to find yourself. I have no right to question your father, but I think you should."

He raised his hands at her in confusion. "Why?"

"Because it's *your* life, not his or mine. You have yet to think for yourself."

His eyes became vulnerable, but he turned away again before Sarah could seize the moment.

This was the only chance she'd ever have to get him to question the temple or his father, so she decided to press the issue. "Do you enjoy Eris as much as Isabelle?"

"No. I keep wondering if I'll ever get over her." He held out a shackled wrist. "She's done this to me . . . over time. I don't even know how it happened. I didn't even truly care for her early on."

Sarah chuckled. "Yes, I remember it all too well. The only reason you wanted Isabelle was to irritate Joel."

"You wanted her to choose Joel, didn't you?"

Sarah hesitated then slowly nodded. "Yes, he didn't love her selfishly at the time like you . . . but that changed too. Joel grew to need her too much."

"I didn't ever need her."

"I know. You grew to love her . . . just because."

He tugged at the chains again. "I don't need her now."

"I know."

He suddenly threw the chains to the ground and yelled.

Sarah drew back at his outburst and waited for him to speak his mind.

"I just *want* her," he finally whispered. "Someone to understand . . . someone to share—doesn't matter now. It's impossible. The only way to be free of her is to hate her."

Sarah searched his face. "Holt, you do have a choice. That's what I want you to see."

He remained silent and closed his eyes. "One more secret, Professor Harte, then this discussion is over."

Hope arose in her spirit. "Yes?"

"If what you say is true about men needing strong women then Joel is more desirable to the temple than before. He has a girl with him."

After some negotiating, the two came up with an agreement in which Sarah mostly held the upper hand—Holt didn't question her antics with Isabelle, and she didn't tattle on him for failing his "assignment" to catch Joel again. But she knew it was only a matter of time before the temple would uncover who the real thieves were. The Templins had delivered Isabelle's letter to Waiz, and the temple's rhydid *actually* belonged to Joel. But any extra time was precious, and she'd take what she could get.

Due to this turn of events, when Sarah spotted Holt leaning over Isabelle in a menacing fashion the next day, she watched only for a moment before intervening. *After all, I have new leverage over the powerful Langston.* Holt had the little blonde plastered against one of the walkway pillars as a nasty tirade ensued. "Ahem! Mr. Langston, that's not appropriate posture or language you're using with Miss Isabelle."

His eyes narrowed upon hearing her, but he quickly drew back from Isabelle and let go of the pillar.

"What seems to be the problem here?" Isabelle looked down while Holt looked up. Quite amused, Sarah put her hands on her hips. "I'm waiting."

Holt exhaled slowly. "There's no problem."

"You're sure?"

"Yes, ma'am."

The three looked at one another then Sarah nodded. "Then might I suggest you part ways."

Holt lifted his head, put his shoulders back, and walked away.

Isabelle huffed loudly as her blue eyes followed him in contempt. "He got a 'C' on the history paper I did for him. I didn't put a whole lot of effort into it since I thought I'd be escaping."

Sarah smiled at her. "I can understand that . . . but don't worry." She patted her hand. "You're still leaving. It just won't be this week."

Chapter 5

TALAN LANGSTON GAZED at the photo of Honey Paisley his assistant had just brought into his temporary office in the West End. "Twenty-one? Who does she think she's fooling?" He raised his head as a pair of boots marched through the doorway. "Ah. You here with a message or to get one?"

"Both, Sir." The young Templin took off his hat and approached the desk. "The headmaster first wishes to know if you have any information regarding the two boys who escaped from the temple last night."

Talan smirked as he leaned back in his chair. "Well, *first*, tell the headmaster he's been misinformed. The two traveling are a young lady and perhaps a young man. I spotted the rhydid sheath on the girl after she got out of my motorcar. I dared not try to retrieve it. If she knows how to use it, well, it would've caused quite a scene—too dangerous especially outside our borders. In any case, I need her trust. She'll soon lead me to her partner." The headmaster's high-ranking general drummed his fingers across the picture and grinned. "You should've seen her—reeking of insecurity. My charms worked like magic."

A deep chuckle outside Talan's office interrupted their conversation. "Good. I'll be sure to tell His Majesty that your *son* misinformed him."

Talan's smirk vanished as the headmaster's personal secretary strode into the office. He hated even looking at the man, from his overweight frame to the scraggly beard hiding the pockmarks on his face.

Secretary Magnus stopped at Talan's desk and cocked his head. The man's beady eyes glimmered as he held his top hat and nodded in Talan's direction. "General Langston."

Talan didn't stand up. "I'm sorry, Holt misinformed the headmaster?"

"Holt was the only one who saw the two fugitives. His post was Moonstruck. So, yes . . . your offspring not only let the thieves escape, but he was also defeated by a girl it seems. Isn't that what you just informed my Templin?"

Talan said nothing in response to Magnus's smug accusation, yet he knew Moonstruck was indeed Holt's post.

The man leaned on his cane toward Talan's desk. "Care to comment on the situation?"

Talan shook his head. Holt was grown. *He will have to defend himself. Hopefully these instances have taught him a lesson—to Never. Fail. Again.*

Magnus let out a dramatic sigh. "Well, that's hardly a surprise, but I have new orders for you that might be."

"Fine."

"The headmaster needs a liaison."

"For what?"

"War. Or, perhaps you'll be more of a diplomat with your good looks and all. Isn't that your front here in the West End?"

"What are you talking about?"

"The headmaster made an alliance with New Waiz several weeks ago. We need a trusted leader on the inside. He wants to know the New Order's secrets."

Talan sat there for a moment, confused. "Now? He . . . he wants me to go now?"

Magnus tossed a blue file onto the desk. "I'm too busy to fool with your questions. Here's your briefing. Read it quickly. You're leaving tonight. There are already three thousand troops there."

Talan looked at him in amazement. "Three thousand? That's more than I agreed to. Does New Waiz know?"

The man pointed to the blue folder then clasped his hands. "My, my, my, you're in the dark. I mean, being the headmaster's prized general . . . he sure has kept some important information from you."

Talan flipped open the folder. "He has his reasons."

"Well, you should know your assignment is quite dangerous . . . perilous actually."

Talan stood to his feet as liquid fire pumped near his temples. "What's that supposed to mean?"

"You and your pretty little face, your cushy lifestyle, your title—they haven't cost you a thing. So, I suggested you have an opportunity to demonstrate the degree of your allegiance." The man's eyes narrowed as he pulled a knife from his belt.

"You have no idea what my allegiance has cost me."

Secretary Magnus slowly ran his fingers over the blade. "Perhaps not, but the headmaster knows, and he's still getting rid of you."

His words unleashed Talan's rage, and Magnus knew it.

The man cackled with laughter. "Come now, Langston, my Templin here would love to see some sport before we send you away on your suicide mission. Show him what a general can do, or, I'm sorry, I mean diplomat. Perhaps you'll inspire him to use *words* as his next weapon."

Magnus pointed the knife in his direction, but Talan didn't flinch. When the young Templin took a step back, Talan made his move. Unafraid, with his jaw clenched he drew near to the man with his arms raised in surrender. "Oh poor, Magnus. Always been the jealous type. You think now, because you're the headmaster's secretary, that you're his buddy . . . but the truth is, you're weak. That's why he really chose you. You won't argue, won't have an opinion. No . . . your job is to say, 'Yes, Headmaster.' Or—" Talan stopped and thumped the knife blade. "I'll bet the most important advice you give His Majesty is what shoes will match his suit."

Magnus lunged at him. Talan twisted the arm that held the knife, causing Magnus to drop the weapon. The secretary gripped Talan's throat with his free hand but was forced to relax his grip when four of Talan's officers surrounded him.

Talan rolled his neck around and stepped away. "Oh, Magnus, remember? *I'm* a general with men at my disposal, but you only have papers that report to you." He bent close to the man's ear. "Magpie, the headmaster gave me the girl, the title, and the prestige because of *who* I am. And, he gave you all that you have because of *what* you are—weak." He held the knife to

Magnus's face and was satisfied when he looked into the eyes of a broken man. He nodded to his comrades to let him go. "Run on home now, Magpie."

Magnus trembled as he backed away and put on his top hat. He stumbled on a chair behind him, then hurried out of the room.

Talan shook his head at his men. "Imbecile."

"General, do you need help going over your briefing?" Talan was surprised to see Magnus's young Templin had stayed behind.

"Coffee. And some books from my library."

"Right away on the coffee, Sir."

"Yes, I'll make a list of the books. I need Waizen history."

The Templin left the room, and one of Talan's soldiers quickly stepped forward. "Shall I accompany Secretary Magnus back to the temple . . . or follow him?"

"Yes, see to it that Secretary Magnus doesn't make it back to the temple on time. In fact, see to it that he doesn't make it back at all."

Chapter 6

AUGUSTINE FOUND HERSELF in a train station that was more open than Crossroads but just as crowded and busy. *Where in the world am I?* She couldn't believe she hadn't asked Talan. She spotted the station's name on one of the walls. *Seda. Never heard of it.* She walked to a map and found Seda was located just over the border of Differe in the West End. As she walked forward to the train platforms she was overwhelmed by the bustling crowds, train whistles, and billowing smoke that flooded the place. Soon a loud voice echoed throughout the station.

"Excuse me, patrons, there has been a change in trains. Facilis passengers will now need to board the number seven train. I repeat, all those traveling to Facilis will need to board the number seven train."

Facilis. That's where Hubert said to go. She knew it was the wrong direction but figured there must be a Waiz train close by. *I'll just get off in a few stops and find one . . . I hope.* Augustine studied the numbers marking the trains and soon found number seven filling up. She shuffled forward with the other passengers until she felt the crowd breaking away from her. The New Waiz fashion scout was making an entrance. A host of condescending and amused glances followed her as she entered the crowded train to Facilis. She pushed her way to the back but found all the compartments full. Finally she plopped down by an older gentleman in the open seating area. She sighed in relief, thankful to be going somewhere. It was at that moment she realized how exhausted she was.

She and Joel had only gotten a few hours of sleep in the past 48 hours. She hoped the man next to her wouldn't mind if she dozed off. Turning to him she realized he already had the same idea, so she settled down into her seat and pulled her hat down over her eyes. She was breathing deeply when suddenly she heard, "Tickets. Tickets, please."

I forgot. Oh, I can't believe I forgot! Panic shook her awake. She wondered if there was a washroom where she could hide, but the attendants were coming from both directions collecting tickets. She froze in fear. *Come on, Augustine, be Honey Paisley. Be Honey.* The man next to her stirred, and she began rummaging through one of her bags. Her heart raced as they drew nearer.

"Ticket please, ma'am?" The young attendant did not seem the least bit impressed by her outfit.

"Well, I put it in one of these bags. It might take a minute . . . if you need to move on." She tried her best to appear aloof.

"I've got time; the rest of the passengers don't. Do you wish to hold up the train?"

She seethed inside at his sneering tone. *Two can play at not being nice, mister.* "If that's what it takes." She dug deeper into the bag.

"Bet you lose quite a few things in something so big."

"I'll have you know it saves me from bringing a whole other bag, thank you very much." *The nerve of this guy.*

"Oh, I was referring to your hat."

The snickers from the other passengers infuriated Augustine, but she welcomed the emotion in light of the true panic she felt. She opened the bag wider in an attempt to appease the mocking audience.

"Wait, what's that? Food? You're a little thief, aren't you?" He grabbed her arm and jerked her out of the seat. The other passengers gasped in surprise.

"Take your hands off me, you brute! I am not a thief!" Augustine tried to break loose from his grip. "Let go of me!"

"You have one minute to produce that ticket, or I'll throw you off this train, thief!"

Augustine jumped when a door slammed behind them.

"Get your hands off her. She's with me."

Joel had one hand on the attendant's arm, and the other held out two tickets to Facilis.

"Yes, Sir. My apologies." The attendant quickly let go of Augustine, and the whole car went silent.

Joel released the train attendant and tugged uncomfortably on the gray sleeves of the junior Templin uniform he was wearing. He squinted at Augustine through a pair of dark glasses and motioned for her to get in front of him. "I have a compartment for us up front. I'll get your bags. Go ahead; I'll follow behind you." He tipped his black officer's hat at the rest of the car. "Excuse us, everyone. Thank you for your patience."

The passengers silently bobbed their heads in response.

Joel bit his tongue to keep from laughing when Augustine marched snootily past the train attendant to the next car. As he followed behind her he had to intentionally divert his eyes from her orange-clad frame. *Yep. That's a double-take if I've ever seen one.* He'd thought the same thing when he saw her enter the train station. It would have been hard for anyone not to notice her. The orange color itself was already in bright contrast to the surrounding passengers' attire; then there was also the curvy beauty on which the orange was displayed. *Okay, enough about that.* It unnerved him a little that he was thinking about her like this. He sighed as he reached out to stop her and open the compartment door. Once inside she scrutinized his face and frame.

"Joel . . . is that you?"

He removed the glasses and smiled.

"I'm so glad you found me! I hated leaving you." Augustine pulled the coat collar down from around his face and hugged his neck.

He stiffened at her touch and briskly patted her back before pushing her away. He caught the flicker of confusion in her eyes but was intent on not addressing her emotions. "Uh, train's moving."

She nodded and quickly took her seat.

"Oh, and I prefer Officer Guy. And, yes, I did think up that name all by myself."

"How original. I must say it's much better than Honey Paisley."

He shrugged then ran his fingers over her sleeve.

She looked up at him in surprise.

"Just wondered what it felt like."

"It's lambskin."

A smirk spread across his face. "You don't say. And the hat?"

"I don't know."

He caught the hint of defensiveness in her tone but was having too much fun to quit teasing her. He pulled at the feathers. "What kind of bird did you have to kill?"

She crossed her arms in annoyance.

"Sorry. You look, uh—" *I mean, really, are there any nice words for this outfit?*

"Like a New Waiz fashion scout? I've been told I'm quite promising."

Joel wasn't sure if she was being serious. "Yes, the clothes . . . they're really, uh . . . well, let's just say I'm speechless, *Honey*."

Augustine finally giggled and threw the hat at him. "I'm ridiculous! I don't even match!"

"No worries; neither do I."

"Yeah, I noticed the hat and coat don't exactly match. What kind of officer are you?"

"A Templin . . . sort of."

"Did you take it from one?"

His expression hardened as he recalled the incident. "Yeah. Well, kind of. The hat and glasses I found—a Templin left them in one of the compartments . . . the rest I stole."

"What happened?"

"I stayed in the compartment until I heard the announcement about two boys. I came running after you but, uh, saw you didn't get off the train. So I went back for my backpack, and a Templin was waiting for me." Joel grimaced. He wasn't happy about how things had happened.

She raised her eyebrows and searched his face again. "Did you use the rhydid?"

"No. Speaking of, we really need to look at Mr. Rutherford's book." He finally lowered his head and confessed, "It was a junior Templin—small . . . he wasn't much of a problem."

Her blue eyes grew wide in amazement. "The room looked demolished."

"I didn't say *no* problem—just not much."

She eyed the gray coat. "I thought the uniform looked a little snug. So, junior Templins wear jackets, and the ranking Templins wear cloaks?"

"Yeah, I guess."

"I'm sorry."

"About what?"

"That you had to fight someone young. Seems easier to give it to the adults—like they know better . . . so they deserve it." She pulled the gloves off her hands.

"Yeah, but in reality I think . . . I think no one deserves it—to be treated harshly. And besides, we're nearly adults, Augustine."

She nodded half-heartedly then looked up. "My turn?"

"Yeah, who got you all dolled up?"

"The ticket master caught me in the kitchen. He seemed to have a plan already—like he knew I'd be there. He smuggled me past the Templins as a waitress and led me to the luggage cars. Guess whose trunk these are from?" She pointed to her three bags.

Joel shrugged. "New Waiz?"

"Madame Bontecou!"

"No wonder they're so big!"

"Oh, stop. She has a shop in New Waiz. Hubert told me I had to have a lot of bags to play the part of Honey Paisley. She's quite horrid, I can assure you, and the Templins definitely think her so."

He stared at her long dark lashes. "Why the painted face?"

"To make me look older."

He nodded. "Suppose it did the trick."

"I walked down the road a bit until a motorcar stopped for me. A diplomat for the West End picked me up. He was quite kind and very glad to rescue me—he said there were bears in the woods! Can you imagine facing another white bear like the headmaster's Sasha?"

Joel raised his eyebrows. There was something different in her voice when she mentioned this diplomat. "Did he give you anything? Ask you anything interesting?"

"No, just his card. Said he'd love to help me again."

The words lit something inside him. "Yeah, I'll bet he would." He was surprised at his own grimace. *Get it together, Joel.*

Augustine looked away from him, and he turned towards the window, aggravated at their situation. *We should be nearly back to Waiz by now—back to Sebastian. And here we are headed in the exact opposite direction.*

CHAPTER 7

THEY'RE NOT BACK yet." The anxious little boy was perched by the window, tracing designs on the glass where his breath had fogged it.

Corwin knew Sebastian wanted to ask him the unthinkable, so he drew near to him. "I'm sure they are only delayed."

"How can you be so sure?"

"Because if they were caught, we'd know. The Templins would quit watching Mr. Rutherford's shop, your parents would inform us, or, when I weigh all the factors—Joel escaping before, his resilience, his drive for you—it's hard to believe he could fail."

"You know what I think, Corwin?"

Corwin raised his eyebrows as he knelt beside his young friend.

"I don't think he can fail because the king's on his side. You know, that Majestic thing. Joel told me he met it in the cave."

Corwin gave a slight nod of approval, then Sebastian let out a loud sigh.

"What is it, Sebastian?"

"Well, what I can't figure out is why . . . why, if Waiz's Majestic is on his side, does he still suffer? You know, the mouthpieces still attacking him?"

Corwin put a hand on his shoulder, knowing Sebastian's question wasn't just about Joel. *No, he wonders for himself too.* Why is he sick? Why had a life-threatening disease been allowed to run rampant in his body if there was something or *someone* powerful enough, and perhaps even good enough, to stop it?

"Sebastian—"

"Please don't answer me in riddles. Just tell me the truth."

The man cleared his throat as he thought of how to answer. "Sebastian, the greatest harm I could do to Joel or you—to your faith, your hope rather—is to conjure up some logical, neatly tied up explanation."

"So what you're saying is you can't answer me . . . can you?" His green eyes begged to be wrong.

"I can, but only with complete humanness and no sort of divine revelation. My intellect, too, Sebastian, longs for your questions to be answered, but my heart refuses to create beliefs around circumstances." He took the little boy's face in his sturdy, thick hands. "So, my best answer is this: I. Don't. Know."

Sebastian fell onto his shoulder as tears streamed down his cheeks.

"I don't know." Corwin pulled him out of the wheelchair and onto his lap. The boy instantly fell into his embrace. "But I don't believe for a minute that your sickness was meant for you to bear. I'm going to do everything in my power to stop allowing evil into Joel's life. He and Augustine are doing everything in their power to stop it in your life. I do believe the king is all-powerful, but we somehow . . . well, we hold the keys to unlock that power. Circumstances change, Sebastian—that's why I don't look to them as a compass for my beliefs. I believe we can change the outcome of our circumstances."

Sebastian sniffed. "For good?"

"Yes, for good."

Suddenly the little boy pulled back from him. "I want to do something. Everyone is doing something for me." He wiped his eyes free of tears. "I want to do something, Corwin. What can we do while we wait?"

Corwin let out a sly grin. "Well now, I thought you'd never ask. I already have a few things in mind." He put Sebastian back in the wheelchair and stood up. "I'm done sitting around too. I think we need to take a look at the scrolls Joel left us. That should give us some direction, but, in any case, I'd like to invite you to be my number one recruit."

"For what?"

"The Thaddean Army." He bowed as he presented the invitation. "Will you join me?"

Sebastian's eyes widened in delight. "Army? What are you talking about?"

"It's an old regime I was in years ago."

"Were you a spy . . . Joel thought you might be. Is it for New or Old Waiz?"

"Mostly Old Waiz at this point, but I feel a strong need to go after those down in New Waiz as well. We need to be united." Corwin gripped the hilt of his sword as he thought about such a task.

"Why? What do you really think is going on here?"

"I'm not sure, but I don't like seeing Templins here. I'm beginning to wonder if their search for Joel is a cover for something else . . . I've seen too many."

"Where? Have you been sneaking out at night? I kind of hope so—it'd be great to tell Augustine I survived by myself."

He thumped Sebastian's knee. "No, I haven't. Though I'm not saying I won't. I spotted Templins at the council meeting."

Sebastian's jaw dropped. "During the murder?"

"They were on the New Waiz side of the river wall. I-I was trained to notice such things."

"You really are a spy!"

"I *used* to be a spy. The army really was just a club of sorts for a while."

Sebastian propped his hand under his chin. "Spill it."

Corwin chuckled then nodded. "I was about eighteen when I was approached by Thad to join him. He found me at a time in my life when it would've been hard to refuse. I was looking down at the Pallas River thinking about my life and how I wanted to end it . . . I wanted to jump."

A young Corwin sat on the stone wall of the Pallas River, dangling his shoeless feet dangerously over the side.

He was startled by a deep voice that called out behind him. "Whatever are you doing?"

"Thinking."

"About?" The voice came closer.

Corwin gave a long hard stare at the Bridge of Miren. "How to get into those towers."

"Get your shoes on, and I'll show you."

Corwin's face formed a scowl. He didn't answer, though the man's offer intrigued him greatly.

"When was the last time you ate something?" The speaker's hand soon rested on the wall beside him. "Your parents are looking for you."

He tossed a rock into the river. "Going back to them isn't an option for me."

"And just what are your options, Corwin?"

He finally turned to face the man. "Who are you?"

A man with a long beard wearing a light blue robe met his gaze. He was at least ten years older than Corwin, and if the cotton robe and beard weren't enough to make him seem a bit peculiar, his dark curly hair sticking out in all directions was.

"Thaddeus . . . but most people just call me 'Thad'."

Corwin cocked an eyebrow at him. "Thaddeus?"

The man grinned. "Yeah, my family has a thing for weird names. They think it makes us different, but I'm pretty sure my hair takes care of that."

Corwin looked away from the happy face in disgust. "What do you want?"

"Nothing. You're the one who's hanging over the wall wanting to know how to get into the towers."

He turned back to him in annoyance.

The man shrugged. "I know how to get in. So, I apparently have what you want."

Corwin stiffened. "Just leave me alone. Did my parents send you?"

"Not exactly . . . no."

"Listen, they've tried everything, okay? I can't do it." He felt anger rage in him as he sputtered out the words.

"Can't do what, Corwin?" The man's gentle tone aggravated him even more.

"Life. Fate doesn't seem to want me to win."

The man went silent and peered down at the river.

"I have no direction, no drive, nothing. You're just wasting your time with me."

"Well, they believe . . . they believe in you, you know."

"Who? What are you talking about?"

"Your parents."

Corwin shook his head. "They're fools."

"Come work for me a few weeks, and I promise to take you to the towers."

A shoeless, homeless, and jobless Corwin couldn't really refuse such an offer unless . . . *I go through with my original plan.* He stared down at the blue water. He had known even before he ran away he wouldn't be able to do it. He'd always needed help to complete anything—taking his life would be no different.

"Come. I'll at least feed you before you make up your mind."

Corwin followed Thad to the east side of New Waiz. The man insisted on creating their own trail through the woods to his home rather than take the service road. Corwin's feet were muddied and raw by the time they reached Thad's cabin. The man reached to open the door then suddenly spun around.

"My dear Corwin, we're on the east side of the river, so where do my allegiances lie—Old Waiz or New Waiz?"

"I, um, I don't really know."

The man nodded then led Corwin inside.

Corwin marveled at the cabin. The walls were lined with sturdy logs and more than a few animal heads. He found himself in a large room containing a hearth, sitting area, and place to eat. He followed a delicious aroma to the back of the cabin where he located the kitchen. A short round woman was cooking something on the stovetop and smiled at them as they entered. Upon closer inspection, Corwin realized she was pregnant.

"Hello, Thad." She kissed his cheek. "And hello, Corwin." She nodded in his direction.

"Uh, Ma'am."

"I'm Lucy. Are you hungry?"

Her smile and the mention of food immediately disarmed him. "Starving."

"Well, sit down, and I'll fix you a bowl."

Corwin made for the table, and Thad soon joined him.

"Lucy, I asked Corwin which side of Waiz we belong to."

"Hm. Any guesses?"

Corwin stared back at her then to Thad's long beard and robe. He pursed his lips and shrugged. "Uh, hard to say."

She nodded as she set a steaming bowl in front of him. "And what about you, Corwin? Trying to hide from both sides by staying in Neutral Waiz?"

Corwin let out a breath of hot air. "I don't need to pick a side. I'm indifferent."

Her fiery eyes flickered with kindness as she poured him a cup of tea. "You mean you don't care?"

He stuffed another spoonful into his mouth. "Exactly. I tend to be more sane that way."

Thad folded his hands underneath his chin. "So, you think by not caring you'll be safe?"

Corwin was silent. *I've got to get out of here.*

"How's that working for you?" Thad pressed again.

"It's not."

"You want things to work out for you? Job, future, family . . . ."

Corwin threw his spoon down. "Listen, Thad, if I knew how to fix myself I would've done it by now."

"Fix yourself *for* something or fix yourself *from* something?"

The compassion Corwin saw in Thad's eyes infuriated him, and he angrily pushed the bowl away. "I'm sure my parents told you."

"What? That you're not like them? That you're not like Old Waiz or New Waiz . . . that you hear things in your head?" The man stopped and threw his hands in the air. "You're so focused on who those things say you should be, or who you're not, that you don't realize, and can't embrace, who you already are."

"I don't know what you're talking about." Corwin stood to his feet. He was grateful for the meal, but he was done being lectured.

Thad stood too. "Oh, but you will . . . Corwin, think about this. You're the only person I've ever met who has even considered there's a way into the towers."

Corwin gripped the table as he looked into the man's dark eyes. "How did you figure out how to get inside?"

"A voice told me."

Chapter 8

JOEL THOUGHT HE was dreaming when he felt the sensation of falling but soon found himself on the floor of the train compartment. "Ouch!" He sat up and rubbed his shoulder.

Augustine hardly stirred.

"I rolled off the—wait . . . the train's stopped." Joel pulled up the shade then ducked underneath the windowsill. "Augustine!"

Her eyes flew open. "What? What is it?"

"They're here! The Templin Guards—right outside the train."

"What? Are you sure you? Are we in Facilis yet?" Augustine grabbed her velour hat and shoved it back onto her head.

Joel panicked. "Oh no, I'm dressed like one of them."

"Joel, where are we? What about your backpack? Don't you have some more clothes in there?"

Both tensed as a loud screeching sound rang overhead.

"All passengers off the train for inspection. I repeat, all passengers off the train for inspection."

Joel looked down and froze. "I'm a dead giveaway."

"Are you sure they're looking for us? I mean, we're in the West End."

"I'm sure."

"How do you—"

"I just know." He clenched his jaw and turned to Augustine. "You gotta get off without me. It's better not to go as a pair."

"But they'll catch you! No, I'm not doing it. I'm not leaving you again."

Both jumped when their neighbor's compartment door flung open.

"Please, at least follow after me. I'll create a distraction. The Templins are bound to look at me." She grasped at the feathers in her hat.

He put his hands on his knees and looked down. *I can't let Augustine be Templin bait. I won't let her do that for me.* He looked up into her blue eyes and sighed. "They'll look all right . . . just not the way I want them to."

She hit his shoulder. "They're not very bright. Come on; you can fool them."

"No, Augie. I . . . you have no idea what they did to me the last twelve years . . . we—you can't get caught."

She ignored his words and pointed to the suitcase. "Do you want to see if I have something in here you could wear?"

"Uh, you think Madame Bontecou has something for me? Doubtful."

"Well, we should at least look. Oh, and you should put these on again." Her hands shook as she pulled the glasses from his coat pocket.

He quickly hung them on his collar.

She frantically pulled a stack of clothes from the bag. "Come on, there's got to be something. Grab anything you might could wear."

Without thinking, he grabbed the first dark object he saw. He quickly unscrewed the top of a medium-sized jar and was delighted to find black goo inside.

Augustine stopped rummaging through the bag and looked at him in shock as he dipped his fingers in the jar and ran the product through his hair.

"What?"

"That's the dumbest thing I've ever seen you do." She shook her head then delved back into the bag.

"Whatever. I'm just nervous. Red hair is a sure giveaway for me. What is this stuff anyway?" He became overpowered by a floral scent.

"Some sort of beauty treatment."

"Well, good to know my hair will be beautiful. Did you find me something to wear?"

Augustine tossed him a gray cloak. "Here, how about this?"

He looked over the cloak in awe. "Where—how . . . why would Madame Bontecou have a Templin uniform?" He marveled at the gray cloak, complete with silver owl insignias on the collar. "This is the real deal—achoo!"

"Ugh, see?" She sniffed his head and wrinkled her nose. "Here, hurry and put your hat back on. Maybe it'll cover the fact that you now smell like a pile of lavender."

Joel was still puzzled about Madame Bontecou having a Templin uniform. *It doesn't make sense. And the emblem is red . . . not the green ones at the temple.*

"Joel, what are you doing? Hurry up and change coats!"

Joel shrugged off his junior Templin jacket and quickly fastened the five silver buttons of his new uniform cloak. "If we keep getting stopped like this we're going to have to get off before Facilis. By the looks of it, these are just little stops in small towns. They're bound to have a whole crew waiting for us in such a big city. I still don't understand why . . . I mean, we didn't even take anything they use. And . . . it looks like we didn't take anything at all." He fastened the cloak around his neck and felt Augustine press several pieces of gauze onto his face. "What are you doing?"

She lifted his hat then pointed to his face. "You wouldn't let me do this earlier, but we're bandaging your face not only because it needs it but because it will hide you. Black hair, bandaged face, Templin cloak. Hopefully that will be enough."

"Just what all does Madame Bontecou have in that bag?"

After Augustine finished taping the gauze she clasped her hands and bit her knuckles. "Oh, Joel, I'm not sure—"

"Let's just wait for a second. Let's just think about what to do. Yeah, let's just calm down and wait."

The two sat in disguise waiting for a plan to form. The anticipation was almost unbearable as their nerves escalated with every creak of their compartment.

Augustine finally broke the silence. "Think we should try to run for it? Catch another train to Waiz?"

Joel shrugged.

"Suppose we have to get off anyway."

He sighed and grabbed one of her bags. "Yeah, let's go."

As they moved into the crowd he studied the passengers to determine if the delay was routine or if it was, in fact, a surprise inspection. This was difficult since most passengers avoided the gaze of someone wearing such official garb. It was as if the seas parted when he and Augie departed the train. *Great, just what we need. More attention.*

"You there, Officer, this way." Another Templin gestured towards Joel then offered him a firm handshake. He bent near Joel's ear. "You don't have to wait over here with these commoners. Sorry to disturb your ride, Sir, but we have orders to search all trains that departed from Differe today." The man began leading Joel off the platform toward a building adjacent to the train station.

"The lady's with me also. May she come along?"

The officer smiled as he looked at Augustine. "Oh, yes, we can make room for her."

Joel felt inclined to hit the guy but remained calm and motioned for Augustine to follow them.

Augustine shuffled forward in her boots. She kept a firm grip on her bags to keep her hands from shaking as she entered the Templin headquarters. She was surprised to find the building full of the same antique art she had seen at Crossroads Station. *Statues everywhere!* She spied not only marble but bronze and wood figurines as well. Much like the temple from the night before, this place chilled her to the bone. Pockets of men were spread around the large room. *Of course . . . no women.* The headquarters was clearly a man's world; she wasn't asked but commanded to, "Sit here, Miss." The officer had guided her to a dark leather sofa situated under a crystal mirror framed by gold leaves.

"May I offer you something to drink? Tea, perhaps?" The Templin gazed at Joel then Augustine.

"One coffee for me. Honey, you want something?"

"I-I . . . ." She stumbled until she caught sight of her reflection in the mirror and remembered to get in character. "Oh! Oh, yes, splendid! Tea if you please. Be sure to bring lots of sugar!" Her tone was so sweet she thought she might make herself sick. She settled onto the sofa then stroked the leather. "Officer Guy, I'd like a jacket made of this stuff."

Joel cleared his throat and shot an annoyed look to a few officers that had turned in their direction. "Fine."

"All right then, what would you have to kill? You're an excellent shot! Hmm, feels like bison leather. You know how I *know* my materials. So, what do you think, Officer Guy? Could you skin a bison for me?" She batted her eyes, while hoping there was such a thing as "bison leather."

"Drink your tea, Honey." Joel sighed before bringing his own cup to his bandaged face.

The way he held the cup, how he was sitting on the edge of his chair, she knew his nerves were racing especially now that most of the room was paying them some attention. It made her all the more uneasy about making her next move as Honey Paisley. She didn't think it would be something Joel would expect. *But I have to for Corwin.* She gritted her teeth and gave his arm a tight squeeze. "Well, if I must, but it doesn't look sweet enough to me, and I dare say I need to wash my hands. I hate the thought of drinking anything after being on a train with so many people—so many possible diseases. My gloves are covered in germs. A washroom if you please, Officer?"

As a Templin led her away from the main room, the other officers began approaching Joel. She smiled to herself when she heard one say, "Pretty face but how do you stand her incessant talking?"

Augustine was careful to study her surroundings as the officer led her to the back of the building. The first room they passed was on the right, and it was full of officers perched around desks and flashing radios of some sort. Others were studying colored pins stuck into maps lining the walls. She casually glanced into the following room across the hall. The office held one large desk, and the entire room appeared to be made of solid wood from floor to ceiling with enormous built-in bookcases.

The back of the building held the kitchen, and it was there she discovered she wasn't the only female in the place after all. A woman and young girl were preparing a host of things in a hot coal-fire oven. The dark fumes had visibly dirtied their clothes, faces, and hands.

"In there." The officer pointed her to a small washroom and turned to leave.

She opened the door and stared inside. *How dare you.* She knew this wasn't what the officers used; the room was filthy. *Poor workers—this is terrible. They look half-starved. In fact, I bet the Templins—*

"Ahhhhh!"

Augustine rushed into the kitchen after another painful yelp escaped from the young girl. She brought a badly scalded hand to her face while the older woman pressed a hand against the girl's mouth. "There now, shush. Shush. Quiet now, mustn't disturb the Templins."

Augustine grabbed the nearest bowl, packed it with ice from the icebox, and filled it with water. She grabbed the wide-eyed girl's arm and motioned for her to put her hand into the water. "It will cool the burn and stifle the pain."

The girl nodded, then winced as she forced her hand into the icy water.

"After you soak it a few minutes, try to keep it wrapped for a bit. Cloth, paper—anything will do."

The two nodded their thanks.

"Oh, and here." She pulled a container of dried fruit and nuts from her bag.

The two ladies exchanged fearful glances.

"I'm not going to tell." Augustine put the container into the woman's farmer bag hanging on the handle of the back door. "Now, from one woman to another, I need some reading material for my next train ride." She returned their puzzled stares with a sly wink. "I very much enjoy reading top secret information. I was hoping you could point me in the right direction . . . ."

The girl looked down at her injured hand then to the older woman. The older woman finally nodded and pointed back down the hallway. "The big wooden office—Officer Chadwick is outside overseeing the train inspection."

She nodded her thanks, then wondered if the two might know the answer to her most pressing question. *Why are the Templins in the West End?*

Joel shot Augustine a stern look as a Templin dragged her toward him. Though a tinge angry, he was relieved to see her. "Where have you been?"

"Well, I finished washing my hands, and, well, you know how utterly horrible I am with directions. I took a wrong turn on my way back." She cocked her head sweetly as Joel took her arm from the officer.

From the looks of the man Joel knew there was more, so he decided to play along in whatever scheme this was. "And? What distracted you this time—fancy curtains?"

"Well—well, I hate to admit it but, yes, you're right, although the furnishings were lovely too. Nothing like the leather here—embroidered silks—couldn't help myself!" She glanced around at the group of officers Joel had been speaking with. "Did he tell you I do fashion?"

One smirked in her direction. "He didn't have to, Miss."

Joel let out a loud sigh then looked at the officers. "I'm sorry. I hope there is no offense taken for my curious companion."

The officers shook their heads.

"Suppose it's that foreign blood that makes her so impetuous. Clearly *you* are not at fault, Officer, uh?"

"Guy." Joel felt an uneasiness settle over him as a head guard broke through the group of men. The man's steel insignia collar plates signified powerful authority.

"Right, well, I'm surprised your rank allows you such company." The man looked at Augustine in disapproval as he pulled a cigarette from his breast pocket.

"Come now, I'm not in Differe. I may choose any pretty face I like for my short-term leave in the West End." Joel cringed inside hating to say such a thing about his friend, but he knew it was expected with this lot.

"Ah, that does make more sense. How long have you been on holiday?" The man flicked his lighter.

"A while."

"You know, Old Waiz will actually fight against Differe in the coming war. I'm sure you heard we're joining New Waiz in their fight." He gazed at Augustine as he inhaled his first drag. "Hmm. Waizen, where does your allegiance lie?"

Joel didn't care for the way the man studied her and felt Augustine move behind him. He wasn't sure if she was afraid or not, but he patted the hand that reached under his arm up to his chest. "Sir, you're frightening my little flower. She will side with me, of course, with His Honor the Headmaster."

"You know His Excellency?" The man blew a puff of smoke in Augustine's direction.

Joel forced himself to suppress his anger. "Only from afar, but his power supersedes him. Anyone would be a fool not to side with him."

"What about your Waizen's so-called Majestic? Any power there?"

"A bedtime story? Power?"

"Waiz is also a bedtime story, but Honey here makes it appear very real."

"If Honey has you feeling scared, Officer, uh . . . ." The surrounding officers laughed as the guard gave his name.

"Chadwick. And I view her as a reminder of what may possibly lie on our path. Waiz is real. I don't plan on being surprised when I march my unit there." He raised his eyebrows and carefully studied Joel's face. "One more question."

Joel held his breath.

"Why the bandages? I overheard you tell my men you'd been injured on one of your latest missions, yet you've been on holiday . . . for a *while*. Plenty of time to heal don't you think?"

Joel didn't have an answer.

Chadwick eyed Augustine once more then flicked his cigarette into a nearby trashcan. "In any case, I suggest you get rid of her quickly for both your sakes. She's in enemy territory with you."

"And just who's the enemy?" Joel was surprised at the firmness in his voice. It was nearly an accusation.

"If you truly serve His Majesty then you should already know."

CHAPTER 9

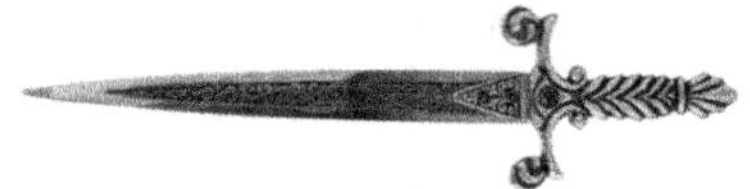

T HAD ENDED UP being right about me." Corwin nodded at Sebastian. "What transpired after going into the towers was something out of a fairytale. I didn't mean to, but I found passion. And that I kindly blame on Thad."

"What was it about him that pulled you out of your mess?"

Corwin took in a deep breath. "The man's passion for life was contagious. Once I tasted it . . . it was a hunger that couldn't be filled. The more I went along with him, spent time with him—the more my appetite grew for life. A purposeful life."

Sebastian pulled his lips to one side. "He seemed really odd."

Corwin threw his head back and laughed. "I wish I had a photograph here to show you. He was one of the few Waizens I knew that never took a side. He simply refused to conform. He was extremely open-minded politically, yet more traditional in his religious beliefs and so on. He played both sides very well."

"What about Lucy? What was she like?"

Corwin rubbed his chin thoughtfully. "I haven't seen her in a long time, but I could never forget her. She was one of the most powerful expressions of love I've ever seen. She loved her Thad, accepted him in spite of all his idiosyncrasies, and affirmed everything about him. She believed in him no matter what anyone else said."

"Sounds like she was kind of strong—you know, like Augustine can be with her opinions."

"Yes, she had no problem stating her opinion, that's for sure, even if Thad disagreed with her. Thad once told me about women being on the councils. Remember, you saw the pictures at the Old Waiz Museum?"

Sebastian nodded.

"They were amazing people. Every time I did something wrong, every time I broke something, every time I ran away then came back, they loved me and never stopped. They believed the best about me over and over again despite my *many* failures. It seems they saw something in me I couldn't see in myself . . . until, well . . . never mind. It's getting late."

"Uh-uh. No way. You have to tell me now or I'll never be able to go to sleep!"

"Well, all right then. You asked me what pulled me out of that dark time. Thad and Lucy certainly helped, but . . . but it was something that happened one night. Something I haven't told many people." He closed his eyes and took in a deep breath. He could still remember what he was wearing that night.

He was running, running fast to nowhere, and surrounded by darkness and woods. His temples throbbed furiously but not from the pace he was moving; it was due to what had just transpired at the cabin.

"They'll—they'll never forgive me," he muttered breathlessly into the darkness. He touched his cheeks and grimaced, tormented by the horrible scene he'd just caused. The toddler's screams echoed in his mind as he dashed forward, running into branches and tripping over vines. A faint sound caught his ear. *Water.* He kept running until he found the riverbank then knelt to dunk his face into the water. He cupped his hands to take a drink then rocked back on his heels, exhausted and dizzy. His eyes fixed on the old bridge a few yards away. *I can just run to New Waiz. Yeah, I can go straight to the train station. I'll go as far away as possible—Differe.*

Corwin felt his chest tighten as the chaos began in his mind. It was as if he had two sides—two voices—fighting for control. One screamed at him to run, and the other begged him to stay. This torment was what he'd fought his entire life; it was like his mind was in a vice, split down the middle. Any outside opinion just intensified the side that was screaming until the other side began blaring even louder for attention.

As he walked to the bridge he struggled for breath. This time it was not only his mind but also his heart that was ripped in two. "This is why I never wanted to pick a side, Thad. I don't want to feel. I want to be INDIFFERENT!" He raised his clenched fists at the night sky. This family had welcomed him without bias, and, for the first time in his life, didn't form an opinion about him. *They just loved me.* If they had a point to get across they asked questions until he was able to come up with his own thought. *They empowered me. But the baby . . . what I just did to the baby. Oh, what have I done?* Remembering the action paralyzed him, and he sank underneath the bridge next to one of the wooden beams.

The water gurgled as it swirled around the beams closest to him. A strong odor reached Corwin's nostrils. It was sickening yet sweet, and he searched the waters to see if something was rotting. By the moonlight he made out a dark tar-like substance fermenting near him. On closer inspection he realized the dark material was contained to a certain area and the water he thought was gurgling was actually bubbling . . . *brewing.* With his mind now curious and fixated on the water, his body escaped its frozen state and walked to the water's edge.

"That's right, My Dear, come have a look," rasped a voice in the darkness.

He yelled in surprise as an older woman appeared next to him.

"Shush, sonny. Hush! You're all right. Just made an interesting discovery."

Corwin stumbled back from her. She was mostly hidden by a dark cloak so that he could only see her lips and some wispy strands of long gray hair flowing out from under the hood.

"You are interested . . . aren't you?" Her voice was sweet and tempting.

Corwin nodded quickly.

"This is my brew." Her lips broke into a sly smile. "It helps . . . people like you."

"How?" His eyes shifted back and forth between the brew and the woman.

"Come closer."

Spellbound by the woman's voice, Corwin obeyed.

"See there." She pointed to the dark billowing water stain. "Look how the darkness is . . . contained." She lingered on the last word.

Corwin stared at the water and felt a longing for something.

"That's what it will do for you." She put a hand deep into the pocket of her robe.

Corwin looked at her in astonishment.

"Come now, isn't that why you're running? From the darkness lingering inside you? It feels like it's growing . . . doesn't it?" She opened her hand to reveal a vial.

"What is it?" Corwin felt all the hairs stand up on his neck.

She pointed to the black water then to the vial.

He hesitated to take it. *I need more answers.* "What will it do for me?"

"It will contain the darkness and make you numb to what's already inside you."

He nodded. "Indifferent."

"Yes, as you long to be."

"I only have to take it once?" He stared at the vial nervously, yet longed to grab it at the same time.

She shook her head. "No, your disease . . . your battle rather, is ongoing. You'll need more." She held it out to him.

He bit his lip and took the vial from her hand. He gazed at the water again, then back at her face. Her smile of pity bid him to take his "medicine."

Corwin nodded and removed the cork with his teeth. The scent caused a shiver to go up his spine. Something screamed at him to reconsider. *I just want to be free. I want to be better.* He told himself to take a drink. He pursed his lips and lifted the vial to his mouth.

"NO!" a yell rang through the air. "CORWIN, NO! NO!"

A piercing scream escaped the woman as Corwin whipped around to find Thad running toward them through the thick brush.

"Throw it down! Now, Corwin!"

Corwin turned back to the woman as she began screaming at him also. "Don't waste it! Don't listen to him! Take it—take it now!"

With shouts plaguing him from both directions, Corwin froze.

The woman waved her emaciated hands in the air. "Chase away the darkness, you fool!"

"No, Corwin!" Thad's voice was getting louder. He was nearly by their side. "Find the light! There's light in the darkness! There's light inside you!"

Thad's words struck their mark, causing something to stir in Corwin's spirit.

"Nonsense!" She flicked a hand toward Thad and turned to Corwin. "You know it's a lie. You know what you've done."

Corwin stood motionless, clenching the vial in his hand, his thoughts at war.

Breathing hard, Thad approached the two cautiously until Corwin stood between them. "You're not looking, Corwin. It's there—the light is there."

"Don't listen to this masterful deceiver. Look down there." Her bony finger pointed at the river. "See for yourself—there *is* no light."

His eyes followed her finger to the dark water. The moonlight illuminated the river for him. He hung his head when all he found was darkness.

"Corwin, don't you see it? Please! Look hard, Corwin."

He sighed and shook his head. "All I see is darkness in me . . . I see your baby and what I've done. I see the moonlight accentuating a contained darkness. That's what I want for myself."

"What moonlight? What are you saying? Corwin . . . there's no moon out tonight."

Corwin raised his head in confusion and gazed at the sky. *Clouds . . . no moon or stars.* He then remembered how dark it had been in the woods on his way here. Puzzled, he slowly turned back to the water. A glowing light, the one he misinterpreted as moonlight, was growing brighter. "It's . . . consuming the darkness."

"NO! NO!" The woman rushed to the river's edge in disbelief.

Corwin threw the vial into the water. As it hit, the growing light burst into flame and leapt out, flinging him backwards.

He opened his eyes groggily after the fall, seeming to awaken from a deep sleep. How long he'd been lying there he didn't know.

"Here." He felt Thad prop him up.

Corwin put a hand on his chest. "I feel different . . . lighter."

Thad chuckled. "You are 'lighter', in more ways than one."

The sun was coming up, and Corwin rubbed his eyes as Thad brushed off the back of his shirt.

"Light is always more powerful than darkness, Corwin. Darkness scatters in the presence of light."

"How did you know . . . ." Corwin trailed off, unsure of what he wanted to ask.

"How to find you?"

Corwin shook his head. "No. How did you know about the light . . . light in me?"

"Why do you think I pulled you off that wall the day I found you?"

Corwin stared into his face and shrugged.

"You were someone who was clearly fighting a war inside himself and against the world. Corwin . . . the light inside you was obvious. Most folks just go about their day never addressing the conflict inside themselves. Where there's fight there's light." The man nodded in confidence.

Corwin still wasn't convinced. "How come . . . ." He looked down at his hands. "How come I couldn't see it?"

"Easy. You were too focused on the opposite. If you search only for darkness you'll find it, identify with it, and eventually become it. But," he pointed his index finger at Corwin, "the opposite is also true. Light brings forth light."

I want to believe him. Corwin inhaled deeply, then closed his eyes in pain. "The baby . . . ."

"It was an accident."

Tears stung Corwin's eyes. "But I was angry. It happened out of anger . . . that part wasn't an accident."

The man paused to clear his throat. Corwin knew Thad was fighting back tears as well. "As for that, I forgive you . . . Lucy and I forgive you. Please, come back with me. We've still so much to accomplish. I see so much potential in you."

Corwin couldn't believe Thad's words. He searched the man's face to see if they were really true. Thad's eyes appeared moist, but even so he offered Corwin his hand.

"I-I can't." Corwin drew away from him.

"So you're choosing to reject my gift of forgiveness. Is that it?" The man looked hurt.

"No! I . . . I—" Corwin wasn't sure what to say.

"To reject a gift is arrogant, Corwin. To receive one when you don't deserve it, well, that's humility . . . takes true courage."

Though Corwin had grown accustomed to such statements, his mind argued against the idea. *It's not fair.* Thad was graciously offering him a way out. He was choosing to move past what Corwin had done. "I-I," Corwin stammered again before lifting his eyes to Thad's, "Thank you."

Thad thumped him on the back then stood up. "Let's go home."

Corwin didn't budge. "Thad, I accept your forgiveness, but I can't—I can't go back. I don't deserve to be forgiven, and I definitely don't deserve to come live with you again."

Thad shot him a knowing look. "Oh, and what will you do now? Carry around guilt? Feel sorry for yourself that you committed such an action? Refuse to forgive yourself? That's arrogant too."

"What?"

"Me," Thad pointed to himself in dramatic fashion, "the victim so to speak, I'm able to forgive you. But *you* . . . you're not able to forgive yourself. Does that make you better than me, Corwin? Higher, perhaps?"

Corwin turned his face away. "Well, no. Of course not."

"Then show humility once more. Forgive yourself. Let it go, Corwin." Thad offered him a hand again and pulled Corwin to his feet. The two stared at one another in silence then slowly made their way back to the cabin.

Sebastian's whisper soon brought Corwin back to his present reality.

"Corwin . . . what happened to the baby?"

CHAPTER 10

CORWIN PINCHED THE crease between his eyebrows and opened his eyes.

The young boy immediately diverted his gaze away from his uncle. "Uh, never mind. You don't have to talk about it. Sorry."

Corwin sighed. "No, I can talk about it. I was outside, and it was dark. I was angry about something. I threw a shovel at the window of their house. And—and through the lights burning inside I saw their little toddler playing just before the glass shattered onto him. Then . . . all I remember is blood and screaming. That's when I ran."

"So, what happened—after the light, I mean?"

"I was different. Changed. I didn't hunt for darkness in myself any longer. Thad used to tell me, 'Whatever you focus on is what you will become, or whatever you give your affection to will define you.'"

"So I'm guessing that's where you learned to talk the way you do. It's all Thad's fault!"

Corwin chuckled, glad to do so after rehashing this part of his past. "I suppose so. In any case, I was his first recruit in the Thaddean Regime . . . though we didn't call it that until after he died."

"What happened to the woman by the river?"

The question unnerved Corwin. "I don't know."

Sebastian looked out the dark window again. "You really think war is coming?"

"It's already here."

He knew his words didn't bring Sebastian any comfort. *Was I right in bringing you here?* The nagging question echoed in Corwin's mind as he thought about what he had seen at the council meeting. "The Templins are here, Sebastian, and something dark is brewing in New Waiz. They've started something in shooting Clovis. They're waiting on something, or perhaps . . . someone." Corwin saw Sebastian shiver as he turned back toward him.

"Are they waiting on Old Waiz to respond or your regime to come together?"

"No, I doubt they suspect either of those. No . . . it's something evil." Though Corwin hated to admit it, he knew the truth. *I can feel it.* He gripped the sides of his chair and sighed deeply. "They want to unleash something with Differe. I'm hoping Joel's scrolls will give us some insight."

"I bet I know someone else who was in this 'Thad' thing with you."

Corwin was puzzled for a moment but welcomed the change of subject. "Who?"

"Haskell Rutherford."

Corwin cleared his throat.

"Ha! I knew it! I can see it on your face. He was in it!"

"Shh! Yes, yes, he was a part of it at one time, but it would take quite a bit of convincing for him to reprise his role." Corwin felt a rock settle in his gut.

"There's a story there." Sebastian sent him a lingering look.

Corwin swallowed hard. "It's not mine to tell."

"Did Thad—was he killed?"

Corwin looked into the eyes of his curious nephew and thought about Thad's death, then clenched his fists. "Much like Clovis. He was framed."

Sebastian sat back and crossed his arms. "You think the New Order did it?"

Corwin nodded. "That's what I suspected. Thad remained heavily involved in the New Order until his death. They began to see him as a threat to their power . . . or, their leader did." He shook his head. "Men and power can be dangerous especially when those in charge forget one of their primary goals should be raising up more leaders. It's a wonder the Order even still exists."

"He was in the New Order? What happened after he died?"

Corwin lowered his head; this part of the story still haunted him. "The army disbanded. His family was ridiculed and abandoned. Dreams squelched. All became quiet and . . . in order."

"He wasn't a good leader then."

Corwin's head shot up in fierce defense.

"You just said yourself that a good leader would replace himself."

Corwin felt the scars of his past being torn open. "No, he was a good leader—a great one. It was his followers . . . it was me. I failed him. I refused to take his place."

"Oh, Corwin." Sebastian moved close to him and put his hands on Corwin's knees. "Why?"

"It doesn't matter now. It's a long story, but what does matter is I'm moving forward. Thankfully, it's never too late." He patted Sebastian's hands.

"Why didn't you take his place, Corwin? Was it me? Was it my fault— you coming to live in Differe for a while?" The look in Sebastian's eyes broke Corwin's heart.

"No!" He emphatically shook his head. "I ran away to Differe. My grief—I let it overcome me."

"The grief of losing your leader?"

Corwin gritted his teeth. "Yes."

Sebastian looked at him pleadingly. "What aren't you telling me?"

He fiddled with the boy's fingers. "One thing you must know about this army . . . we all carry these." He held up his rhydid to Sebastian.

"But—but I don't have one."

"It's all right. What I want you to understand is that we . . . we all needed them."

Sebastian froze. "The mouthpieces . . . voices in your head?"

"Yes, that would be one of the reasons. Though some . . . some people just had illnesses."

"Healed . . . they were healed?" Sebastian's voice was barely audible.

Corwin nodded. "Yes."

He gasped, and Corwin saw hope spread across his whole being. He gripped the folds of Corwin's shirt. "I want to know more."

"You will, but I still have to figure out how to raise this army."

"Oh, right. Well, you need a caychura—a meeting with the Majestic. You need something supernatural."

"Yes, and perhaps a little spying."

"Spying? On the New Order?" Sebastian's eyes grew wide with delight.

"Something evil is lurking down in New Waiz. I feel it getting stronger." He gripped his rhydid and instantly thought of Joel. "We need to find out what it is."

Sebastian nodded. "That would give the army a purpose to band together for sure."

"Well, we've got to start somewhere. In any case I think we should start contacting a few folks to seek out interest." *That will be no small task, considering how I abandoned them all . . . .*

"How about Mr. Rutherford?"

"Perhaps, but right now I'm more interested in seeking out someone who's already on the inside." Corwin stroked his beard as he thought of such a meeting.

"Who? Can I come?" Sebastian unlocked the wheels on his chair.

"Thad's son."

Sebastian looked up at Corwin in disbelief. "His son?"

"Yes, the one who shot Clovis."

CHAPTER 11

ANDI WAITED UNTIL the Watchmen crossed the bridge nearest to his childhood home before moving from his hiding spot in the woods. New Waiz's security, known as the Watchmen, rarely crossed to this side of the river. *It's me they want . . . no other reason for this many to come this way.* He crumpled the wanted poster with his name and face splashed across it and threw it onto the ground. He hadn't been surprised to find he'd been named chief suspect for the murder of Clovis Macon. *That stupid redhead kid. I haven't seen his picture anywhere. He probably tipped them off.* As soon as he'd returned from Differe, he delivered Isabelle's letter to a Templin in the Adams Kalona. It was there he saw the first poster. Following this discovery he bolted to safety—*or what I thought was safe*—but the posters were in New Waiz too, and the New Order was nowhere to be found. The group that now called him a member had abandoned him, so he'd had to find solace in one of the towers above the Bridge of Miren. When he spotted a group of Watchmen head for the east side of the Pallas River early this morning, Andi decided it was time to move and find out about his missing comrades.

He waited patiently until seven of the Watchmen walked back toward downtown. He grabbed an arrow from his quiver and paused. To kill a Watchmen would be risking his citizenship. *How many are left? Who sent them? Are they here just to collect me for the trial? Did they go to mother's?* He needed answers before he made the next move. The surrounding area was quiet; few people resided east of the river. *Unless you're an outcast.* He carefully made his way through the woods to his mother's home. The log cabin was tucked between a fair amount of brush and trees, but the real thick of the woods was located behind the place. Andi shook his head at the cabin as he got closer. Between the decaying roof, the worn wood door, and iron-barred windows, he thought the place resembled more of an old jail than a home. *Can't even remember the last time I was here to see mother . . . or Arianna.* Though he was good to send his mother and sister every extra penny he earned, he wondered how he'd be received with the Watchmen visiting just moments before. He rounded to the backside of the cabin and smiled to himself. His mother forever insisted, "Only strangers use the front door, Andi. The back door's always kept unlocked for you."

He shuffled through dried crunchy leaves and kicked off any that had stuck to his shoes as he reached the back door. He took in a deep breath, softly knocked on the door, and gently pried it open.

"Mother." He kept his voice quiet as he entered the kitchen. "Mother, I'm home," he tried again when silence met him. Soon a short, plump woman came into view. Her usual broad smile that always accompanied open arms was instead displayed by a timid frown indicating something was wrong. Her eyes darted to the left wall, then back to him as she waved from across the kitchen floor.

"Is Arianna here?"

She shook her head "no" and started wringing her hands nervously. Her eyes darted to the left wall again, then she carefully pressed two fingers against her lips.

Andi nodded this time and pulled the bow from behind his back. *Two Watchmen in the house; I should've waited longer.* He grimaced at having put his mother in such a position . . . *again.* She'd already been through several of these predicaments because of his father. He sighed when she motioned for him to put the weapons away.

"She'll be back later."

Cowards! Why aren't they coming out to arrest me? He waited for his mother's next clue. "Well, I was hoping to catch her. She asked me to take her fishing by the river."

"She still takes the long way home. You know how afraid she is of the snakes by the river."

Andi raised his eyebrows. *Watchmen are waiting for me at the river too? Why so many?*

She pointed to the door and nodded. "I'll tell her you came by. Please be careful."

He looked down at his quiver strap and nodded behind him. "I'll be fine. See you in a few weeks."

After he closed the door behind him, he grabbed an arrow and quickly concealed it under the left side of his jacket. A series of questions flooded his mind. *Are there more stationed outside the house, or is it just the two inside? How many are at the river? Have these two been here since the murder? Were the others just checking in? Where is Arianna?*

A branch snapping to his right grabbed his attention. He pressed his back against the cabin and got his bow ready for the arrow in his left hand. Whoever was approaching seemed less cautious, as the noises grew louder and more consistent. He drew the arrow, cringing inside knowing he'd have to aim to kill. *Wounding him would only lead to another trial . . . then I'll certainly be found 'guilty.'*

Just before the guard was about to pass into his line of fire the footsteps stopped. Andi grew anxious at the silence. His eyes darted around the woods as his fingers kept the string of his bow tight. A humming sound . . . then piercing pain in his leg brought him to his knees. He groaned in pain as the bow fell from his hands.

"Ha! That'll teach you to—" the voice stopped as the individual came around the corner.

He spotted a seventeen-year-old girl, one often called his twin. Andi ran his hand to the spot that was searing with pain. He looked down at his right calf. *A dart.*

"Andi?" His sister stared at him, then looked at the cabin in fear. She rushed forward and breathed his name again. "Andi." She spotted the dart in his leg and beat her head with her fists. "Oh no! I didn't know it was you. I promise I didn't know it was you!" She shook as tears filled her dark eyes.

Andi grabbed her chin. "Arianna, calm down. What's in this?" He clutched the dart, wondering how long the tip was.

"No!" She frantically grabbed his hand. "It will spread if you remove it. Can you still feel your leg?"

"It feels like there's fire running through my veins." He grasped the side of the cabin in pain.

"It's—it's, well, it's, um, enervo."

"Good grief, Arianna!"

"I know! I'm sorry I . . . well, I thought if I paralyzed the thief he wouldn't be able to steal from us anymore."

"Thief? Who? Who gave you the enervo?" He grabbed her arm, and a bulging muscle flexed underneath his grip. Puzzled, he suddenly noticed a much stronger frame had replaced his sister's thin appearance. He then remembered the healthy state of his mother inside the cabin. *They certainly haven't been starving . . . what is someone stealing?*

"Just forget it! Forget that for now. The Watchmen! Andi, you've got to get out of here."

He nodded. "Right. Go in and tell them you passed me near the river . . . heading toward Old Waiz." He rose to his feet, then cursed in pain.

"Okay, I-I'll tell them. Don't touch that dart until I get back."

With Arianna providing a distraction inside the cabin, he took the opportunity to move into the woods. He was sure she'd have told him if there were more Watchmen nearby. His leg tingled with numbness as he limped into the thick woods behind the cabin. *I wonder if I can make it to the cottage.* The trail to their family hunting cottage was so overgrown Andi wasn't sure he'd be able to find it. *But if that's the case, neither will the Watchmen.* Every few minutes he stopped and held the flesh around the dart. It was turning black and growing numb to his touch. He cursed again and hoped his sister had an antidote for the poison infecting his leg. Just as he lost feeling completely, the cottage finally came into view a few yards away. Andi hobbled to the door dragging along his limp leg. He pushed it open and hit the floor with a thud. Desperate for relief, he pulled himself across the floor to the whiskey cabinet and grabbed the first jug he saw. He uncorked the bottle with his teeth and brought the burning liquid to his mouth.

"Andi, don't!"

He craned his neck and found Arianna walking inside with a satchel bag draped over her shoulder. She took the bottle from his hands and helped him to the couch. "Whiskey settles you. I need you awake. You can have some later."

He fell back on the couch and stared at the thick roof above him. His dad had built the cottage, and it was much sturdier than their home. Andi often camped out in the old place as a young teen pretending he knew the man. He would search around the one-room cottage for clues about his father—anything the man would've left behind. But all Andi knew of him was a string of differing tales—traitor versus hero, weak versus strong, crazy versus wise. He closed his eyes, knowing the real story would forever be a mystery to him.

"Wake up!" Arianna shook his arm. "Besides, you have some explaining to do."

He startled and opened his eyes. "Mother . . . is she safe?"

"She's fine. The Watchmen left—believed my story. Would've been too suspicious if we both disappeared into the woods. May have led them right to you." She began to cut the fabric of his pants surrounding the dart.

Andi looked down at the projectile in his leg and remembered he had some unanswered questions. "Who's been stealing what? What's been going on?"

She stopped cutting, looked at him in silence, and grabbed something else from the bag.

He gripped her arm. "Answer me."

Arianna raised her eyebrows as she removed his hand from her bulging bicep.

"And where'd these guns come from?"

She flipped her long black curls over her shoulder. "You've been gone a while. A lot has happened."

He sensed a bitter tone in her voice. "Have you been getting the money?"

She softened and patted his hand. "Why, yes. Yes, of course. Always."

Andi's eyes widened as she drew a syringe out of her bag. Attached was the longest needle he'd ever seen. "Do you know what you're doing? Arianna, what's going on? Please tell me what's happened."

She chuckled at his stiffened posture. "Don't worry; this isn't going in you. It's a slow release dart. I'm going to try to remove what's left of the enervo before it reaches your leg." She unscrewed the head of the dart and stuck the needle inside.

He wiped sweat beads from his brow as he watched the needle draw out a clear liquid, then a bit of blood.

Arianna quickly measured the liquid. "Oh, thank goodness. Less than half the drug made it into your leg."

"Yeah, great. So, do I get to keep the dart or what?"

She leaned back and cocked her head at him. "For now. At this point it's saving your nerves. If I take it out the enervo will spread into your nervous system, and, uh, your brain won't be able to talk to the nerves in your leg."

He sighed. "Which would make my condition permanent."

"Andi, I'm sorry. I didn't mean to, I . . . ." She stopped and fidgeted with a piece of gauze in her hand.

He wasn't much for guilt and gently kicked her with his good leg. "I know you didn't. It'll be fine. Don't worry about it . . . however, I am worried about you. Please—"

"No, you first. I want to hear if the rumors are true. And, um, I'm going to have to bind this too, so you might want to talk and get your mind off it. I don't want it to spread any further."

"Sounds just lovely. Suppose I can have my whiskey now?"

She nodded.

"What have the Watchmen told you and mother?"

"That you're wanted as a witness in the murder trial for the Old Order's head councilman. Oh, what's his name? Clovis Macon. I-I figured if it were true that might mean—"

"They don't want me as a witness."

She bent down toward his face, eyes wide with anticipation. "Well?"

Andi turned away just to spite her.

"Come on! Well? Ugh, you're so stubborn." She grabbed his face and searched his expression for clues.

He put her off a few more moments, yet was so impressed with her earnestness that he finally broke into a grin and spilled the news. "Member."

"Hoorah! A member of the New Order!" Arianna stood up and raised her hands to the ceiling. "Now that's a much better reason for a drink." She fetched two glasses along with the whiskey.

She beamed at him, and his cares felt a little lighter.

She clinked her glass against his. "Cheers."

He finished his drink in one gulp then pointed to the dart in his leg. "Arianna, come on now . . . tell me what's been going on. Where'd you even get something as potent as enervo?"

She looked down, then back into his eyes in a way that made him wonder if he wanted to hear the answer. "I made it."

Andi sat upright. "You—you what? Is *this* what people are stealing from you?"

Her silence answered his question.

He gritted his teeth, fearing the worst. "You're selling it aren't you?"

"Maybe."

"Drug dealing? Arianna, are you mad? They'll lock you up for years if you're caught!" A deep pain filled his heart as he looked at his baby sister. *After all I did to take care of you . . . after all I've done to protect you—*

"Judge all you want, but at least I didn't kill anyone."

Her remark stung deeply as he viewed Clovis's murder simply as an assignment from the New Order. He sighed, unsure of how to respond.

She crossed her arms over her chest. "It's a good living. I've met loads of interesting people. Some of them have even been training me to build up my muscles—they're the ones who gave me these guns."

"You're being naïve, Arianna. And you're not fooling me . . . those arms aren't just from working out." He held his hand over his eyes, hating to ask his next question. "Are you mixing enervo and something else . . . are you taking it?"

"No."

Andi breathed a sigh of relief.

"Not that one."

"Arianna! What else are you selling?" Andi suddenly thought of his mother. *What does she think about this? Is she taking something too?*

"Andi, what I'm selling is of small consequence. What's of real value is who's buying. I won't be going to jail anytime soon." Her dark eyes narrowed as she pulled a vial from her bag. "I'm taking fortis."

"An enhancement drug." He pinched her arm. "Not very shocking."

She pulled away from him. "It was recommended to me."

"By who? Some addict?" He shook his head in disapproval, blaming himself. *I was gone too long.*

"No . . . unless you think your boss is one.

"What? What are you saying?"

"I'm saying that the head of the New Order is one of my biggest buyers. Yeah, Andi, you heard me right. It's Emil Marcell."

Chapter 12

J OEL WAITED UNTIL they had been on the train for several minutes before shooting Augustine an angry look.

"What? You're going to kill me? You can't believe I wandered off? You're furious I'd risk blowing our cover?" She threw a hand in the air for effect. "Well, go on."

Joel started to open his mouth but felt her hand cover it.

"But wait. What's this?"

He watched her pull a folded piece of paper from her glove.

"Oh, and this, and this?" She proceeded to produce several tightly folded papers from varying places around her body.

He finally sighed at her satisfied smile. "Pretty pleased with yourself, huh?"

"I am." She nodded.

"You're not off the hook yet. If you ever pull something like this again—" He shook his head at her. "Yes, I'm furious with you."

"So furious that you can't even think of a punishment for the next time?" She playfully kicked the toe of his boot.

He wasn't amused yet. "Why'd you do it?"

"Corwin. He told me if we ended up anywhere important to look for clues or at least try to sabotage the search."

"He knew they'd be searching for us . . . ."

"I don't know about that, but the Templins are most definitely looking for whoever stole the rhydids. Anyway, remember how the lady from the Inquiry Desk at Crossroads said the 'Joel' in her picture had brown hair? Someone had to have changed that. I was hoping to do something like that and throw them off."

He put a fist to his lips and shook his head again. "You risked getting caught."

"I was just doing what Corwin said."

"I don't care what Corwin said. It was just plain stupid."

"What? Are you serious?"

"Well, I didn't tell you to do it, so don't get mad at me."

"Why not? You're mad at me. Besides, you just called me 'stupid'."

Joel had heard enough, and he threw his officer hat at the seat across from him. "Any other orders I should know about?" She shrunk back, and he was instantly filled with regret. He realized the person he was really mad at was Corwin. The man had not only kept much from both of them, but had also obviously created secrets between the two. He swallowed hard, knowing he wanted to reconcile. "Augie, listen . . . it's just the risk, well . . . it's Sebastian. Every time you risk getting caught his life is in jeopardy. I understand what Corwin may have told you, but he's not here, and I say you're too valuable to risk getting caught."

Her eyes softened, and she looked towards the floor.

"Oh, and I'm sorry I had to make up what I did in front of the officers about . . . well, you know. I wanted to pulverize them for the way they treated you."

She sat back and crossed her arms.

"You can hit me if you like—if it will make you feel better." He winced, pretending to brace himself.

"It might . . . but you've been beaten enough on my account already."

He leaned back in his seat, wishing to avoid such a topic.

"Joel, I-I'm sorry too. I honestly didn't think of Corwin's idea until we were inside. There wasn't time to explain. I was hoping you'd just trust me."

"This has to stop between us. The secrets. I know neither of us wants to divulge much of what's behind us, but as much as we don't want to . . . we've got to come clean or miscommunication will doom us."

Her lips formed a smirk. "Doom us? Really?"

"You know I always go for the dramatic. All right, all joking aside, let's be honest with each other." He leaned toward her and put his hands on his knees. "I'm all ears."

She put her hands on her hips. "Me? I have to go first?"

"I'm only being a gentlemen. Ladies first, Augie."

"Uh, that hardly seems fair!"

"Perhaps, but it's true, and I must hold to my character." He gave her a firm salute.

"Yes, well, your *pretty face* wishes you'd go first."

He made a zipper motion across his lips.

She fidgeted under his silence and eventually let out a breath of hot air. "Fine then, ask questions if you want, but the gist of what Corwin told me is how to help you when the mouthpieces come and what I just told you about the Templins. Oh, and Corwin also said if the Templins discover I'm with you they'll—they'll somehow use me to get to you . . . meaning—"

"If they figure out you're a girl we have to separate. Yeah, I know. That's why I decided to separate the first time."

"I see. Well, what else do you want to know?"

"Sebastian—what's the deal with him and the rhydid?"

She shrugged in sadness. "He's sick, dying really. There's no cure for him . . . whatever it is seems to be spreading."

Joel felt like he'd just been punched in the gut. "Why . . . why would you say it's spreading?"

"He used to walk unassisted. He used to be bigger, stronger . . . actually growing. I—" Her mouth clamped shut, and she turned away from him.

"Augie? Augie, it's okay you don't have to—"

"There's a lot there . . . 'behind' as you mentioned . . . but anyway, his breathing got worse, and, well, he was catching pneumonia and infections all the time with the freezing temperatures in Differe. So, like you, we escaped to Waiz."

He waited to see if she would go on as he digested the information.

"I'm not exactly sure about the rhydids. There's some connection between them and the Majestic. I forget most of the rubbish Corwin told me about it before we left."

Joel raised his eyebrows at her lack of faith.

"Listen, it's obvious they hold some sort of power, but there's something . . . really one more thing you should know. Sebastian, well, he's worth it. He's worth trying anything at this point in my mind."

Joel nodded.

"But . . . we've tried this before. We've tried the whole king Majestic thingy. It didn't work, and I don't want to talk about it."

"Did you have a rhydid?"

"I *said* I don't want to talk about it, but at least now you know why I'm skeptical."

Joel nodded and begged himself not to pry anymore, but he couldn't help asking one more question. "Augie . . . are you Waizen?"

Her face fell flat. "My uncle's from there, so of course I'm connected. I mean, look at me."

He looked over her dark features again then stopped on her blue eyes. He suddenly recalled Officer Chadwick's advice to ditch her as well as the officer's overall disdain of Waiz. It seemed not only Differe, but even the West End didn't think well of Waiz. *I've got to get her out of here!*

Augustine interrupted Joel's racing thoughts. "Ahem. I do believe it's your turn to share."

"What? Oh yeah, about my secrets. Um, let me think . . . well, Corwin also told me to separate if we needed to. But, uh, it was more in reference to making sure you got back to Sebastian—not protecting me. He also said not to take Isabelle as 'the bait.' You know, get the rhydids and get out of there. He mentioned a lot of stuff about the mouthpieces and the king, but I won't bore you with that." Joel was ecstatic to finally have the opportunity to bring Isabelle up in conversation. Nothing had been said about her since Augustine had revealed it was Isabelle's ticket he was given during their first escape from Differe. He waited in anticipation as Augustine scratched her head and pursed her lips in thought.

"Tell me why you need your rhydid?"

He was naturally disappointed by this question but hid it well. "Corwin says I need it to fight the mouthpieces."

"Should we look at Mr. Rutherford's book now?"

"Not yet. I think we need to come up with a plan for what to do when we get to Facilis. But first, what's your verdict on me? And, uh, Isabelle and you . . . is that a closed subject too?"

She gave him a long look then piled the stolen documents onto her lap. "You already had my trust. Here, we should read these to help us form a plan."

Frustrated by her answer, Joel begrudgingly took one of the papers and carefully unfolded it. He attempted to study it, then sighed as his weakness exposed itself.

"What's wrong?"

"It's not a map."

"So?"

"Corwin didn't tell you . . . about, well, my reading."

"No." She took the paper from his hands.

He was relieved she said nothing else.

"Scoot over." She moved to his side of the compartment and pointed to a stamped circular seal with her pen.

Joel's eyes widened. "The eagle seal? The head of the Differian Democracy . . . he's in on this?"

"You would think, but it's not Preceptor Muse." She pointed to the signature at the bottom of the page. "Can you read the signature next to the seal?"

Joel stared at the letters and broke into a sweat. "Uh, the first word's too long."

"You're right; it's two words. Let me break it apart for you." She covered half of the word with her hand.

"Well, it's an 'h'?"

Augustine's nod encouraged him. "Yes, now use your gift. The only thing Corwin mentioned about your reading was that you were gifted or something—that you could see beyond the words."

He felt her curious blue eyes bore into him as he took a deep breath. He didn't exactly know how to use the "gift" the king had mentioned to him in the caychura. He just knew that before the cave he could barely read anything, yet now his reading somehow seemed to be improving every day. He had looked at the cave's ceiling unable to read, but when he saw the image behind the writing the message had suddenly become clear. So, in an attempt to recreate his experience in the cave, Joel studied the eagle stamp for any markings or clues. He jumped back when he thought he saw the bird's wings flutter on the page.

He was surprised to feel Augustine's hand calmly grab his arm. "You're all right. Try again." She held the paper in her hand and gave him a pen.

Sweat trickled down his forehead as he leaned forward to study the symbol again. Instantly he saw the wings of the eagle expand and start fluttering again. He didn't jump this time but watched and waited. The wings flapped and slowly began to change shape. The feathers turned into fingers, and Joel saw thumbs joined to outline the bird's head. The bird had become two flapping hands, and all became clear. Joel lightly traced the image with the pen—the jewels covering the hands, the 'h', and the last word on the page. "Headmaster Dark."

Augustine looked back at him and smiled. "That's right. Very good."

He grabbed the paper from her and devoured the words on the page. "I can read it, Augie. I-I can read most of this. The headmaster sent this out to the entire Templin guard."

"Great. We're becoming even more popular."

"Uh, yeah, that's one way to look at it. The letter's notifying the guards in Differe, the Southern Regions, the Northern Regions, and Waiz . . . since when are there Templins in Waiz? Anyway, they're all looking for us. Says I'm a fugitive, and the other *boy* is my accomplice. It—"

"How come *I'm* the accomplice?"

"We're 'armed and dangerous,' but don't worry, we're to be kept alive if captured. There's even severe punishments if we get killed."

"Well, that's nice. Suppose I'm glad my death would be rectified. Does it say anything about what we've done?"

"We took temple property. 'All trains traveling to Waiz as well as trains departing from Differe will be checked. Trains to the West End, particularly those heading to Facilis, will also be searched.' Wonder what that means—the 'Facilis' part?"

She grabbed another piece of paper to read. "Don't know. Do you know anything about Facilis?"

Joel scratched his head. "Yeah, one of my professors used to talk about it a lot . . . something about politics. Obviously it's in the West End—I think it's the capital. Uh, maybe it's pretty much neutral when it comes to laws and stuff, but—"

"Joel! Joel!"

He covered his ears. "What? I'm right here."

The train suddenly started braking, and both turned their heads to the window. Augustine gasped and turned back to him in horror.

"Augie, what? What is it?" Her expression unnerved him.

"They're checking all trains going to Facilis! They keep stopping them. They're trying to catch us before we get there."

Joel stared back at her puzzled, tapping the pen against his mouth. "Uh, I know. I just told you that."

"Listen. 'Headmaster, about the legal issue you spoke of in the West End, this is what I have discovered. If the fugitives journey to the West End, legally the region will have to release them to Differe; however, if they reach Facilis they will become property of their political system. In fact, any fugitive may take up residence in the capital and claim political refuge. Facilis's political justices require that any inhabitants of the region receive an impartial trial. Bottom line is as you feared—we will be unable to touch them.'" Augustine looked up at Joel as the train came to a halt.

He grabbed her shoulders. "If we get to Facilis they can't touch us."

"Which means they're going to do everything within their power to stop us."

He shot a quick glance toward the compartment door. "Come on, we're getting off. Let's—"

"Ladies and Gentlemen, to expedite our journey and limit your delay, we ask that you stay in your seats. Templin guards will be inspecting the cabins shortly. Thank you for your cooperation."

The two looked at one another as the overhead speaker clicked off. Neither said a word, giving Joel enough time to think of a plan—a plan he couldn't share with Augustine. He pretended to doodle on the headmaster's letter, then stood up and grabbed his backpack.

"Okay, you stay here, *Honey*. I'm going to another compartment."

Her face lit up in protest.

"Uh-uh. You'll be fine. I'll see you after we start going again." He tipped his hat as she waved in obvious irritation. "See you soon."

Augustine stiffened as she heard the compartment doors banging around her. She hid the papers again and fell back against the seat. *I need sleep.* It seemed at every juncture there was something to get anxious about— something to keep her adrenaline up. They had yet to have a break. *We have to get to the rhydid, we have to get to the Waiz train, and now, we have to get to Facilis. I'm so tired.*

"Miss?" A Templin stuck his head inside.

"Officer." She nodded coolly.

"Traveling alone?" The man gazed over at Joel's empty seat.

"There's no one here."

He nodded and closed the door.

She waited until the train jerked forward before fishing out the only piece of paper they had yet to read. *Thank goodness we're leaving.* She gazed out the window and found the officers filing toward another Templin office. *Interesting.* Being deeper into the West End, it was certainly disturbing seeing Differe's guards so far from home.

She looked the other way and noticed one guard going in the opposite direction of his group. The man was walking in step with the train further up from her compartment. *There's something familiar about the way he walks.* He suddenly thrust his hands into his pockets and stopped to lean against a post. Augustine gasped and pressed her hands against the window in disbelief. She held her breath as her car drew nearer to him. Tears welled up in her eyes as her hands pounded the glass. "No, no, no!" Joel seemed to notice her and pressed the pen she'd given him against his lips, then turned away. She didn't know how they had come to know each other so well, but she read his gesture immediately and grabbed the headmaster's letter he'd read to her. *He had read . . .* She hadn't even had time to explain to him how she knew he'd be able to read. *And it wasn't from what had happened in the cave.* She opened the paper and found Joel's "doodle."

> Augie, sorry to leave you. They're not looking for you. Hide in Facilis until you think it's safe to go to Waiz. Meet at the caychura like Corwin said. You can do it. J

Tears streamed down her face. "No! Why? Joel, I need you! I don't know how to find the Waiz train. And Sebastian . . . he's counting on me." The worst of it she couldn't say aloud, but she didn't have to. A cold voice in her head spoke it instead. "You. Are. Alone."

She shivered inside. She hated being alone, but this time was different. Her heart ached. *Do I . . .* she stopped herself and closed her eyes. Joel's smiling face greeted her. He took her hand and started swinging it. "You can do anything. I know you can." She shook herself awake and grabbed the last unread document from her lap. The paper fluttered to the floor as she jumped to her feet. Her hands pressed against the glass once more. "Joel! Your father! He knows you've escaped!" It was no use; the train station was nearly out of sight. She sighed. "Oh, Joel. He's looking for you. He's coming for you!"

Chapter 13

SEBASTIAN, WAKE UP."

Sebastian rubbed the sleep from his eyes as Corwin pressed a hand against the bedroom window.

"They're starting to watch the house."

Sebastian bolted upright and spotted a Templin guard standing near a tree at the end of Corwin's drive. "Did they follow you back here?"

Corwin shook his head. "I don't think so. But it's all right . . . I wasn't able to accomplish anything."

Sebastian gave his uncle a questioning look. He had gone to New Waiz during the night.

"Andropolis . . . he's . . . I suspect it's the Order's doing . . . ." The man scratched his head. "Though I can't understand why . . . ."

"Corwin!" Sebastian swatted at him. "Stop giving me pieces. What happened? What did you find out?"

"Oh, sorry. There's a warrant out for his arrest, but I'm positive he's hiding." Corwin leaned forward and rested his forearms on his knees.

Sebastian sighed. *There goes that idea.* Both sat in silent frustration at their failed plan.

Sebastian turned his gaze to the morning light outside then back to the Templin. "Are there any more?"

"I'm not certain, but I think there are a few in the woods behind the house."

Panic surged through Sebastian at the mention of the woods. "Oh! Oh no! The mouthpieces!"

Corwin returned his cry with a puzzled look.

"Remember? That's where they got Joel when I got sick." He recalled the moment vividly, being unable to breathe and Joel being sent to get the alabaster herb for him . . . yet not returning. He knew it was the real reason Joel had decided to go back to the temple. Sebastian could still hear his voice, "As much as I don't want to go, I think of that moment, and . . . well, I never want that to happen again."

Corwin finally nodded in remembrance. "It won't be the same for the Templins, Sebastian."

"Why not?"

"They won't notice them . . . ignorant fools."

Sebastian raised his eyebrows.

"Sorry . . . what I mean to say is the mouthpieces control them. Joel only notices them because he's fighting against them . . . he recognizes they're trying to control him."

"Hm. Sounds kinda like your 'darkness'."

"Yep, except Joel realized on his *own* what they were saying wasn't true."

"That's not true! He needed you to help him, and he needs the rhydid. Everyone's listening to something. And, you know it doesn't do him a lot of good to just recognize their lies—he's got to actually quit believing them."

Corwin smiled at him. "Come up with that on your own?"

"Sort of. Don't be mad . . . ." He paused until Corwin held his hand up in promise. "I started looking at the scrolls Joel left."

"Oh?" He appeared impressed.

"Yeah, but more on that later. We have Templins to worry about right now. Think we should head to the cave?"

"That's why I woke you up. We need to make a different plan. Get dressed. We're going to see Mr. Rutherford."

"What?" Sebastian poked his head through the shirt he was pulling on. "But it's so early."

"He'll be up."

Sebastian looked at his suitcase. "Corwin—"

"Yes, pack a lot . . . I'm not sure when we'll be coming back."

"What about the Templin?"

"If this is his post, he'll stay put and just inform his contacts we've left . . . or he'll follow us." The man shifted his rhydid sheath around his waist, and Sebastian hurried to pack.

Corwin's mountain house was located near the base of the mountain where Joel had found the caychura, so it took over an hour to reach Mr. Rutherford's shop. Sebastian rode on Corwin's back most of the hour and, though he hadn't meant to, fell asleep for most of the journey. When he was bounced awake he realized he had no idea why they were going to see Mr. Rutherford. "Corwin?"

"Yes?"

"What are we doing?"

"Going to get some information. Just follow my lead." The man rang the front bell until they saw a dark shape emerge from the back room.

Sebastian's eyes widened. "That's not Mr. Rutherford."

"Shh! It's all right."

Sebastian peered over Corwin's shoulder to see a twenty-something year old man draped in a gray Templin cloak. He gave Corwin a tight squeeze.

"Can I help you two? The shop's not open for a few more hours."

"Yes, I'm looking for Haskell, or Mr. Rutherford."

"Oh, well, he's—"

"You're pretty early for work aren't you?" Corwin pressed hard against the door, and the Templin's eyes zoomed up to Sebastian.

"Yes, I suppose I—"

"Does Haskell know you're here? He's a very good friend of mine."

The guard quickly smoothed his robes. "Uh, yes, he's letting me stay here."

Corwin stepped forward and pressed the door back further. "Hm. Doesn't sound like him."

The young man shrugged in response, but Sebastian knew he was intimidated.

Suddenly Corwin punched the door, and the young man tumbled backwards onto a display case. The Templin hurried to his feet again and rushed to the bottom of the stairs leading to Mr. Rutherford's rooftop.

Corwin made for the stairs and muttered over his shoulder. "Hold on tight."

The Templin held his hands out in protest. "Stop! You have to leave. We're not open yet."

Before Sebastian knew what was happening Corwin let go of his legs. He clutched Corwin's shoulders as his uncle grabbed the front of the Templin's cloak. His jaw dropped when Corwin picked the young man up and dangled him in the air.

"Put me down!"

Sebastian expected Corwin to drop him, but to his surprise Corwin walked up the stairs holding the guard in front of him. When the three reached the top, Corwin kicked open the door and dropped the young man onto the roof floor. Sebastian looked around and couldn't believe his eyes. The rooftop garden was no more! The lush plants had been replaced with satellite equipment and dozens of dark metal trunks.

The Templin scrambled to his feet and attempted to keep Corwin from moving forward. "You're not supposed to be up here. You—you had better go."

Corwin grunted in his direction and pulled the rhydid from his belt. He held the tip of the blade to the Templin's throat when the young man reached under his cloak. "Get your hands in the air, fool. Sebastian, jump down."

Sebastian's slid off Corwin's back as the Templin cringed in terror.

"Listen to me! You've got to get out of here!"

Ignoring the young man's request, Corwin walked over to a trunk and threw open the lid. "Empty? What's the meaning of this?"

The Templin went into a panic. "Stop! Don't open those! Please!"

Corwin marched back over to the young Templin cowered in fear and pulled the back of his cloak, forcing the young man to look at him.

"Where is he?"

"Wh-who?"

Corwin growled and pulled the cloak tighter. "Don't make me ask again."

"We're—we're not sure. Honest!" The man screamed when Corwin dragged him backwards across the roof floor.

Sebastian looked at the stern expression on Corwin's face and wasn't sure whether to cheer or to be afraid.

"The boy just vanished! We thought you'd know where he was. That's why we've been watching your house. That's why we took over the shop, hoping he'd come back here."

Corwin let go of the man's cloak, dropping him onto the hard gravel and bent over him. "I'm looking for Haskell. Where is he? Be quick about it."

"Oh, him. He—he just left . . . okay, fled. He didn't really have a choice once we took over the shop."

"Where did he go? I'm sure some of you followed him."

The man scooted back against one of the trunks. "He was followed to Neutral Waiz. That's all I know."

Corwin made his way back over to Sebastian and picked him up. "We'll see ourselves out." He tipped his hat before walking back down the stairs. He took Sebastian straight into the washroom from the rooftop. After looking around a moment he grabbed a chain with a jeweled stone from a wooden peg. He stuffed the object into his pocket then walked over to the counter. "Might as well grab some breakfast while we're here. Let's get a few things and eat in the park."

After Corwin opened the door, Sebastian slid down his back. "I want to walk."

"You sure? Have you got your braces on?" Corwin bent down and peered into his green eyes. "You know I'm still the same Corwin, Sebastian. You don't need to be afraid of me."

Sebastian nodded and crossed his arms. "I know. And you know what else? I was kind of scared of the Templins, but now I know they're nothing to worry about."

"Good. You did very well back there—a true blue soldier."

Sebastian rolled his eyes. "All I did was stand there."

"You were helpful. You noticed his Templin garb and gave me a good squeeze to alert me."

Sebastian shrugged. "You would've figured it out."

"You held on when I told you to. A good apprentice can follow instructions . . . instructions that aren't fully disclosed. You had to use your instincts."

Sebastian finally accepted his praise and grinned at him.

"And, you've got a head start on me with the scrolls."

The stream of compliments gave Sebastian the courage he needed to ask a question he'd been harboring. "Um, Corwin?"

"Hm?"

"Are all the Templins we've seen here just for Joel? Your house, Mr. Rutherford's, and the ones at the council meeting?"

Corwin's face hardened.

There he is—Corwin the spy again.

"Something's going on. They forced Haskell to leave . . . I hope he's all right. We've got to find out why so many are here."

Sebastian then asked the question he wasn't sure Corwin could answer. "If it's not Joel, then what does the temple want with Waiz?"

CHAPTER 14

TALAN LANGSTON DIDN'T waste any time. The cunning general reviewed his briefing from the headmaster, collected his entourage, and was on the next train to Waiz. His four men sat in a compartment together while he sat in one alone. He had a stack of books on Waiz history and laws to research. He stared at the stack then decided to go through his mail first. He opened an envelope that was delivered to him just prior to leaving the West End.

> General,
>
> The deed you requested has been performed at this time. Secretary Magnus died at the hand of his own knife near the Differian border. The West End is sure to be at fault if accomplices are suspected, but any investigation should confirm the death was a suicide.
>
> Yours in Allegiance,
> Officer Preffet

Talan reached into his breast coat pocket for a lighter. He lit the paper on fire and dropped it onto his silver lunch tray. He glanced at *The Differian Post* situated on the seat across from him. *I can just see the headline tomorrow: Headmaster's Secretary Commits Suicide. Just like Dark wanted.* He didn't expect any affirmation for following his master's orders, but Talan had been confused as to why he'd been called to Waiz right in the middle of his investigation of the rhydid thieves. *And never mind that the West End is on the brink of a revolt.* He decided to keep his discoveries about the fugitives or fugitive—*I've only seen the girl*—under wraps until he returned. He was suspicious of his master's silence . . . even that it had been Holt who let the two escape. He rubbed his temple. *Either way, I'm the one who put the effort into the investigation. I intend to be the one to reap the benefits.* He put the lighter back into his pocket and thought of the last time he was in his master's presence. An impressed grin spread across Talan's face when he remembered someone else had been there too . . . .

"Andropolis, you've made no mention of the Southern Regions. What is Marcell saying about them?" Talan gestured to the wall map in the headmaster's office as he walked toward the hooded apprentice from New Waiz.

"He doesn't believe they will be as eager to become involved as the Northern Regions will be . . . initially. Since his first plan is to control Old Waiz, he has called for their aid and yours." The young man's deep voice held a commanding presence.

"Ah, I see. He plans to surround the Southern Regions just as he will first do to Old Waiz." Talan clapped his hands in admiration. "Fear—a most powerful tactic."

Andropolis shrugged. "I suppose. The most difficult part of that plan is controlling the seas. I think the region that controls the sea will hold the most bargaining power."

Talan moved closer to inspect the emblem on the young man's green cloak. "Are you a soldier?"

"No, just an apprentice for the New Order. My father . . . he was in the service."

"Mine too. You'd do well to follow in his footsteps."

Talan turned slightly and suddenly pulled the short sword from his belt. Andropolis's sword was pointing at Talan's neck before he even had time to thrust his forward.

"Very good." Talan stepped back, impressed at the young man's readiness. "Let's see your skills."

Talan made a gesture toward himself, and the two bowed to one another. Andropolis stuck out his long sword and made a swipe at him.

"Feeling me out, eh?" Talan missed his blow and soon metal clashed on metal as the two attempted to disarm each other. Before long Talan became aggressive, moving forward and forcing Andropolis to back away. Once he had him in a corner, Talan took the opportunity to take several sharp swipes at Andropolis. He gloated when his last swing caught Andropolis's left arm but was surprised when the young man didn't flinch. The general became more assertive, and after a few more blows he successfully knocked Andropolis's large sword from his hand.

He pointed the short sword at Andropolis's chest and winked. "Bigger doesn't necessarily mean better, now does it? Surrender?" A massive blow to his chest from young man's boot sent him flying backwards onto the floor. Talan's attempt to stand became futile when the hooded agent dropped a knee into his chest and punched the arm holding the short sword. Soon the young man held Talan's own sword at his neck.

"Big or small—I can work with either." Andropolis lowered the sword and lifted his knee off Talan.

Talan coughed as he sat up in shock.

The headmaster's hands clasped in delight. "Impressed?"

Talan rubbed his chest. "Very. Are all agents of the Order trained such as you?" He took Andropolis's hand and stood to his feet in amazement.

Andropolis smoothed the folds of his cloak. "Yes, but few complete their training."

"I see." Talan turned to the headmaster. "I like the plan. I'm pleased to assist in both revolts."

"I'll see to it that you do participate in both the one in Waiz and the one in the West End, Langston. Agent Andropolis, you have our token of allegiance. I'll send for a junior Templin to take you to the young lady with the letter. I do appreciate you delivering it to my associates in Old Waiz."

Before Andropolis walked out the office doors, Talan called after him, "Don't deliver letters forever, Andropolis. You're a remarkable swordsman. You'd make a fine soldier."

He waited until Andropolis was out of earshot then threw his hands up in the air in triumph. "Is that one of them, Master Dark?"

"No, not that I know of. That one . . . he just has natural talent." The man stroked his dark mustache. "I have a feeling Marcell is saving them. Yes, the Black Ferox will make a debut that is fierce, flashy, and public—the best methods for driving fear to gain control."

Talan nodded in agreement.

"That's where you come in. Our troops have been flooding the east side of the river in Waiz for the past few months . . . pity a few died from inoculating them with the deadly nox strain."

Talan tensed at his words. As a general he took the responsibility of his men very seriously. The needless taking of lives angered him, and though he said nothing he was sure his expression gave his opinion away.

"Oh, come now, Langston, the troops needed a reason to want the zavis drug. In any case, I need you to secure their allegiance to Differe. They get the drug from Waiz, but their allegiance is strictly to Differe. There seems to be some discrepancy as of late. I don't want them turning rogue. They will listen to you."

"So, Marcell has his small team of Ferox, and we will have our army of these black guards." Talan scratched his head. The whole plan sounded good in theory, but his gut told him otherwise. *There's way too much room for error. I don't like this.*

"Yes, he thinks our army is there to help his precious Order . . . *his* Ferox super humans. I need you to convince him of this. I need you to get on the inside of that Order. I need you to play nice and make friends . . . very good friends . . . with Marcell."

"Of course. I will do all that you ask. As always, it is an honor to serve you, Headmaster." Talan bowed in allegiance.

"I chose well in you, Talan. I have never regretted it. I need you to get into the Bridge of Miren's towers. They will try to convince you there's no way to reach them, but there is. Find out how then contact me. Otherwise, wait to hear from me."

Talan nodded again.

"In the meantime, stir things up in Facilis. I want the West End scattered and scared." He stopped and chuckled. "Hungry if need be. The city will fall easily if its inhabitants feel powerless."

Talan raised his eyebrows. "That's pretty much been accomplished with the taxes."

"I'll send a full description of your orders for Waiz through Secretary Magnus when it's time to move." The headmaster leaned forward over his desk. "And, Talan, see that he doesn't return."

Talan saluted him. "Killing that fool will be my pleasure."

"One more thing before you go. Do you wish to see Holt before you leave?"

Talan looked down at the headmaster's fingers drumming around his glass of scotch. He thought through his answer carefully. He wanted to see Holt, but the failure surrounding the young man indicated the headmaster would disapprove of a response like this. So he kept firm instead as he looked into his master's inquiring eyes. They were ready to give out approval or disapproval. "I'll see him after he restores his family name by completing his first assignment."

As Talan now sat on the train to Waiz, he somewhat regretted not seeing Holt that day. The boy had failed again by not catching the fugitives who took the temple rhydids, but worse than that he had lied about the girl. He was sorely disappointed in his son. *It's that pitiful girl, Isabelle. She's poisoned his brain.* In his last letter to Holt, he'd made his opinion of Isabelle very clear: "This Isabelle is nothing but a pretty voice, not even a pretty face. Quit listening to her brainwashing songs. She's making you weak. Eris Brunell, now that's a fine catch."

Women. Such trouble, yet so delightful. He smiled as he thought of his wife. He couldn't remember the last time he had seen her. When he thought of her long blond hair, fair skin, and piercing blue eyes he understood why Holt had such a weakness for the likes of Isabelle Chanton. She was not only the spitting image of Sylvia, her mother, but also her mother's distant cousin whom he'd married. Most of the Chanton women had these physical traits as well as a gracefulness that most other women had lost. Holt may have a weakness for women, but Talan couldn't imagine he'd let the "Honey" character he met escape on purpose. *However, I can see the brawn overriding brain with her too.* She could've tricked him with her charms just as Talan had done with her.

As he prepared to undermine the New Order, he promised himself to rid Holt of his weakness. He vowed to teach him to choose duty above all. That was the only voice he should ever listen to. After all, the young man had yet to realize his assignment to watch Joel had been chosen for him long before the two had ever stepped foot onto the temple grounds.

Chapter 15

"EMIL MARCELL!"

Those had been Andi's last words before he passed out on the sofa. Arianna had been glad to have his full attention . . . if only for a moment. Now his chest was rising and falling with rapid breaths. She put a hand on his hand. "You're gonna be okay. I'm sure I can make something that will help you." She knew he would disapprove of her activity over the last few months and dreaded telling him the whole story. *But after all he's done for me . . . I'll have to.*

Andi, eight years her senior, had practically raised her. He was her brother and "not my father" as she'd told him on many occasions, but he had played both roles . . . which meant they fought on both fronts. They had only each other on the east side of the river, and, for the most part, she'd always looked up to him. Perhaps they loved each other, but she felt like their relationship was based more on mutual respect. They had learned to survive together.

As long as she could remember, the Watchmen had come once a quarter to collect a property tax for living on the east side. When Arianna was older she saw it more as penance for her father's disgrace to New Waiz. After all the stories she'd heard about him from the gossips in town, she thought the Order's allowing them to even live in New Waiz was generous. The man had gotten into the New Order's inner circle then sold their secrets to Old Waiz. Most said he'd gone mad. Arianna wasn't sure where her mother stood on the subject. The woman had never said a bad word about him, yet she also never disagreed with negative comments said about him in public.

After Arianna and Andi found out about their father, they made a pact to care for their mother the way their father never did. For Andi, this meant joining the New Order. So it was no surprise on her thirteenth birthday when his years of service at the Marcell mansion landed him an apprenticeship with the New Order. He had barely looked back to say goodbye and had only come back twice, for a day or two, in the past four years. He had been faithful to send them money, but following his last visit the taxes had increased, which meant less money for food.

Arianna had checked the post every day hoping for something from Andi, desperate for him to send extra money for them. She even did her best to fish, but being deathly afraid of snakes she hated going to the riverbanks alone and most days didn't last long. By the time the second cool season hit, her mother's sacrifice of giving up part of her meals to Arianna was becoming fatal. Arianna still vividly remembered the desperation that had clutched her then and the futile effort to get help for her mother.

"Please! Oh please, you have to help me." She shook with fear as she banged on the glass window of the medical clinic.

The receptionist shook her head, refusing to open the window and allow her inside. "You don't have any money."

Arianna's cheeks flushed as judgmental scoffs rang out from those in line behind her. "I know, but I can pay you back. My brother's an apprentice of the New Order, and I'll receive his check within the week." She knew this would mean having to forgo paying the property tax this month, but she figured they could hide in their old cabin.

The woman shook her head in phony sympathy. "No, Dear, his puny check wouldn't be enough."

"But, please . . . I don't know what else to do. Can I work for you? I'll do anything!"

"No, thank you." The woman looked past her at the next person in line. "Move aside for the next patient, please."

Arianna's shoulders drooped in defeat. She headed back home, disgraced and empty handed. As she reached the last stretch of buildings on her road, she heard a hiss. *A snake!* She panicked and searched the ground. She soon realized the hissing was coming from an older woman trying to get her attention. Arianna cautiously moved toward the old hag, who was standing by a worn out cart. Arianna spied an assortment of mushrooms, greens, leaves, and objects her mind couldn't place. She kept a safe distance.

"Momma's got nox?"

Arianna's insides churned at the sound of the woman's raspy voice, but she managed to nod in response.

"Burning with fever, pale, unable to eat . . . how far gone is she?" The woman looked at her from underneath her hood with concern.

Arianna could barely bring herself to say the words. "Sh-She's become unconscious."

The woman smacked her old cracked lips together. "No wonder you're scared. You should be. She's close . . . and what will you do without her?"

Arianna's teeth began to chatter. The terror of her reality made her feel like she couldn't breathe.

"There. There." The woman bent down and started rummaging through the bottom of her cart. "Got something for her . . . but she'll have to keep taking it." The woman pulled out a glass bottle of dark blue liquid. Arianna read the label.

"Venom . . . s-s-alus? Oh, I can't!"

"If you want her to live you can. Yes, it's true she won't be able to get off it, but . . . it'll save her life." The woman shrugged and held out the tonic.

Arianna looked around to make sure no one saw the illegal poison extended to her. "What do you want in return?"

"Your help. Meet me under your bridge tomorrow morning."

Arianna nodded, and with her hands shaking, grabbed the bottle. She ran home only to find her unconscious mother paler than the white sheets covering her. She pulled the bottle from her pocket and stared at the dark letters on it. Guilt settled onto her as she unscrewed the top and her mother moaned.

"You're giving her this without her consent . . . in her weakest moment."

She jumped at the voice that sounded in her head, but quickly fought back. "But it won't be her last." And with that she poured the illegal liquid into her mother's mouth.

After her mother recovered, Arianna lied to the woman, telling her the blue liquid was a vitamin the clinic had given to her. She met with the old woman at the bridge and apprenticed under her until the woman was . . . well, gone. After her first round of tonics, pastes, and pills were ready she found the old woman's cart and set it up on a corner just down from the medical clinic. The location turned out to be the perfect selling spot. And though Arianna confiscated all of her mentor's supplies near the bridge, she dared not go back to the place where she'd received her first lesson. She even found another way home down river where the water was low enough to cross over. It appeared to be an unknown path, so she eventually hid most of her stash near there on the east side of the bank. One afternoon after her first few months of selling, she crawled up the bank to stash her unsold goods and check on her latest brewing concoctions.

"Let's see, anti-itching paste over here. Two more weeks on these herbal tonics. This flu tonic looks about ready." She looked down and scribbled in her personal notebook.

"How about some salus venom?" A hand covered her mouth. "Don't scream," said the male voice. "I just need some information. What happened to the old lady? She was my partner, and she seems to have gone missing."

Arianna struggled against the man's thick arms, but they held her tighter. She bit his hand and elbowed him hard in the ribs. A kick to his groin area finally allowed her to get loose. He growled behind her as she took off running into the woods. Tears of fear and frustration rolled down her face as she ducked under branches and spun around trees. She pressed through the thick brush as she went deeper and deeper into the woods. Her wet blurry vision sent her stumbling over a freshly cut stump, and she startled as an armful of firewood fell at her feet. She tried to backtrack, but it was too late.

"You there! Stop! Hands up where I can see them." A uniformed officer aimed an axe at Arianna's chest.

She raised her quaking hands as a group of armed men stood to their feet. Her eyes darted nervously as they looked at her, more in curiosity than in anger, for her intrusion into their camp. A guard broke through from the back of the group. He was not dressed in black coats like the others, but in a long gray cloak with several medals pinned on either side of his chest.

She shuddered. *He must be the leader.*

He motioned for the men to drop their weapons as he walked past them. "Well, Lass, what are you doing so far into the east side of Waiz?"

His smile calmed her slightly, yet she remembered her reason for running and quickly looked behind her. "There was—there was a man chasing me."

The others started sitting down when their leader beckoned her forward.

He had the bluest eyes she'd ever seen. She shot him a puzzled glance. "Are you Watchmen?"

"No, this is His Majesty's army, and I'm their Templin. We're from Differe. Have you heard of it?" He sat her down on a large rock.

She shook her head. "Where is it?"

"Far west and north."

She sat down in silence, fumbling with her hands and far too afraid to ask any more questions.

"I have only seen my men in these woods. Why were you being chased—"

"Captain! He's lost consciousness!"

The man hurried in the direction of the voice. Arianna turned to find dozens of men lying in a tent a few yards past the camp. She rushed after the captain, startling the other officers. "Sir! Pale, unconscious, fever? I mean, Captain, do your men have nox?"

"Aye, the weather change has many of them all messed up . . . among other things. This Waiz . . . it's an odd place for us." His firm expression faded as he let out a long sigh.

Arianna pulled her lips in tight. "I have something that could help them."

He looked back at her with raised eyebrows.

"I make tonics and such."

"Illegal tonics!"

Arianna squealed when she realized the man who'd held her captive moments earlier was lunging for her.

The captain moved in between them just in time. The guards held out their weapons once again. "And, who are you, Sir?"

"Rufus. The girl's with me."

Arianna jumped behind the captain. "I'm not with him! He was the one chasing me. Please don't believe him!"

The captain stepped toward the man. "What do you want with her?"

"Nothing. Well, I'd like to know where my partner is. We dabble in tonics as well. Last time I saw her she was headed to meet this one."

All eyes fell on Arianna. She looked at Rufus as he rubbed his grimy hands together.

"I, of course, want to know about my partner because it's hurting my business being shorthanded and all, but uh, more than that, Marcell, the head of the New Order, wants to see her."

"Is that so? I have a meeting with him later today. I'll take her." The captain didn't budge when Rufus moved forward in protest. Soon the dirty scoundrel was surrounded by the other guards.

"Fine." Rufus shot Arianna a dirty look as he rubbed his groin area then walked away.

The captain rubbed his chin and led her into the sick tent. "What's your name?"

"Arianna."

"I'm Captain Myron. I'll take you to Marcell, but I'd like some of your medicine for my men. What else do you have?"

By the time the two left to meet Marcell, she'd filled enough orders to eliminate her need to sell by the clinic entirely. She was pleased but wondered if she might have to train others to help her fill such a large order.

She stared at the back of Captain Myron's cloak as she followed him. *It's okay that I'm helping him . . . the Templins . . . this Differe place . . . especially if Marcell knows about them . . . right?* She hoped she'd be reassured after they all met.

Captain Myron stopped her at the edge of the woods and held out a piece of cloth. "I'm sorry. Where we meet must be kept safe."

Though terrified to be led blindly by a man she hardly knew, Arianna nodded and quickly slid the cloth over her eyes. She heard metal being moved several times, water trickling every few seconds, and then her terrain seemed to change. It felt like she was walking in something smooth, narrow, and dark.

After twenty minutes of fumbling in the dark she saw light and heard a voice she recognized. "Arianna, what a lovely surprise. You are so grown up."

Arianna removed her blindfold to find Emil Marcell sitting at a rectangular table in a dimly lit room.

"Hello, Master Marcell." She curtsied then nodded.

"How did you find Captain Myron? Or did he find you?" The man beckoned them to the table.

The captain removed his hat and stretched out his hand to Marcell. "She was running from someone named Rufus."

"Ah. Yes, he's looking for his partner." He shook the man's hand and turned toward Arianna. "Seems you stole his business . . . or something."

Arianna gripped the back of the chair in front of her. "I didn't steal anything."

"I believe you, but his partner is still missing. Do you know anything about that?"

She avoided his eyes and attempted to dodge his question. "I can make anything she can . . . could."

"I'm not interested in buying . . . yet." Marcell drummed his fingers on the table and tried again. "What happened to his partner, Arianna?"

She broke into a cold sweat. The same trembling that began at the bridge started again, and Captain Myron helped her into a chair.

"Arianna? Are you okay?" He gently patted her face.

She began to cry as the trembling continued. "I can't . . . I can't."

She saw Marcell leaning over her. "Shush, it's all right. You don't need to keep it in, Arianna. Tell us what happened at the bridge."

That's when all fear turned to rage. She still couldn't explain it. "I DON'T WANT TO TALK ABOUT IT!"

CHAPTER 16

JOEL WATCHED AUGUSTINE'S train roll away from the station. The sight of her hands plastered against the compartment window troubled him. He knew her greatest fear was being alone, but he silently begged her to see his action for what it was—a guarantee that Sebastian would get the rhydid. He turned back toward the station building to search for an area map while admitting to himself that he would undoubtedly miss her. A few months ago he'd have done anything to part with the haughty brunette, but now, as the train's whistle blew in the distance, it was as if he had just said goodbye to his best friend. His loud sigh was met by a surge of hope when he spotted a framed map right outside the station. He hadn't given up on making it to Facilis.

He leaned in to study the map. He could not read the words well but was able to make out the roads and a few symbols represented on it. He thought of Augustine's words and reviewed the map more closely. "Nothing. Some gift I have." He deciphered he was in the West End and northwest of Facilis, which he assumed was the largest dot on the map, but that was about it. There didn't seem to be much between this place and Facilis. He chided himself for not continuing on the train. *Maybe there wouldn't have been any more stops.*

"Officer?"

Joel turned around and was surprised to see another Templin near his age. He straightened and stuck out his hand. "Officer Guy, from Differe."

"Officer Dillon, from Galanne."

Joel noted a thick accent and paused, knowing the place sounded familiar. He stared at the young man's pale skin and brown eyes then the symbol on his cloak, which he didn't recognize. He honestly couldn't remember where Galanne was, but decided not to give that fact away just yet.

"Yous going to go to the city?" the officer pressed in broken Differian.

Joel nodded, but his puzzled expression must have indicated that he didn't quite understand the young man.

Dillon laughed and shook his head. "My Differian is not so good. Let me try again. Yous want a ride to first village? We have extra." He motioned behind them.

Joel still wasn't sure what he was trying to say, but riding sounded better than walking. He nodded quickly. "Yes. That'd be great."

The young officer pursed his lips and looked at him with a slightly raised eyebrow. "I do not ask, er, uh, like Differian Templins to ride with us, but at least, I mean, few are young like yous."

Joel stuck out his hand again. "Thanks. I really appreciate the offer."

This time Officer Dillon raised both eyebrows in obvious surprise. "Another first. A polite Differian." He motioned for Joel to follow him. "Come on."

Joel walked north of the station for some distance until he and Dillon came upon a group of young men. A gray wooden fence stretched out a few acres on either side of the group, enclosing fields full of hay bales. The break in the fence where the young men were congregated led to a white horse stable. Joel stared at the motley crew. *These guys are Templins?* Most of their cloaks were unfastened and thrown over their shoulders as the gang sat straddling or leaning against the old farm fencing. Their cloaks were gray like Templins but had what Joel guessed was the Galanne symbol on the front—a red feather crossed with a black horse. A few in the group appeared to be mere boys. Joel and Dillon came upon a variety of happenings, with smoking and talking being the most popular while others drew quietly in notebooks. The youngest were playing games with a small ball.

"Officer Guy," Dillon announced Joel to the group. To Joel's surprise no one acknowledged his existence—that is, not until Dillon finished. "From Differe."

Every activity came to a screeching halt, and all the officers silently moved forward to inspect Joel more closely. He fought the urge to run as more than a dozen officers soon circled around him with grim looks.

"Young," one said.

Another nodded and spoke in Galannic. This was followed by several other remarks in their native tongue to one another.

"Enough." Dillon waved them away from Joel. "He is good I think."

Joel felt a rush of relief as the group began to back away.

"Ride before or after dinner?" A young boy searched Joel's face for an answer as he tossed a ball back and forth between his hands.

Joel then realized the officers were all looking to him for instruction, even Dillon. "Hey, I'm your guest. I leave when you want to leave."

"See, I told yous. He is good." Dillon nodded, and a few others nodded slightly in approval.

"Give Differe Paz." One grinned as he flicked a cigarette to the ground.

"Come." Dillon beckoned Joel forward. "Sorry, uh . . . ."

Joel waited patiently as he figured Dillon's pause was an attempt to translate his words.

"Differian Templins train us. Not good. It was not good." Dillon's tone and ill expression told Joel more than his words could probably ever convey.

He followed him into the stable. "Who's your leader?"

Dillon looked away and took a deep breath. "He is dead."

Joel's posture tensed. *Great. Just great.*

"Well, Guy, this is Paz."

Joel forgot his questions when he stared into the stall where Dillon was pointing. Paz was a reddish-blond horse with a white-striped nose. Joel marveled at its size; at six feet and an inch tall, he was still looking up to the horse's back. The horse pranced before them in what little space the stall had. The creature's strawberry-blond mane and tail swished magnificently as he approached Joel in obvious curiosity.

"Uh, hi, Paz." Joel moved forward and tentatively stretched out his hand toward the massive creature. Paz snorted in response then jerked back against the stall and began to prance again.

"Stallion. Spirit, this one. I think yous like him." Dillon smiled in admiration.

"Sorry, what? What are you saying?"

Dillon furrowed his brow and pointed to Paz. "Paz, he is your ride."

My ride? Oh . . . my ride.

Joel stayed with Dillon until it seemed the clan was ready to leave. Dillon assigned the youngest of the group to saddle Joel's horse for him. Joel faked a protest but was relieved when Dillon insisted.

"I will do for you." The boy smiled at Joel, waving away his help.

If the Differians were so awful to these guys . . . why are they helping me? Maybe they're hoping I'll fall off and break my neck. He looked at the stirrup the boy held out for him to climb onto Paz and swallowed a big gulp.

Once mounted, Joel squirmed around in the saddle trying to get comfortable. *Some padded pants would be nice right about now.* To his surprise, once again, the group looked to him for direction after everyone was saddled. He wondered if he should tell them he was just a young officer like the rest of them, but he thought better of it. *Keep your status. Keep some control.* "Officer Dillon, lead the way."

The pale-skinned officer beamed and led the parade of stocky beasts onto the road. As Joel followed between two riders, he wondered where in the world they were going. Wherever they were headed, he sure hoped it was in the direction of Facilis.

Thankfully Joel managed to keep Paz in the riding line for over half an hour. He thought he was doing pretty well. Though enormous, Paz proved to have a pretty smooth gate. He took to Joel easily, and it seemed Joel had retained much of what he learned as a child after all. He couldn't tell if the others were impressed or indifferent at his ability.

A sad smile crossed his face when he thought of his riding teacher. He could still see his mother in the corral, playfully chasing him with her riding crop. Her long red hair and a bright smile very much resembled his own.

"Why are you running away from me?" he heard her call to the younger version of himself.

"Because you're going to smother me with kisses! I'm too big for that, Momma." He always ran as fast as his little legs would allow, but it was no use. She caught him every time and, indeed, covered him in smooches.

"You miss her?"

Joel jerked the reins, startled by the voice that was becoming more and more familiar. It was the good voice; the one he thought might be Waiz's Majestic. *You know, I really don't like how you just show up whenever you want.*

"Have you been trying to get my attention?"

Only a dozen times or more. Joel was met with silence, which he now understood meant he was supposed to answer the original question before any conversation ensued. *Sure I miss her. Who wouldn't? I was fine before . . . well, she died.*

"Yet, you're still running away from embraces, I see."

What? Augustine? That wasn't running away. I left her for her own safety.

Dillon circled back to Joel interrupting his conversation. "We are close. There is the village of Baithe. See the stone wall?" Dillon pointed far across the pasture they were about to enter.

In the distance Joel could see the stone wall, but whatever was behind it was too obscured by woods for him to make out much more. Joel nodded. "Great. What are your plans?"

"We are meeting with the Differian Army there, of course."

Paz bolted across the pasture before Joel was able to hear anymore. He immediately lost control of the reins and threw his arms around Paz's neck. "Paz! Paz, you've got to slow down!" He finally caught a rein, and the horse instantly turned in a circle. On his second circle, Joel let go of the rein again when he started losing his balance. "Paz! I'm not asking you to go faster. Slow down! Slow down, Paz!" The horse seemed to ignore his pleas but responded right in step with Joel's pounding heart. Paz was out of his control and running at full speed toward the woods.

Calm down, Joel. He won't slow down until you calm down. Joel thought of his mother again and moved his hands from Paz's mane to the saddle horn. *Breathe, Joel.* The image of his mother radiantly riding about with her eyes closed burned into his mind. Scary as it was, he forced himself to do the same. He felt disoriented and even more terrified with his eyes closed. All he could focus on was his body being jostled about, until he remembered the secret—*breathing. Just breathe in and out.* To his amazement he began to relax. Joel slowly let go of the saddle horn and put his arms in the air. The wind buzzed around his body. *I'm floating.* He opened his eyes in triumph, just before he hit the ground.

Joel watched Paz run ahead into the woods. *Well, that was stupid.* He stayed on the ground for a moment to catch his breath. *What just happened? What did Dillon say to me before Paz took off? The Differian Army?* Joel wasn't sure what meeting the army meant, but the words sure seemed to have spooked Paz. *Or was it me?*

During Joel's confusion Dillon rode up, jumped down from the saddle, and rushed over to him. "Okay? Yous okay?" He looked over Joel with concern.

"Yeah, fine." Joel brushed off his cloak, and Dillon offered a hand to pull him to his feet.

"Told yous. Paz have spirit." He sighed as they headed into the woods to retrieve the horse. Paz was still breathing hard but had stopped in front of a group of tightly knit trees. He turned his head toward the two of them and jerked it upright when Dillon reached for the reins. "Do not be stubborn, Paz." Dillon reached up high to snatch the reins. "Not good. Not good, Paz."

"No, it was my fault."

Dillon ignored Joel's comment and led the horse out of the woods for him.

"Dillon, what's your business with the Differian Army here?" *Might as well see what I've gotten myself into.*

"Well, that is who we are." Dillon pointed to his cloak and looked at him in curiosity. "We are part of the army for Differe."

"But the Templins trained you . . . you aren't part of the Templins?" Joel suddenly realized he had no idea what the difference was between Differe's army and the Templin Guard.

"Yes, that is true. Templins train us for the army—that is why we wear the cloaks and not Differe's black army coats. Our emblem shows we have no ranking inside your army. The army belongs to, er, the Templin Guard."

Joel shrugged. "So why not just call yourselves Templins? I'd imagine it would give you a few more perks."

Dillon looked at him in shock. "Yous . . . unusual, Templin Guy."

Joel looked past him to find the other horse and riders approaching.

"Yous do not seem to follow the same, uh . . . rules as our master Templins. They tell us 'Templin' is a status or, er, ranking you get by fatherhood."

Joel furrowed his brow at Dillon. "Say what?"

"No, not fatherhood, Dillon," a rider called out from behind. "Birth. You must be born a Templin."

Dillon lightly tapped a finger to his temple. "Right, birth."

"They own the army?" *Differe's army is controlled by the Templins—some small group of elitists?* Joel could hardly believe it. He quickly turned his face away from the dozens of riders eyeing him suspiciously. He now understood why they had treated him, the supposed high-ranking Templin, the way they had. He had to know more and pointed to his Templin badge. "Why then? Why do you fight for us . . . so far away from your homes?"

"Papa."

"Sisters."

"Momma."

"My Marie, ah, my love," was the last reply before silence hit the group.

Dillon eventually took a step toward him. "We fight for our families— for our villages in the Northern Region."

Joel wanted to spit on the ground at hearing these young men dedicate their service to a bunch of hypocrites for the people and places they loved. He took in a deep breath to control the rage bubbling up inside him. *They are deceived.* His arms flexed in anger, but he kept himself in check. "Well, your families and villages would be very proud of your service to me. Let's ride to meet the army." Their faces surprised him. His words of affirmation seemed to have made them come alive. He nodded to Dillon to give him a leg up.

CHAPTER 17

AUGUSTINE CROSSED HER arms in annoyance as the officer searched her compartment. "How much longer to Facilis?"

"Well, this is the last checkpoint. It normally wouldn't take this long, but there've been extra stops today."

She rolled her eyes. "You're telling me."

"Yes, well, you should be there in the next half hour, Miss." He tipped his cap and ducked out.

Augustine sighed in relief as she peered out the window to see the officers disembarking the train. *I'm not sure my nerves could have handled another stop.* As the train started up again she decided to pull out Mr. Rutherford's book that would tell her about the dagger pinned to her side—the one that was supposed to save her brother's life.

She drew the book out of Madame Bontecou's bag and blew her lips apart. "Okay, little brother, let's see how a 'Compilation of Thoughts' can help you." As she studied its cover, she discovered the founder of Waiz—Theodore Waiz himself—was the author. She shrugged, flipped open the book, and found an inscription on the inside cover. "To Haskell from Thad." Her brow furrowed. *Thad.* The name sounded very familiar to her. She racked her brain for a moment before deciding it would come to her as she continued searching through the book.

She glanced over the table of contents and noted the chapter titles were simply the names of the objects they had learned about at the Old Waiz Museum—caychuras, sacred stones, tenehs, rhydids. She thumbed through the pages until she arrived at a section that displayed drawings of several swords. A few resembled the daggers she and Joel had obtained while others were varying sizes up to full-length swords. The rest of the chapter was divided into three parts: Where to Find, Who can Get, and How to Use.

She stopped for a moment, wondering if she'd be able to figure this out on her own. Joel had been such a help to her in figuring out the unknown . . . or unseen. She tried to look at the words on the page then stopped again finding her thoughts drifting back to Joel. *Why can't I get him out of my mind?* Watching him read the letter earlier had been amazing. Corwin told her what Joel had seen in the caychura. Corwin had said, "The Majestic told him something—that he will be able to see what others cannot. If Joel chooses to believe these words, he'll be empowered to access this gift. Try it with him." Augustine was skeptical about being able to decode words by simply using symbols on a page or, in the Majestic's words, "Looking between the lines." But Corwin assured her that Joel had been able to discern the phrase, "Every warrior needs a weapon," by only seeing a warrior with a sword on the cave's ceiling.

At first Augustine wasn't sure she believed Corwin, yet after spending time with Joel she knew he could see things others could not. *He can see inside people's souls. He somehow knows what's there . . . how to charm them.* She'd seen him do it with Madam Bontecou, Mr. Rutherford's customers, and the Templins. *And me.*

So, even though she wasn't sure what to make of this whole Majestic thing, she had loved seeing the gift work when he was able to read the letter only by seeing the eagle. She twisted her mother's ring around her finger wondering if she could believe in this Majestic being . . . again. She reasoned with herself that she would do anything for her brother.

She smoothed her jacket and gave the hilt of her rhydid a tight squeeze. "Joel, why am I still thinking about you?" She looked down at Haskell's book and realized it was partly because she missed him, more than she wanted to admit. There was so much more she wanted to know about him. The letter she had intercepted at the Templin's office led her to believe Joel's father was aware of his first escape from the temple and was now threatening to blackmail the institution. She wondered what the man knew. It seemed to her the temple had done his father a big favor in letting someone like Joel inside the school. She and Joel had just begun sharing secrets of their past before he left the train. Now that he was gone, she only felt a tiny sting of guilt about not revealing one secret—one she was sure he was dying to know about. *Isabelle.* She knew he had to wonder how the two knew each other. Didn't he realize she clearly resembled someone they both knew? She glanced at the empty seat across from her and sighed. *What if I never see him again? I don't even have a picture of him.* Then she remembered something and her spirit soared in triumph. *Oh, yes. Yes, I do. The temple file!* Every secret she wanted to know about Joel was sitting in one of her bags . . . just waiting for her to discover.

The Galanneans rode to the stone wall of Baithe in silence with Joel in front. Dillon thought it best for the Differian Templin to lead them into the village, and Joel felt he had no choice but to oblige. He tried his best to look proud as they entered the village's stone wall. The place resembled a Waiz kalona but was even smaller, and, from the looks of it, poverty stricken. The homes he passed held only thatched roofs and were less than desirable. *No glass in the windows? Dirt floors? Is the West End poor?* Curiosity swept over him as the group approached the nearly empty village square. The shops lining the square were in dire need of repair and a thick coat of paint. The group rode through the square and turned into the courtyard where the army was stationed. Joel felt his blood boil as he eyed the chapel in front of him in perfect condition. Its stained glass and pristine white walls mocked the village's surroundings. The Differian Army perched out front only fueled the fire burning inside him. His hands clenched the reins tightly. *Joel, you're just supposed to get to Facilis. All you're supposed to be thinking about right now is getting to Facilis.*

The "army" was comprised of twenty middle-aged men just standing around. The officers were clearly from Differe, wearing black army coats and white officer hats with Differe's black flag stitched across them. Joel was pleased to find the group impressed at their riding up.

"What's this?" One of the older soldiers stepped forward to approach Joel and Paz.

Followed by his ragamuffin group, Joel wanted to rip the clean, obviously well-fed, man's face off. He bit his tongue to calm himself. "This is a young regiment from Galanne. Their leader is dead, so I accompanied them to meet your troops."

"We've been expecting them. You're late." The man cast a look past Joel at the foreigners. "How did you find them?"

"On assignment. Got off the train in Penwell, and Officer Dillon here, well, I guess you could say he found me." Joel shot a nod of respect in Dillon's direction.

"Hope it's been no trouble to you, Sir, especially if you were on assignment. These foreigners aren't familiar with your ranking and authority. Whatever your orders are always take priority." The man scowled and started towards Dillon. "Boy, did you distract this Templin officer from his orders?"

Joel and Paz intercepted the man before he could reach Dillon. "Are you insinuating I'd actually *take* orders from him, soldier?"

"Well, no, Sir, I just wanted to make sure these Galanneans were—"

"I only take orders from the Templin Commanders or the headmaster himself." Satisfaction filled his emotions as the soldier began backing away. "This troop did me a favor. I'm riding for Facilis, and this village happened to be on my way. I needed a horse, and they gave me one. They honored me with the position of leading them. They honored the Templins—isn't it against our code to perform any duty without a leader?" Joel had no idea how the words kept coming out of his mouth, but he was glad to find his speech silenced the other officer. "Where are the stables?"

"Uh, just down this road and outside the wall. On a small farm. I'll take him if you like. I'm Officer Evans." The man motioned to take Paz.

"No, we can find it. I'd like to see where my horse will be kept. We'll return in time for dinner." Joel nodded then spurred Paz forward.

As the group reached the dilapidated barn, Joel caught his first glimpse of the village's inhabitants. The residents' poor appearance was almost predictable judging from the looks of the place. The two young men who met them at the stables were dirty, skinny, and wearing clothes that appeared several sizes too small. The one who took Paz from Joel suffered from a terrible cough.

He wondered if he was supposed to tip him and watched to see what the others did. As expected, each Galanne officer took in and unsaddled his own horse. He was the only being served like a king.

Joel walked out of the barn and eyed what must be the farmer's house. It was made of gray cinder blocks with wooden scraps covering the windows and roof. He spotted an old wooden barrel next to the footpath of the house, and smiled as he looked at the flowers springing up in its center. Glancing around at the farmland, he noticed it was in worse condition than he would have thought. He looked back at his group, busy with their horses, then turned and walked toward the barrel. He stuck his fingers into the dark soil and took in the deep violet, yellow, and blue clusters growing happily inside the makeshift home. There was something he liked about flowers. His mother always seemed to have them scattered in her hair in most of the pictures he'd seen of her.

A door opening from the house diverted his attention. An older woman waddled out with her back to him. "Let's go! Come on, Noor. Time to work in the fields."

"Coming!" a child's voice called from somewhere outside the house. "Here I am, momma!"

Joel watched a little girl, he guessed near the age of six, run out from behind the house towards the footpath. Her tousled hair was the color of his own—flaming auburn. Her pale angel-kissed skin was scarcely hidden under the ragtag dress she wore. She spotted Joel at the barrel and instantly buried her face in her hands. He was surprised at the wails that came next.

"Noor, Dear. Noor, it's alright, Dear." Her mother rushed over to pick up the little girl who had fallen to the ground in sobs.

"No, no! He's going to take them. He's going to kill them!" Noor lifted her face off the ground and stared at Joel with contempt. Her mother turned and spotted Joel for the first time.

Joel looked down at his Templin uniform then turned to find his men and the farmhands approaching. Each held a solemn look as they studied the little girl and her mother behind him. Joel stuffed his hands in his pockets as he focused his attention back on Noor. She slowly stood as her mother wiped her tears. She took the little girl's hand, but Noor looked at Joel again and broke free from her mother's grip. The girl raced toward him with her fists out. Dillon jumped in front of Joel, but Joel had just enough time to push him out of the way. He stood ready for the blow, but nothing happened. With her fists still out, the redhead slowed her pace and marched toward him until he backed away.

"These are *my* flowers."

"Noor!" Her mother ran toward them in horror.

"Don't you take them. Don't you kill my flowers!"

Joel stood tongue tied at the little girl's fiery words until her mother fell on her knees between him and Noor.

"I'm sorry, Master Templin. My daughter is foolish and rash. All we have is yours."

Joel grimaced inside. There's no telling what the Templins did here. He was a tyrant. A round of questions ran through his mind. *Did the Templins do this to the village? Are they controlling the West End? Is getting to Facilis a lost cause after all?* The last question left him with a sick feeling in his stomach. *Augustine.*

"Noor, apologize to the Templin. We beg your forgiveness, Sir."

At eighteen, the title of "Sir" made him want to laugh. He finally shook away his confused thoughts and tried to make amends. "I'm sorry, Noor. I didn't mean to disturb your flowers. I was just admiring them. You've done an amazing job. Which one is your favorite?" Joel looked over her mother's head hoping Noor would answer.

Noor wasn't disarmed by his words and sniffled in silence. He was about to try again when she blurted out, "The violet."

He nodded and softened his tone. "Do you put them in your hair?"

"Sometimes."

Joel bent down and offered his hand to the woman kneeling in front of him. Noor's mother was startled by his gesture but allowed him to help her up. "Thank you for the use of your stables, ma'am."

She nodded in silence.

"Is there anything you need in return?"

The group behind him gasped.

The woman shook her head. "No, it is our honor to serve you."

"We need food."

A farmhand waved his hands and tried to cover Noor's mouth. "Noor, hush. We don't need anything, Sir."

Silence fell over the group once more. "Well, thank you again." Joel nodded and walked away from the barrel.

CHAPTER 18

AT DINNER IT became evident where all the food in the village was. Joel chewed on his turkey leg and decided to determine if his suspicions were correct. "Where did all this food come from?"

"Some from Differe and some from the village. The place is out of money. Can't pay the tax for us to be here in money, so they pay us with food." The soldier raised his glass then took a gulp of wine.

"Why would they *pay* you to be here? Aren't you employed by the Templin Guard?" Joel was beginning to realize how little he knew of army and Templin politics.

"Well, like I said, some of the food's from Differe. It's supposed to be taxed in order for the people to receive it."

"But I'm assuming they can't pay the import tax if they're out of money." *This isn't making sense.*

The man shrugged. "Right, so they pay us with food."

"Wait . . . so they're paying you *for* food *with* food? How does that work exactly?"

A soldier a few seats down from him leaned forward. "Not very well for the villagers."

The whole table then weighed in on his conversation, with the Galanne men seemingly fixed on him. "What's their motivation in keeping you here?"

"Safety, of course. They have no means of protecting themselves."

"From what?" Joel heard his voice grow louder as his anger festered.

Officer Evans stood to his feet. "Lawlessness. You should know that better than anyone else, Templin Guy. Without rules and regulations the village would be in utter chaos. There'd be no food for sure. We keep the order."

"You're keeping the food." He knew his response was too quick when the conversation went silent. *Joel, you're a Templin. Keep it together.* "Sorry, I just hate you're not getting the money for yourselves and the Templin Guard. Uh, well done in using what resources you have to keep the peace." *I shouldn't . . . but I have to know . . . one more question.* "And chapel . . . is the village attending?"

"Oh, yes, Master Templin, every service. See how the building has been kept up in honor of the headmaster?" The surrounding soldiers beamed at him.

Joel could hardly believe his ears. He looked at the faces awaiting his affirmation. He then realized these soldiers weren't the ones behind this evil. They were simply doing what they had been told. *It's like they don't have a choice.*

"But they do," replied a voice in his head he knew wasn't his. His heart fluttered. He'd been longing to hear more from this voice ever since his meeting in the cave. The brief conversation on horseback as he left the train station hours earlier didn't count in Joel's mind.

Where have you been?

Joel wasn't surprised when the voice ignored his question. "They do have a choice, but someone will have to tell them that."

I don't want to be the one. I've got to get to Facilis. Joel put his head down and took another bite of food.

"That choice will only affect one person."

Joel nodded to himself. *Yeah, keeps things easier that way.*

"Does that mean you do not wish to travel with Augustine once you reach Facilis?"

Okay, you got me . . . in fact, I think I can feel you gloating.

"I might be."

Joel laughed to himself. *All right, not exactly. I'm fine keeping one companion.*

"What about Sebastian? Corwin? Mr. Rutherford? Dillon and his men?"

Joel stirred the food on his plate with his spoon before responding. *I didn't ask to lead any of them.*

"You weren't asked. You were chosen."

"What?" Joel sputtered aloud.

"Templin Guy?" Dillon leaned across the table. "Okay?"

Joel waited and heard only silence in his head. "Yeah, fine."

Several hours later, most of the soldiers were inebriated from the wine and had retired for the evening. Joel wasn't tired—his head swirled with all the information he had learned. He wondered when the best time to sneak away would be. The black grease in his hair and bandages were only going to last so long. He walked toward the stables again, feeling a little guilty as he planned another escape. He knew he'd have to steal Paz. He found the stallion in the largest stall toward the back of the barn. "Paz. Hey, boy." Paz snorted back and moved toward him, clearly looking for a treat. "Sorry, I don't have anything. I just wanted to say thanks for the ride today. You're a good boy." He patted him, then walked outside behind the barn. The moon was bright and full as he leaned on the gate that led out to the pasture in front of him. "You were chosen," the words echoed in his head. *Why didn't I get a say in that?* He walked around the side of the barn and saw a shadow out front. Joel calmly put a hand on his rhydid.

"Who's there?" He heard someone call.

Joel cautiously moved forward. "Just Templin Guy. Was checking on my horse."

An older farmhand came into view. "Oh, sorry, Master Templin. How did you find your horse?" The man quickly leaned a pitchfork against the barn.

"He's perfect." Joel glanced over at the pitchfork then back to the farmhand. "Guarding your food?"

"What little we have, Sir."

"When did the village run out of money, and how's the rest of the West End fairing?"

"Ran out two winters ago. By then the community had become so dependent on the rations Differe was sending that the farms, our main living here, were almost completely finished. We had to keep the officers here . . . for protection. There used to be only two until . . . people do foolish things when they're hungry."

Joel nodded and waited for the man to continue.

"You probably know more than me about the rest of the West End. Facilis is safe, of course, but most of the West is ravished with famine, and Differe's Army."

"Due to the tax?"

"That and it hasn't rained. Crops have been poor the last few seasons."

"Where are your people? This place seems nearly abandoned."

"There's no real need for anyone anymore 'cept for farmers." The man shrugged. "No one can trade. There's . . . there was just no reason for any of them to stay."

Joel heard the pain in the man's voice. He automatically thought about how Waiz originated—an abandoned city. He sighed. "What a mess."

The man rubbed his hands together. "You disapprove of your government?"

Joel didn't answer but handed him a small sack of food he had taken from dinner. "Give this to Noor."

Joel's shoulders drooped as he walked toward his posh Templin quarters for the night. *Disgusting.* While the rest of the crew slept under haphazard tents, he would sleep inside the chapel in his own room. *I won't know what to do with all that space, or with a bed for that matter.* The abandoned village made for a quiet and lonely walk back to the square. It was almost eerie as he passed by the empty, darkened homes on the road. *The people just left.* He couldn't believe what he'd just heard. What he couldn't understand was how the smallest region in the entire land was invading the West End and the North with this much force. *How are they doing it? It's like—*

A rustling in the grass just off the road stopped his thoughts and legs. Joel took a guarded step forward and heard nothing. He quietly drew his rhydid and took another step, fighting the urge to run straight into the grass. He would no longer be running away from his fears. When he heard the grass rustle again he made himself known. "Someone there? It's Templin Guy." There was a tweeting sound on the opposite side of the road in response to his words . . . or to the rustling grass. *Great.* Joel kept walking, but picked up his pace a little. Suddenly he realized the rustling to his left was keeping pace with him. His nerves escalated as the tweeting to his right grew louder. He wondered if he should make for the chapel, but quickly thought of a better idea. He sped up to nearly a jog, then whipped around and broke into a full sprint back toward the stables. Just above the noise of his heavy breathing he could still hear whatever was following him in the grass. With pursuers on both sides, he was forced straight. Joel made for the illuminated stable door and eyed the pitchfork. The rhydid in his hand felt small in relation to the panic he felt. *The door! The door! Make for the door! Come on!* He was there. He threw it open, heart pounding, shaking from whatever unseen objects were gaining on him. He blinked in surprise at the scene in the stable, then something struck his head and he crumpled to the ground, quickly sinking into a sea of darkness.

Chapter 19

JOEL WAS STARTLED awake by a freezing sensation. He opened his eyes and felt his body convulsing in shock. His surroundings were blurry. *Where am I? Can I move?* He blinked his eyes a few times to gain focus and moved a hand but barely felt it. It was as if his body was frozen or asleep or both. A splashing noise distracted him when he moved his hand again. *I'm soaking wet.* Joel squinted down at his body. He was nearly stripped of all clothing and in a small pool of water. He raised an arm out of the water finding it whiter than usual. The fingernail beds on his hand were a deep purple. To his dismay he spotted his feet and his toes were a bluish gray tint, confirming what he was feeling. *I'm freezing. I'm freezing to death.* "Augustine!" he cried out as he struggled to find feeling and strength in his legs. There was a shuffle to his left. "Augustine, are you there?" His brain felt like mush, and he knew something was wrong about calling out her name. *Wait, she's gone. She's on the train. I'm in—I'm in . . . where am I?* A familiar animal sound gave him a big clue. *A horse. In the stable. Running. The stables.* The thoughts coming to him were a mess, but he soon remembered the hit. He moved his hand to the back of his head. There was a tender lump where he'd been struck. "Ugh." Joel squinted when he thought he saw shadows moving around him. "Who's there? What do you want with me?"

"Yous hush! Can't yous see there is an emergency going on?" A voice hissed at him.

Joel furiously blinked his eyes. *Nothing.* He frantically rubbed them, hoping something would begin to make sense. The shadows finally came into focus enough that he could distinguish the outline of the stables and the bodies moving around. He heard groaning coming from his far right. When he looked down again, he realized he was in one of the horses' water troughs.

Joel flailed his arms. "Get me out of here! I'm freezing! Hurry*!" Are they trying to kill me?*

"Then yous will think better than to spy on us again!" came a sharp reply.

Joel shook his head in confusion.

"Yous spy. Yous traitor!"

"Yous no Templin!"

"We follow yous tonight!"

"Hush, I can't get the bleeding to stop. Stupid hinge. Blast!"

Joel heard several more voices argue in another language.

The Galanne clan? Right . . . yes, I remember. "Dillon? Dillon are you there?"

"Shut up, spy!" Someone moved towards him.

Joel soon saw Dillon standing in front of him with a knife . . . *no, a sword.* "My sword!"

"Not anymore." He could feel the young man's glare.

"What is—" Joel stopped, wondering why the sword hadn't disintegrated like Corwin's had when he had taken it at the Marcell House. Joel pulled away when he felt the weapon touch his chest. "Why?" He gasped through chattering teeth.

"Yous tell us why." Dillon pulled a small mirror from his pocket.

Joel saw a ghost white figure with blue lips, no bandages, and flaming red hair.

"Yous has been in disguise. How are yous?"

"Uh, cold."

A young Galannean shook his head at their leader. "No, Dillon. *Who. Who* are you?"

"Right." Dillon nodded. "*Who* are yous? And, who is this Augustine yous been going on about?"

"Obviously his girl. The way he's been shouting for her the past hour." The group let out a few chuckles.

Going on about her . . . for an hour? "Please, let me explain."

"Shut up all of you! Byron's fainting. We have to get it off him!" screamed a voice on Joel's right again.

All words came to a halt as a frenzy began.

"Wh-what's happening?" Joel was shaking uncontrollably.

Dillon's younger brother came into view. "A trap—a metal trap."

"Do not talk to him, Ian!"

The groaning to his right continued as Joel heard the voices of those trying to keep whoever was hurt conscious.

"He's bleeding too much."

"Wake up, Byron."

"Here, try this pry bar."

"Nothing is working!"

When all fell silent, Joel felt hopelessness settle over the room. He caught a glimpse of the rhydid in Dillon's hand again. "Wait, I can open it."

No one moved.

Joel attempted to stand up. "Do you hear me? I can open the trap!"

Dillon came back over to him.

"The sword—my sword will open it."

Dillon looked at him with disgust. "I already try it, spy."

"It's—it's not an ordinary sword. It's a rhydid." When his comment was met with more silence he tried again. "It only works for the owner. I know—I know you don't believe me, but I've seen it open metal locks. It's—"

"A trick," a Galannean interrupted.

"No, it will work. Let me at least try. Please?"

"Spy!"

Joel looked back at Dillon and shook his head. "Dillon, you're right. I am a strange Templin because . . . I'm not a Templin at all, but I'm no one's spy either. I'm trying to get back to Waiz, but . . . I have to get to Facilis first in order to ensure safe passage."

"Lies. No listen, Dillon."

"I've been in the Templins' service, but I'm running from them. It's true. I want to be free of them."

Dillon clutched the rhydid to his chest. "Yous no make sense. Leave the Templin service?"

Joel struggled to find his footing but pushed up with all his might and shakily stood up. The young men instantly surrounded him. "Yes, because this is what they've done to me." Joel winced as he hobbled to turn around and display his heavily scarred back to the group. When he turned around again some had backed away while most others had dropped their stance, but Dillon remained firm.

"Why should I believe yous?"

The groaning man in the corner answered for Joel. "He brought us food, Dillon. A whole bag. That's why—" The man gasped and coughed before he could finish. "H-h-he was just returning from the deed when you found him."

Dillon's eyes narrowed. "This is true?"

Joel stiffly climbed out of the trough. He grimaced as he walked toward Dillon. "Just let me try."

Dillon looked around at the others before conceding the weapon. As he did, the others drew their own weapons, keeping them aimed in Joel's direction. Joel limped toward the farmhand he'd met only a few hours before. Sharp needlelike pain filled his every step. He moaned and shook as he moved forward. He found the farmhand lying on his back on several bales of hay. The metal animal trap was clamped shut around the man's leg, soaking his pants in blood from knee to ankle. Joel studied the trap for a moment. The man was breathing rapidly as Joel decided on the best place to insert the sword. His arms shook as he placed the sword tip inside the hinge of the trap. As before, the hinges sparked and the trap instantly swung open.

No one moved at first; they just stared at Joel. "Don't just stand there!" Joel motioned to them. "His wounds need to be cleaned and wrapped. We've got to get the bleeding stopped. " Joel took the sword and cut the pants off the man's leg, exposing his torn bloody flesh.

After the man lay resting and out of danger, things settled down around the stables. Joel was draped in three layers of blankets and given a spot by the heater. Underneath the layers were his wet shorts and the rhydid. Eventually Dillon brought him a hot bowl of soup.

Joel shook his head. "Not hungry."

"Yous must." Dillon shoved the bowl at him.

Joel crossed his arms. "How do I know you didn't poison it?"

"It is not for food. It is a Galanne remedy . . . keep yous from catching cold." Dillon shoved the bowl at him again, and this time Joel took it. "Galanne—"

"To freeze, frozen."

Dillon appeared impressed. "How did yous . . . yes, that is what it means. My home is cold . . . very cold. What we did to yous is a game where I come from. Yous are very strong to survive so long."

Joel slurped a mouthful of soup and breathed deeply. "So how do you win this *game*?"

"Oh. Well, there are two or more in the water. Last one in the water wins." Dillon bit his lip sheepishly and turned his eyes to the open trap lying on the floor.

"Those are illegal aren't they? Can't imagine the Templin Guard being okay with the people catching food they don't know about."

"Not really. We see them in every stop, and the Templins do nothing."

"Why?"

"Because so fews know how to live without them. A few traps is hardly a threat."

Joel knew his face looked confused because Dillon tried again.

"There are enough people who cannot survive without them— powerless."

Joel nodded in understanding. "Then why are you hiding him in here? The Differians probably have a doctor among them." Dillon was about to open his mouth but Joel continued, "I mean, it's incredible . . . they're controlling the food supply simply by controlling the tax . . . how are they doing that? How are they even stationed outside their own region? Sorry—just thinking out loud."

Dillon sighed. "That is not the worst of it. Yous hear us say we fight for family . . . our people . . . remember?"

Joel nodded in recollection. He expected Dillon to say more, but the whole room went still. He searched the faces of Galanne's young men and found most were turned toward the ground with cold expressions. "Yes, you said you were fighting for your father."

Dillon swallowed hard and nodded.

"So . . . where are they?"

No one uttered a peep.

"H-hostages? Blackmail?" He was so angry he could barely get the words out.

Dillon's eyes and the faces of the others answered his question.

Joel clenched his fists. "Dillon, where are they? Where did Differe take them?"

"Trompè."

CHAPTER 20

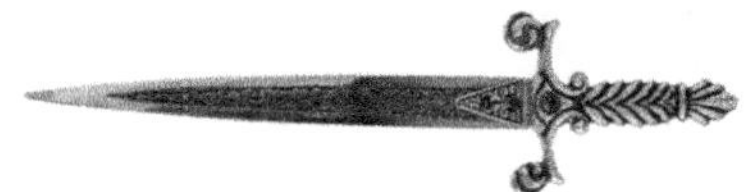

AUGUSTINE FINALLY ARRIVED in Facilis late in the afternoon. Exhausted from her travels, especially lack of sleep, her first order of business was to find a place with a bed and a shower. The Waiz track was underground, and she hurried to follow the exiting travelers up several flights of stairs. Unlike most of the small stations she had been through that day, the Facilis station was magnificent in size. It was old, yet dramatically different than the dark and dreary Crossroads Station in Differe. The entry room had an airiness about it and was filled with light. The floor to ceiling windows allowed the setting sun's rays to shine throughout the station. As Augustine gazed around the room, she thought of her mother's pastel pink purse in her bag. The station's arches, counters, and doorways were covered in blush, lavender, peach, and sage colors that made her feel happy for some reason, and suddenly she was eager to step outside.

The station appeared to be in the middle of downtown Facilis, much like Crossroads Station in Differe, though this station was standing across from a park rather than being completely surrounded by buildings. She smiled as a horse drawn carriage entered the park across the street from her, hooves clopping against the cobblestone walkway. She leaned against one of the large columns of the building trying to figure out what to do next. She watched the large groups of people walking past the station for a few minutes before finally deciding to join them. *You can do this. You can do it for Sebastian.* She was surprised, as she walked among the crowd, to hear different languages as well as her own being spoken. Curious, once her group was stopped on a busy street corner, she took a moment to study the people around her more closely. No one seemed to pay much attention to her wild orange ensemble, as most others had done that day. *But they should.* The ladies' clothing and accessories differed greatly from hers, yet they were anything but drab. In fact, their clothes were much more to her liking than what she was wearing. The clothes wrapped around the women were silky, smooth, light, and above all, feminine. Their makeup was simple, yet in all her travels thus far, she would deem them the most beautiful people she had ever seen. She tried not to stare at the beauties as she crossed the streets beside them.

Focus, Augustine. She wondered what part of the city she was in and if the whole place was part of the political hub. She only hoped she was safe. Soon the whiff of a delicious fragrance easily distracted her again. *Oh, yum!* She soon became fascinated by the shops lining the streets, particularly the patisseries. She stared into each window front with delight. *Oh, look at the clothes! Cheeses and breads. Such lovely flowers. A store just with shoes?* She was in heaven.

The crowd she kept following seemed to be going around the park, which appeared to weave in and around most of downtown Facilis. The tall buildings surrounding the green area were lovely and historic. It was as if she was in a fairytale of some kind, strolling beside a romantic park surrounded by old palaces. She gasped in awe as electric lights suddenly lit the streets around her. *Spectacular.* She was spellbound until the lights reminded her it would be dark soon. *Come on, you've got to make a plan . . . . Sleep. Get some sleep, then decide.*

Searching the street for a kind face, she spotted an old man and his dog people-watching down by the next park gate. Augustine took a deep breath as she headed his way with a horde of others. "Uh, excuse me, Sir?"

He turned to her in obvious surprise and smiled. "Lost?"

She was relieved he spoke her language. "Uh, new. I'd like an inn close by if there is one."

His smile became wider, and he chuckled. "Your fancy get up had me fooled. You're not a city girl are you?"

She shook her head, hoping this would buy her some pity, help, or both.

"We don't have inns here, but we do have something like them. They're called hotels."

Augustine nodded in embarrassment. She knew what a hotel was. *They're for rich people.*

"And, yes, there are several, but for a first timer like yourself I'd recommend the one in Dunn Square."

Augustine thought of the square in the Adams Kalona. "Oh, you have a square here?"

"Not square, but squares. The city is filled with them. Dunn happens to be my favorite. It's a bit old, but the price will be fair. And, there's a lovely patisserie there."

"You sold me at patisserie."

"Come on, I'll walk you there. I can tell you a little about Facilis on the way." He stood up and untied the dog's leash. "I'm Earl, and this is Jack." Earl was a thin man and looked to be in his early sixties. His white hair was unconventional, unkempt and somewhat long for someone his age, but he had a kind smile and that was enough for Augustine at this point.

"Hello, Jack." She patted the dog's black head. "I'm Au—I mean—I mean . . . ."

The man shot her a curious look.

"Honey," she finished quickly. "Honey Paisley."

He gave her the same amused look all the others had upon hearing her false name.

She blushed and decided to find out a little more about her guide. "Are you from Facilis?"

"I'm from the Southern Regions, but Facilis has been my home for over thirty years. And you know what?" He stopped and gave her a knowing look.

"Hm?" She turned to face him.

"It hasn't changed a bit. Well, I mean, obviously some things have changed, but as far as the look and feel of the place, it's relatively the same. A man my age who's had many ups and downs comes to really appreciate stability in a place."

Augustine nodded in understanding.

"Well, now." He started walking again. "You must be from Waiz, I suppose."

"Yes, that's correct." *Honey's from New Waiz anyway.*

"Yes, I could tell by your complexion and, of course, your dress." He winked at her and smacked his lips. "I would guess New Waiz, but you seem like a small town, kalona kind of girl as well."

She raised her eyebrows at him. "You know quite a bit about Waiz."

"Been there a few times. I get around."

"What's your occupation if you don't mind?"

"I don't mind at all. We're turning off here—down this main street." Earl pointed away from the park toward a bustling street of pedestrians. "I'm retired. In my younger years I was a scout for a travel agency."

"A scout?" She took Jack's leash as the man bent down to tie an undone shoelace.

"Yes, it was my dream job. I was paid to travel the world."

Augustine pondered his words. She wasn't sure if a job like that sounded exciting or frightening.

"Basically I visited different areas and searched out the best places to eat, stay, and, you know, what attractions to seek out then wrote about them in travel books or pamphlets. Sometimes I provided tours for people."

"How interesting. How long did you do that?" She motioned she was fine to take Jack for the rest of the walk. *He makes creating a path in this busy crowd much easier.*

"Oh, about seven years, then I took over the agency, but then the government took it over."

She knew the latter statement wasn't positive by his tone. "Which did you prefer, planning trips for tourists or for the government?"

He chuckled and gave her a small bow. "I like what I'm doing right now the most."

His goofy bow and sense of humor immediately made her think of Joel, and Earl caught her smiling to herself.

"Ah, I'm reminding you of someone? This way." He led her off the crowded street to a block of buildings. They walked under a beautiful arched entryway that was so large it took up the first four floors of the building, and she soon found herself in an opening.

"The square."

She watched Earl take a bow again. "Are you meeting this man in Facilis? I'm guessing he's a man . . . about your age?"

She heard his teasing tone and laughed at his calling Joel a "man." She nodded. "I hope so, but I'm not really sure."

"He'll come for you. I'm sure of it. Now then, take in Dunn Square."

Augustine walked forward and was thankful Earl stopped to let her take in the surroundings. The square was, well, a square—a square of adjacent buildings facing one another. The ground was covered with large square stones interspersed with black antique lampposts and grown palm trees. A statue of a woman pouring water from a jug into a trickling fountain held the middle view. All the buildings boasted similar archways to the one she had just walked through; however, she found open-air restaurants and shops just past these arches. The floors above were decorated with old wooden shutters, window boxes, and tiny iron-barred balconies. The buildings were cloaked in stone and marigold colored brick.

She felt Earl take Jack's leash. "What do you think, Honey?"

She took in a deep breath. "It's magical."

After settling into her room, Augustine threw open her windows and leaned over the balcony. The square smelled as delicious as the dish she had just bought from one of the restaurants below. The cool night air brought a fresh breeze into the cozy room Earl had helped her get for the next few nights. He promised to give her a tour of the city, so she had taken his card. *But mostly because I feel like he'll know the best way to get back to Waiz.* She took a bite of her pasta and prided herself on how well she'd done by herself. *You were right, Joel. I did it.* A sound in the distance caught her attention. She spotted a man with long dark hair sitting on the side of the fountain strumming a guitar. The light from the fountain exposed his dark skin. *It's darker than mine.*

Curious, she studied him further. The man stood up, coughed, and stamped out a cigarette. He made his way to the restaurant across the square from her room, strumming as he walked. She smiled as he started singing a Differian song in his broken accent for the restaurant crowd below. A Differian song in this square seemed ironic to her. He croaked out a few more songs until he noticed her staring down at him. Once he did, he walked over and stood right below her balcony to play for her. Augustine followed suit by throwing down some coins to him as she had the seen the others from the restaurant do. She ate her pasta to his mesmerizing tunes, and then he bid her goodnight.

She closed the balcony windows and was more than happy to change her clothes and scrub off her makeup. As she sat down at the small desk in her room, she wondered how long she should wait before catching the train to Waiz. *Corwin said if we didn't meet up in five days we'd meet at the cave.* In any case, she knew he'd wait for her. He had no choice—*not with Sebastian.* Her body pleaded for sleep, but Joel's bound leather file lying in front of her begged to be opened. She ran her fingers over the cover and quickly untied the leather strips holding it together. She grabbed the cover flap then paused. *This feels wrong. I'm about to see things that even Joel hasn't. This information is private . . . but what if I don't see him again? Should I wait for Corwin?* Of course her plan had always been to read it, but when she thought she was returning to Waiz with Joel she figured she'd just give the file to Corwin. *Enough. Just open it.* The file was packed full of documents. The first thing she saw was the picture of Joel and his parents that she had slipped inside at Moonstruck.

His mother was a redhead like Joel. *He has her smile.* His father was holding him on his shoulder. Both parents were looking at Joel, appearing captivated by the little boy. She placed the picture on the desk and studied the file's cover page. "Temple File of Joel Reagan. Temple Property." There were a few dates and signatures near the bottom of the page.

The next page was Joel's acceptance letter from the temple. She scanned the paper for an address. She wondered where Joel was from—he'd never said, so she had just assumed Differe, but the letter about his father looking for him led her to believe otherwise. *Nothing.* She struggled to turn the page. There was something attached to the acceptance letter. She found a lengthy assessment following the letter and quickly flipped to the results page.

"Holy smokes!" She covered her mouth in shock.

Dear Master Reagan,

    We have scored the entrance assessment that was given to Joel at our office in Differe. We are delighted to tell you that he more than exceeded the requirements requested by the temple. In fact, Joel scored the highest of any student that has ever been accepted. His ability to comprehend and problem solve at his young age is remarkable. The manifestations you are concerned about we fully believe he will outgrow, as the trauma of his mother's death is still quite fresh. He displayed some normal behavior one would expect with such a trauma, such as refusing to play with the toy train station. We fully believe the temple will only serve to enhance his skills. We recommended annual follow-up testing over the next few years. We are glad he is able to follow in his late mother's footsteps by attending her alma mater. Hopefully this will be a comfort to him. As we discussed, the worst possible situation is for the boy to be isolated. His peers may not relate well to the genius level he displays, but the temple will make every attempt to give him opportunities to make friends.

Genius level? He can't even read.

CHAPTER 21

I’*M NOT COWERING, I’m surviving.* Isabelle hid behind a brick column and waited until Holt was out of sight. At first she thought he was only mad about the paper grade, but since that episode his behavior had become even more despicable. And, unfortunately, she hadn’t been lucky enough to have Sarah rescue her over the past few days. The worst of it was that Holt had joined Hertz Marlis, the menacing head Templin, in his ruthless pursuit to antagonize Isabelle. She was trying her best to be invisible, but it was hard to avoid them because of the covered walkways that connected the campus buildings. Her choices were to pass by or walk in the snow. She shivered and touched her neck as she stood in her hiding spot. *Thanks to them I need a scarf more than ever now.* Touching her bare neck made her mind drift back to the day before. She hated thinking about it, but the scene had been one of her most traumatic encounters to date.

"Eris, what do you think of Isabelle?" The blonde heard Hertz sneer as she walked past the group on her way to class.

Isabelle preferred not to hear Eris's answer and turned away just before someone stuck their foot in front of her. Isabelle stumbled forward, flinging her textbooks across the walkway. After she pushed herself off the cold ground, she looked up to find out who had done such a thing.

"Well, she's quite clumsy . . . obviously."

Eris's cackle rang in her ears as Isabelle gazed up at the face peering down at her. *Holt.* She was surprised how badly it stung her heart to discover it was him.

"No, No. That's not what I'm asking . . . ." Hertz shuffled toward her. "No, I mean, in terms of . . . attractiveness. How would you rate the little vixen?"

Isabelle tried to ignore their stares as she began collecting her books.

"Oh. Well, I suppose she's not *all* ugly."

Isabelle fought the urge to glare at the girl for her rude comment.

"Of course she isn't. You can't forget she was attached to your hunk of meat for years."

Isabelle was shocked Hertz would admit such a thing. *He's just trying to get a rise out of Holt.*

"She has pretty hair," a younger student interjected.

"I didn't ask your opinion, you little nobody. Go on, Eris. Holt's past love . . . is she as pretty as you?"

Eris seemed to hesitate. "Well, like I said, she's not all ugly."

Yes, how ugly can you say I am with Holt standing right beside you? Isabelle felt both Eris's discomfort as well as her stare.

"Her hair . . . um, if it were gone she'd be no match for me."

Hertz smacked his lips. "I agree."

Isabelle finally turned to them and watched Hertz lift a knife from his belt. She frantically searched around for a professor as the three closed in on her. Her heart quickened as Hertz held the knife out to Holt.

Isabelle shut her eyes and pounded the pillar in front of her, eventually stopping the memory from replaying in her mind. *I have to find a safe place. A place they wouldn't dare set foot in.* Besides Moonstruck she knew of only one other place. A place she hated.

She easily snatched a clean surgical gown from the Infirmary's laundry bin behind the building. This wasn't the first time she'd escaped to this place. Draped in her white camouflage, she pressed through the emergency room doors and into the Infirmary's corridors hardly noticed. She headed toward her and Joel's mainstay—the Psych Ward. *I don't want to go through the access door. I need to take the stairs so I can just end up directly on the floor.* After entering the code to the stairway door, she proceeded to the third floor.

She shuffled onto the floor, keeping her white hooded head away from any prying eyes. She marched past a very quiet nurses' station, then stopped completely. The main lights were off, and all monitors shut down. *There's no one here!* She didn't know whether to feel spooked at being all alone in the Psych Ward or elated to have found a new place of refuge . . . *at least until I can get to Waiz.* She decided on elation after remembering what she and Joel used to do every time they left the floor. She threw off the linens and did a victory dance in her own honor. She could almost feel Joel dancing right alongside her. "A way to keep sane," he always told her, clearly mocking the Infirmary's methods. The nurses didn't agree but never stopped them either.

She smiled until she shook her head and felt her chin-length hair. The smile quickly became a scowl as she put her hands on her hips. It was then she realized she was not alone and quickly threw the white linens back on. Her heart pounded as she eyed a light glowing underneath the door of a room down the hallway to her left. She moved closer to listen for voices, and upon hearing some, was surprised to find them very familiar.

"It's time to take action," she heard Dr. Pryderi state firmly.

"What do you suggest? Let out a bunch of zombies? It's not time yet! Besides, we don't even know where he is!"

She had never heard Professor Louis yell like that. *What's going on in there?* She inched her way down the hall to find out.

"Stop arguing. His father will put the pressure on Dark. That's sure to give us more options."

Sarah? You're here? What kind of secret meeting is this? She slipped into the room next door and found a chair to get comfortable in. *I'm ready to eavesdrop.*

The professor continued, "Speaking of James, when do you think the letters were delivered?"

"Had to have been several days ago," Sarah replied.

Professor Louis cleared his throat. "Yes, that sounds about right. That's when I intercepted the alert to the Templins."

"They won't dare enter the Southern Regions . . . ." Isabelle leaned her head against the wall as she waited for Sarah to finish. "But I think Master Reagan knows he'd be in danger if he came here."

"He's got plenty of enemies in Differe. That's certain." Professor Louis's voice became softer.

"Have you—have you heard from him?" Sarah asked quietly.

"No. He knows it's too risky. It's all right, Sarah. I never made him any promises regarding Joel. He . . . ," the man hesitated, "he knew why I was really stationed here."

Isabelle heard Sarah sigh.

"I've had my share of long nights . . . thinking about Joel. I-I know he's all right. He's endured enough to show himself strong, but I sometimes wonder if he ever found out about me . . . being here . . . just standing by and watching." The professor stopped there.

"It was the perfect plan," Dr. Pryderi chimed in. "Hide him in the enemy's camp. One day he'll understand."

Understand what? Why hasn't Sarah told me about Dr. Pryderi or Professor Louis being on her side?

"Still doesn't make me feel right about watching my own flesh and blood be tormented for over a decade."

As Isabelle heard Professor Louis utter these words, she felt even more confused. The group went silent for a moment, and she wished she could see through the wall.

"All right, enough about Joel. We can't do anything there until we hear something. Listen, what's Dark saying about the West End? There seem to be ties in Differe's plans with Facilis *and* Waiz somehow," she heard Dr. Pryderi say.

"Well, I already told you Langston's orders. He's probably on his way to Waiz right now." It sounded like the Professor was presenting papers.

Holt's father? What's he doing in Waiz?

"He's bound to charm more than just Marcell," Sarah quipped.

"Of course, that's precisely why Dark sent him," Professor Louis growled.

"All right, Emerson, enough. Stop being so negative." Isabelle was surprised at the firmness she heard in Sarah's voice.

"Sorry," the professor retreated.

"Just calm down and tell us about the West End."

The professor sighed. "You're right. They're after Facilis. It's the political power of the free world. All the regions abide by its laws and standards."

"So they just plan to march in there and take it?"

"Sarah, they're already on their way," Dr. Pryderi let out.

"What do you mean?" Isabelle thought she sounded confused.

"Why do you think Trompè is the fullest we've ever seen it? And, mind you, many of those are foreigners from the Northern Regions . . . ," the doctor trailed off.

Sarah didn't answer.

"How do you think they've come to acquire the funds to send so many troops and supplies to Waiz?" Professor Louis added. "The Temple—"

"Headmaster," Pryderi interrupted.

"Is taxing the villages in the West End and the Northern Regions."

"On what basis?"

Yes, what indeed . . . .

"Safety," the men said in unison.

"From what?"

The room went silent again until a recollection hit Sarah. "Oh," she finally let out.

Oh? Oh what? Isabelle was anxious to know.

"Yes, so you see, they're already holding control in most of the villages and cities in both regions. They've also acquired troops from both places by, well . . . blackmail."

"Trompè," Pryderi let out quickly.

"See! Now that's why I think we can do something. Not everyone in Trompè is, well, you know, infirmed." The professor sounded pretty adamant.

Dr. Pryderi seemed quick to cut him off. "No, it's too risky. There are too many at that mental institution that *are* infirmed. They need a leader."

"They need a rhydid," Sarah claimed.

"I know, I know, they need Joel. He's the only one." The Professor was obviously frustrated by this notion.

Sarah chuckled. "I feel a bit sorry for the fellow. A lot of people need him."

Dr. Pryderi seemed to agree with her. "Hm. Yes, this eighteen-year-old kid has no idea how many people are counting on him."

"Eighteen? Where do you think he is?"

Isabelle very much wanted to know the answers to the professor's questions.

Sarah answered his first one. "He had a birthday recently."

Dr. Pryderi took a stab at his second one. "That's a tough question. There's been no word from Waiz to Dark, no word from the Templins—they searched every possible train he would've been on. My guess is he's on foot somewhere. Headed back to Waiz?"

"Then I'm with the doctor. We have to wait until we know something about his whereabouts before we take action," Sarah concluded.

"That could be weeks!" Isabelle was startled by the professor's roar.

"We've waited this long. A few more weeks aren't going to be detrimental," Dr. Pryderi replied in a raised voice.

"Don't start lecturing me on how long, Ravi. I know he was your favorite, but I was just sticking to my position."

"Just like a Templin." Isabelle knew the doctor meant the words as a barb.

"How dare you!"

There was some commotion as Sarah intervened, "Enough! Stop it! This is helping no one, and, if I remember correctly, we agreed to forgive the past."

"That doesn't mean—"

"I know, 'forget,'" Sarah interrupted Dr. Pryderi.

The room went silent again, and Isabelle wondered what stories must lie in the past.

"My apologies, Emerson. I'm sorry for accusing you of something that is so obviously against what you stand for."

"Accepted. I'm sorry as well for lashing out. I suppose it's the guilt I feel."

Isabelle sat back and crossed her arms. She had never heard grown men apologize to anyone.

"Well, the past is forgiven, and one day Joel will understand," Dr. Pryderi assured him.

Professor Louis's calm voice seemed to agree. "Yes, all right then. We will wait until we hear something. We are certainly on the brink of breakthrough for so many."

CHAPTER 22

"TROMPÉ! THEY CAN'T do that!" Joel shuddered at the thought of these comrades' loved ones lying comatose in such a terrible place. He shifted his attention back to the metal trap, realizing he hadn't gotten an answer from Dillon as to why the injured farmhand was still in the barn. "Why are you hiding Byron from the Templins? The trap . . . is it theirs?"

The group went silent, and Joel knew he was on the cusp of discovering another secret. "How was your Templin leader killed?" The grim expressions and eyes darting away from his confirmed his conclusion. "You killed him."

"It was accident!" one let out.

Dillon's younger brother stepped forward. "My fault."

Joel shook his head at him and shrugged. "You can tell me. I've already told you I'm not a Templin. In fact, I hold a great deal of hatred toward them. Why else would I steal their food and bring it down here? Do you honestly think a real Templin would do such a thing?"

One of the younger farmhands sitting next to the injured man stood up. "Who are you then?"

Joel stared back at the young man and slowly shook his head. "It's better if I don't say. For me and for all of you. If—if you don't mind I'd like to keep Paz, but I'll be leaving your company in the morning."

Dillon squinted his eyes in confusion. "Leave? Why?"

Joel grasped the handle of his rhydid. "It'll be safer for you without me."

Joel awoke the next morning feeling quite well and gave full credit to Dillon's soup. He was still in the stables, but the troops were gone. He wondered if the Differian Army would be expecting him at breakfast. *I've got to get going.* His belongings were sitting near the door, and his clothes hung on a line. After dressing, he went around back to search for a water pump to fill his canteen. As he filled up the pouch, he thought of Augustine brushing her teeth on the Hallie Farm in Waiz. Every time she came into his mind he told himself she was fine and in Facilis, and hopefully heading to Waiz in the next few days. He assured himself he had done the right thing in leaving her. She was safe, and that meant Sebastian was safe also. *I want her with Corwin, though.* He didn't like the idea of his pretty little friend being on her own.

That was another thing that had wrecked his thinking lately. He tried to convince himself that nothing had changed about her. He was closer to her now, no doubt, due to all the time they'd spent together. So, he figured that was why he felt more protective of her. But Dillon's words from the night before still echoed in his mind. *I went on about her for an hour?* Every now and then he also thought of Isabelle. He was aggravated at himself for not having the guts to press Augustine about their connection. Isabelle seemed the same in his mind, but he knew something had changed in her as well since he'd last seen her. She was running away. *She was running away to find me.*

"You're spilling water all over yourself."

Joel jumped back, startled by the voice. He huffed and shook the water off his clothes and hands. He turned to find little Noor looking at him with her curious brown eyes. "Good morning, Noor."

She wrinkled her nose at him. "Your hair . . . it's the same as mine."

"Yes, it is."

She covered her mouth with a finger. "It's a secret."

Joel crouched down beside her. "Yes."

"Just like the food?"

Joel nodded.

She eyed the bag at his feet. "You're going away."

He nodded again.

"I . . . I—" She shyly looked away from him.

Joel shuffled around until she finally looked at him again.

"I don't want you to go."

His brow furrowed. "Why not?"

"We need a nice Templin like you to keep helping us."

"Oh. Well, Noor, I'm not a Templin. I fear it'll be more dangerous than helpful if I stay. But . . . Dillon and his group will help you."

Disappointment filled her eyes as she pressed her lips together and nodded. "I won't forget you."

Joel felt relieved when she scurried off to the front of the stables. *Just what I need, one more person depending on me.* He walked into the barn and was grateful someone had prepared Paz to be saddled. "Good morning, boy. Ready to head out?" He rubbed the white stripe on the horse's nose.

Paz snorted in response and swished his tail.

"I comb him for yous, Sir."

Joel turned to find Dillon's brother behind him holding Paz's saddle. "Thank you, uh, what's your name?" Joel reached out to take the saddle.

"No, I can do it. My, uh, name is Ian."

"Good. Ian, teach me how."

Dillon's brother nodded and grinned slightly. "Yous really are no Templin."

"Nah." Joel shook his head. "I mean, I've ridden before, but I was young and didn't saddle them much myself." He slid open the stall door and gave Paz a pat on the back.

"Here. First yous put on the saddle pad." Ian handed him the object, and Joel adjusted it accordingly. "Then yous put on the saddle and girth."

The two worked together until Paz was fully saddled and bridled. "Good thing you like me, Paz. You made that pretty easy." Joel jumped off the stepstool and folded it up.

Ian led Paz out of the stall then put a hand up. "I shall tell yous what happen before yous leave. Paz has a tattoo on his lip. In case the Templins find yous . . . Paz is my old leader's horse . . . yous need to hear the story."

Joel nodded.

"Differe, the Templins, take us from Galanne . . . after they take father to Trompè."

Anger flashed through Joel at these words. His face must have shown it, because Ian stopped there until Joel motioned for him to continue.

"Well, the Templin in charge of us was like the rest of them—mean, cruel."

I know all too well.

"He take us from, er, village to village in Galanne to collect the tax and people . . . and more volunteers for our group. Once we got out of Galanne, he take us to Differe for training camp. We boys became men. We learn . . . we learn to survive."

Joel clenched his jaw as he looked into the eyes of Ian, who couldn't be more than twelve.

"Our first mission was to guard a village in the West End—like this one." He pointed to the ground. "Hungry, poor. One night a man stole bread for he family. The Templin leader teach us fear as army tactic. He make us use."

Joel cracked his knuckles as he took in the words. "So, your Templin leader made an example of the man."

Ian's eyes brewed with fire. "He did try. He did not succeed."

"It was you . . . you killed him."

"It was an accident." Dillon suddenly marched up with several others.

"Dillon was in charge of the man's punishment—taking he daughter to Trompè."

Dillon gritted his teeth. "I refuse . . . I could not do it. I could not do to someone what I suffer . . . am suffering."

"The Templin start to beat Dillon, so I grab a big, uh . . . rock. It kill him."

"Wow." Joel couldn't say anything else. Nothing came to mind.

"Yous say yous be a danger to us if yous stays, but we . . . we might be more of danger to yous."

Joel chuckled slightly at the irony of Dillon's words. "Seems we were meant to meet. Thanks for helping me get this far. I hope I haven't delayed you in, uh, whatever it is you're up to." He went to mount Paz but felt a hand on his shoulder.

"The traps—we hide them because theys are ours."

Joel turned back around, and Dillon locked eyes with him.

"Yes, we are helping the villages. We shall teach them how to survive. The Templins shall leave thinking they are in control, but the remaining survivors . . . they shall band together."

"And this village, Baithe, is no exception, I guess?" Joel had to admit he was impressed.

Dillon nodded. "Yes, but it will be easier with yous, though. They think yous are a Templin, so they shall leave faster. They will leave the village in your control."

I know what you're trying to do. He turned back towards Paz. "I can't stay. I've got to go."

"To Facilis . . . to your Augustine?"

Joel didn't answer, but mounted Paz instead.

"Stay. Help us, and we will get yous to Facilis."

"I really can't wait."

"Better for yous to ride in with troops. We can help yous."

Noor's face came into view. *This is more trouble. More defiance . . . messier.* He turned Paz forward, forcing him to face the young men surrounding him. They had turned their own suffering into someone else's gain. They were fighting for others when it seemed no one had fought for them. Joel knew he had done what he needed for Sebastian and Augustine. *If I leave . . . it will be only for myself.* He sighed. *Stupid conscience. What should I do?* He gripped the rhydid and instantly thought of Sarah. *I'm free because someone else helped me . . . risked for me.* He was still unsure what to do as he dismounted Paz. "All right, here's the deal. Now you need to hear *my* story. If you think I'm more of a help than a danger I'll stay, but the group decides. Not me."

"Deal."

The group voted unanimously in favor of Joel staying after he finished recapping his story. He had purposely left out the part about Trompè fearing they would ask questions—questions he didn't want to answer. He agreed to stay and help them, but had one stipulation. He would not tell them his real name. He figured it was still too dangerous for him and for them, so the group decided to stick with "Templin Guy."

Noor and her family had also cast their votes. Saving Byron's life and giving them food had more than earned Joel their favor. He couldn't help but notice Noor's mother's eyes when he told his story. Tears swelled several times as she listened, yet he knew they revealed compassion, not pity.

"You are so very brave. What you have endured has not been good, but *you* are. It has not been kind, but *you* are. It has been unbearable, but *you* bore it. *You* have fought . . . and, I believe, *you* have won."

Joel shook his head, smiling faintly at her words. "Not yet, but I hope I'm on my way."

The others nodded in approval of him. "Well, you won our Galanne game."

"The freezing water game?"

"Yes, maybe we shall call you our Galanne champion, our frozen chosen?" The group burst into laughter.

Joel's smile grew wider as he laughed along with them. He couldn't deny his heart ached after losing Augie's companionship, but in turn for keeping her safe—*free*—he'd been provided, for the first time in his life, a group of male comrades. Glancing around at the grimy faces of his new friends, he felt more proud than he had in his whole life.

Shortly thereafter, the group filled a restaurant kitchen on the square to prepare a meal for Differe's soldiers. Joel stood next to the stove near Noor's mother, whom he had learned was named Violet. She turned up one of the flames and patted his hand.

"You made no mention of your family. Do you have any family?"

A pain struck deep inside him. He'd not had a family besides Isabelle and Sarah since he was five years old, and then it had become Augustine, Sebastian, and Corwin . . . *for a while*. And now the group standing in front of him had embraced him. Joel eyed each face curiously as they waited for him to say something. He finally just shrugged. "Yeah, I suppose I've had an ever changing family of sorts. I don't really belong to anyone. I don't even have a last name on my temple file that I know of."

A farmhand named Gus brought over a hot frying pan. "I know you can't deny what you saw in the cave, but do you ever have doubts . . . doubts about something that you can't see?"

Images of the past few months flashed through his mind—the mouthpieces, the escape, the murder, the cave, Sebastian almost dying, the rhydid. With all the ups and downs, everyday seemed to bring reasons for him to hope and reasons for him to doubt. He had even been hit with doubt regarding whether the Galannean's plan to free Baith from the Templins would work. Here was a destitute family and a rogue army unit serving their enemy breakfast. This group of young men was attempting to break the Templins' bondage over the region, yet they barely knew how to provide basic care. He knew he'd made the right decision in choosing these people over himself, anyone could see it was noble, but he knew deep down something was churning in him. He finally nodded at Gus. "Yes. Definitely."

"How do you push past them . . . how do you keep believing?"

Joel shook his head at Gus. "What other choice do I have? To give up is . . . ." He stopped when a rush of air blew across the room and scattered a pile of fresh greens. Goose bumps rose on Joel's forearms, and he looked around to see if the others were feeling what he was. He jumped as an electric jolt flooded through his body. The others rushed toward him but were pushed back by something invisible. "Wait, it's all right. I hear something . . . I know I hear it." He looked into Dillon's eyes. "Do you hear it?"

He shook his head. "No."

Joel gritted his teeth in disappointment. "The singing. I hear the singing again."

"I do not hear it, Templin Guy . . . but I *feel* it."

It seemed as if an electrical current was floating around them. Joel's eyes pleaded to Violet. "Do you hear it?"

She nodded. "Yes . . . yes, I hear the words."

Noor tugged on her sleeve. "What's it saying?"

Violet eyed Joel nervously.

He nodded at her. "Go on. I can't make it out."

Violet took a deep breath and clasped her hands. "All right. The voices are saying, 'Empower the weak.'"

The words poured into Joel's spirit like fire. He suddenly felt more alive and knew right then leading this group of villagers and the Galanneans was something he'd somehow always wanted. He faced the group and saw the eyes of the others held the same zeal he now felt inside. "Why are you here? How many villages have you helped? Who are you really?"

Joel watched a sly grin spread across Dillon's face. "Yes . . . there is much for yous to know. Violet . . . she call to us."

"Called for you? What does that mean . . . exactly?" Joel saw the others held Dillon's same grin.

Dillon rubbed his chin thoughtfully. "Hmm . . . yous will think it crazy."

Joel matched his intense gaze. "Try me."

Chapter 23

JOEL WATCHED AS the villagers served the Differian Army the meal he had just helped prepare. He ate alongside the troops, disgusted by their gluttony. *I can't take this much longer.* Back in disguise and the captain being satisfied by a full stomach, Joel made his move. "Officer Evans, I understand you have other assignments that require your unit to move out. I assume these matters are much more important than the likes of this place."

"Right you are. I've been waiting for weeks to leave this pigsty. This is the best meal we've had the whole time." The man lowered his voice, "You don't think they've been hiding food from us?"

Joel's palms grew sweaty as he tried to cover his culinary tracks and change the subject. "Hardly. We both know there's not enough to hide. Where are you headed next? With so few living here in Baithe, my comrades and I can clearly handle the village. I'll send for a lower ranking Templin to take my place in the next few days. He could probably do fine on his own." Joel let out a chuckle and stroked the green Templin emblem on his cloak for effect.

The officer shoved in a few more bites then stuck out his hand. "All right, Templin Guy. Baithe is all yours." He stood up and motioned to his troops. "Gather our supplies. We'll move out after lunch to the Facilis gates."

"Ah, joining the political business there?"

"Of sorts. We're guards by nature." Evans drew close to Joel's face and flashed a sinister grin. "We'll be staking out the gate."

The grin made Joel nervous. "Doesn't Facilis have its own guards for those matters?"

"Nope. Those merciful idiots let anyone in. The headmaster thinks he's got a lead on those two boys who escaped from the temple a few days ago."

His blood was pumping now. "Oh?"

The officer smacked his lips. "Pretty easy guess. Where would you head if the law was chasing you?"

"Somewhere . . . I could be pardoned."

"Exactly."

The sinking feeling in Joel's gut was still there as he watched the group ride away. His jaw clenched in frustration at the situation. He told himself Augustine was safe. *She's a girl, not a boy. She's safe . . . she's gotta be.*

"Come." Dillon's voice interrupted his thoughts.

Joel followed his new comrades back down the road to the stables and further tailed Dillon into the field behind the barn. It was then Joel noticed the rest of the group had stayed back at the stables—except for Violet, Noor, and Byron. They were walking beside him. His anxiety about the Differians guarding the Facilis gate lessened as he remembered the scene from the kitchen earlier. The group had united as something supernatural took place. The singing host had chanted a mission for them. Joel repeated the words over and over in his mind before deciding to add his own spin on their song. *Take down the enemy by empowering the weak.* He pondered his new phrase as they walked farther away from the barn. His enemy, the headmaster, had always called him "weak" and "crazy," so he was more than interested to uncover what Dillon told him might appear "crazy."

He glanced over at Violet. "Calling?"

She winked at him and nodded.

Dillon eventually stopped, and Joel rounded beside him. The young man began unbuttoning his cloak then his shirt. He reached inside the shirt and pulled out a small object. Joel moved closer since Dillon didn't seem to mind his curiosity. Dillon pulled a chain from around his neck and held it out for Joel to see.

Joel gasped. "A sacred stone." He stared in awe, for unlike the others he'd seen—*it's real.* The greenish blue rock covered in rows of rings was thin and round like a medallion. Joel shook slightly when he instantly felt a burning sensation near his face. He tugged his ear and twisted his earring. It must have been the first time Dillon had noticed it because he shot Joel an odd look. Joel held up his hand. "It was my mom's."

Dillon furrowed his brow and shrugged.

Joel waited, but the group just stood there. "Uh, now what?"

"Something new." Dillon pointed to Joel. "Get the rhydid out."

Excited and nervous, Joel lifted the dagger from its sheath. He held it out to Dillon, but the young man quickly pushed it away.

"Wait. I will show the other way first."

Violet drew a jagged rectangular object out of her pocket and came forward. It was also attached to a chain, but this chain was longer and much thicker. Her weapon was made of slick black material and had shimmering pearl colored writing etched across it. Joel looked at Dillon's sacred stone then to Violet's thicker tablet. An image from the Old Waiz Museum came to mind— the black rock burned with an inscription. *What in the—*

"Ready?" Dillon motioned to Violet then looked to Joel.

Joel gripped the rhydid and looked back at the barn. He spotted the rest of the group now hanging around the fence, waiting for whatever was about to take place. He turned back to find Noor and Byron covering their ears. Joel wondered if he should do the same. *No, I want to hear this.* He nodded at Dillon to proceed.

The two started swinging their objects in the air as if preparing to throw a pebble from a slingshot. Joel marveled as a howling wind began swirling around them. The winds, seeming to come out of nowhere, began spinning along with the tablet and sacred stone. Seconds later he found himself in the middle of a small cyclone, and the screaming winds brought him to his knees. As he held his ears, it felt like his right one was blistering. He twisted his earring again. When the winds died down, he stood to his feet completely breathless. "How—how far away can that be heard?"

"At least to the next village." Noor smirked as she removed her hands from her ears.

Joel eyed the objects again. "Uh, you have some more explaining to do."

Dillon and Violet exchanged amused glances.

Joel took the object from Dillon for closer study. "First of all, where did you get those?"

"Village or region leaders have passed them down for generations."

Joel turned to Violet. "So, yours is really your husband's?"

She held out her black tablet to him. "It's called a barique. And, yes, that's right. He didn't want it to leave the village."

"Or fall into the wrong hands. Dillon, you're the leader of your village?"

"My father is the ruler of Galanne in the Northern Regions."

Joel's jaw dropped. "How then—what—where are his men? How did he get taken to Trompè?" His mind suddenly felt fuzzy.

Dillon's face hardened. "He did not get taken. He went willingly."

Joel stroked his chin, puzzled for a moment, but then the action became clear to him. "He sacrificed himself for your people."

"Yes, it was him or several hundred." The young man sighed before hurling a rock in disgust.

Joel looked at the sacred stone again and sighed too. "That's why you're really doing this, because of—"

"It is not revenge, Joel." Everyone in the group froze at Dillon's interruption.

"How—how—" Joel dropped the stone and started backing away from Dillon. *He knows my name. I need to run. They know who I am somehow!*

Violet reached out towards him. "Joel, wait."

A fuse was lit inside him, as he thrust the rhydid at them. "Let's get something straight here, right now. I want answers, or I'm gone. Do you understand me?"

"I'll tell you everything—I promise. But first I need you to do something. I need to see something. We need the rhydid. Please. Please, help us."

Joel didn't budge at Violet's plea, but shoved the dagger back into its place. "What? You're asking me for a favor? It'd better be worth the exchange of all your secrets." *I can't believe I was so deceived!*

Byron moved between them. His face was stern as he pointed to Joel's rhydid. "Well, don't fall, for one thing. Just take that and hold it up this time. I don't think it's too much to ask. We'll let you take Paz if you decide to leave."

Joel was so mad he didn't want to participate in the show, but curiosity beat out his pride. *And I'll need Paz.* With a grand scowl on his face he walked between Violet and Dillon. "Fine." He caught the two's concerned glances, but Dillon gestured for Violet to begin.

Joel closed his eyes and spread his feet apart to brace himself for the roaring wind show. As the sounds grew louder, he uncrossed his arms from their sulky position and slid his hand to the hilt of the dagger. Anticipation built as he pulled the rhydid from its place. He squinted through the rushing winds and held the dagger out. Nothing seemed different than before. Disappointment crept over him. *Who are these people? How do they know me? Have they lied to me the whole time?* As the questions swirled in his head, he realized something humbling. *Guess I planned on lying to them the whole time too until Byron got hurt. But—but that was different. It was for their own safety, just like Augustine.*

"Are you glad you left her?"

You again with the same question. Can't you see what's going on here?

The voice responded to his thoughts with silence.

Yes, I'm glad I left her. She would've wanted to be safe, so she could get to Sebastian.

"Are you sure? You didn't give her a choice." He somehow clearly heard the voice amidst the cyclone. "In fact, you haven't given anyone choices around you."

The faces of his group flashed before his eyes. It was true he hadn't given them the opportunity to choose whether they wanted to stick by him or not. His first instinct had been to leave Baithe in order to protect them. *Great. I'm just like the temple . . . eliminating choices. But I don't want to control anyone—*

"Then don't."

I—

"Empower them, Joel. You have the choice. And, for the last time, are you glad you left her?"

"No," he finally whispered aloud. "I'm not glad I left either one."

"Raise the rhydid."

Joel lifted the dagger into the air above his head. Instantly the winds funneled into a skinny tornado with the top reaching the sky and the bottom Joel's dagger. He could hardly believe his eyes. The funnel grew more turbulent and powerful as it got thinner. Suddenly it became a flash of lightning and quickly disappeared, followed by a huge thunderclap that sent them all flying to the ground. Joel opened his eyes and looked up to find the floodgates of heaven opening over them in a torrential downpour. He wiped the water and black hair dye from his face. The four rose from the ground, soaked from the rain and covered in mud.

Dillon motioned for everyone to head back toward the barn.

Joel nodded in agreement and hurried to stick the rhydid back into its sheath. He put the tip in perfectly, but the rhydid wouldn't budge. "Ugh. Come on." He glanced up at the others hurrying for shelter ahead of him as he tried again to shove the dagger into its spot. Oil and water ran into his eyes as he pulled the weapon back out to examine it. "What's wrong with this thing?" Then he saw it. The rhydid was no longer a dagger.

CHAPTER 24

AUGUSTINE WOKE TO the sound of raucous cheers the next morning. She rubbed her eyes and peered through the darkness. *Is the sun up?* Even the crack of light beneath her curtains seemed dim. She tumbled out of bed and walked over to the window, wondering how early it was. She peeled back the drapes and squinted at the square's clock. *It's afternoon! How did I sleep so late? I was more exhausted than I realized.* She sighed and turned her eyes to the stormy rain clouds overhead. *Might as well get back in bed.* Another burst of cheers finally turned her attention back to what had gotten her out of bed in the first place. *What's all the fuss about?* The square was full of people holding different colored umbrellas. The closed umbrellas were mostly being used as dancing props while the open ones were being twirled about by the owners. *What in the world?* In the middle of the square she spotted two men wearing large colorful masks that covered their heads and part of their chests. Each clutched a walking stick and was shaking it about. Augustine walked out onto the balcony, surveyed the scene, and looked up at the gray clouds again. "They want it to rain."

Joel shook off his cloak and pulled at the shirt stuck to his skin. "Well, that was exciting." He was alone in the barn; the others hadn't followed him inside. He wasn't sure why everyone seemed mesmerized by the rain. The water pounded on the roof above him as he wiped a smudge of black oil from his face. *Time to get this off.* He stripped down to his shorts and headed back out into the rain. *Won't be the warmest shower, but it'll work.* The rain was coming down so hard he almost thought using soap would be a waste. He spied some black oil running down his chest. *Augustine would insist on soap.* He smiled when he remembered her shoving it into their backpacks in Waiz. His smile turned to a frown as he recalled the words he'd just heard in the cyclone. He wet the bar and took a whiff. *It smells like her.* He hoped with all his heart she was on the train to Waiz today. He tried to push the thoughts of her away, confused about what he was beginning to feel for her. He looked at the bar of soap as the voice's words from earlier ran through his mind. *Next time . . . if I find her again . . . it'll be her choice to leave me.* As he came to this conclusion, he heard a rowdy hollering from around the barn. He was in the middle of lathering up his hair when he marched over in the direction of the ruckus.

Every Galannean and villager from Baithe was dancing and parading about in the rain and yelling "Hoorah!" Joel held the soap to his temple in amusement until the group noticed him. They stopped abruptly and gaped at him in silence. The rain, the celebrating, him stripped down with his hair tousled in soap—it only took a few moments before the group burst into laughter at him.

Joel even chuckled himself as he stepped forward and playfully pointed his finger at them. "You're a mess, you bunch. Your leader should at least look clean—I'm a Templin, after all."

The group hooted even louder.

"Come, our Templin is right. We shall wash up. Pass the soap." Dillon began stripping down, and the others followed suit.

Joel held the soap to his chest for a moment. He wanted to keep it as a reminder of Augustine, but he knew she would insist on sharing so he let it go.

Later, when all were clean and dry, Joel suggested they go to the chapel. He was ready to hear how they knew his name.

"Why the chapel?" Byron limped over to him.

"Because, it's the largest place in Baithe. It can house us all comfortably in order to make a plan. It's really the perfect meeting place."

"And, yous like the idea of fooling the Templins at their game—using their meeting place against them." Ian gave his ribs a hard jab.

Joel winked at him. "Perhaps."

The rain had lessened to a light drizzle when the group made its way to the middle of the village. The once dry dirt roads were muddied and overflowing with water. Joel scuffed the mud off his shoes on the doorstep of the chapel before going inside. The large room had a high ceiling that made the perfect resting place for the adorning steeple outside. A circular stained glass window looked down from the front wall, with the sidewalls holding smaller circular panes. The chapel didn't have pews like the temple but rows of green cushioned chairs.

Joel twisted his lips as he glanced at the windows. He turned to the group and shrugged. "Let's make a circle with the chairs." He, for one, had zero desire to stand in front of them. If they were to make a plan, he wanted each person to have an opportunity to participate. *Ahem, if you're listening, 'Voice,' I want each person to have a choice.* He picked up the first chair and turned it around. The group members obliged him and soon were sitting around facing one another—except Violet, Noor, Byron, and the other four farmhands.

Joel stood up and motioned to the villagers sitting behind the circle. "What's the problem?"

Byron waved his hand. "Oh, we're not part of your group . . . you know, in the service."

Joel raised his eyebrows. "Maybe not, but you're part of this village which means you are part of this plan. Get up here."

The five men hesitantly rose from their chairs and came forward.

Joel sat back down as the others moved to make room for them. "I suppose it's time to be a bit more honest with each other. It's vital, really, in gaining one another's trust."

"Not really." Dillon shrugged. "We trust yous in faith."

"Fine." Joel felt his posture stiffen. "It's vital for me then."

Dillon propped a hand under his chin. "Fine."

"I want to know more about Galanne. Your father."

The young man's head rose in pride. "Galanne is on the Northwest border of the Northern Regions and Differe—"

"I know where it is. It's in the uppermost corner of the Northern Regions, but your Nothern Regiment guards the entire region's borders instead of Differe because . . . oh, something like . . . it's been guarded by the Galanneans for hundreds of years and your people are known for their loyalty, blah, blah. I heard all about it in my history class." He rolled his eyes at them.

Dillon drew back and crossed his arms. "Hm. Then I will not give yous anymore history lesson."

Joel grimaced, realizing he had just offended the entire group. "Sorry, I don't know why I'm being so defensive. Oh, but maybe it's because you already knew my name, and you still tried to freeze me to death in your Galanne water trough game."

Tension mounted at his words, yet Joel's sarcastic apology was more or less ignored.

"Yous know the history, but not the latest news."

"I'm sure. I didn't get a lot of news from my prison at the temple." He didn't know why he was feeling so angry.

"The borderlines has been fought over with Differe for the past century. Only in the last decade has it turn more, er, uh, violent."

Dillon now had his attention. "Violent?"

"Yes, troops fighting on the borders, threats from the headmaster—all sorts of violent tactics."

Joel leaned forward. "Like what?"

"Curses," Byron whispered.

Joel threw his arms in the air. "You gotta be kidding me—that stuff isn't real."

"Yous being disrespectful!" a Galanne let out.

"Well, you're not telling me anything!"

"We are trying to help yous!" Another yelled as some of the group rose to their feet.

Joel stood up too. "You lied to me."

"We should no let you have Paz. Such a poor rider," another piped in.

Dillon finally stood up. "I should have not taken yous from the train station."

Joel took a step toward him. "You practically froze me to death last night."

"I should have let yous freeze." He moved towards Joel as well. "Augustine is betters off without yous."

Joel thrust his rhydid out.

"Stop! Joel, stop! Listen to yourselves. This isn't you!"

All turned to find Violet standing on her chair. She shook her head at them. "It's—it's this place." She gazed around the chapel. "It's been used for power and control so long . . . if you're not careful you take it on yourselves." She paused to let her words sink in. "Joel, I know you want to be a good leader. Look, you've broken the bondage of hierarchy by making a circle. Now, be quiet and listen. You must listen and know their side of the story—how they know you. Dillon, Galanneans, remember your loyalty to patience and kindness. Be gracious to those living in ignorance as you once were."

As much as Joel disliked being referred to as "ignorant," he was glad to see the Galanneans return to their seats. He put his rhydid away and stared at Violet in disbelief. *She's right about this place. It's time to turn the tide—it's time to turn this power for good.* He had formed a circle, but there was more that needed to change to bring a greater shift. He motioned for the two sitting beside him to move their chairs over, and the whole group shifted. Joel brought in two more chairs and exited the circle toward Violet and Noor. He extended his hands to them.

Violet eyed his hand curiously. "What are you doing?"

"Breaking more bonds. We would be honored if you will join our group."

The two looked at him in shock.

"Violet, you've been running this village since the day they took your husband. Come and take your place with us. You too, Noor."

"Oh, Joel . . . no, I couldn't—"

"You must. If we're going to defeat the temple then we're going to have to change the rules . . . all of them."

Though she still seemed bewildered, Violet took Joel's hand and nodded to Noor.

Soon all three were back in the group, with Violet on one side of him and Noor on the other.

Joel looked at Dillon. "All right then. I'm listening."

CHAPTER 25

G OOD MORNING, HEADMASTER." Holt slid the mail carrier's
delivery into the headmaster's file box.

"Ah, good morning." The man barely lifted his eyes from the papers
scattered across his massive desk.

Holt stood in the doorway of the office holding the man's breakfast
tray. He noted Headmaster Dark had spent most of the past few days at his
residence rather than working from his study on campus. It was a longer trek
for Holt, but he didn't mind much. *It's much nicer than the study.*

The home was fully staffed to cater to the headmaster's every whim,
and that service extended to his Templins. Even a junior Templin was served
well in the place. Holt felt his palms begin to sweat. *It's so warm in here.* The
blazing fireplaces in every room were certainly a welcome change from his
drafty classrooms and dorm. In reality, he'd actually only seen the back part of
the house. He always used a back door that led straight into the kitchen. Each
morning for the past week he had picked up whatever the headmaster ordered
for breakfast and delivered it along with Differe's newspaper and his office
mail. The headmaster was either in his dark mahogany-adorned office or sitting
in the grand room.

Holt preferred the grand room to any room he had ever seen. It had a
fireplace that could hold several large adults inside. Above the fireplace mantel
was a painting of the temple grounds. The odd painting always caught Holt's

attention. There was no snow in the picture. In the far corner of the room, a white baby grand piano stood across from an old spinning wheel. Past the spinning wheel, two small white bear heads were mounted to the wall. The rest of the walls were fashioned with glass cabinets or small wooden shelves. Everything they housed appeared little, expensive, and breakable. He wondered why the man had so many. He looked around the office but was distracted by the headmaster clearing his throat.

"Let's go to the other room."

Holt grabbed the mail back from the box and placed it on the breakfast tray. He walked into the grand room and placed the tray on the round ottoman in front of the fireplace. The headmaster shuffled behind him, and, when he turned to help the man, Holt noticed he had yet to shave or dress. Puzzled, Holt led him over to the couch. "Are you all right, Headmaster?"

The headmaster sighed as he plopped onto the plush floral pattern. "Just old. That's all."

"Can I get you anything else, Sir?" Holt eyed the tray to see if anything had been misplaced.

"Sit." The man pointed to the wingback chair behind Holt.

Holt removed his gray jacket and sat down.

The headmaster picked up a fork and started pushing his food around. "Can I trust you, Holt? I trust your father a great deal. Are you of his caliber?"

Holt was taken aback by the question. "I-I—"

"Be confident, boy! You're nearly of age, and it's time you grew to act that way—live up to your name. Your name is so great . . . grand . . . it's powerful in Differe. Don't let such a name go to waste, but don't let it go to your head either."

Holt nodded, not sure where the conversation was going. His secret hope of being promoted lasted less than a second when he saw the headmaster's eyes fill with suspicion.

"My men keep no secrets from me." He put his fork down and leaned forward with his hands on his knees. "Do you know why, Holt?"

Holt broke into a cold sweat. *This is a test. Don't fail. Don't fail. Don't break and tell him about Joel.*

"They tell me the truth to gain or build my trust. I will not have anyone working for me that I do not trust. Do you understand?" He picked up his coffee cup.

Holt brushed a curly brown lock from his forehead and nodded quickly.

"Good. Now, is there anything you wish to tell me?" Dark brought the hot cup to his lips, providing ample time for Holt to answer.

No. Don't you dare give yourself away. No. Just say no, Holt. He heard himself utter a firm "no" out loud.

Dark picked up the knife on the tray, his serious expression unchanged. "Read my mail to me."

Holt froze. His eyes drifted to the letters on the tray. He knew he was about to open a pile of top secret information.

"Have you gone daft, boy? Now!" Holt noted the headmaster's hands shook as he started buttering his bread. This only heightened his own anxiety, yet he also felt concerned for the man as he took the first envelope from the stack. The envelopes were all large and official looking. Holt had never been asked to do such a task and felt excited but terrified at the same time. *Maybe I'll read something about my father.*

The first letter was from a law office in Differe. Holt began reading the letter line by line until the headmaster grunted at him.

"Langston, just give me the gist. I don't need all the details.

"Uh, yes, Sir." Holt quickly scanned the contents of the letter, thankful it was only one page. "This is from Magistrate Chanton's lawyer. It appears the man is on his deathbed. He—he wishes his granddaughter Isabelle to return to her family following his death. He plans to give his fortune to them . . . unless . . . unless you refuse to comply with your prior settlement. He, uh, he promises to release the whereabouts of the ovo if you will set her free." *What? Isabelle's grandfather is a magistrate? How could my father not approve of her upbringing? Does she know he's dying?* His head was swimming in confusion. *And, set her free . . . I don't understand.* He dared not ask such questions. He had seen the rage that followed a Templin being too nosy.

"Next." The headmaster motioned for Holt to move to the next piece of mail. "Been waiting for that fool to go on—he's a thorn in my side, as is that girl. Glad to know I'll finally get what I've been waiting for all these years." He wiped his mouth with a crisp white napkin and raised his eyebrows. "I hardly have any use for the girl now that her old friend is gone."

Holt felt a chill run up his spine at these words. His father must know what's going on. *That's why he urged me to end it with her. He must know the headmaster's plans. He wouldn't want me to cross him.* The more he thought, the more he wondered if he could convince his father otherwise. All the hate he'd been showing toward Isabelle melted at the reality he'd just discovered about her. He realized his anger had simply been a cover for his true feelings. *A prisoner? Her family has a fortune? I miss her . . . I'd do anything to have her back. Scar or no scar, long or short hair. I-I love—*

"Holt, I don't have all day."

"Oh, of course. Sorry, Sir." He lifted the next envelope from the stack. He was delighted to see his father's name signed at the bottom of the document but hurried to get a quick overview. "This one is from my-er, General Langston."

"Continue."

"Yes, he's informing you that he made it to Waiz." Holt's eyes widened. *It does exist!* "Uh, he's meeting with Marcell, the head of the New Waiz Order, and will let you know of his plans as they develop. He's sending out his scouts to communicate with the army instead of meeting them himself. He—"

"Smart. The Waizens will be less suspicious that way."

Holt looked up from the paper. "Right . . . that's exactly what he said."

A smirk crossed the man's face. "What else did he say?"

"As soon as the merger is made and the army's set, he will take the new group of Ferox with him to Facilis. He—he believes the city will fall quickly."

"Very well. That all?"

"It is." But it wasn't. His father had asked the headmaster to give Holt his regards and that he hoped the man would allow Holt to meet him in Facilis for some on-the-ground training.

"Well, just throw that one in the fire." There was something eerily calm about the headmaster's tone.

Holt froze for a moment then quickly put the paper into the fire. *Father will ask again if he really wants me there.* "Headmaster, there's just one more here."

The headmaster propped his feet onto the ottoman. "Yes, read that then grab the telegrams from my desk."

"Yes, Sir." Holt suppressed a gasp upon opening the last envelope. "It's, uh, it's from Trompè."

The man shook his head at him. "Holt, unless you're beneath those at Trompè I suggest you toughen up. You need never be afraid of those weaker than you."

He pulled his gaze away from the headmaster's piercing stare and swallowed hard. He had only heard rumors about Trompè, but it sounded like a place right out of a ghost story. He had ridiculed Joel enough to know the redhead had been there. He thought Isabelle had been there too but had never wanted to ask her about it. "Uh, it says all the hostages are contained. They ask you to send them no more until they have, uh, more money . . . it seems they're running out of room. They prefer not to house the patients in the caves as, uh, you suggested. That's, well, that's about it."

The man reached out to see the letter. "Fine. Hurry. Papers off my desk."

Holt rushed into the man's office and grabbed the file of telegrams from his desk.

"Here, Sir." Holt sat back down and flipped open the file to the first page.

The man rubbed his dark mustache and leaned back against the couch. "Go ahead. Read a few."

The headmaster's all too calm demeanor, plus the fact that he was reading top secret information, made Holt feel beyond uneasy. He couldn't keep his hands from shaking as he held up the telegram. "Galanne has fallen into our hands. The entire west border of the Northern Regions has now fallen to the Differian Army. High profile hostages have been taken, removing hope and encouraging fear—"

"Fear. A fabulous war tactic, my young friend."

Holt nodded and went on. "The polluted rivers have cut off the region's main water and food supply. Many have starved to death." Holt stopped there. He lifted his eyes to find the headmaster stroking the cushion next to him.

"Go on, Holt."

"The West End is nearly finished . . . it hasn't rained in months. The crops are yielding nothing, devastating all villages, livestock, and the inhabitants. Again, high profile hostages have been taken to Trompè, and many of the villages have been abandoned with refugees fleeing to Facilis. The city will be full when Differe attacks." Holt stopped again, not wanting to continue this time. *Where's Hertz? The guy thrives on this kind of information.*

"Headmaster, this just came for you."

Holt was relieved to see the headmaster's housekeeper enter the room with a telegram. *Good. Maybe I can leave now.* To his dismay, the headmaster instructed her to give it to him. His heart sunk as he opened the letter. "Urgent news. There's been heavy rain all over the West End. Also, unfortunately, Trompè miscounted and only has three hostages with medallions—"

"That means the rest are being used!"

Holt jumped at the man's outburst.

"Go on then, Holt. Quit stopping so much!"

Holt took a deep breath and tried to compose himself. "We believe even with the ones left available, they could not force the rain on their own. We await your instructions." He folded the paper as the headmaster stood to his feet.

"Holt, you must understand that Waiz exists."

"Right, my father—"

"We rulers of Differe keep it a secret from our people, because . . . well, Waiz is too soft. They give their people choices, free will or what have you. Do you know where this has led them?"

Holt shook his head.

"To a divided city and an impending war. They are becoming weak. Differe, on the other hand . . . we keep things orderly, controlled. We keep the power only in our leaders' hands. That way the power in our region is retained."

"Does Waiz have a power, Sir?"

The man clicked his tongue. "With the news of this rain, it would appear so. Unfortunately for our world, Waiz politics spread at its initial founding. The Waizens took their freethinking ideas into every region. Everyone embraced their policies at first . . . yet, Differe eventually had enough sense to reject such freedom and even Waiz's overall existence."

I'm so confused. Waiz started our world? What?

"We, Differe, rejected Waiz and its ideals, and then . . . we waited. And now, every region is ripe with weakness. Our world needs leadership. It needs Differe."

Trompè, the hostages, the starving villages . . . it was beginning to make sense now. *The regions have been made weak by force.* "Differe has taken the Waizen leaders from these regions to Trompè."

"Very good. Though the Waiz 'epidemic' started a long time ago, most of the leaders aren't Waizen. They're actual citizens of their lands but just adhere to the old ways."

Holt glanced down at the telegram again. *But they're fighting back.* "They made it rain."

"Impossible!" The headmaster pounded his fist on the fireplace mantel. "We've taken too many people and all their special tools. The rest with power are our allies. Most have disbanded . . . no, it's—it's something or someone else." He looked up at the colorful painting then slowly turned to face Holt. "The rhydid. The boy. The boy has the rhydid."

"Sir?"

"Holt, I let you read those to me because I trust you. Remember our discussion earlier?"

The hairs on the back of Holt's neck stood on end.

"I'm going to ask you one more time . . . should I trust you?"

Sweat beads formed on Holt's brow. "Sir?"

"Who came and took that rhydid—who took that sword? Who chained you to the wall, Holt?" The man walked to the far end of the fireplace.

Holt had never felt so afraid in his life. He realized in that moment he had never been nearly as brave as Isabelle or Joel.

"Tell me." The man stopped and turned his back to him. "TELL ME!"

Holt lowered his head in shame. He couldn't even speak Joel's name. The clamor of iron he heard near the headmaster made his insides turn. He finally lifted his head when he heard the headmaster shuffling back in his direction. The man locked eyes with him as he stuck a black iron poker into the fire. Holt gripped the arms of his chair and grimaced. He knew when the iron became hot, it was meant for him.

CHAPTER 26

TALAN LANGSTON AND his men were fascinated upon their arrival in New Waiz. The station didn't look anything like Differe's Crossroads Station. Talan felt as if he had entered an enormous circus tent. The temperature inside the place was warm, and he immediately removed his cloak. Above him, a tough fabric stretched across the ceiling. The roof had been dyed differing terra cotta shades and stood in peaked rows above the station. The same fabric covered the station's glass walls and was anchored in the ground outside the building, much like a tent.

Talan and his four men followed a young officer, who had escorted them off the train, to the station's exit. He studied the officer's green hood and cloak. "Andropolis?"

The officer stopped and spun around. "You know him?"

"Well, yes—met him in Differe. Sorry, just saw your cloak and thought you might be him."

The young man removed his hood, revealing that he was most certainly not the dark-haired apprentice. "Much has happened since then. Have you had any contact with him since Differe?"

Talan mocked the Green Cloak's authoritative tone with his own. "No. I'm much too busy to correspond with letter carriers."

The young man's mouth twitched as he pulled his hood back on. "He's wanted for murder."

Talan clasped his hands together. "Is he now? I must say I'm impressed. And I suppose 'wanted' means he hasn't been caught?"

The hood turned around in silence and motioned for them to continue following.

This one seems angry. Does he know about our troops on the east side of the river? "May I ask who he killed then?"

The young man didn't answer, but it didn't matter this time. Talan remembered. *That's right! The Old Waiz leader. Andropolis was the one chosen to bring the tension needed to start the war.* Marcell's plan seemed to have worked out perfectly. *Incredible!* Talan still couldn't help wondering if Andropolis was, in fact, one of the Ferox. In any case, he was ready to meet these respected warriors. He wanted to see both sides. *I want to measure Differe's soldiers against the Ferox of Waiz.*

"Afternoon, General Langston."

Talan's hand dropped the drape he was holding, and he turned from the window. He looked across the immaculate Waizen government office to find a man in a navy business suit. His features were sharp, and his charcoal gray hair was styled neatly to conceal a receding hairline. Shrewd eyes behind a pair of small circular lenses bid Talan to come around the desk and away from the window.

Talan cleared his throat and moved toward the center of the room. "Yes, I was just enjoying the view."

"Ah, right. Not used to seeing the water. We will get you and your crew out on a boat this week."

Talan nodded politely. "If we have time that would be excellent."

"It will be my city's pleasure to honor our new diplomat from Differe." The man extended his hand and Talan shook it. "Emil Marcell, Head Council for New Waiz, leader of the New Order."

"Talan Langston, Master Templin and Secretary General of Differe's army." Talan paused to take a small bow. "And, now, His Majesty's diplomat to New Waiz."

"Sit." Marcell gestured to the modern "U" shaped couches surrounding them and nodded for a young man to bring over a silver tray. "Please, have a drink."

Talan carefully sat on the bizarre blue couch. He found the modern furniture most uncomfortable, yet smiled and sipped his drink respectfully. "This drink is inspired. Did you concoct it yourself?"

Marcell chuckled and set his cup down on the white leather coffee table. "Headmaster Dark was right about you—you are quite charming, most handsome as well. The people will love you."

Talan awkwardly leaned back on the couch and considered ways to bring up the Ferox.

"I have a proposed agenda for you. Here." Marcell slid a piece of paper across the table between them.

Talan leaned forward again and studied the schedule. "A host of parties and charitable gatherings . . . this hardly seems like work."

"Oh, I can assure you it is. You will be presenting new political ideas to very opinionated men . . . though, persuading their wives shouldn't be a problem."

Talan bit his tongue as Marcell raised his eyebrows at him. The man's infatuation with his looks was beginning to feel degrading. "I meant, Master Marcell, that this hardly looks like a challenge. I was hoping to be more involved in some of your battle tactics. It's the general in me, I suppose."

"Right. Well, *diplomat* is your official title, so the hobnobbing will be your primary role."

Talan scratched his head, frustrated at the man's quiet, commanding tone. "Will I take my men to these gatherings?"

The man shook his head. "No, that would look too threatening. You will attend with me or another colleague of the New Order."

Talan raised his drink in agreement and took the last sip. *Great, I'll have babysitters.*

"I'm sure the Headmaster informed you of the ideas we are proposing?"

"He did. I read over the briefing on the train."

"Good." Marcell smiled and stood up, and Talan followed his lead. "I will see you this evening. One of my apprentices will see to it that you have everything you need for yourself and your men."

"Thank you, Master Marcell. I will see you tonight."

Talan ventured into the bottoms of New Waiz before feeling it was safe for him and his men to discuss his plans without causing suspicion. And they also all wanted a closer look at the Valtina Sea. Finally assured no one was following, Talan led the men to a spot by the stone wall nearest to the beach.

"How was your meeting, General?"

"It was telling." Talan rubbed his chin and pulled out the proposed agenda. "Marcell is arrogant. This will work well in our favor. He says my primary role is to play the dazzling, charming diplomat. I'll be sure to play my part all right . . . in fact, I'll play it a little too well." He grinned at his men as he passed around the schedule.

"You mean, get the people to trust you more than they do Marcell?"

Talan nodded. "Exactly."

"What about our men, General Langston?"

"I didn't mention them. I'm not sure what Marcell knows in terms of the number and locations of our troops here. I need his full trust. I didn't want to bring it up prior to us meeting with Differe's army. I need to figure out what Waiz knows about our men. If he knows how large our numbers are, we'll say the army is here to prepare for the takeover of Old Waiz . . . yes, perhaps they needed time to adjust to the climate change."

"When will we meet with them?"

Talan sighed as one of his men handed him back the itinerary. "Looking at this, it seems impossible to find a time."

"In the middle of the night?"

"There's an off chance those Watchmen would see us. I have a feeling the Green Cloaks will be watching me . . . maybe even the Ferox. I can't be seen doing anything suspicious. I'll probably need to send you four to the meeting point without me. You must ensure you are not followed."

"You want us to join them, Sir?"

"No, I'll need you soon enough. At present they're only allowing me to be 'diplomatic' with an Order colleague. So, until I get more information from these gatherings, there'll be no assignments for you in terms of what I briefed you on in the train. First I need to discover who's in the Order, where they meet, and such . . . then I'll need you with me. In the meantime, I need you to do what I cannot—meet with Captain Myron. I'm hoping he will have an idea as to Marcell's plans with the Ferox and his overall thoughts on this coming war between the North and South."

Talan stared into the mirror with his razor in hand and began making strokes along his face. Tonight was his first party, and the assignment seemed easy enough. He'd be escorted by Marcell to a gathering at the home of one of the big industry owners. Talan knew the party host owned one of the tall buildings downtown. *Does steel manufacturing, I think. I'll give the paper another look after I finish shaving.* He looked in the mirror at his foamy reflection then down to the small photo frame he'd placed above the sink. The frame held his wife's picture. He wished she were here. He much preferred having her on his arm rather than show up as Marcell's commodity, yet he knew in reality she'd be even more of a trophy to them. He splashed water onto his face, and her graceful blue eyes stared back at him as he patted his face dry. He looked into the mirror again and his image began to blur. Talan rubbed his eyes in an effort to clear them. He stared back into the mirror, but it seemed foggy at the edges. He closed his eyes. *Great. It's worse than before. Maybe they just need to rest for a moment.* After a few deep breaths he opened them again, only to find the fog spreading to the mirror's center.

He squinted at the glass until he couldn't see his reflection anymore then jumped at the sound of the condensation on the mirror dripping onto the floor. He gripped the sink below, blinking furiously as he scanned the room. *You're losing it, Talan. Get a grip. The Headmaster trusted you to come back here.* Talan turned back to the clouded mirror and shuddered as the object turned pitch black. A snake-like hiss rang out as a black mist began pouring from the mirror. He drew back, suddenly disoriented by the engulfing mist, but a form growing and taking shape inside the mirror instantly drew him back in. He waited breathlessly until the silhouette of a woman wrapped in glistening golden material appeared. The silky fabric was draped in perfect folds around her face, but a thin veil hid her features. Talan sucked in a tense breath as the mist blew across the beads of sweat forming on his forehead. The hissing stopped when a white light rose behind the woman. The light began pouring out toward him, overpowering the dark mist. He backed away, plastered against the bathroom wall as the woman began to unveil her face. Talan gasped and tears crept into his eyes as she smiled shyly back at him. He stepped forward and gripped the sink again. The woman put her hands on her heart then held them out to him.

"Choose me," she whispered softly. "Talan, choose me . . . choose us!"

He couldn't take it any longer. He scanned the room and grabbed a silver vase from the back of the commode.

"Talan!" he heard her voice cry.

Eluding her gaze, he hurled the vase at the mirror, raining down shattered glass all over the bathroom. He was relieved to hear his men come running into the room.

"Master! Master!"

"Are you all right?"

"Your hand—you've been cut!"

"I'm fine. I just—just—I—"

"You're so pale. Come sit down, and we'll wrap your hand."

"Stop, I'll get this mess." His oldest soldier moved him from the broken shards to the easy chair in his suite.

Another one was soon at his side. "Here, drink some water." The soldier pressed a cold compress onto his bleeding hand. "Should only take a moment to stop the bleeding."

Talan leaned heavily against the back of the chair. "Thank you, friends. Sorry for the mess."

"What happened?"

"No more drinks from Marcell. Curse this place." He shook his head and straightened in his chair. *Pull yourself together, Langston. You're their general.* "The past. The past was attempting to sabotage me, or perhaps distract me from my duties. Sometimes . . . I forget . . . ."

"General?"

"Sorry, yes. Sometimes I forget the past is dead."

CHAPTER 27

AUGUSTINE WAVED FROM her balcony when she noticed Earl and Jack walking around near dusk again. "You must enjoy evening walks."

He looked up at her and smiled. "Never been much of a morning person. Come down. Be my dinner date tonight." He beckoned her with his hands.

She nodded and was in Dunn Square in no time.

"How was your day?" He shook her hand politely.

"Lazy." She bent down to pet Jack. "The rain kept me in bed most of the day."

"Perhaps you needed the rest."

"Oh, I know I did. I was thankful for a dreary day."

"You weren't the only one." He nodded to the square as she stood back up.

"Yes, I noticed the celebration. Why so much excitement over a little rain?"

Jack tugged on the leash, and Earl motioned for them to take a walk. "Well, it hasn't rained in a very long time. Most of the West End has been devastated, because the harvests prior to the drought were already less than fair. That's why Facilis is a bit overcrowded right now." They stopped under one of the stone archways. "To the park?"

Augustine nodded. "Sure. But, Earl, why has everyone come here?"

"Facilis is the capital, Honey. Whatever assets the region has left are stockpiled here. Most of what grows or is produced by the villages is imported here for selling anyway. Just hasn't been as much to buy lately."

"So, most of the villagers have sought refuge here?"

"Yes . . . the capital seemed prepared for it in many ways . . . to provide for everyone here, I mean."

His suspicious tone unnerved something in her. "Uh, is this a safe place . . . for the villagers or even an outsider like me?"

"Yep. There's plenty for everyone. And, now it's rained."

She didn't like how quickly he answered. "Earl, why hasn't it rained?"

His eyes darted away from hers. "Oh . . . I . . . who knows?"

She hurried to keep pace with him. "No, I'm thinking you do, or you at least have a guess."

He went silent, but she knew she had his attention.

She rounded in front of him. "And, if you can't answer then at least tell me what made it rain today."

"There's a lovely take-out vendor in the park. Why don't we have dinner there?"

She didn't budge at his ignoring her request.

He finally raised his eyebrows at her. "It's quiet and secluded. I'll tell you my thoughts in exchange for yours."

She was surprised when he took a step closer to her. "My thoughts?"

"Yes." He moved closer still and gripped the side of her coat that had the rhydid hidden. "On what's underneath this."

Augustine's heart pounded when she felt his hand touching the object. She looked into his eyes. They were kind, disarming, yet curious. She desperately needed a friend. She remembered Hubert and thought, like him, Earl being here seemed almost too good to be true. Had the man been put on her path for some reason? In any case she knew with his travel experience, he could get her out of the city. She finally nodded. "Dinner in the park sounds nice."

Augustine found a grassy spot near a few lampposts and spread out a blanket provided by the café in the park. Earl had insisted he order and pay for dinner. Augustine was intrigued by the smells coming from the café and soon realized how hungry she was. She looked at the black dog sitting beside her. "I haven't really eaten all day."

"Well, I'm glad you'll be hungry then."

Augustine was delighted to see Earl approaching with two baskets full of food.

"Honey, I want to share a taste of Facilis with you."

"Well, it looks like a feast. No, Jack!" She shooed the interested canine from her basket then took a look inside. "I don't think I've ever tasted any of these before. Tell me about them."

"The fruit actually came from the trees inside the park—mangosteen. The rice is from our fields and is blended with saffron. The bread is made of cornmeal flour, and the meat is quail."

"Thank you. I know I'll like it all." The two ate quietly for a few minutes until Augustine announced her verdict. "I was right. It's all delicious!"

Earl chuckled with pleasure. "Oh, be careful; it's a bit damp from the rain." He pointed to a spot off the blanket.

"Suppose you'll answer my questions now?" She smiled at him.

"Ha. Well, I suppose so. I'll start off by saying I watched you get on the Facilis train in Seda. I was a few cars down with Jack."

"Really?"

"You were hard to miss in that bright orange."

She was done pretending she actually liked the outfit. "Ugh. Yes, I suppose so."

It seemed hard for Earl to hide his amusement. "Anyway, I got off the train here in Facilis then saw you looking a bit lost as you wandered across the street with the crowd. You were different in dress, of course, but there was something different about your demeanor as well. I thought it was very brave of you to walk up to a total stranger and ask for help. I sensed a great strength about you. When you reached to pay for your room last night I spotted your dagger."

Augustine weighed the words of his story carefully. She didn't think there was any reason for him to lie to her. *He hasn't tried to take the rhydid. I'm sure he did see it last night. I would've been too tired to even notice.*

"The hilt of the sword was something I instantly recognized from drawings I've seen in my travels abroad. I can't quite remember the details, but I'm hoping you can refresh my memory."

Augustine pursed her lips and cocked her head sideways. *Not so fast.* "Rain first."

Earl took a deep breath. "All right then, the ruler of the West End met with Differe's government leaders over a two years ago about combining the two regions' assets or goods, meaning Facilis and Differe would begin to export items to one another.

"Differe doesn't export items."

"Well, it appears Differe changed its mind for a short while. It sounded like a good plan on the outside—there was the opportunity for overall economic increase; however, Differe proposed taxes be taken on all imported goods."

"So both sides have to pay taxes on whatever is imported from the other region?"

"Exactly. A treaty was signed by both regions, agreeing to the taxation of imported goods. There was, of course, a small clause in the treaty as to the legal ramifications if taxes could not be paid. It was risky for the West End— as I mentioned, our farms were already struggling. But most voted in favor of the trading agreement, because by that time we needed many of the resources Differe was offering. The West End only hoped it could sustain a fair enough harvest to compete with the import tax on Differe's goods. So, when the rain stopped the food shortage began and the taxes rose, which drove many people from the villages to Facilis. As part of Differe's stipulations, Templins or Differian soldiers have been stationed in the villages with unpaid taxes. I fear the future of the West End has now become dependent on Differe."

"So, now the West End is full of Templins and Differe's army . . . and Facilis is full of refugees." Her eyes widened when a ghastly thought dawned on her. "When was the treaty signed?"

"Uh, just over two years ago."

"When the rain stopped!"

Earl's eyes darted away from hers. "Precisely."

Augustine clutched a hand over her heart. "You think Differe has something to do with it not raining? But . . . that's impossible . . . isn't it?"

"It just seems like too much of a coincidence. You see, I think each region has been given certain privileges . . . powers, if you will."

She thought he was beginning to sound like Corwin and figured that was a good thing. "What's the West End's power?"

"Peace and prosperity between the government and its people."

Augustine didn't understand how that was powerful, so she tried again. "What's Differe's power?"

"Education, learning—words . . . to help or to harm."

A shiver ran up her spine. "To harm in this instance." She pictured the rain dancers she had seen in the masks earlier. "A curse. Earl . . . you think Differe cursed or cast a spell over the West End—a curse of no rain?"

His worn hand patted hers. "It's okay, Honey. Don't be frightened, but, yes, that's exactly what I think. So, you see why it's hard for me to answer your question about this being a safe place for you or anyone else very honestly."

"Right, because why would Differe want everyone in Facilis . . . it would make more sense if the people were driven into Differe. Unless . . . unless, Differe plans to—to—why yes! That's it! All the soldiers here—Earl!" She looked at him in fear.

"Shh! I know . . . I know." He squeezed her hands then sighed.

"Earl, I've got to get out of here before Differe takes over. I have to get back to Waiz."

"Not possible today or tomorrow, Dear. There are no outbound trains on the weekends."

"My brother—" She unbuttoned her coat to reveal the rhydid. "He needs this."

"Magnificent." He studied the object as she held it out to him. "What can you tell me about it?"

"I have a whole book on it if you're interested."

"Yes, of course." He nodded as he took the dagger from her.

"Earl—" She closed her eyes and swallowed hard.

"What is it, Dear?"

"Why did it rain *today*? If Differe kept the rain from coming . . . then who brought it?"

He shook his head and shrugged. "That's what I think everyone would like to know—Differe *and* the West End. Whoever or whatever it was has words more powerful than Differe's. With this kind of shift . . . the future of this city and our region may have just changed."

Chapter 28

ISABELLE'S TEETH CHATTERED in the cold night. Both Langston Hall and Thymes Hall had been evacuated by a group of Templins. There had been no explanation for the piercing alarm and being roused from their sleep in the dead of night. Students from both dorms were covered in an array of mismatched clothing, with their nightclothes having been hastily covered with whatever warm items they could grab. Isabelle had pulled on long johns under her gown, thrown on a sweater, wrapped a scarf around her neck, grabbed her heavy coat, and stepped into her snow boots before making for the foyer.

A man had ushered them out. "This way. This way, ladies."

She eyed his gray Templin cloak and noticed he wasn't from the temple. His bright red pins were different than the normal green ones of a temple uniform.

The cold stung her eyes as she walked with a few others to a fire. She was glad the junior Templins had taken the liberty of starting several in the courtyard between the dorms. *Can't believe I forgot my gloves.* She held her hands near the blazing flames and noticed Eris and Holt making for a fire across from hers. Eris was smiling, but Holt was not. *He never seems to smile anymore.* She had watched the couple from afar over the past few weeks. The girl dangled on his arm every second of spare time he was off duty. She babied him, bringing him anything he needed. *And many things he doesn't.* The more Isabelle studied them, she knew deep down Holt was more annoyed than affectionate towards Eris.

He rarely said thank you for the silly objects she brought him. Just the other day she'd brought him a pair of goggles.

"Holt! Look what I found in the combat arena! No one has a pair quite like this."

Yeah, I wonder why? Oh, maybe it's because it stays mostly below freezing around here. Who has a need for swimming goggles?

"Here. I brought you some gloves. You'll catch a cold without them." Eris's words interrupted Isabelle's memory.

Maybe she's not as dumb as I thought after all.

Holt continued holding his hands over the fire instead of taking the gloves from Eris. Isabelle was puzzled by his actions. She noticed he typically obliged the girl at least with a gesture; he rarely spoke to her. In fact, he seemed to stiffen when she fawned all over him, *nearly unresponsive*. Even so, she was surprised he was ignoring her tonight.

"Just like his father," she heard Sarah's voice in her head. "The man has become so infatuated with his call of duty that his emotions are guarded and unexposed in the face of others, even those he claims to care for." Isabelle had seen this for herself in Holt's letters from his father. "It has been detrimental for Holt," Sarah had told her.

Isabelle often wondered what this response had done to Holt's mother. She had never met her mother's distant cousin, but the woman had sent Isabelle several letters during the time she had been with Holt. She had seemed kind, happy even, at their family being brought together by the two of them. Isabelle knew that Holt also received correspondence from his mother. She was the affirming one, *but it doesn't matter . . . that's not who Holt wants it from.* She frowned as she looked into the fire, remembering her last journal entry.

"It seems expected of mothers to be affectionate—you know, women being the caring ones. You're looked down upon if you don't show emotion. However, with men, though the need seems even more desperate, they may start off as lovers but end up warriors who place duty over relationship."

She knew Sarah would chide her for penning such negative words, but she had tasted the reality of them over the last few weeks. Holt betraying her, the Headmaster using her as bait, Joel being unwilling to take her with him, Dr. Pryderi and Professor Louis clearly using her and Joel for something, and . . . who else had she encountered? *Oh, yes, the Green Cloak.* He had even hurt her by being deceived into the Headmaster's plot. *Yet, there was something different about him.* The scars he bore made him seem different than the others. Joel and Holt had their share of emotional scars, and Joel some physical, *but they're not on their faces for the whole world to see.* Maybe it was a mixture of empathy and pity she felt toward the Green Cloak. She wasn't sure. *Doesn't matter. I'll probably never see him again.*

She turned her back to the fire when she felt Holt might be staring at her. His gaze startled her now. As unresponsive as Holt had been with Eris, he had been just as mean toward her. His eyes seemed full of hate when he gazed on her. He pushed past her after most classes, slamming her into the side columns. His tripping her and allowing Hertz to use her for sport was humiliating, but cutting her hair might be unforgiveable. She now seemed to be an easy target whenever he was around. She had blackmail on him, of course, but couldn't let anyone else know that the bait scheme had worked. Joel had indeed returned, but as Holt had told Sarah, he didn't have Joel . . . which meant he was unwilling to help Isabelle escape as he had promised. Since the incident with Joel, she and Sarah had spoken to each other only in class. They decided to lay low for a while; however, after hearing the conversation in the Infirmary, Isabelle wondered if Sarah was really waiting to find out Joel's whereabouts. *I'm on my own until then.* The information Isabelle knew she needed lay in Moonstruck in her old locker. She hadn't dared go to the scene of the crime just yet. But now, standing out in the freezing cold, she decided it was time to plan her next move. The vision of the Pallas River she had seen in Sarah's picture brought warmth more powerful than the blazing fire in front of her. *I've got to get to Moonstruck. I have to find Joel!*

"What are you thinking, Master Joel?"

Joel knew Violet was referring to the pensive look on his face. He turned his gaze away from a saddled Paz. "That this could be stupid. That this plan is not a real plan at all. That we'll be leaving these villagers—you—to their deaths."

"Don't think such things! The Templins may come back, and they may rule over us again, but now we're equipped. You have empowered us, Joel."

Joel had been in Baithe several days with the Galanneans. In that time the group had managed to plant the fields, teach the farmhands how to set and catch food with the animal traps, and Joel taught Violet everything he knew about cooking. *And . . . I made it rain.* In fact, he had made it rain several more times. In addition to the rain, he had been greatly enlightened by Dillon's "history lessons."

He was grateful to Violet for having made him see reason during that first meeting. Joel had swallowed his pride and quietly listened to Dillon's tales—ones the temple had never told him.

Dillon had started his lesson with a question. "Yous know the four regions?"

Joel reminded himself to be polite. "Uh, yeah. Differe, West End, Northern, and Southern Regions."

"Right, do yous know how the regions came to be?"

Joel thought for a moment and shook his head. "I guess I thought they'd just always been around."

"That is what the temple tells yous. The King of Waiz—"

"There's an actual king then?" *I knew it! The voice. I'm not crazy.*

"Yes, of course. Joel, there is a whole world outside the regions."

He was stunned. Joel had never thought of a world beyond the region maps he'd always been shown.

"So, yes, there is a king in Waiz, but it was not Waiz a long time ago. It was just, uh, place. A piece of land, but it is the best place. Yous have been there so you know—green hills, mountains, valleys, ocean, rivers."

Joel stopped to think about it. Waiz really did boast the best land of all the regions. He nodded at Dillon. "Yeah, fit for a king."

"Yes. Well, the people have one and only one. He was the first and last king—there has been no more."

Joel marveled at finally having heard the truth about his world for the first time. "What happened?"

"Well, the people chose him to lead. It was, umm, what is the word . . . oh, ironic. He was of simple means . . . poor. Just a miner. But his deeds were so kind it earn him favor with all the people. He went to discover the rest of the four regions, but he did not take over."

"He didn't take over the rest of the lands? What kind of a king does that?"

"No, he leave his best men and women to rule instead. He leave many families in the West End, also Northern and Southern Regions. But . . . he leave only one in Differe—that is how it got the name. Differe is a family name."

"What?" Joel could hardly believe his ears.

"Well, that's what we think." Violet leaned forward. "We're not exactly sure how Differe got its name. It pulled out from the World Alliance a long time ago. The other regions had multiple groups leading, so they settled for more generic names, but many of the places are from family names."

"Galanne, Facilis, Baithe, all family names?"

The group nodded at him.

"What happened to him—the king, I mean?"

"After the regions were stable, he decides to go into a mining cave on the mountainside in Old Waiz. He—he never comes out."

Joel sat back and crossed his arms. "A cave? He just disappeared? Is that why so many people look in the mountains for caychuras . . . they're . . . they're looking for him?"

"Yes, many try to go after him in the caves, but none find him. After this hope was gone, so the city fell and region disperse everywhere."

Joel stood up and put his hands on his head. "Yes! Yes, that's what happened! I understand, I think. Then—then Theodore Waiz came, found the old abandoned city, and founded Waiz . . . and—and, he claimed to find the king . . . sort of . . . through the caychuras. Am I kind of on the right track?"

Violet flashed him a big smile. "You're doing very well."

"So, this king . . . he just vanished? That's, well, it's a bit unbelievable."

"Do not worry, Joel. We, even yous, have proof he is real. He leave a few things behind with the families in charge. He give certain tools to the regions."

"Your sacred stones."

Dillon pulled the object from around his neck then pointed to Joel's sword. "Your rhydid. We hear about yous escaping from the temple the first time. The Templins tell us about it. It was easy to figure out yous were this Joel after yous told us about your escape."

Joel was relieved to finally understand how they knew his name. "So, what are all of you exactly? What are you doing?"

Dillon held out his stone to Joel. He slowly took it then handed over his rhydid. Violet offered up her black tablet as well.

"How do they work . . . how many are there? How did you know they would make it rain?" Joel's mind filled with questions as he examined the objects.

"My father did not have time to tell me much. Just that they have power. I see him swing the stone before. The first time I did it was after our Templin die, the wind and noise scare us half to death."

Noor giggled and Violet grinned. "But, Joel, don't let them fool you. I think what scared them more than that was seeing another wind tunnel go up in the distance."

"The 'calling' you mentioned."

"Yes."

Joel gave his comrade a smirk. "It's not so crazy, Dillon."

Dillon shrugged.

"So, were you 'called' to Baith? Did you see it in Penwell? Just before you met me?"

"No, before then. We were in route when we find yous. After yous were hit in the barn, we try the stone and barique together that night. It was more loud . . . more powerful."

He looked back at Violet. "So, when you took me to the field . . . you weren't sure it would rain?"

"We hoped it would. After all, you'd gotten that from Differe. They're the ones who seem to have a hand in this evil spreading across the regions. I wondered if your rhydid could do something to break their power."

"You think Differe is causing the drought?"

"Joel, think about it. They're stripping leaders away. Most have had their kingly weapons confiscated. It's like something is trying to take or diminish the powers of each region . . . to do something . . . or quite possibly to use them."

Dillon gripped Joel's shoulder after Violet spoke. "See? What we are doing is empowering the regions. Banding together to help the people under darkness. We bring hope and light."

"Hope and light? What does that have to do with anything? These people need food. They need it to rain on their fields! What darkness? The mouthpieces? The mouth?"

Dillon shook his head. "I do not know, but it is a growing power. Taking over borders, taking leaders hostage, bringing drought, war brewing in Waiz. It is some evil force—something working against good."

Joel looked back at Dillon and grimaced. "Well, that's nice and unsettling. So, uh, your plan so far is to go from village to village . . . teach them how to be self-sustaining?"

"Yes. And, now we bring rain *and* a Templin. Pretty good, eh?" Ian gave him two thumbs up.

"Well, I certainly like the idea of ridding the villages of the soldiers."

Meetings like this continued for nearly three days, with Joel discovering more of the history he never knew about. He soaked up every story they would tell him about their parents, grandparents, and so on, regarding their encounters with caychuras and mouthpieces. Many of their forefathers had never seen the king, but they served him . . . holding on somehow. Joel was astonished at these stories of faith. As he listened, the word "empower" continued to resonate with him. Imprisoned his whole life, he thought he was running to Facilis to become free, but he was beginning to believe he might already have what he was seeking. He finally felt free in his mind.

When Joel knew the primary work in Baithe was done, that the villagers were equipped to survive, it didn't make it any easier to leave the people with whom he had formed such a fast and deep bond. He was sad to leave. As he stood ready to mount Paz, Noor approached Joel with a handful of her flowers.

"Well, I guess this is goodbye."

Noor stepped forward and stretched out her flowers to Joel. "You have to wear them, you know."

"Yes, of course." He grinned at her as he tucked them into his front pocket. He looked at the saddled Galanneans facing the road ahead of him and shook Byron's hand before taking Paz's reins. The man gave him a leg up.

"We can't thank you enough, Master Joel." Byron and the other farmhands nodded their thanks.

"I wish you'd quit calling me that, Byron."

"Just send the word, Joel. We'll follow you if you need us," Violet called over his shoulder.

Joel turned around to give the people of Baithe a final farewell. He gave the group a small wave then looked past them. *What . . . .*

Horror filled every one of his senses. On the horizon, a dark mass seemed to have swallowed the sky and was growing . . . moving. Joel stared, immobile and bewildered.

The darkness! It's real. It's here. It's coming for us! He glanced around at the others, searching their faces for signs they had caught sight of the mysterious dark substance headed toward them. "Get on!" He motioned frantically to Violet and Noor. "Now! Get on a horse! Hurry! Hurry, everyone!"

The villagers and riders looked at one another in terror.

"Listen, we've got to run! You can't stay here!"

Violet took one look in the dark cloud's direction and quickly obeyed. She grabbed Noor and put her on with Dillon. Byron helped her up to ride with Joel, and once the rest were mounted their leader circled the group with Paz. "We're running! We're running!"

"What is that?" Ian's voice trailed off as he stared blankly, the billowing darkness reflected in his terrified eyes.

"I don't know, Ian, but we're not staying to find out. What's the nearest village?"

Byron leaned around one of the Galannean riders. "Darit . . . but, Joel, they didn't respond to Dillon's call yesterday."

All looked to him and Violet. He heard her voice close to his ear. "Joel, we'll follow you. Just say the word."

Joel clucked to Paz then stared at his men. "All right. Darit it is."

CHAPTER 29

AUGUSTINE OPENED THE pages of Mr. Rutherford's book and smiled as she thought of him. Though their last meeting had been less than cordial, she knew the man truly cared for her. She hoped Sebastian had visited him since she and Joel had been away. *Sebastian. Hopefully I'll see him soon. He would absolutely love this city. And he would love Earl, too.*

She was back in the park eating breakfast, as she and Earl had planned to meet later in the day. "Right, not a morning person," Augustine had kidded him. She was tempted to tell him her real name but knew Joel would disapprove, so "Honey" had stayed.

She bit into a mangosteen and flipped to the chapter on rhydids. Since there were no outbound trains until tomorrow she decided to spend her time discovering as much as she could about the rhydid. "Where To Find." She was surprised to discover the text filled less than a page.

All rhydids were gifts from the King, who distributed them among the four regions. Most rhydids that were distributed outside of Waiz have been destroyed. The ones remaining in Waiz are generally passed down from generation to generation. It is believed that the North Corner (known as Differe today) destroyed its rhydids when it revoked its allegiance to Waiz. Rumor has it that the only one left in the North Corner is inside the Temple of Differe

178

Chapel. It is the supposed rhydid of the region's founding leader and preserved in remembrance of his rule.

Augustine's eyes fluttered to the handwritten notes surrounding the text.

> An inside source has confirmed this rumor. There is a rhydid in the chapel, but is it locked down not only by natural means but supernatural as well.

She wondered whose handwriting she was reading on the page. *Mr. Rutherford's? Or the one who gave him this book? What's his name?* She flipped back to the front page. *Thad.* She pulled the rhydid from its sheath. The memory of retrieving the dagger replayed in her mind often—being unable to dislodge it without Joel's help, Sarah unable to remove her hand from the object . . . .
She turned to the next section. "Who Can Obtain."

> As with the other Waiz gifts of power given by the King, most rhydids are passed down through generations by family members. If one has no family or offspring, he or she may gift the object to whomever they deem worthy. One in possession of a rhydid should hold to the Waiz laws and share the faith of our forefathers; otherwise, the object will become powerless.

She still wasn't sure about this king. He had let her down before, yet she had certainly witnessed the power of the rhydid. *I opened the locked door at Moonstruck . . . and I broke Joel's chains. But wasn't that because I believed in the rhydid . . . not the king?* She read on.

> With most of Differe's rhydids destroyed, if there is indeed one in the Temple Chapel, the only persons who could obtain it from such a place would have to have supernatural means.

Again, she was thankful for the notes scribbled around the text.

There's a spell on the rhydid. I have it on authority there's more than one—that the rhydids were not actually destroyed, but taken and combined into this one rhydid. It's dark magic.

Dark magic? More than one? Well, I suppose I understand that. I have one and so does Joel. We . . . or Joel . . . broke the spell? But it replaced itself, so . . . no, it's not broken . . . but perhaps we overcame it?

She flipped the page to the "How to Use" section. *Finally, this is what I really need to know.* She finished the last bit of her biscuit and was puzzled at the words she saw on the next page. *Oh, I must have missed a page.* She flipped the page back then forward again. Her eyes darted down to the page numbers. *You gotta be kidding me.*

"Gone—completely ripped out." She sighed as she followed Earl into the capitol building for lunch. "The one thing I need to know."

"Well, Honey, the other information is helpful too."

She gripped the hilt of the rhydid then held her forehead in her hands. "Do you think it's still under a spell? I mean, the one I have?"

"I wouldn't think so. You wouldn't have been able to get it—wasn't that what the spell was meant to do? Hide all rhydids in one? But, wait, before you answer." He opened the doors leading to the terrace. "Come. Enjoy the view."

Augustine saw the large city gates of Facilis below. Being so high up, the guards below looked like miniature blue spots walking about. She could view the vast farmlands of the West End for miles. Shielding her eyes from the sun, Augustine gazed at the tiny groupings of buildings in the distance and marveled that several outlying cities and villages were visible from here. She set her hands on the terrace wall. "Oh, amazing. Thank you, Earl, for bringing me here. You have proved to truly be a gifted guide."

He smiled at her compliment. "You have a way with words, Honey."

She gritted her teeth as she turned from the gorgeous view and was led to her chair. Once seated, she responded to Earl's statement with a revelation. "Earl, I-I didn't get this." She looked down and tapped the rhydid's sheath.

"My friend, he—he got his own then helped me retrieve this one. I honestly don't think I could've gotten it by myself. There's . . . there's something very special about him."

Earl propped a hand underneath his chin. "That's an interesting piece of news. Where is he?"

"We parted in Penwell. He left me. Said it was too dangerous for us to be together—I mean, continue traveling together. He's escaped from the Temple of Differe . . . twice. The second time was with me." The rest of the story flowed out as the two waited for their food to arrive.

"So, we need to get you to Waiz," Earl let out after she finished.

She nodded and sighed.

"What is it?"

"It's just . . . I can't stop thinking about what you said yesterday—about the rain, about someone's voice being stronger. My uncle, he's not a careless man. He put me in Joel's care because he trusted him . . . saw something in him. I can't tell you the countless times he's impressed me with his words, especially in light of how juvenile his manners are."

Earl shot her a confused look. "Your uncle or your friend?"

She chuckled. "Both really. Joel—he's got a way with people. He sees everyone the same, draws out the goodness in them . . . oh, but don't get me wrong—he's not perfect. He's obnoxious, irritating, and can be a bit of a know-it-all."

Earl seemed quite amused by her latter statement.

"Sorry, what I'm trying to say is . . . he broke the spell of the rhydid or Differe's spell. He broke Differe's curse over Facilis. I'm sure it was him. My uncle would've known about this, about him."

Earl straightened and raised his eyebrows. "You think your friend is the West End's savior . . . the rainmaker?"

She looked over the vast landscape again and nodded. "I'd sure say it's possible."

"He may have the power to do so, but what's his motive, Honey?"

She turned back toward him. "Well, for one thing, he hates Differe, or the Templins really. He'd do anything to cross them, but . . . he'd also do anything to help if he could. He got his rhydid—my rhydid—for my brother, not himself."

"Hmm. A noble man. You think highly of him."

Augustine blushed. "Mind you, he still drives me crazy, but, Earl, he did go back to a place he hated for my family. I can hardly ignore the facts about his character."

Earl pursed his lips and gave her a wry smile. "Oh, and what does he think of you?"

She looked away from him again, and, as she did, her jaw fell open. She gasped and covered her chest.

"What on earth?" Earl rushed to the terrace wall.

Shouts and murmurs from the terrace grew as others hurried toward the wall alongside them. Dark smoke rising in the distance brought an eerie shift to the sunny day they were enjoying.

Earl raked his fingers through his gray hair. "Differe."

Augustine covered her mouth and grabbed Earl's hand. "What are they doing?"

"Exactly what they have been. Whatever game they're playing hasn't changed."

"What do you mean?"

"They're driving everyone to Facilis to take over. And now I'm wondering if they also want your Joel driven here."

"He's got to get here before the city falls to Differe. He's got to be warned. Oh, what do we do?" She buried her face into his shoulder.

"He's not alone out there, Honey. And, we need to make sure he's not alone when he gets here. We need to tell the people of Facilis—the West End— who the rainmaker is."

Augustine wasn't sure she agreed with Earl.

"Think about it, Honey. Spreading the word about Joel should be easy. Facilis is already dying to know who made it rain. All we have to do is figure out how to expose Differe's plans."

Augustine shook her head and shrugged at Earl. "Any ideas on how to do that?"

"Yes. Come with me."

The two soon found themselves down in the courtyard between the capitol building and the city gates. The guards barely seemed to notice them as they marched through the middle of the place.

Augustine clutched Earl's arm. "Why is the gate shut? And the whole area is swarming with guards."

"Why indeed? I'll let you ask the front guard when we get close. Yes, that one up in the left tower. Just follow my lead."

Augustine felt nervous and excited at the same time.

"Excuse me, guard, we'd like to go out to get a better view of the building if you don't mind. My little friend here's an artist."

The guard glanced down at both of them, unmoved by their request.

"We'll only be a few minutes."

The man looked to the guards lining the gate then back at them in silence.

"Master Guard, I'm a Waizen and was told I'd be safe here. If this is true then why is the gate closed? Should I—should I be afraid, Sir?"

The man seemed to soften at her words and sweet tone. "Well, Love, due to the taxes we're now involved with, we've invited the Templins and their power into our region. Facilis is the only place in the West End unaffected by Differe's power. We intend to keep it that way."

Augustine clasped her hands and brought them under her chin. "So the Templins aren't allowed inside, Master Guard?"

"Absolutely forbidden, as is Differe's Army."

She smiled brightly at him. "You're good to do that. I think they have evil intentions."

"You're not the only one with that mindset, Miss." He sighed as she looked pleadingly towards the gate. "I'd rather not let you out, Love. It's dangerous. They're waiting for an escaped prisoner of theirs."

Augustine tried to appear calm. "Oh?"

"Yes, they have his banner draped just outside the gate on our walls and all over the West End. Strange, though. He's quite young."

Augustine's eyes darted to Earl's face before she looked back at the guard and approached his ladder. "Oh, Master Guard, is he a redhead? Is his name Joel?"

His eyes widened in surprise, and he knelt down. "You know him?"

"He's escaping Differe's evils. He saved my life."

"Yes, we've heard of his escaping . . . as well as a few other rumors."

"Promise me you'll consider letting him inside if he comes."

"You have my word, Miss."

How many did you get?" Augustine ushered Earl and Jack into her hotel room.

"Oh, I can't see a thing."

"Sorry. Hold on." She stumbled to the bedside table and turned on a lamp.

Earl glanced at her in surprise. "Are you all right? Have you been waiting for me in the dark?"

"No, but—sorry, I-I blew out the desk lamp when I heard someone, well you, on the stairs. I've been followed before. Guess I'm a little nervous."

"It's fine, Dear. Well, to answer your question, we only got two."

She started to help him untangle the fabric bundled in his arms. "We? Who helped you?"

"Seems 'Master Guard' took a liking to you. His name is Simon. He helped me snatch these off the outside walls from inside the courtyard. It was fairly easy."

"Perfect! I'm sure it was easy with his access to the gate towers. And, the Templins wouldn't think anyone in Facilis would want their warrant banners. I suppose in addition to liking my charming self, Simon was more than happy to aggravate Differe."

Earl chuckled in response.

She crossed her arms while gazing at Joel's face sketched across the banner. "Did you tell him what we were doing?"

"I did."

"Did he believe you . . . about Joel?"

"Not sure, but I believe he'll think it over. I'm inclined to believe he agrees with what you said about Joel escaping Differe's evils. Did you get the paint, Honey?"

"Got it. Black, thick, and ready." She popped open the paint can and grabbed the bag of brushes.

"How are you, Dear?"

She felt his hand on her shoulder. "Beg your pardon?"

"Joel, your brother, the confusing rhydid . . . how is Honey holding up?"

Augustine realized she hadn't really stopped to think about how she was feeling. She was focused on getting Joel to safety and getting Sebastian the rhydid. She sighed and looked back at the banners. "A bit weighed down, but hopeful. After all, I have you and Jack. But enough about that. Come on, there's no time to waste."

As Augustine and Earl painted into the night, she noticed the man was unusually quiet. "What are you thinking about?"

He looked up from the banner. "Well . . . I'm thinking about the possible outcomes this message could bring."

"I just hope it brings safety for Joel."

"Hm. You don't know Facilis. This is a statement, Honey. It's a claim—a claim the guards will back."

"Why do you say that?"

"Because the word of Joel's escape from the temple is spreading. That's why I really think Simon helped us. The rumor of him being the rainmaker has already taken flight with the guards."

"Well if the news is spreading won't that work in Joel's favor?"

"Yes, but . . . but you have to understand he will also put our city— our whole region—in danger."

"But Facilis has always hosted criminals, er, I mean refugees, looking for justice or . . . right?" She wasn't so sure now.

"It's a divided issue, Honey. That's the reason Differe was even allowed into the West End in the first place. The political councils aren't currently in agreement on the issue of Differe or housing refugees of other regions."

"What!" She looked at him in dismay. "How do you know all this?"

"I'm sorry."

"Stupid men on these stupid councils. They're not accomplishing anything by arguing. It's as bad as Waiz not getting along." She plunged her brush into the dark paint again and sighed. "But, Earl, he made it rain . . . maybe."

"What I'm trying to tell you is not everyone will like that, Honey."

She ran her fingers through her tangled waves. "Now you've got me worried."

"Don't worry. It won't help a thing. We're still going to do what we think is right, no matter the probable outcomes. We'll do our best to convince the city to turn Joel's way, but I believe it will be him—the man himself—who will persuade the masses to support him."

"Hide him, you mean."

"More or less."

Augustine sighed again.

"Stop, Honey. Keep your hopes up. But I must tell you, the more I keep thinking about your situation—Joel, you, Sebastian—well, I think in honor of your friend Joel's wishes and for your brother, we need to get these banners posted and get you to Waiz as quickly as we can."

Augustine didn't like this plan one bit. She wanted it all. She wanted Facilis to believe her and to hide Joel. She wanted justice for him so he would be released from Differe forever. She wanted the councils to agree that Differe was evil and to drive the troops out of the West End. She wanted to get to Sebastian, but she wanted to do it with Joel.

She tossed the rope that held Earl's side of the banner several balconies over from hers. Once both sides were secured, the two draped the banner down the front of the hotel. *Maybe I could just wait for him a few more days.* She glanced around the sleepy square, hoping the masses gathered there in the morning would look up at her room and believe. She met Earl down in the square to venture on to their next location. Before they walked away she looked up at Joel's face and read her handwriting.

An Escapee From The Temple of Differe: The West End's Rainmaker.

CHAPTER 30

JOEL STOPPED THE group when he made out Darit's stone wall in the distance.

Dillon rode up beside him. "What is it?"

"Templins." Joel pointed to the flag hanging outside the wall.

"Then we just stick with the plan." He nodded to Joel in encouragement.

"The plan has to be tweaked now." Joel looked back at Violet, Noor, and the others. He hadn't intended for them to be part of the plan. "Dillon, call to Darit. Let them know we're coming."

"Joel? Yous sure yous want to be so obvious? They did not respond last time."

"Yes. Between the black smoke and the calling cyclone, I'll bet the Templins will be more than happy to leave the village to me." Joel sighed as he jumped down to help Violet off Paz. "I want all of you from Baithe to stay here. We'll come for you once it's safe. Ian, leave your water and rations with them." He looked at the dirt road with contempt and picked up a moist clump of dark clay. He took off his hat and ran the substance through his hair.

"It's still kind of red," he heard Noor say as he put on his hat. He turned to face her. "Oh, but the hat makes it very sneaky, Master Joel."

He winked at her and took her outstretched hand. "Come on, let's move the horses back from Dillon calling to Darit."

He and the others marveled again as Dillon's sacred stone created the wind cyclone. Noor gave Joel's hand a firm squeeze after it was over, and he bent down toward her. "Never gets old, huh? Just think, one day it'll be you out there." He was confused when the little girl shook her head.

"No. I don't want a barique. I-I want a rhydid . . . like you."

His face beamed as he looked upon Noor's fiery expression. "Yes, seems it would suit you better. Perhaps that's exactly what you'll use." As Dillon returned to the group, Joel secretly hoped that someday there would be a way for Noor to have her desire met.

Inside the wall, Darit appeared to be in the same shape as Baithe, but with more people. As Joel and the Galanneans entered the courtyard, a chill went up his spine when he spotted a familiar face plastered across a hanging banner. He wondered if the others noticed it yet. The townsfolk eyed them nervously as they passed through the square. *I wonder if they think we're bringing the black smoke?* Just as with Baithe, the Templins and soldiers were camped out in front of the chapel, looking useless as usual. Joel gritted his teeth in anger as he neared the lounging men. "What's the meaning of this?"

The loafing men stumbled to their feet. "Wha-what's happening? Who are you?"

"Templin Guy. Who's in charge here?"

"I." A middle-aged man stepped forward. "Templin Shaelip."

"Differe demands taxes from these inhabitants, and the means for Differe to acquire these taxes is by you enforcing the law." He cued Paz to ride into the group of soldiers. "Is this how you ensure Differe gets paid—by sunbathing in front of the chapel? And by paid, gentlemen, I mean your salary."

"I-I, well, there's not much here. We've sent the hostages to Trompè, but there's famine. There are no goods for us to collect. Please, what can we do?"

Joel was glad to see he had their respect. "Oh, so I suppose the clouds of rain missed Darit? Have your people planted in the last few days?"

"Uh, well, the rain—our orders didn't really correspond . . . ." Templin Shaelip scratched his head.

"I assume you've taken note of the black smoke on the horizon?"

"I, well, yes." The man wrung his hands nervously and gestured for Joel to follow him inside the chapel.

Joel jumped down from Paz, handed his reins to Dillon, and followed the Templin inside.

Templin Shaelip motioned for Joel to sit down in one of the pews beside him. "Is it time, Sir? Is it time to move everyone in?"

Joel was delighted to hear Differe's plans firsthand. "What do your orders say?"

"We're only here for him—the kid on the banner. I just got back from Waiz—followed his trail there back to here. I'm not involved in the siege of Facilis."

"Do the people of Darit know? Does the West End know?"

"Not the truth. They think we're here just as you said, for the taxes. We just arrived two days ago."

"Right, sorry to put on such a show back there. Need the people to think we mean business." His heart was pounding in anticipation of hearing more news. "You sent the other guards on to the next village?"

"No. They're waiting outside Facilis. There are more than seventy troops waiting near the gate . . . ."

"Templin Shaelip, who's guarding the remaining villages?"

The guard ignored his question. "It's to stop him from getting inside . . . to safety. Even if the city falls, the people will hide him."

"You know this for a fact?"

"Yes, they're expecting him. They're already looking out for him."

Joel sat there dumbfounded. "What's the headmaster saying?"

"Only that he's armed, but we'll have no problem stopping him. He should be alone."

"How does he propose to stop him? I'm only involved in the siege."

"Well, the darkness—that smoke—will either kill him, or it will drive him into our hands. There's no way around it. The only options for him are darkness or Facilis—death or arrest."

"It would seem it's time to move the people in. I doubt Differe wants the blood of that many villages on their hands. The headmaster sent this black poison for just one person? Seems extreme."

The man shrugged in response. "He'll blame the smoke on the kid."

"May I ask you a personal question, Templin Shaelip?"

"Fire away."

"What does the headmaster really want with this character? Surely it's not just about him breaking the rules?"

The man chuckled in recognition. "I agree. The headmaster is hiding his real reasons, but I feel certain we will know very soon." He looked at the stained glass surrounding them and got a twinkle in his eye. "I think it's partially the weapon the boy carries—above all else we're supposed to retrieve it—but I'm also inclined to believe it's beyond that. In fact, I'm wondering if what Facilis is already saying is true."

Joel held his breath. "And what's that?"

"That he's the rainmaker.

After Joel convinced Templin Shaelip his orders were to gather and escort the remaining villages to Facilis for the siege, the man and his soldiers left to join the other forces waiting outside the city gate. Joel's group stood in the middle of the square and took a good look at the remaining fifty villagers. *I wonder how many are in Trompè?* None would look him in the eye; they stood silently by their shops and carts. Even the children were mute. Joel hated the sense of hopelessness he felt among the people. He broke the silence with an order. "Ian, go get the rest of our group. Take Paz with you."

The young man nodded and headed away from the square.

Joel still held the entire group's attention. "All right, everyone, please listen. The smoke on the horizon is deadly. We have to get you to Facilis along with the remaining villages. There's no way around it, and there's no sticking it out either. Gather what you can—gather what you need—then we'll head to the next village. I doubt any of the villagers between here and Facilis have any idea the smoke's poisoned."

"But it's been raining of late. Perhaps it will drive away the smoke, Sir." A young woman moved toward him, but the hand of an elderly man snatched her backward.

"Shh! Erin! Forgive my granddaughter's outburst, Master Templin. She knows not of what she speaks . . . she's not had enough . . . I mean, we've had plenty of water, but—"

"We're starving is what he means." The woman broke loose from the man and straightened her tattered dress.

Joel forced himself to withhold a smile as he looked upon the slender, daring brunette. Her dirty face and disheveled hair made her appear as wild as her untamed tongue. He thought of Noor and Violet. *Their leading men have all been taken from them. The women have to fight for the villages now.* He slowly walked over to her and raised his eyebrows. "What else do you have to say?"

"We're not leaving here. We're not leaving our land. Not with you . . . not without . . . ." She stopped as tears swelled in her eyes.

Joel looked at her with understanding. "If you stay, you'll die and give your hostages no one to come back to." He reached up to put a hand on her shoulder.

"Don't you touch her!" The old man barreled around her.

"Joel, look out!"

Joel heard Dillon's warning just in time, allowing the man's pitchfork only to slice the fabric of his cloak.

"You stay away from her." The old man kept the pitchfork aimed in Joel's direction as several other men from the village stepped forward to surround him.

"Joel! Joel!" His troops awaited his lead.

Joel remained silent and threw open his cloak.

"I didn't even scratch you, you softy."

Joel gripped his rhydid.

The villagers of Darit rushed forward. "Get him! He's got a sword!"

"Joel!" His troops raised their weapons.

"Wait! Just wait!" Joel lifted his rhydid and, to everyone's surprise, threw it on the ground. He raised his hands in surrender.

All the eyes surrounding him drifted to the rhydid, but the pitchfork owner kept his aim. "Who are you?"

"They keep calling him Joel!"

Joel's men lowered their weapons. "He's our Templin leader."

Erin stepped beside the old man. "Papa, he's the one on the banner. He's the one Differe wants." She threw Joel's hat off, and the group drew back in shock.

"He is our leader. Our hero. He will empower the village of Darit." Dillon was finally at his side and motioned for someone to come forward.

Joel felt someone grab his hand. He was relieved to find Violet standing next to him.

"Yes, Darit. He has restored Baithe. He is the one who made it rain."

Chapter 31

SEBASTIAN SMILED TO himself as he and Corwin rode toward the same tavern they had gone to after Clovis Macon's murder. Though he wished Joel and Augustine were with them, his heart still pumped with excitement. He and Corwin were on a mission—a mission that could save Waiz.

The ride down from Old Waiz had been uneventful, with Corwin sleeping most of the way. Sebastian knew the man had been gone most of the night before. In fact, it was the first time he could remember anyone leaving him alone somewhere. It made him feel independent somehow. *Corwin must trust me a lot to let me stay by myself.* He thought of how mortified his parents would be to know such a thing. He honestly hadn't thought much about them since arriving in Waiz. He barely knew them. They had worked sunup to sundown since he was born. *I don't blame them, though. It's my fault, really.* He knew the financial strain his illness had put on the family. There wasn't even a name for his condition—a condition doctors had never been able to fully explain. Shortly after he'd been born, something happened that forced him right back into the hospital. Augustine told him she couldn't remember the exact details, being so young, but that it had something to do with difficulty breathing. However . . . what he didn't find out until this year was that maybe, just maybe, the past years of pain could have been avoided altogether. His memory flickered to life as he recalled the visit to the doctor.

"Good morning, Augustine and Sebastian. Sebastian, I can't believe how much you've grown since I last saw you." Dr. Pryderi, his physician for years, reached out to shake their hands.

"Well, it's been a little while since you've seen me, but really, Dr. Pryderi, it's not like I've grown since I was eight years old." Sebastian gave him a knowing look, and the man motioned for him to get onto the exam table.

"Well, I've certainly missed you both. They've got me doing most of my rounds at the Temple Infirmary now."

Sebastian grinned. "Do you ever see Isabelle?"

The doctor hesitated to answer when Augustine grunted and turned toward the wall. He nodded slowly and pursed his lips together. "Well, yes . . . though not nearly as much as I used to. She's doing well in her studies, and she's one of the finest soloists they have."

The good news about his sister brought warmth to Sebastian's heart. "That's what she always wanted."

The doctor nodded again. "She's quite beautiful. Much like you, Augustine."

Augustine didn't break from her silent stance.

Sebastian tapped his chin and showed the doctor his signature grin, always slightly mischievous. "Does she have a boyfriend?"

"Yes, I think so. She's had her choice of suitors, that's for sure. But, now then, let's talk about you. Tell me how you've been while you follow this." Dr. Pryderi began slowly waving a penlight in front of his eyes.

"Okay, I guess. Some days it's easy to move, easy to breathe. Other days it feels like I can hardly do either."

"Uh-huh. And how many 'easy' days are you having?" The doctor started triggering pressure points with his hands.

Sebastian winced. "Ouch. About half and half."

"That's not true. He's getting worse."

Both stopped to give Augustine their full attention.

"It's true. He's—well, you're turning blue now your breathing gets so labored. Some days he won't even let me touch him his body hurts so bad. I'm—I'm afraid the steroid shot isn't working anymore. Perhaps . . . ." She stopped there and started wringing her hands.

The doctor looked at Sebastian with obvious concern then took a step in her direction. "Go on, Augustine."

"Perhaps a stronger antidote would be more beneficial."

"Augustine! I'm not taking the salus venom! I'm not doing it. I'll die before I put it in my body! You know it's addictive—it only means I'd never really be well."

She pressed past the doctor and got right in his face. "Well, that's exactly what's going to happen if we don't do something!"

He looked away from her, knowing there was truth in her words. He sighed in frustration. "Well, so be it then."

"No! I'll not let you concede like that. Not when there's something that can help you. You—you can't die. You can't leave me!" She marched back over to the doctor for help.

"You and being alone! Sometimes I wonder if you really love me, or if it's just that you're too afraid to be by yourself." His anger was showing now.

"Enough! Augustine, sit down. You know better."

She obeyed the doctor and smoothed her dark hair away from her eyes. "Yes, I'm sorry. I'm sorry for upsetting you, Sebastian. I'm sorry for upsetting him, doctor—toxic emotions trigger his condition. I know."

"No, Dear, that's not what I'm referring to. Yes, emotions can be toxic over time, but that doesn't mean you hide from them. Sebastian will be just fine if he gets angry now and then—might even do him some good. If he, or anyone really, stays angry, well that's when it becomes a problem." He eyed both of them, appearing amused at their banter. "No, I'm referring to your suggestion of the salus venom. There's no guarantee it would ever work, and the risk of side effects far outweighs the benefits. And, Sebastian is, by far, old enough to voice his own opinion. He's the patient, not you, and he gets the final word."

Sebastian felt quite satisfied by this. He was looking smug until he saw Augustine's face. Tears streamed down her cheeks as she nodded in agreement. He held out his hand to her. "I love you, Augustine."

She smiled through tears and took his hand. "I love you, too."

"I know . . . I know . . . sometimes I think you love me too much."

The room fell silent, and Dr. Pryderi grabbed his stethoscope. "So, what can we do to get you better? I don't wish you to concede easily either." He pressed the cold object against Sebastian's bare chest. "You're taking all the herbs we have here, but that's not saying much due to our cold climate—not much can survive these temperatures. You'd really fair better someplace warmer."

Sebastian shook his head at him. "Like where?"

"Really, any of the other regions would do. Even the Northern Regions would be better for you than Differe."

"We—we have an uncle in Waiz."

"Waiz?" The man seemed very interested in the piece of information Augustine had just delivered.

"Y-y-yes. I promise, it's real. He lived in Differe for a while before going back. He sends us presents from there. I know most people don't agree it's real, but it's on all the old maps. I think people have just forgotten about it . . . or, or maybe just Differe has."

The doctor nodded slowly. "Corwin."

Augustine clasped her hands in delight. "Yes! You know him?"

"I do . . . he offered to take you to Waiz shortly after Sebastian was born. In fact, he told me the offer would always stand."

His words felt like a blow to Sebastian's stomach. "What?"

Augustine looked at the floor.

"What? Are you sure? What stopped him?" Sebastian crossed his arms, not sure he wanted to know the answer.

"Well your parents didn't want to be separated from you, of course. They . . . they thought it was best for you to stay here—to raise you in Differe."

Augustine put a hand to her hip. "No, they didn't. They stayed for Isabelle to go to school."

Sebastian wasn't sure what to think when the doctor didn't defend his parents. He didn't want to think the worst of them or Isabelle. He was glad she was at the temple. *She's our sister after all. But if the doctor is correct . . . my parents . . . . I . . . I can be better someplace else?* "All right . . . so I'm old enough to speak for myself. It's time to take Uncle Corwin up on his offer."

Corwin had responded right away, even offering to take Isabelle with them. If she was ever even aware of the offer, Sebastian didn't know. He couldn't believe what he'd needed all along had been right within her grasp. The rhydid could help him in some way. He wondered if she knew this . . . and, if she did, why hadn't she come with them?

CHAPTER 32

S EBASTIAN?"

"Oh, you're awake." He caught his breath.

"Yes, and our ride has been stopped for ten minutes. Are you all right?"

"Oh? Yes, fine . . . just, um, thinking about the scrolls. I want to tell you about them."

Corwin nodded. "I know. It's almost time."

As the two walked into the old tavern to connect with an old recruit, Sebastian's heart raced. He spied the same table they had occupied with Augustine last time. He was surprised, however, when Corwin led him over to the bar instead. He followed, irritated that his braces creaked loudly across the room. By the time he reached the long wood-stained bar top, the bartender and customers were eyeing him curiously. The bartender didn't speak to them but gave Corwin a few quick glances as he fixed drinks for some others. After a few minutes Corwin leaned over the bar, forcing the bartender to stop and look him in the eye.

"You just gonna keep staring, or are you gonna order something?"

Sebastian shrank back at the man's abrasive tone, but Corwin pushed forward.

"The usual."

The man gritted his teeth and grabbed a short glass. "Fine. Who's your friend there? He want something?"

"This is Sebastian."

The dark-haired man stopped what he was doing and bent over the counter to get a good look at him.

Sebastian hesitantly stared back at the burly man, puzzled as to why he was being scrutinized.

Corwin cleared his throat. "Um, Sebastian, would you like something?"

He nervously raised his chin at the bartender. "Yeah. Yes, I do."

"What'll you have?" The man leaned back to finish making Corwin's drink.

"You pick. Make it something special."

The bartender pursed his lips in disapproval and handed Corwin his drink.

"Here, let me help you up here." Corwin's sweaty hands grabbed Sebastian's as he pulled him onto a barstool.

What's wrong with him? Why's he fidgeting so much? How does this guy know his "usual?" "Corwin—" The man put a finger to his lips.

"Here." The bartender shoved a glass between them.

"What is it?"

"Ginger beer."

"Beer?"

"It's fine, Sebastian." Corwin nudged him to take the drink.

"Thank you." Sebastian studied the fizzy amber-colored drink then took his first sip. "Hm. Pretty good." He was thrilled to see the bartender slightly return his smile. "What's your name?"

The man seemed surprised that Sebastian spoke to him again and remained silent.

"You know mine."

The bartender brought around a set of empty glasses and smacked his lips together. "Dade."

"What's the tavern's name?"

Dade squinted down at Corwin. "Your friend asks a lot of questions."

"Of course, I do. I'm a thirteen-year-old kid from Differe."

He watched Corwin's jaw clench as the entire tavern went silent and turned to stare at them.

Oops.

Soon Dade waved the drying cloth he was holding at his customers. "It's all right. He's just a kid visiting his uncle . . . everyone have another round. It's all right. Have another round on the house." Folks slowly turned their chairs around and went back into conversation. Dade grabbed Corwin and Sebastian's glasses and emptied them.

Corwin raised his hands in protest. "I wasn't finished."

Dade leaned back over the bar and lowered his voice. "What are you trying to do—drive away my customers? You just cost me another round. Get out of here."

"I'll pay you for it."

"You've already cost me enough for an entire lifetime. Get out, Corwin."

"No, we need to meet. It's time."

"The last thing I need right now is trouble. Clovis being murdered. Did you see about Thad's son? He's probably rolling over in his grave."

Corwin straightened and cracked his knuckles. "Oh, get a hold of yourself. Trouble's already here."

"Yeah, and your kid knows why so many of his troops are here?"

"He knows something."

Dade slammed his fist down on the counter. "Get out."

"Dade, come on. We've got to figure out what's going on. The whole region may fall—then what?"

"Get out, Corwin. And take your friend with you." He pushed his fist near Corwin's chest.

"The drinks." Corwin grabbed his shirt pocket for change.

"I'll cover it. Just get out." He opened his fist and moved to the other end of the bar.

Sebastian felt defeated until Corwin gave him a thumbs up. Curious, Sebastian followed his gaze to where Dade's fist had opened. The man had left them a key.

"So, now what are we going to do?" Sebastian looked up at Corwin, who was leaning against the river wall with his pipe dangling out of his mouth.

"We wait. We have to wait until it's dark to use Dade's gift."

Sebastian moved toward the wall and put his hands under his chin. The rushing sound of the Pallas River drew his eyes to the blue water below. "Tell me about Dade. He didn't seem too keen on us being there. I don't think I even noticed him the first time with Augustine."

"I'm sure he was wrapped up in the murder situation at the time, but he was there . . . he's always there. We don't mingle unless there's something to say to one another." He pulled the pipe from his mouth. "Since I went straight to the bar, it was probably obvious I had something important to tell him."

"You know him—he knew your 'usual'."

"Yes, he was in Thad's league with me."

"He didn't like you."

Corwin peered out over the wall. "Well, you have to remember, Sebastian, that I left the league when they needed me most. I abandoned them . . . ."

"When you came to Differe?"

Corwin gripped the sides of the wall with force. "Yes, when I ran away to Differe. I took the lead for a while after Thad was killed, but life became . . . complicated. My, uh, my personal life greatly began to affect my leadership."

"What happened?"

The man hid his face from Sebastian. "Well, the group suggested I take some time off to, uh . . . to recover. It was during that time that I escaped to Differe. I left them."

Sebastian tugged at his sleeve. "Did you write to them? Did they know where you went?"

"Yes, I told them about you, Augustine, and Isabelle. Of course, they didn't believe me when I returned later . . . without you."

Sebastian's eyes widened in recognition. "That's why Dade looked at me so funny when you told him my name!"

Corwin finally turned back to him and smiled. "Absolutely. You just being you gave me some credibility today, and I certainly thank you for it."

"You're welcome." Sebastian waited to see if Corwin would say something else. When he remained silent, Sebastian decided it was time to discover the truth about his last visit with Dr. Pryderi. "What happened in Differe while you were there?"

"Oh, well . . . it didn't go as I had hoped. Being such a free spirit, I hardly got along in Differe. Too many rules—too much pretension."

"Even when you're poor?" Sebastian guessed Corwin's latter remark referred to his mother, despite their social class in Differe.

"Yes, Sebastian, even if you're poor. But that's all in the past now . . . or that's the attitude I'm hoping the league will extend to us."

"So, we're having a meeting with the army? How are you sure they'll come?"

"Well, Dade still has a sterling reputation with the group, and I have his key." He pulled the object from his pocket. "This will alert them of the meeting."

"How?"

Corwin smiled at him. "You'll find out soon."

Sebastian sighed in dissatisfaction. *There's so much I want to know.* He moved closer to the man. "Corwin?"

"Yes?"

"What happened? I mean, I get why you left Differe—it's rules and stuff, and, after all, Waiz is your home—but what happened that made you leave Waiz in the first place?"

The man's facial expression didn't change much, but he also didn't answer right away.

"Corwin, you can tell me anything, you know."

"I can't tell you."

Sebastian didn't try to hide his disappointment at the quick reply.

"Sebastian, listen, it's not that I don't trust you—I do. It's just . . . that part of my life involves other people . . . people who could be hurt if the information was shared. Does that make sense?"

"Yes, I think I understand, but—" He tried to keep words he had held inside for weeks from coming out, but in the end he failed. "I bet it's about Augustine."

Corwin cocked an eyebrow at him and turned back to the wall. "Why do you say that?"

"Just a guess, but I think it's a pretty good one."

Corwin drummed his fingers on the stone wall. "Hm. Interesting."

Very interesting. Sebastian's reasons for this guess resonated even more as he pictured Augustine standing beside them. *She has your smile.*

CHAPTER 33

J OEL STOOD HEAD to head with the old man holding the rhydid at his
throat.

"Where did you get this?"

Joel grimaced, careful not to move under the blade's sharp tip. "Uh,
the temple."

"Harding, enough of this. You have my word." Violet still had a hold
of Joel's hand, but he felt her let go. She held out the black barique to the man.
"You have my husband's word."

Harding drew the sword back and gasped. "He—he . . . ."

"Trompè," she finished for him. "Why didn't you respond to our
calling?"

"Violet, we couldn't. All of our sacred bariques were taken with our
hostages."

Joel scratched his neck as Harding studied Violet's barique. "Is Differe
the only place that doesn't know about these things?" He was both glad and
frustrated that the man knew what his rhydid and Violet's barique were.

"Is this why Differe wants you?" The man examined the hilt of the
rhydid then handed the small sword back to Joel.

"That, and I escaped from the temple."

"Twice." Ian gave him a wink.

"How'd you know it was there? How'd you get it?"

"They can tell you everything you want to know." Joel motioned to the group behind him. "But, listen, I'm serious about leaving. In this disguise I was able to hear Differe's orders. The smoke is deadly."

"Why are they driving everyone to Facilis?" Erin cast him a worried glance.

Joel clenched his fists. "Sorry, I suppose that's my fault. They're after me. I have no idea how they know I'm here . . . how they know I took this. I mean, it replaced itself."

All eyes looked at him in wonder.

"But there's no time for that story now. They're waiting for me at the gate—a host of troops. Smoking me out, so to speak."

Erin stared down at his rhydid. "I'd want you too, if I knew you could make it rain."

Harding followed her gaze and stroked his chin. "What do you plan to do?"

Joel shrugged. "Travel to the rest of the villages. Drive out the Templins as we did here. Get the people to safety."

Erin closed her eyes and shook her head. "How can they do that—not warn us, leave us to die?"

"Why are you so special?"

Joel shook his head at Harding. "At this point, I kinda wish I knew."

The group went quiet with all of Darit's eyes on Harding. He finally nodded. "We should go. We should help warn the other villages."

Joel held up a hand. "No, go on to safety. We'll take care of them."

The man shook his head. "No, Baithe didn't play it safe in helping us. And, Violet's the only reason I'm convinced about you. You'll need us." He extended a hand toward Joel.

"Thank you, Sir. How can I help your people get ready?"

"Well, we've heard a few rumors about the boy who escaped from the temple. Is it true about your cooking?"

The caravan only took two hours to prepare, as there was hardly any surplus to collect. Joel prepared what food he could for the group, and soon all the villagers were loaded on their farming wagons, norracs, or on horseback. With the darkness engulfing what lay behind them and moving closer every hour, he knew time was running short. Ever present was the vision of seventy

Templins waiting just for him, and Joel forced the thought from his mind again and again.

"Paz ready, Joel." Ian handed him the reins.

"Thanks. Where's Dillon?"

His brother cracked a smile and tilted his head to the right.

Joel spotted Dillon talking with Erin. The two were smiling as he packed the flatbed wagon portion of her norrac. Joel raised his eyebrows and chuckled a little. It gave him hope that his friend could find a little romance in such a dire situation. "Dillon!" He waved over to him.

The young man perked up and headed toward him. "Yes?"

Joel looked back to Erin then punched Dillon in the shoulder. "Nice."

"Ow! I do not know what yous are talking about." He rubbed his shoulder and smirked.

Joel turned him away from the others. "Dillon, I need you to do something for me."

Dillon's expression fell upon hearing Joel's serious tone. "I am not going to like this . . . am I?"

Joel looked at the ground and kicked the dirt. "Having these villagers as your witnesses about the smoke is enough. You don't . . . you don't need me—"

"Joel, it is not true."

"Stop. Listen to me. I can't put the rest of the villages in danger. What if . . . what if while the Templins or army try to capture me, somebody . . . ." He ran his fingers through his hair. "What if a kid gets hurt? It's not worth it, Dillon. I'm not worth it."

Dillon kept a sharp gaze and shook his head. "Why are yous not going to tell them about Differe sieging Facilis? Yous might be leading them to death anyway."

"Well, they're certainly dead if they stay here, but I figure in bigger numbers they have a better chance to fight Differe. Besides, Differe's only taking over Facilis if I'm there."

"Yous do not know that for sure."

"Stop. Just take this." Joel shoved his Templin cloak and hat into Dillon's chest.

Dillon shook his head and pushed Joel's full hands away from him.

"Be the one to lead them. You can do it, Dillon. I know you can." He held the clothes out again. Joel was baffled when Dillon ignored him and walked back over to Erin's norrac.

The young man climbed high atop the carriage portion and clapped his hands. "Attention, attention, please."

All commotion stopped, and every eye turned toward the young man.

"Joel says I am to lead the rest of the villages to Facilis. I shall be the Templin."

Joel felt himself shrink back as the crowd shifted their gaze to him.

"He knows following him is risky, but he must think yous are idiots and have not thought about that."

Joel's jaw dropped, and he vehemently started shaking his head at the crowd.

"So, Darit, would yous like for me to lead yous on in safety . . . or," he turned to Joel, "would yous prefer Joel lead yous?"

The group looked back and forth between them in confusion.

Joel's anger stirred as he stared in Dillon's direction. He rushed over to the norrac. "What are you doing?" He gritted his teeth and faced the crowd. "Everyone, please disregard Dillon's words. I, uh, I don't think you're idiots." He turned back and glared at his friend.

"They do not want me to lead, Joel. They . . . we, we want yous."

Slightly pouting at having been reprimanded so publicly, Joel mounted Paz and led the group onto the road. He pulled back into the crowd once everyone was moving. *I didn't want to abandon them. I just wanted to keep them safe.*

"Like Augustine?"

Joel bit his lip in frustration. In seeing Erin, he was very much reminded of her. *Reminded of how much I miss her. I hope she's in Waiz with Sebastian by now. Maybe I can get back to them . . . but would she even want me back with them after leaving her?* He wondered what he would do once he got to Facilis. *If I can make it in. No, I can't think like that. Wait! Wait . . . who asked that?* "Like Augustine." It was nearly the same question he had heard before he raised his rhydid to make it rain. *Right. Choices. These people want to follow me, but—*

"You don't want to give them the choice."

Right. I thought that was you again.

"Why do you keep having trouble with this?"

Joel gripped the reins tighter. *You ask a lot of questions.*

"It's for your own good."

Fine then, so I'm eliminating choices.

"Why?"

Because . . . because it's helpful. I'm helping people make the right decision—the safe decision.

"I don't see you making any 'safe' decisions."

What do you mean?

"Disguising yourself as a Templin, joining a rogue army group, making it rain, saving villages, journeying to a place where you'll be caught . . . ."

Joel couldn't argue with the voice.

"How is that okay for you but not for others? It's probably even more costly for you."

I know.

"You do know you may get caught?"

I know.

"In fact, you may lose your life."

I said, I know. He'd been trying to shove this reality away for the last several hours.

"Then why are you doing it, Joel?"

Didn't you choose me or something? Isn't this really your doing? You're not giving me any choices.

There was a long pause, and Joel worried he had offended the voice.

Please, I'm sorry. It's just, because . . . because it means something. This place, these people—they mean something.

"To you?"

Not necessarily. But they do to someone else. Just like Augustine means a lot to Sebastian.

"Is it worth the risk?"

He thought of Augustine then caught Noor staring back at him from her horse in front. *Yes. It's worth it. I've . . . I've never been able to help anyone.*

"The freedom you feel from escaping the temple and its evils is contagious, isn't it?"

I suppose so. I can't help but want to give it away . . . to repay them for their evils.

"Your freedom birthed many choices for you. And, Joel, I haven't made you do anything. You can leave them anytime you please. But answer this, why do you think these people want to follow you?"

Joel hesitated. He wasn't exactly sure.

"Why won't you give others a choice?"

Joel sucked in a breath. *I don't know.*

"They believe in you, Joel."

The words terrified something inside him. *Yeah, I'm not sure that's a good idea.*

"Every leader makes mistakes. Don't be afraid to lead because of it."

I'm not afraid of that. It's just . . . I'm not sure a person who's been, well, you know . . . He couldn't bring himself to say the word.

"Crazy?"

Paz startled when he shuddered. "Easy, boy." *Yes. I'm pretty sure if they really knew about me I wouldn't be leading for long.*

"Augustine knows."

Yeah, you keep bringing her up.

"So, they are worth it . . . ."

Yes.

"They believe in you."

Great.

"You don't believe in yourself."

Joel stayed silent.

"They look to you because they *need* a leader. A true leader with no rank, no pretension, but someone who shares their values. You find them worth the risk—valuable—so they trust you."

Fantastic. Joel hoped his sarcasm would end this part of the conversation. *Just tell me what to do.*

"Why don't you give them the choice to follow you? I know you're still thinking of how to leave them. What are you afraid of?"

If you know so much then you tell me.

"They are worth it?"

I've already answered that.

"Yes, but not about yourself. Are you worth it?"

Chapter 34

AUGUSTINE STOOD IN the enormous Capital Square with Earl and Jack. "Look! Another group is approaching." They had seen Templins and soldiers coming in droves during the past forty-eight hours. She bent down to scratch Jack's head. "Where do you think they're coming from?"

"Let's get closer. I think we'll be able to hear this one."

Augustine nodded. "It's worth a shot."

The Differian group had nearly tripled in size and was no longer hidden in the forests off the road. Most soldiers lined the sides of the road while the Templins guarded the outside of the city gate. Facilis soldiers also stood firmly before the gate, though from inside the city. Augustine noted the leering eyes of the Templins on the other side. *They know they're not wanted here—by the Facilis guards or the people.* Augustine caught Simon's eye as the two approached the gate, and he made a slight nod in their direction. They moved near him just in time to see the head Templin from the oncoming group arrive at the gate's entrance.

His horse pranced about as he peered through the gate. "Where are our banners?"

The Facilis guards returned his question with silence.

He turned to his fellow comrades. "What's the meaning of this? Why are there so many legions here? Someone bring me something to drink. We look ridiculous!"

"I agree."

Augustine suppressed a smile at Simon's sarcasm.

A Differian soldier brought the Templin a cup of water. "Sir, the banners went missing a few days ago, but no one knows where they are."

He turned to the Facilis guards again. "How many people have been let in since the banners went up?"

They didn't answer again.

"Only a few, but none have come out." The soldier refilled the man's cup after he gulped the drink.

The head Templin dismounted and strode up to the gate right in front of Simon. He gripped the iron bars.

Augustine gasped and moved behind Earl when she realized it was Templin Chadwick, the horrible man she and Joel had met at the Templin headquarters.

"And what do you know, soldier? What are they saying inside the walls about all these men out here?"

Simon cleared his throat. "They're a bit puzzled as to why you're piled out there . . . looking to catch a boy."

The man spat on the ground. "Ha! Let them think that then, but this boy is dangerous. Do you hear me, Facilis?" His voice grew louder. "The purest leader, our headmaster, wants this so-called 'boy' for heinous crimes! Do not let him into your city!"

Augustine was suddenly pushed from behind. She turned to find the Capital Square filling up with people. It was mostly young adults like the ones she had seen celebrating the rain in Dunn Square. She glanced up and saw older generations of people standing on the terraces and balconies of the capitol building behind them.

Templin Chadwick looked up and cupped his hands around his mouth. "Do you hear me? Do not think of hiding someone so vile! He must be punished for his crimes! He's armed with a great danger!"

"Is that why so many of you are here?" A young man behind Augustine pressed past her.

"Yes, just how weak is your army that you need so many to fight one boy?" another from the crowd jeered.

Chadwick appeared astonished at their tones. "How dare you! My allegiance is to the headmaster. I follow his orders with great loyalty. I do not question him. This is how we Templins serve, you fools!"

The younger crowd pushed toward the gate, pressing Augustine and Earl forward as more taunts were thrown out.

"With that kind of talk we're inclined to let this fellow in!"

"Hear, hear!" The crowd cheered.

"We might need his weapon!"

The crowd cheered again.

"You wouldn't dare go against the headmaster's orders!"

Differian soldiers began running to the gate as the crowd grew louder.

"We've seen the truth about him—about your banner—you wicked lot!"

"We know who he is, and we intend to let him in!"

Earl and Augustine exchanged surprised glances. *It worked.* She couldn't believe it, but the crowd was for Joel. *They believed the banners! They believe he's the rainmaker!* She glanced back at the fiery young crowd. *They'll protect him . . . but I'm not so sure about the older ones.* She glanced up again at the groups leaning over their balconies in silence. It was as if they were poised in deep thought as the crowd below continued arguing with the Differians.

Templin Chadwick finally focused his attention toward the older crowd. "What say you, up above? Wisdom, speak!"

A host of whispers suddenly ran through the crowd.

"Look! He's here."

"The Vicar!"

"The Vicar is on the Midway Terrace."

Augustine looked up to where everyone was pointing. The Midway Terrace was more than halfway up the capitol building and was the longest and narrowest terrace of all, protruding from the building like a platform. She stood in awe with the rest of the crowd as a man with a long white beard came into view. His ivory robe and silver staff attested to the honor his position held. He put a hand on the terrace wall and leaned forward. "Templin, what is the meaning of this smoke?"

The crowd went silent as the sound of the man's booming voice flooded the square.

"It's lethal, Your Honor, bringing our fugitive to us."

The man stroked his white beard. "He is so valuable that you would choose to take the lives of our villagers in this region?"

"He is destroying your region by being here. Your Honor, it's his very presence that has brought this evil into your land."

"I see. And how do you propose to keep our people safe—warn our villages?"

"Facilis residents will remain safe by staying inside the gate. The smoke will not come inside. Considering the attitude of your younger inhabitants, I think it best no one leaves the city as well."

The old man grasped his silver staff with both hands. "You hold us hostage then?"

"No, I keep you in safety. The smoke, or if necessary our army, will kill anyone who tries to flee the city."

Trapped! So much for getting to Waiz.

"Our villages, Templin?"

"Don't worry, Vicar. The Templin leaders will flee if the smoke comes too close. Your people will be free to follow them."

A commotion behind the Templins turned Augustine's attention away from the old man. A young Templin was barreling down the road on horseback.

Chadwick shook his head. "What now?"

Everyone seemed to hold their breath as the young man jumped off his horse and ran toward Chadwick.

"Ma-master, how—how—" The young man was clearly out of breath. "How many legions have come in today?"

Chadwick shrugged. "I have just arrived myself. I have no idea. Now, calm down." He whacked the boy on the shoulder.

Another soldier stepped forward. "We've had nearly a hundred soldiers, I'd guess."

Augustine grabbed Earl's hand.

"It's—it's a trick. It's a trick, Master." He grimaced as Chadwick gripped his shoulders.

"What on earth are you talking about?"

"Speak up, you below," the Vicar bellowed. "I fear this news involves our villages."

Chadwick looked up at the old man then got in the young Templin's face. "Speak loudly."

"You were relieved by Templin Guy, right? A young man with several other young comrades . . . in fact, you all were."

The Templin leaders looked at one another in confusion then slowly nodded their heads in unison.

"Well, it's the same man—the same young Templin each time. He's been going from village to village leading the people here." The young man started trembling and gripped his shoulder where Chadwick had been holding him.

"Well, you see, Wise One, your villages are safe after all. Someone's leading them here to safety." Chadwick nodded up at the man then turned back to the young Templin and spoke quietly. "Who is he?"

"He's not one of us, Master. When I say he's leading the villages, I mean he's their leader. I just happened to stay back in Butler. I saw the other villagers—hundreds of them—hiding far behind him. Their numbers will match ours by the time they get here."

Chadwick knew the crowd closest to him had just heard this news as well. "Hm, that's noble, I suppose. Some farmer disguising himself as a Templin to get these villagers to safety."

Simon hit the iron bars with his spear. "They'd better be safe, Templin. They'll be mostly women and children."

"As long as they're agreeable, there will be no reason for anyone to get hurt or . . . not reach the gate."

"I'm not sure they'll cooperate, Master," the young Templin interjected. "I don't think they'll hand him over." He let go of his shoulder and unbuttoned his coat, wincing in pain.

Augustine finally saw the ripped fabric his hand had been concealing. She covered her mouth when she saw the gash on his arm.

"A woman did this."

Terrible as it was, the words made Augustine feel empowered somehow.

Chadwick shot a glance in Simon's direction. "Well, if they use violence we will have no other choice but to respond."

"Wait, don't you see—" The young man stumbled and began trembling again.

Chadwick motioned for two soldiers to help the man up. "Come on, let's get you taken care of."

"No!" He pulled away from the guards. "You need to plan, Master. You must get ready."

Augustine saw fear in the young man's eyes.

"Don't you understand? He's the one—the one we're waiting for. Their leader . . . they call him Joel."

CHAPTER 35

JOEL GAZED OUT across the fields in front of him. The smoke had thickened and was covering the villages they had left behind. This was the last stop before reaching Facilis. He watched a rock fly over the fence and turned to find Dillon walking up to him.

He clucked his tongue when he reached Joel. "Wow, what a sight."

Joel kicked the ground with his boot. "You know, I've seen mouthpieces, but this—" He stopped and pointed toward the darkness. "It's even more evil looking."

Dillon shrugged. "Maybe because it is bigger?"

"Maybe. I . . . you know, when I was in that cave, I was so intent on finding the king—"

"Desperate, yous mean." Both young men chuckled.

"Yeah, that too. When I saw those mouthpieces screaming at me, and then I remembered the song . . . my name—"

"The one the heavens sing to yous?"

"I don't know who sang to me, but yeah, that one. I think because I was focused on something else . . . it's like it, I don't know . . . ."

"It is like anything, Joel. What yous focus on yous give the most power."

Joel turned to him in surprise. "Well, listen to you."

The young man winked at him. "I know a few Temple, uh, laws. Yous should not focus on the smoke, but on the people and the Facilis road."

"I know. I was just trying to figure out a way . . . like if we made a cyclone and sent the smoke a different direction."

"The direction of the winds are not predictable—way too dangerous."

Joel nodded when he felt a hard nudge from Dillon. "Yeah, I agree. Just thinking."

Silence passed between them, and Joel returned his gaze to the fields. A few moments later he felt Dillon step sideways and stare him up and down. Joel turned and threw his hands up. "What?"

"Yous shoulders are sagging."

"That's how a fugitive typically looks."

"But yous are a Templin."

"It's only a disguise."

"Yous a leader."

"Uh, that's a disguise too. Just don't tell anyone."

Dillon pursed his lips and looked at Joel's shoulders again. "A leader's shoulders do not sag."

"Who says?"

"My father, and he is a fine leader. Yous got a problem."

Joel sighed in annoyance at Dillon's pointing fingers.

"I know how to fix it. He show me how."

Joel crossed his arms sternly, communicating he didn't want help.

Dillon raised his eyebrows. "Oh, now yous are being stubborn?"

Joel gritted his teeth. "I don't think my posture is an issue."

"So, I suppose Augustine would prefer yous ride into Facilis hunch over, yes? Looking like a failure?"

Joel's jaw opened in rebuttal, but he stopped to hear the young man out. "Okay, what's your point?"

"Yous are carrying too much."

Joel shrugged in confusion.

"Why are yous here?"

Joel scratched his head. "Uh, you asked me, or the people asked me to lead them."

"Hm. They say they would follow yous . . . so yeah, guess they did make yous the leader, but yous did not have to say yes."

Joel looked down and rubbed his jaw line. *Why did I say yes? Why didn't I just leave . . . get to Augustine?* He gripped his rhydid and remembered. In the midst of the cyclone of the first rain, he realized he had two choices. He could choose himself and impact one or choose others and impact many. "Seems to be more purpose in greater numbers of people."

"Purpose for what?"

Joel peered at the darkness again before answering. "Life. Selfishness is lonely. I was given a choice. I *chose* to say 'yes'—that's why I'm not sitting here complaining about the group following me. You're right. I could've said no, but I said yes to leading them."

"Who give yous the choice?"

Joel shook his head at him and smiled. "Sure you're not from Waiz? All right, Dillon. Something, maybe even someone, helped me recognize I had a choice."

"Then yous really just say yes to that something. Yous are only responsible to that one someone. Take off the others."

Joel leaned on the fence, recognizing that he indeed did feel heavier than he wanted. When he closed his eyes all he could see was Noor's face. *I have to leave. I can't put her in harm's way . . . but . . . is it worse not to allow her to choose her own fate . . . with or without me?* "I don't want to control, Dillon. Not like the headmaster. People may make mistakes . . . make a choice I think is wrong, but I'd rather take the risk of allowing them that freedom."

"Good. We Galanneans make our choice. Here." Dillon pretended to take something off Joel's shoulders and put it on the fence. "This is me and my men. Do not carry us. We follow yous freely. We shall take care of ourselves and those yous lead. We shall not look to yous for power—we look to the king. Yous are no different than us."

"Feels lighter already." His words were flat, but he admitted to himself there was perhaps some truth in what Dillon was saying. He continued listening as Dillon removed unseen burdens one by one. By the time they turned to leave, Joel was standing a little taller. He gripped his rhydid when he saw a crowd rushing toward them.

"Joel! Joel!" He heard the terror in the voices of the young boys running out in front.

Joel knelt down, ready to meet them head on. "What is it?"

"A Templin! A junior Templin!" One cried to his left.

"I got him!" Erin came running up behind them with a pitchfork in her hand.

"He spied. He came back for something," came another.

"It's all right. Where is he?" Joel stood up and saw Erin's pitchfork was stained with blood.

Their heads shook in dismay, and Joel felt the weight return to his shoulders.

"He's—he's gone. He got away."

Joel bit his cheek. "What did he see?"

The oldest boy stepped forward. "He saw all the people gathered near the square. He was on a horse."

Soon another boy was by his side. "Yes, we saw him riding up. He asked for guards . . . then he saw—he saw all the people—even the ones coming up behind."

Joel saw fear spread across both boys' faces. "It's all right. Go on, tell us the rest."

The older one nudged the younger. "He was afraid then. His horse reared on its two legs. We—we tried to just tell him we were all getting away from the smoke and hurrying to Facilis."

The smaller boy balled his fists and looked behind him. "Oliver goofed up though. He told our secret."

Joel spotted a boy around seven years old, with tears streaming down his face, hiding behind the others.

Dillon sighed loudly next to Joel. "What happen?"

The little boy bit his lip, unable to speak due to his flowing tears.

The older boy shook his head. "The Templin asked who our leader was. Oliver . . . he said it was a Templin named 'Joel'."

Erin put a hand over her heart as she tried to console Oliver. "He knew right away who you were—I could see it in his eyes. I grabbed the pitchfork and tried to block him from leaving, but all I did was give his shoulder a good scratch."

Joel grimaced at the turn of events, but more so in response to Oliver's remorse. He broke through the boys to get to him. Joel scooped up the child and took him away from the crowd. He carried him just outside the village's wall near a group of trees that would provide them both some shade and privacy.

Joel plopped the boy down on the ground then sat beside him. He leaned his back against one of trees and looked out at the approaching dark air. He closed his eyes and sucked in a breath. "Oliver, where's your father?"

The boy sniffed. "Trompè, Sir."

Joel's muscles flinched in anger. If he made it into Facilis alive, he was intent on finding out why so many had been taken there. "I'm sure he misses you. I haven't seen my father in a long time either."

"Is he in Trompè?"

"No. He's—he's at my—his home." Joel hesitated, not wanting to go on about the man who had left him at the temple. "He doesn't know where I am."

"I'm—I'm sorry about—"

"Stop. No apologies. I brought you out here to tell you a secret."

Oliver frowned. "I'm not good at keeping secrets."

"Oh, I don't believe you. Besides, I bet your father would want you to try again. I bet you can keep this one."

He dried his eyes and looked at Joel with curiosity.

Joel smiled down at the dirty face. "Well, as crazy as it might sound, Oliver, I have to thank you."

"Thank me?"

"Yes, now I know exactly what I need to do."

Oliver wrinkled his nose in confusion.

"Yeah, sometimes too many choices . . . though it's nice to have options . . . sometimes it's just plain easier to have one."

"Uh, is this about getting all of us to Facilis?"

"Very good. You're not only trustworthy, but smart." Joel winked at him. "Yes, it is. I want it to be the safest route possible for everyone. And, with the Templins looking for me . . . well . . . ."

The boy's eyes became sad again. "You think we'll be safest getting there without you."

Joel nodded while glancing at the smoke. "Yes, I do. They think you'll hide me . . . and fight them, which you probably would, and—"

"And, people would get hurt."

Joel nodded again. "I've been watching the smoke, Oliver. Timing it. It'll be here in a few hours. If everyone leaves now, you'll be in Facilis by the time it gets here, giving the Templins plenty of time to search the group for me . . . which they most certainly will do."

Oliver fidgeted with a few leaves on the ground. "You could just go and turn yourself in?"

Joel shook his head and grinned. "Nah. That's not my style. Plus, the people wouldn't let me."

The little boy shook his head in agreement.

"So, thank you for blowing my cover. I needed a reason to leave and keep everyone safe—that's the secret part." Joel motioned for Oliver to stand up.

"What will I tell them?"

"That I left. I abandoned you. I won't be back. Tell them it's time to get to Facilis. The smoke is rising—there's no other way. Can you do that for me?"

Oliver shot him another frown. "I don't think they'll believe me. What about your men?"

Dillon would be furious with him. He grimaced as he thought of a way to convince the group to move on. "Take Paz for me, and here's my Templin cloak and hat. That should convince them. All right?"

The boy shrugged. "You're not really giving me any other choice."

"That's not true. You can stay if you like. But I have choices as well, and I've made mine."

CHAPTER 36

AUGUSTINE JERKED EARL'S arm to shake him awake. The two sat on the highest terrace of the capitol building. The square below had cleared somewhat, due to Facilis's daily siesta. The chatty young people were perched near the guards below, while the older folks among the terraces had retreated inside the capitol building. Augustine had yet to ask Earl about the old man with the long beard. As she sat across from the man who could be her grandfather, she couldn't help but feel aggravated with all the regions. *Why is it that the older and younger generations are so segregated? The pattern seems juvenile, embarrassing even. It's like watching a bunch of arguing school children. I mean, after all, the groups are attached to one another in some form or fashion. The older had to have given birth to the younger . . .* She looked at Earl again, who hadn't budged from his deep sleep. *He's different, though . . . hasn't lost his fire.* "Come on, Earl. Wake up." She shook him again.

His eyes fluttered open. "Hm. Yes?"

"You can see them now." She nodded outward beyond the gate. In the far away distance she could make out a group of people. "There—there are more than I thought there would be."

"Well, there are nearly twenty villages nearby. I'd imagine, just as Differe suspected, they will be matched in numbers."

They watched as the Differian Army began lining the road on either side.

"What do you think they're doing? Their line must stretch out for over half a mile."

Earl shook his head. "Doing a search I suppose. Look."

Augustine squinted to see what he was talking about. A rider had met the approaching villagers. There was a brief conversation, then the group moved forward in pairs. By the time they reached the guards each person was walking single file down the line.

"Wow, that's thorough." Her heart beat faster, wondering if Joel was somewhere in the group coming toward her.

Earl got out his binoculars. "I'm sure your Joel is well disguised . . . if he's with them."

"Yes, I'm sure—I'm sure you're right. I suppose you can finish your nap. It'll take them a while to get here." She propped her elbows on the pillar in front of her as they waited for the first villagers to enter Facilis. She took the binoculars as the first group entered the gate, searching their faces and those beyond. "Oh, Earl! Something's wrong. They look—"

"Differe . . . yes, it's worse than I thought."

"Oh, why haven't they come until now?" Augustine was mortified at the filthy, weary people coming into the beautiful city of Facilis. She thought of the first time she met Joel. *He was skinny, but . . . at least he was clean.* Just like him, these people looked grossly mistreated. She finally looked away and gave the binoculars back to Earl.

She turned her attention to the young zealots below. They were taking the villagers by the hands, and half an hour later the square was full of refugees and food. Augustine looked through the binoculars again when the guards fiercely shut the gate behind the last one who entered. *They know Differe has done this to their people.* When the Templins remained standing in command outside the city walls, it was obvious they didn't have their prize.

Augustine jumped when a thunderous clap arose below them. She leaned over the wall to find the bearded man standing on his platform again. The people went silent as all eyes above and below locked onto the man.

"Good citizens of the West End, I welcome you to Facilis. May it be a refuge for you during this difficult time in our region."

The people remained silent.

"I see there has been no capture outside our gates, so I must ask if you are hiding the person the Templins want. Please inform our guards, for I will need to know how to proceed if there is such a situation in our midst."

Augustine squinted as a yell escaped from a young woman below. "Sir!"

The old man raised his hand for her to speak.

"Joel is not with us! He abandoned us in Butler. We have his horse—registered with the Templin guard." She motioned to a golden horse nearby.

A Facilis guard marched over and raised the horse's lip. "Yes, Your Honor, it's registered."

"Very well, then. Thank you, young people, for providing care." And with that he retreated.

Augustine turned and stared at Earl.

"What?"

"Well, first of all, I'd very much like to know what that is all about." She pointed to where the man had stood.

Earl smiled wryly. "And?"

"And, secondly, Joel didn't abandon them." She twisted her mother's ring around her finger. "He saved them."

"Stupid woods." Joel removed his bag and unsnagged his pants from the briars entangling his feet. He wanted to follow close behind the villagers, but traveling in the woods beside the road proved more tedious than expected. He was now a quarter mile behind them. He was sure Dillon had a map, but Joel had no idea if there was more than one road to Facilis. He figured it was best to keep the traveling group within his vision. *I can also make sure they get in safely.* He knew the Templins were waiting for him and would most certainly post a few in the woods, so he marched awkwardly against the brush with his rhydid out. He chastised himself for learning so little about the West End's capital. *I should've asked about the roads. I should've asked about alternative routes. Is there just one entrance? Focus, Joel. It doesn't matter. You've got to be ready for anything.*

He tried to keep his thoughts together as he pressed onward, but they drifted mostly to women. He hoped Augustine was safe and with her brother. As often as she had entered his mind, he was now certain he wanted to see her again. He wanted to give her choices. *I want her to be the one who leaves me next time.*

Every time he made out the group ahead, he thought of Noor and Violet, wanting them safe in Facilis. And then there was Sarah . . . and Isabelle. *I'm still confused . . . about both of them.* Sarah had risked her very life for him, yet he wasn't sure why. He knew being with her for so many years had earned him a soft spot in her heart, but he'd also tried her patience for the most part. *It's like she knew something about me, my future. I don't understand it . . . yet.*

His thoughts about Isabelle were just as baffling. For the first time in years, she suddenly seemed to see past the tormented boy she had once known. *She wanted me to save her . . . she wanted to go with me this time.*

His reflections were derailed when a branch snapped behind him. Joel's head turned sharply toward the sound. All was silent. He darted forward, hacking away at the tangled woods with his rhydid. A call heard to his right left him frozen for a moment. He turned around again and thrust his sword out. *Silence. Nothing.* He thought of running across the road into the woods on the other side. His jaw clenched as reality hit him. *If it's Templins, it'll be no use. They'll be covering both sides of the road.* He knew all evidence pointed to his being followed. Heart pounding, he turned back around and moved forward toward the road. *If I can just make it to the road, maybe I can make a run for it. Come on, go!* He moved rapidly, watching his rhydid glow hot as fire and slice through small trees. He had no time to marvel when he reached the edge of the woods. Instead, he hoped to confuse his followers with his next move. He suddenly turned away from the villagers and ran back toward the approaching darkness.

He ran two miles until he realized it was becoming difficult to breathe. *The smoke.* He was facing it head on. He dodged into the woods on the other side of the road and stopped to catch his breath, clenching a hand against his chest in pain. His lungs burned like fire and his thoughts became foggy. Suddenly he was draped in darkness.

"My eyes; I've gone blind! The smoke has blinded me!"

"Yous sure about that?"

Joel reached forward and felt a cloth in front of his face. He pulled on it and saw a Templin cloak fall to the ground. He looked up and was shocked to see a group of familiar faces. All were staring at him with unfavorable expressions. Joel bit his lip then knelt down to pick up his cloak. "Uh, yeah, guess I deserved that."

"Yous deserve worse than that in my opinion. I think we shall send yous into Facilis with no clothes." Dillon raised his eyebrows at the others.

"Be quite a sight for his Augustine," another echoed.

"The Templins would like."

Joel stood to his feet. "Be too much of a sight for her, I'm afraid."

Dillon shook his head at him. "Yous are an idiot. Yous would have not made it without getting caught."

"Guess I was just gonna take my chances. I've slipped by them a few times now."

The grumpy group was unmoved by his response.

He cleared his throat. "But, extra cover is always good. I'm sorry. I . . . I made a mistake." He stuck his hand out to Dillon, but he didn't take it.

"What mistake, Joel? I want to hear it."

"Oh. Well, that Erin is clearly able to protect the villagers without you."

Dillon smiled faintly but maintained his steel gaze. "I mean it. Yous leave us in secret, and just after we talk about choices. Yous took our choice."

"You're right . . . I'm sorry. It seemed like the right decision. I don't . . . I don't know how to do this."

"How to do what?"

"Let you all give your lives for me, for this." He looked down at the rhydid.

"Joel, yous have the thickest head I ever know. We choose this. We choose yous. We choose the King." His eyes searched Joel's for understanding.

Joel held his gaze and nodded. "Forgive me?" He gripped Dillon's hand and looked to the others, who nodded their agreement.

Dillon smiled and released his hand. "Glad we found yous when we did. We are doing this for the villagers too. They need a leader, so we are protecting yous, Joel."

Joel sighed. "Suppose I need protecting at this point. Is the gate the only way into Facilis?"

"According to map, yes. I hear of some underground tunnels, but I know—" The young man went into a coughing fit.

Joel whacked him on the back. "It's the smoke. It's getting harder to breathe, even with it so far away."

"No time to find tunnels. Deadly smoke. What was yous plan?"

The group gathered around to listen.

"I've been timing the smoke. It's moving faster—half a mile every hour now. How much farther is Facilis?"

"Three and a half miles."

"It'll be there by late afternoon. If it's truly meant to bring me in, yet deadly at the same time, I figure the Templins will have to flee at some point."

"That is pretty risky. Yous shall be exposed to it."

Joel rubbed his chest. "We've already been exposed to it."

"True."

"I think between the smoke and the army fleeing that it'll be chaos, and I could slip inside. And now, with all of you, we can create even more of a diversion."

He was glad to see the group beaming back at him.

"It is still risky but the best chance of yous getting in . . . maybe they do not know . . . yous could—"

"What else are you thinking? You have something else?" Joel was open to suggestions.

"Yes . . . now that we are together. I think we should combine our resources near the gate. The West End *and* Differe's army will be watching. We can give them a show."

Joel smirked, knowing full well what resources he was referring to. "Exactly what I wanted to do in the first place."

"I see!"

Joel looked up and saw Ian high in trees above them.

Dillon glanced upward. "How many?"

His question was met with silence.

"Well, Ian, how many is the army?"

"Uh, too many to count."

Joel grimaced. "Great. Just great."

"They line both sides of the road, and the villagers are moving in one by one." The boy let out a hacking cough.

"Come on down, Ian. We need to move on." Joel felt the burning sensation in his chest moving into his eyes.

Dillon pointed at Joel's cloak they had thrown at him. "We shall take off the flashy stuff. We all need to look the same. We shall confuse them."

It was then Joel noticed they all had on their old Templin army cloaks with Galanne's red emblem marked out. "What did you do?"

"Black ink. It is fine. Probably wash out. Put yours on."

Joel was stunned. They had given up their last bit of dignity from their homeland for him.

"Your hat too, redhead."

Joel chuckled nervously. "Of course, so nice of you to remind me."

Dillon tipped his hat in response.

The group moved forward gradually, keeping watch on the darkness behind as well as the road beside them. As Joel pushed through the brush with the others, he thought back to walking along the edge of the woods by the frozen lake with Augustine. He glanced at his watch every few minutes to make sure they were keeping pace with the poison on their heels. The young men did their best to keep quiet, muffling coughs and wiping tears from their burning eyes. The Templins were now within their sight. Joel heard himself begin to wheeze. *This is terrible, but at least it will make them move.*

Joel felt Dillon grab his shoulder. "Look!" He pointed up ahead. "They are moving down the road."

"Perfect." Joel's voice had turned hoarse, and he glanced back at Dillon when he heard Ian start hacking again. The boy was coughing so hard that he appeared to be choking. Joel grabbed Dillon's cloak. "Come on, take him. You can leave now and be safe, Dillon!"

Dillon brushed Joel off. "I cannot. Yous need me for the plan."

"Screw the plan! It's not worth it."

"It is . . . yes, it is, Joel. I-I fine." Ian was speaking between gasps of air.

Instantly reminded of Sebastian, Joel searched the ground for the blue alabaster herb. Once each man had a bud in his front pocket, the group rallied to move forward again.

"Joel, army moving!"

Joel looked ahead and watched the soldiers retreat to the city gate. *How on earth are all twenty of us going to pull this off?* He lowered his voice so only Dillon could hear. "They'll probably arrest you for helping me. You really don't have to do this . . . not for me."

He jabbed Joel in the ribs. "Who says I am doing it for yous? I am just trying to impress Erin."

Neither smiled at his joke. "I'm not sure we can stay here much longer. I'm—I'm—" Joel's own coughing interrupted him this time.

Dillon handed him his container of water.

"Thanks. I'm not sure we can get as close to the smoke as I thought."

"No, we got to be strong. We got to wait it out. We shall move forward, but stay with the plan."

"But, Dillon—"

"Joel, the plan is all we got."

The group continued forward, just inside the woods, until the hordes of soldiers guarding the city gate were in full view. Something happened then that no one had expected. A steady south wind caused a shift in the timing of the approaching darkness. The eerie cloud was gaining speed. Joel shot his men a concerned look. "It's closing in." His chest heaved. *It hurts to breathe.* In a matter of minutes the cloud would be chasing them right into their enemy's arms. "Dillon, Dillon," he croaked, his eyes streaming with tears. "Let's make for the road. We'll bring it with us."

CHAPTER 37

AUGUSTINE PEERED DOWN at the sleepy square. It was still full of people, but most were sitting on the ground or standing quietly. The villagers seemed reluctant to leave, as did the ones who welcomed them. Augustine guessed why. *He's coming. They're waiting for him.* She'd expressed this thought to Earl as well. Shivers went up her spine as she saw the wall of black smoke approaching. She felt Jack put his head on her lap. The black dog seemed to know she needed comfort. She bent down, rubbed behind his ears, and kissed him. "You're a good friend." He licked her face in return.

Earl had assured her the lethal cloud wouldn't reach them, and as she looked at the people below she was grateful they had not been lost to the poison. *Looks like they've been through plenty.* She'd been scanning the crowd with the binoculars the last few hours in hopes of seeing her dear friend disguised among them. There was no sign of him. *I suppose that makes sense. If they're waiting around, it can only mean he's really not with them. Unless . . .* She turned to Earl, who was reading Mr. Rutherford's book. "Earl, do you think he's really here and they're hiding him? Do you think they're trying to throw the Templins off?"

He glanced up from the book, pursed his lips, and looked toward the road. "Uh, I don't think so." He dropped the book and reached for the binoculars.

Augustine squinted to see what he was looking at. Anger rose in her when she spotted a pack of Templins coming down the road. "It's like they're literally bringing that darkness with them. It almost looks as if they're enforcing it."

Earl handed over the binoculars. "They must have been hiding in the woods waiting for him."

She set her eyes behind the glass rims. "The smoke has driven them out." She focused in on the men and startled Jack when she stood to her feet. She removed the binoculars, looked out toward the road, then brought them to her eyes again. "Young ones. Very young, in fact."

"Something's going on. Look at the army below."

She removed the binoculars again, discovering the Differian army was gathering and stirring just outside the gate. She brought her lips to one side and decided to zoom in on the approaching group once more. They were quite young, some looked no older than Sebastian. The tall one in the middle stuck out to her. Something was familiar about the way he walked. *It's that slight swaying.* He ran his fingers by the sides of his hat, seeming to tuck up his hair. Then she saw the object in his hand. "Simon. I have to get to Simon."

"Put that up until yous need it. Gives yous away." Dillon clambered to stand in front of Joel's rhydid.

Joel grimaced at his own foolishness. What if they had arrows after all? He'd just made himself an easy target.

"Do yous think they fooled? Do yous think they see Templins?" One whispered from behind.

"Who knows, but I bet we look pretty threatening with the smoke behind us." Joel's voice cracked as he spoke.

Ian coughed beside him. "Yes, nothing like using enemy's own weapon against them."

Joel tried to smile. He knew his comrades were feeling the same pain in their bodies as he was. They marched in tempo with the smoke following just behind them. The group would have just enough time to pull off their scheme. Joel only hoped they wouldn't die in the process.

"Dillon, are you sure?"

Dillon nodded firmly. "Tell the men to stand outside the cyclone and make a run for it." He then turned to Joel, his eyes bloodshot and lips and face bitterly chapped from the nasty fumes. "I think we shall win, Joel, but just in case, serving yous is an honor."

A sound from the gate distracted them both. Joel's ears buzzed as he attempted to make out the words of the Templin standing in front of the army.

"Halt! Stop right there! Give up our fugitive, and we'll give you safe passage. We know you have him!"

"Do not respond." Dillon grabbed a handful of Joel's cloak to keep him from breaking away from the group.

Joel turned to him and pointed to his dead vocal chords. *Can barely respond even if I wanted to.*

The Templin called to them again.

His comrades stayed in line next to him. None even flinched. These boys were some of the bravest souls he'd ever known. Joel cleared his throat and leaned forward to get their attention. "Move forward." He could barely force the words out. "Move forward, then run for the gate in the chaos. Show the Facilis guards the Galanne badge inside your army cloaks."

Each eyed him nervously but nodded in obedience.

The Templins lining the gate kept shouting orders, but he couldn't hear what they were saying anymore. His hearing was fading. The Galannean troop spread forward as he and Dillon stayed side by side.

Dillon gasped for air as he reached under his clothes for the sacred stone.

"Listen to me, Dillon."

The young man squinted at him.

"Hold your breath until you break away from the cyclone."

Dillon motioned that he couldn't hear him.

Joel quickly gestured for Dillon to hold his breath.

Dillon nodded he understood.

The head Templin hadn't moved from his stance, but Joel saw the rest of the army beginning to back up. Just as the dark air drifted across their boots, Dillon swung his stone in the air, and Joel gripped the hilt of his rhydid. They had never used just their two weapons together, but both agreed it'd be enough to forge a way for them. *It has to work.*

Joel held his breath as the dark smoke engulfed them, working itself into a spinning frenzy. The normally shrill winds were faint to his ears. Their comrades stood just outside Dillon's masterpiece. Joel held up his rhydid and watched lightning pierce through the black cyclone to his sword's tip. He pointed the sword toward the Differian Army and moved away from Dillon. Lightning crashed down from outside the cyclone just over the army's heads. Just as the two had hoped, the winds followed the direction of Joel's lightning rod. He and Dillon rushed forward with the black spinning fog as his men sprinted toward the gate. Joel's lungs screamed for air as he and Dillon surged forward in the swirling winds. He had to breathe. He sucked in a gasp of toxic smoke just as Dillon stumbled. Joel rushed to his side. He placed his rhydid in the young man's free hand and forced him up.

Chaos was now in full force. It was a mess of black coats and gray cloaks running around like madmen. Some fled the gate in fear of the dark cyclone spinning toward them. Others were chasing Joel's comrades, while some Templins began fighting each other in the utterly confusing sea of coats. Joel and Dillon spun off in opposite directions. Dillon kept up the diversion with the rhydid and the stone. Now weaponless, Joel only saw one option. *Keep running or get caught.* Though they had succeeded in creating chaos, even causing a good portion of the army to flee from the gate, the Templin guards still appeared to be coming at him from all sides. The ones behind were catching up to his full-on sprint, and if they didn't catch him the ones coming from the left and right would snatch him before he reached the gate. His fingers fumbled as he undid the buttons on his cloak. He swung the strap of his bag from around his chest to his neck. The four Templins chasing him from all sides soon turned to eight then to sixteen. *I'm close. I can see where the gate opens.* He spotted the Facilis guards in their light blue coats just inside the gate. He squinted to see if they were letting his men inside, but the poisonous smoke blurred his vision. The gate ahead danced and shifted heights. Joel zigzagged his way towards it, partly from feeling disoriented and partly to confuse his pursuers. *But they know where I'm headed.* He was almost there when a voice distracted him, someone moving inside the gate.

He could barely make out the female voice. "Joel! Joel!"

The Templins closed in on him just a few feet shy of the gate. He was surrounded, and a blow to the head sent him sprawling to the ground. He pushed up from the concrete, ready to surrender. *I have no choice.* He peered between his capturer's legs as he struggled against more blows. Through blurred vision, he made out black flashes entering the gate and saw the Facilis guards, now bluish blurs, beckoning him forward. *Wait . . . they want me to win.*

He felt an arm being pinned behind his back and instantly clutched the other to his chest. Four Templins hovered over him as they brought him to his feet.

In one swoop with his free hand, Joel flung his bag over to the gate, distracting the Templin holding his arm. He fought loose as the two on his sides grabbed his cloak, which he shook off to break free. He dashed under the Templin's legs in front of him and rolled across the six feet between him and the gate. Hands quickly pulled him inside.

He frantically turned around to be sure he was safe, only to find the blurry blue uniforms standing in position before the Templins itching to get inside the gate. He smiled weakly, assuming their faces scowled at him for eluding them once again. His hearing, now muffled by the smoke or the blow . . . he wasn't sure, still made out the same voice that had called his name just before.

"Joel, Joel!"

He turned around to find a young woman pushing through the guards. She seemed familiar, but he wasn't sure who she was. She drew nearer yet became more blurry. He could hear her talking to him, but nothing was clear. He startled when she touched him. She stroked his arm, caressed his face, and seemed to be touching him all over. He gazed down at her in bewilderment.

Who is this woman?

She held him in her arms, and he in turn clung to her. She looked up at him and brought a hand to his face again. He felt her wiping away the tears from his burning eyes. *I'm safe. She's safe.* He rested his forehead against hers as his heart calmed and breathing slowed. When he pulled away he saw his blood smeared against her forehead.

"Oh." He lifted his hand to wipe away the stain. As his fingers met her soft skin, he bent down to make sure he got it all off. He didn't know if he was seeing things. As his face neared hers, his eyes studied her forehead then drifted to the only thing he could make out for sure—her penetrating blues eyes. His lips found hers just before he collapsed in her arms.

CHAPTER 38

AFTER ANDI REGAINED consciousness the night of his injury, he had made Arianna tell him what had happened in his absence.

"Why didn't you tell me the tax went up? That means you've had less money for food!" Andi grimaced, feeling remorse for having been so wrapped up in his work.

"What good would it have done? You were sending us all you could." She pressed a firm hand against his chest to lay him back down and proceeded to tell him about their mother contracting the nox disease.

He tried to comfort her, wiping away tears when she confessed to giving Lucy the salus venom. Andi tried to remain calm. "She—she looks well."

"Yes, she was better within the week."

"Does she know?"

"She . . . she doesn't say, but you and I both know she's no fool." Arianna lowered her head only to have Andi's tender hand lift her chin again.

He looked at her intently. *Could I have prevented you from making these choices? Oh, Arianna.*

"I learned to make the salus venom . . . even a few others. Suppose I became an apprentice of sorts, like you." She smiled at him.

He shook his head at her. "What's this about Marcell being involved?"

Her smile turned to a sly grin when he mentioned her boss's name.

Andi gripped her shoulders in a vice. "I'm gonna kill him—I'm gonna kill that spineless pig!"

"Stop! Stop it! What are you thinking?" She struggled against him. "It's not like that! He's given me a job! Andi, that's all, just a job. "

He only relaxed after she repeated the same lines again. "It's not a job—he's using you. He's using the drugs as a method of control. Can't you see that? He holds the drugs—the bargaining power to get what he wants from Differe's Army. You do realize he's using you to control those men?"

"He's allowing me to serve the New Order, Andi, the one my father disgraced. Come on, like you're not serving them to redeem our family name? You're doing the same thing as me, except I'm not casting stones. So quit judging me for the way I'm going about it."

Andi looked away from the bitterness in her eyes. The happy girl he'd left seemed to have had her soul stolen, and he couldn't help but wonder if he might be losing his own.

She let out a loud sigh. "I'll finish the rest of my story, but then it'll be time to tell yours."

"Fine."

"I'm not sure of the original purpose for Differe's Army being here, but after I met with Marcell that first time with Captain Myron, their numbers increased dramatically. They've been pouring into the forest on the east side of the river—hiding out—waiting for something . . . ."

"Something or someone?"

Arianna shrugged.

"Well, you have to know something. I mean, you've talked with them . . . since you're selling there. Are they serving the New Order or Differe?"

"I just give them the drugs."

Andi wasn't convinced. "Are you giving them fortis—making them stronger?"

"At first they just asked for common disease meds. Seemed most of their men had a difficult time adjusting to our climate. But, uh, yeah, then they started paying for fortis and others. A good bit of them also asked for placid. It's a calming drug. Something about silencing voices."

"I could use a dose of that."

"Anyway, now you know why I had to involve others. I needed help to keep up with the massive orders."

Andi was still having trouble putting all the parts of her story together. "Why does Marcell want to buy drugs from you and sell them to Differe's Army?"

A hint of guilt spread across her face. "Because they're addictive."

"I knew it! It's a power play, but it still doesn't explain what the Differians are doing here."

Her jaw clenched as she cracked her knuckles. "I think I can answer that. Marcell's been training a bunch of us . . . ."

Andi was not impressed. "In what? Dart throwing, perhaps?"

She bit her lip. "Among other things."

"Arianna, I don't like this . . . even if it is Marcell. Please, tell me what's really going on." He grabbed her hand, and his fatherly tenderness seemed to unarm her. "Did you . . . did you see something, like it was your imagination?"

Her face darkened at his questioning, and when she turned away he was sure of the answer.

"What happened? Arianna?"

Silence.

He leaned forward. "It scared you, didn't it?"

"Stop. I don't want to talk about it."

He reached out for her. "It scares me too, sometimes."

She pushed him away. "I DON'T WANT TO TALK ABOUT IT."

"It's a gift, you know." The two startled as their mother, Lucy, entered the cottage. "I suggest you lower your voice, Arianna."

Andi read kindness despite her scolding as she walked over and put a hand on Arianna's shoulder.

"Sorry, Mother. Are you feeling well?"

"Fine. What happened?" She looked at Andi sprawled on the couch.

He pointed to the dart. "I was mistaken for a Watchman."

"Oh dear! How's the pain?"

"Subsiding." He was thankful she didn't scold Arianna again, but he knew it wasn't in her nature to pile on guilt.

"Good." She looked around the little cottage then stared back at the two of them. "Well, I must say I'm a bit jealous. You've both had the opportunity to catch up on your lives."

Arianna shrugged. "Only me. Andi's said nothing about himself."

"Did too! I've been promoted to a member of the Order, Mother."

Lucy nodded slightly. "I'm glad for you, Andi, if that's what you want . . . but I'm confused. I'd think the Order would protect you from the Watchmen . . . not that you need it. The two at the house were petrified when they heard you come inside. Seems your apprentice training scores have given you quite a reputation."

"I'm confused, too, Mother. I don't want to lead the Watchmen to the Order, but I'm not sure how to contact any of the members."

Arianna stood up. "I can take care of that. I'll see Marcell in a few days."

Andi narrowed his eyes at her. "You meet with him regularly?"

She rested her fists against her hips. "Yes, I told you, for my training. Pharmacology isn't my only job."

Andi clicked his tongue at her. "Yeah, but you never told me what is. Training for what?"

"I'm training to be a Black Ferox. It's a special forces team for the Order."

Andi's brow furrowed suspiciously. "I don't believe you."

"I don't care what you believe. It's the truth. Here's the deal. Differe's joining us to take out Old Waiz. We're being trained to work alongside them."

Andi found the excitement in her voice revolting. "How many are you?"

"A lot."

"Mother, what do you think about this?"

Lucy folded her hands. "It doesn't matter. Your sister's old enough to make her own decisions."

Furious, Andi hurled his whiskey glass at the wall. "Mother, you can't be serious?"

Arianna gloated and kissed her mother's cheek. "I'll be back to check on you in a little while. Don't worry, Andi, I won't tell anyone you're here. I'll try to find out what Marcell wants you to do." She grabbed her bag and looked at the shattered glass on the floor. "Try not to make any more messes while I'm gone.

Andi watched in disgust as his sister left the cottage. He was relieved to see disappointment on Lucy's face. "Mother!"

"She made her decision the day she decided to pour that concoction down my throat."

Andi sighed and ran his fingers through his dark hair. "But it saved your life."

His mother's face softened as she brushed a curly lock from his forehead. "I'd always choose honor before compromise even if it meant death, Andi."

Anger burned against his sister as he thought about her selfish act. "Sorry, mother. I-I wish I would've known. I'd—I'd—"

"Have tried to save me? Tried to save her? Sometimes it's painful to let those we love make choices, but it's how we grow."

"She needs guidance."

"She's getting it from Marcell."

"Absolutely the wrong source!"

She appeared amused at his outburst. "Isn't he your boss?"

"Some boss. He's left me to be found out for some reason."

She looked down and patted his hand. "It's true then about Clovis? The Order must be proud of you."

He pulled his hand away and punched the couch. "Mother, how can you show no judgment? I killed someone."

She looked at him in surprise. "Wasn't it in the name of duty?"

He stared down at his hands. "I suppose . . . but it doesn't settle well with me now. It seems . . . wrong."

She lifted his chin and showed him a wry smile. "Then you clearly don't *need* my judgment."

Puzzled, he stared back at her face.

"What's more powerful? Me telling you what I think you did was wrong, or you coming to that conclusion on your own? Would you have really cared what I thought? Come now, what would you have said if I'd scolded you—a grown man?"

Andi brought his lips to one side. "I'd have been angry . . . defended myself."

She chuckled. "You know yourself pretty well."

He sighed. "Oh, Mother, what do I do now?"

She pulled something from her coat pocket. "For starters, read this letter from the Order. They dropped it off a few days ago."

"They didn't forget about me!" Relief washed over him until he saw his mother's look of disapproval. He down looked at the letter but didn't take it. His feelings were conflicted as he thought about the murder, Marcell, the drugs, Differe's Army, and his sister . . . *and Isabelle, the mysterious girl in Differe.* "I'll just wait to see what Arianna finds out from Marcell."

"Good, because I have something else you may be interested in reading." She slung the bag from her shoulder onto his lap. "Dig deep into it."

Andi obeyed until he grasped a leather bound book. The book was thick and bound tightly. He began untying the leather strips. "What is this?"

"Open it and see."

The pages were full of sketches, maps, and journal entries, but he didn't recognize the handwriting. He turned to the front and opened the inside flap. The book fell from his hands when he spotted his father's initials. He sat up and stared at the book on the floor. "I thought—I thought everything was burned. I-I didn't think any record of him was left."

"I didn't know the evils of the Order back then, but he did. Once he was ready to expose them . . . well, he became a target."

He was astonished. "Expose them? How?"

A hand pressed against her heart. "He found light."

CHAPTER 39

ANDI'S MOTHER WOKE him from a deep sleep as she fumbled with the door and shuffled inside the cottage. She removed the hood of his father's old cloak after placing a bag of food on the counter. He hadn't seen her wear it in ages. After the New Order dismissed them to the east side of the river, she wore it every time she went out. Andi also wore one, but it was to cover his scars. He'd always figured his mother's reasoning was due to the grief and shame she felt from his father's mistakes. But after reading the man's journal he wasn't so sure. He had devoured the book after his mother left him that day. He'd figured "light" was the same thing as "dirt." *And, boy was I right.* Like the murder he'd performed, his father had gotten dirt on the Order and had been ready to come clean. *Maybe I'm more like him than I realized.* He rolled over and ran a hand down his leg. "It's gone!"

His mother nodded from the kitchen. "Arianna took it out last night."

He rubbed his eyes. "I don't remember . . . she drugged me."

"Probably."

"What are you doing here? I told you I had plenty of food. It's dangerous for you to be here."

She waved her hands in the air. "Just bringing more food and supplies . . . if you want them."

He finally smiled at her. "Well, I am hungry."

"I'll make some breakfast."

He sat up and attempted to stand. He put all his weight on the good leg then slowly shifted to the other side. "Ouch!" The wounded leg was stiff and sore. *And it still feels numb.* He grimaced at the loss of sensation and pain when he took his first step. "Great. I've picked up a limp."

"Hopefully it'll get better. Perhaps the feeling will return once you've used it again. You're lucky—should've paralyzed the whole leg."

He shook his head in annoyance. "Seems a bit harsh, even for a thief."

"There's an antidote . . . but it's addictive."

He straightened and nodded in understanding. "Guess she knows me better than I thought."

"It would seem so . . . but do I?" She shoved a satchel bag toward him.

He raised his eyebrows at her and slowly opened the bag. He was surprised at its contents. "What's all this for?"

"It's the supplies I mentioned."

"Supplies?" He looked at her in disbelief. "To run?"

She looked to the stove and began to shake.

"Mother? Momma." He reached out and wrapped his arms around her. She laid her head on his chest and began to cry. He sighed. "Where would I run to? Old Waiz? Differe? The sea? There's no place for me to go. I don't have a choice. I can't run."

She clutched him tighter. "Oh, Andi."

He grimaced in understanding. "You don't think the Order will save me at the trial?"

She shook her head. "They might. But not truly . . . not for free."

"What do you mean?" He searched her tear-stained face.

"If they spare your life it will cost you. You'll owe them. And they will see to it you pay them back."

He somehow knew she was right but decided there was no use discussing it further. "You knew all along the New Order was in the habit of collecting souls, didn't you? Don't worry about me, Mother. Arianna. I'm more concerned about her. She's . . . she's gone."

"What's this about collecting souls?"

Andi faltered. "I don't know. Just seems like I'll be selling my soul if I consent to them any longer. There are things I'm beginning to feel deep on the inside . . . like something's trying to come alive . . . or break free." He sighed and held up his father's journal. "I think I'm going crazy."

His mother grabbed his face. "I wouldn't say that, especially if you're starting to feel 'alive.'"

"Whose side are you on, Mother?"

"On whatever side that keeps making you feel free."

He wiped another tear from her eye. "I meant to thank you for the book."

She looked down at the bag of supplies. "I'm afraid it's only served to fuel a fire, one that had already started in you."

He pulled away and gave her a curious look. "And how do you already know what I'm going to do?"

She playfully bopped his head. "I'm your mother!"

"Then you know I can't run. I don't have 'light,' but I have my integrity—"

"You mean pride."

"Yes, some of that too, with maybe some stubbornness mixed in. What a well-rounded man you've raised." She finally smiled again. It felt so good to break free from the tough persona of the apprentice trying to prove his worth to just being himself again. His mother's love had led him back to who he truly was. He grabbed her shoulders. "Momma, I can't run."

She smoothed the folds of his shirt. "Well, you at least don't have to face your enemy on an empty stomach. Let me get breakfast going."

He nodded and let her go. "Besides, I don't plan on facing them until I can get this leg stronger . . . but it's probably time I opened their letter. I figure I should see what they're expecting me to do."

She crossed her arms with a look of apprehension on her face. "Uh-huh, but not necessarily what you *will* do."

"But, of course." He opened the envelope and slowly unfolded his assignment. He eyes widened in disbelief. "I can't believe this!"

Just then the door burst open. "I got it!" Arianna bent over to catch her breath. "I got your orders! The members want you to turn yourself in. They want you to go to trial." She paused, surprised the two didn't seem the least bit shocked at her news. "Uh, it'll be the biggest scene in Waiz's history."

"Oh?" Lucy clasped her hands politely.

"Well, yes, it's the Ferox's first mission."
"The trial?"
"Yes, we're going to take out the Watchmen."

CHAPTER 40

LONG AFTER THE sun went down, Corwin and Sebastian ventured into New Waiz. Sebastian was mesmerized by the electric lights and loud streets. The array of colorful clothing, eclectic music, and delicious smells dazzled his senses. He was thrilled when Corwin picked him up and pushed through a crowd onto one of the partying streets. Sebastian eyed the stage of musicians blaring from the middle of the street as the crowd nearby danced wildly to the folksy tunes. Corwin shouldered past the stage to a shop called "Madame's Boutique." The music became muffled as the two entered the boutique, and Corwin put Sebastian back on the ground. He whirled around only to find himself among the frilliest looking clothes he'd ever seen. "Oh, my!"

Corwin chuckled until someone familiar walked up.

"May I help you with something?"

Sebastian instantly recognized the thick accent but was still shocked to see Madame Bontecou. She had been their guide at the Old Waiz Museum, and she also happened to be the largest woman he had ever laid eyes upon.

"Oh, Corwin! What a surprise. I hope it is a good one." She eyed him cautiously then spotted Sebastian. "Oh, hello there. Sebastian is it?"

Sebastian nodded quickly.

"You look well." She smiled at him and looked back at Corwin. "I had a feeling I'd be seeing you down here at some point."

Corwin cleared his throat and straightened his tunic. "Glad to see you've spanned both cities with your influence."

Sebastian held back a smirk wondering if "spanned" was a pun for her size.

She pursed her lips and folded her hands. "It has its benefits."

"I was hoping so."

Her eyes darted left and right. "Oh?"

Corwin lowered his voice. "Yes, I need your help."

"Of course." She gestured for them to follow her to the back of the shop. She stopped right outside a closed door. "You are welcome to use the box. Do you have the key?"

"Yes, I got it from Dade today."

She raised her eyebrows at them. "Impressive you could convince him, but I suppose Sebastian here revived his faith in you."

"And what about you, Charlotta . . . might you believe in me again?"

She looked away from him. "I-I cannot deny . . . I've seen the children . . . you're here now, so, yes." She bent down and stared at Sebastian. "Yes, I trust you. Perhaps . . . perhaps it was unfair before."

"How do you mean?"

She stood back up and faced him. "You weren't ready before, but . . . now, you're more than ready. I don't think anything will be able to stop you."

Sebastian saw a surge of confidence spread across Corwin's face.

Corwin took her hand. "Thank you."

She nodded quietly and unlocked the door behind them. She seemed surprised when Corwin didn't release her hand and go inside.

"I do need the box, Charlotta, but I need more than that from you."

She tilted her head and furrowed her brow as her brown eyes grew curious.

"If we're going to succeed in even reforming or being a force . . . then I want it to be a family affair this time."

Her brow slowly unfurled in bewilderment. "Wh-what?"

"Yes, I should've listened to you in the first place. It was a mistake to ignore you before. I'm—I'm so sorry. Please, do me the honor of joining the regime this time." He moved her hand between both of his.

She looked down at their clasped hands. "You're—you're serious? I-I don't know what to say."

"Say yes. Say you'll join me and you'll convince the rest of the women—the wives, sisters, daughters, and sons. I want everyone included this time."

Sebastian saw she still looked uncertain. "Madame Bontecou, I'm in it now, and I'm not even from Waiz. I'm just a kid, but look—I helped get Dade's key, and now you're even willing to let us use your box, though I have no idea what that means. Come on, join us . . . and please, when you recruit your women, or families, I'd like a few people my age."

She couldn't hold back a small giggle. "I, well, yes. I want this. Yes." She finally put her other hand on Corwin's. "Where to start?"

"How many can you convince to come tonight? I'm going to signal for 4 a.m."

"The tavern?"

"Of course."

Madame Bontecou shut her eyes tightly. "Okay, make it three, and we'll be there by four." She removed her hands from Corwin's and made room for them to go behind the door.

"Good. See you then." Corwin motioned for Sebastian to follow him.

By the way Madame Bontecou squeezed his shoulder when he passed by, Sebastian knew something big had just transpired. Something wrong had been made right. Corwin was ready. He wondered if his uncle would publically ask the group's forgiveness when they met, and if any of the old group would actually show up. Would they be as receiving and forgiving as Madame Bontecou? Would they hide like Mr. Rutherford? Would they be as unfriendly as Dade? He wasn't sure, but he knew Corwin must believe it was worth a try.

They made their way past boxes, mannequins, and clothing racks to the right side of the storage room. The walls bore no insulation and displayed the building's rows of pipes and wires. Corwin pointed to a small metal electrical box that Sebastian assumed was "the box." Corwin slowly opened it, revealing several rows of switches. The bottom of the box held a slot for a key.

"All right, Sebastian, we're about to signal the others." He pulled Dade's key from his pocket.

"How's it work?"

"This box isn't for the stretch of buildings on this street. It actually houses one of the main electrical lines for a good portion of New Waiz and Neutral Waiz. All of these switches can turn the power on or off at the workplaces and residences of the old league members."

"It's a signaling mechanism. The key allows you to move the switches."

"Exactly. Now, I just plan on flickering the power on and off. How many times do you think I should do it?"

Sebastian bit his lip and thought for a moment. "Oh, three. Three times, so they know what time to meet at the tavern."

"Right again." Corwin inserted the key and stood back. "Would you like to do the honors?"

Sebastian made out the tavern's outline from the torches lit near its door. "Corwin, how will Old Waiz know to come?"

"They won't. But I have a feeling several have fled like Haskell. We'll have to go ahead and meet then contact them afterward. They're more likely to agree to rejoin once the others have banded together again."

"Do you know what you're going to say?"

Corwin stopped walking and grabbed the side of a tree.

Sebastian waited for him to speak, but he said nothing. "Corwin?"

"No, I don't know, but it will come to me once I'm standing in front of them."

"How are you so sure?"

"I'm not, but it always worked that way before—I just had to be willing to take the first step." He sat down and leaned his back against the tree, beckoning Sebastian to join him. "May as well get some rest while you can. I don't want to go in until it's time. We indicated three to Dade, so we'll not trespass on his property a minute before."

Hours later, Corwin shook him awake. "Let's go."

Sebastian stretched from his sleep and rubbed his eyes. He was surprised when Corwin picked him up. "Stop, I can walk."

"You'll need some help." Corwin carried him off the main road and away from the tavern.

"What are you . . . where are we going?" Sebastian, now wide awake, cringed before he asked his next question. "You—you aren't leaving are you?"

"No, but we don't use the front door for our meetings. That would be foolish." He turned onto the road that housed the back of the hotel where Joel had been seen the day of the murder. A short walk later he rounded to the back of an old barn down the street. He slid the barn door open and put Sebastian down. "Sorry, I guess you could've walked that part, but I needed to be extra quiet. I don't want to be noticed, let alone followed."

Sebastian knew he was referring to his squeaky leg braces and understood. Even the drowsy animals seemed to hear him follow Corwin into an empty stall. "Sorry, guys, go back to sleep."

Corwin swept hay and dirt away from a circular frame. The man bent over and slid a round metal lid across the ground, revealing a black hole in the stall's floor.

"Wow! A tunnel!"

"Let me get in first. Then I'll help you down." The opening was barely big enough for Corwin to fit through, and once underground he turned to help Sebastian begin his descent. Once both were safely inside, Corwin climbed back up the metal ladder and pulled the lid back over the entrance. It was pitch dark in the tunnel until Corwin pulled a light out.

Sebastian couldn't determine the source of the light. "What is that?"

"Later." The man then put a finger to his lips and picked him up again.

Sebastian wondered what the need for silence was, but he didn't question his guide. As he was carried along, he noticed old burnt torches hanging on the tunnel walls, but none were lit. It was damp and dripping like the Waiz train platform at Crossroads Station, except this tunnel went many directions. Corwin eventually stopped at one of the ladders and started climbing with Sebastian on his back. Moments later they were inside Dade's tavern. The place was empty. Corwin checked his watch and Sebastian grimaced. Then Corwin's light went out.

CHAPTER 41

"YOU ALWAYS WERE early. Give me a hand with these."

Sebastian squinted and made out Dade's silhouette from across the room. He was pulling dark tarps down over the windows. He stopped and pointed toward the tunnel. "Did you leave it open?"

"Yeah. Sebastian, go around the bar and set out some glasses. I'll help Dade finish the windows." They worked in silence until the clock chimed three.

Dade moved over to the bar. "No one's here."

Corwin thumped him from behind. "We're here."

"True." The man grabbed a barstool and offered one to Corwin.

Sebastian smoothed his hair back and grinned. "Something to drink, gentlemen?"

"Black coffee for me." Corwin playfully saluted him.

Dade nodded as well. "Me too. Mugs are in the cabinet behind you. Coffee's back on the stove."

Sebastian stood on his tiptoes to grab two mugs then hobbled over to the flaming stove. He filled up the mugs and set the black kettle back on the stove, banging as he did so. He was startled by the noise but noticed he didn't spill a drop of liquid. He set the mugs on the bar and heard the clanging again. This time he realized he wasn't the culprit. His head swiveled toward the tunnel. There was a dim light, murmuring voices, and a few more bangs.

"Hurry up. It's open!" Someone shouted from the bottom.

Sebastian's jaw dropped as twenty men near Corwin's age began exiting the dark hole. His hands shook as he handed Dade the coffee mug and found that Corwin had vanished.

One man grabbed a stool next to Dade and smiled at Sebastian. "I'll have some of that."

"Me, too, friend," came another.

Soon Sebastian was pouring a dozen or more cups of water and coffee for the men. He was shocked to see around fifty more had poured into the room a few minutes later.

"Darn tunnel backed up with the lot of us. Sorry we're late," one motioned to Dade.

"Suppose it takes us longer than it used to anyway," another cracked.

"No worries." Dade joined Sebastian in serving the men and grabbed his arm when both had their backs turned to the bar. "Where's your uncle?"

Sebastian bit his tongue. "Uh, don't worry. He hasn't chickened out. I'm—I'm sure he just wants to make an entrance."

Dade sent him a wary glance then motioned to one of the men. "Everyone's here. Cover the entrance."

The man went to move the cover when suddenly a yell came from below. "Wait! Wait, please!"

The old Thaddean Army looked around at each other, trying to discern who was still missing. An older man emerged and was immediately followed by someone else, someone young.

The member holding the cover looked at the older man in shock. "Gage! What are you doing?"

The older man wiped his brow nervously. "Bert, I-I can explain."

"You'd better. How dare you bring a Watchman here!" Bert dropped the hole cover and started toward the young man until Gage blocked his way.

"What have you told him? What does he know of us?"

Dade rushed past Sebastian. "Stop, Bert! Give the man some room and a chance to explain."

"Yes, it's true, men. I brought my son with me tonight. Gideon's a Watchman, but he doesn't serve the New Order. He refuses to have ties with them. He chooses to serve New Waiz alone. He's . . . he's a good man. He's served the Kendrew name well."

The room went completely silent, giving the man the floor.

"He has information that we need about Marcell, Differe's defensive tactics, and those blasted Templins snooping around harassing our members in Old Waiz. He's come to help us."

Bert shook his finger in Gage's face. "For a price, I bet. You want information about us, don't you? How do we know he's not serving both sides—a spy?"

The young man stepped out from behind his father. "I swear to it. I'll swear to it by blood . . . on the Kendrew name." Gideon pulled his knife from his pocket.

"That won't be necessary, Watchman Kendrew. I know a spy when I see one."

Sebastian watched as the entire room transferred their attention from the Kendrews to the staircase behind the bar.

"It was good of you to bring him, Gage."

"Er, thank you, Sir."

Sebastian finally turned around. No one moved as a hooded Corwin, looking much like the "brown heap" he'd first seen him as in Crossroads Station, walked down the stairs.

"I thank you all for coming tonight, or this morning . . . whichever suits you."

The group of seventy men eyed Corwin then looked at their neighbors in confusion.

"I believe Waiz needs us again. I'm sure you saw or heard the news about Clovis's murder. It appears our old leader's son is to blame . . . or perhaps he was framed."

The room gasped, and Sebastian wished Corwin would hurry up and remove his hood. The suspense was almost too much.

"None of us can deny Differe's growing presence here. Between the Templins and the soldiers, something's brewing. But these dangers are not my real reason for calling this meeting tonight. It was time for me to do something." Corwin stopped to clear his throat.

"Who are you?"

"That will become evident soon enough. First, I wanted to tell you how humbled I am to be in the presence of such great men. Your allegiance to our league, each other, and your families is truly remarkable." Corwin stepped off the last stair and sighed. "I didn't realize what I had years ago in all of you. Truth is . . . you all believed in me. I knew it. I felt it. But the reality was . . . I didn't believe in myself. So for the second time in my life I wanted to run away from Waiz. This time, with no leader to stop me, I succeeded."

No one stirred as Corwin stepped toward the bar.

"A day doesn't go by that I don't regret leaving you . . . abandoning you. The wake I left was so great it destroyed this union. So, first things first, I've gathered you all here to ask your forgiveness for my actions. I pray you show me grace I don't deserve . . . for now, I'm ready. The time is here. I'm ready to serve you—to serve Waiz."

Sebastian heard the quick intakes of breath as men beside him began to catch on. A chorus of whispered exclamations swept through the crowd.

"It can't be!"

"Wouldn't dare show his face here again."

Sebastian listened to the murmurs around him and silently willed the men's hearts to soften. *Just hear him out.*

"I do deeply regret my actions regarding you men; however, I do not for one minute regret having gone to meet my—my—" The man seemed to falter. "To meet my family."

Sebastian was all smiles when his uncle turned to face him.

"You questioned Gideon, but did none of you notice the youngest person in the room?"

Sebastian felt himself turn red as all eyes in the room fixed on him.

"Gentlemen, I want you to meet my amazing nephew. His name is Sebastian."

Silence lingered for a moment, then frantic whispering broke out among the men.

Gage was the only one brave enough to move toward him. "Corwin?"

No one breathed as the man removed his hood and turned to face the group.

"Corwin!"

"Corwin Atticus!"

"It's the old spy!"

Chapter 42

THE REVELATORY SHOUTS in the tavern quickly turned ugly.

"This is why we're here?"

"I'm leaving!"

"Why should we ever trust you again?"

"We don't need a leader!"

Bert's accusations soon became loudest. "How did you get the key?"

Dade stepped beside Corwin. "I gave it to him."

"Why? Why on earth would you do such a thing?"

"Because!" A man from the back of the tavern stood up and began walking toward Corwin. "Because we need a leader. Nothing has happened since ours left. Come on, men." He gazed around the room. "We haven't even met, yet three flickers and we're here again. All of us knew Dade had the key, but . . . but none of us ever did anything. No one took the lead." The man stopped in front of Corwin, and Sebastian was shocked to see it was Haskell Rutherford. "I believe that's because the role of leader was always meant to be yours. We need you." He turned to face the group again. "And, Waiz needs all of us."

Haskell stuck out his hand while the rest of the men absorbed his words. "Corwin, I forgive you, Brother. Welcome back."

The moment was powerful. Corwin's eyes were teary as the two men shook hands and embraced.

"If Haskell can forgive you, then I can too." Dade put a hand on his shoulder, and Corwin nodded at him.

Other group members began stepping forward, whereas Bert and a few others didn't budge. Half an hour later the room was still divided regarding taking Corwin back as leader; however, all had agreed to reform the league.

Bert crossed his arms. "I think we should debate for a while."

The group even argued whether that was a good idea. A solid knock on the tavern's back door shifted their focus.

Corwin walked toward the door. "You can debate as long as you want, but the rest of my league is here, and I intend to get started."

Bert chased after him. "What do you mean? Who else have you invited without our permission?"

Corwin put his hand on the door handle. "Dade gave me this space tonight, Bert. You can stay and join us or find another place to meet. Oh, and, gentlemen, be sure to give up your seats if necessary."

Sebastian burst into laughter at the sight of women and children entering the den of men. The old league was in shock while the women coming in droves beamed like Corwin's light. The most satisfying moment was watching Bert's wife approach the man.

"What's the meaning of this?" His rigid stance fell when she kissed his cheek and a young boy embraced him.

Madame Bontecou was the last to enter, and Sebastian supposed Corwin's action then began to make some sense to the old league.

"Welcome." He gave her a slight bow.

She nodded her thanks.

"You are brilliant. Were you seen?"

"No. We came from the woods. Couldn't use the tunnels. Don't know the way."

"We'll teach you."

"Corwin, what's going on? We need an explanation." Bert stood by his wife, holding her hand, and his tone was much more civil.

Gage stepped up and put a hand on his son's shoulder. "I get it. Stronger in families."

Corwin chuckled. "That, and we're not getting any younger. I should've listened to Charlotta long ago."

The rest of the men seemed to understand. The crammed room became quiet again. It was evident the people were ready to meet, ready to listen to their leader. All except one.

"Bert? Have you reached a verdict?"

He looked at his wife and children then nodded in Corwin's direction. "You've got us."

"Good. Again, thank you all for coming. Thank you for leaving the past behind so we can move forward. We're all a good deal changed since the last time we met, so let's drop all expectations and assumptions of one another. Think well of each other. Take some time over the next few days to get to know one another again. Let's begin with you, Gideon. Tell us what you know."

The young officer moved to the front of the bar next to Corwin. "Well, I mostly patrol by the Valtina Sea near the bottoms. You'd think my low ranking would mean the Order wouldn't fool with me, but there's been quite a bit of activity going on down there."

"Like what?" A voice interrupted.

Gideon stopped until Corwin nodded at him. "Go on."

"What I mean to say is, I've been made privy to a few New Order meetings. I didn't realize the council and the Order were two different things."

"Yes, 'the council' is a fake—simply paid to show up and say whatever they're told."

A chorus of uproars rang out in the room. Corwin waved his hand at the group. "Gentlemen, please let Gideon continue."

"The activity I mentioned is happening more on the east side of the river. There's the usual riffraff with beggars and scoundrels tearing up properties, gambling, but I started noticing lots of activity near the bottoms bridge across the river. No one really uses it. I mean, the only people that even go to that side of the river do so just to hunt or fish. But I . . . I began to see a large number of individuals crossing the river after dark and coming back hours later. It didn't sit right with me. First, they wore all black leather, and, second, when they returned they seemed, well . . . different."

Corwin jumped in. "Different how?"

"Harder, intoxicated . . . yet not. It was strange, but I obviously had enough sense to realize something wasn't right. So, I decided to disguise myself as one of them."

The room held its breath in anticipation.

Gideon eyed the group of women and children and bit his lip. "They, uh, this group is buying medicine. Very strong and addictive medicine."

"Who's their leader?"

"They said Marcell; however, that's not all that will interest you in this matter. They're not the only buyers."

Corwin closed his eyes in dismay. "Differe."

Gideon nodded. "Yes. Apparently you've noticed them on the east side."

Bert stepped forward. "Are they bringing the medicine in?"

Gideon shook his head. "No, it's very much homegrown. Differe wouldn't have access to it—they can't. It's—"

"We'll talk on that later. What happened in the Order meeting you were taken to?" Corwin shot Madame Bontecou a concerned glance then nodded to Gideon.

"As silly as it sounds, I think the Watchmen are being watched. Whether it's by Differe or the New Order I can't say. There are plenty on either side. Now, these are strictly my suspicions, but the questions they asked me . . . well, I'm getting ahead of myself. First, Marcell came to my post at the bottoms and asked if he could meet with me in secret. I obliged him, of course, but he insisted I be blindfolded and gagged. Alarmed as I was, I still trusted him. I was questioned once I arrived in the dark room."

"About being disguised?" Sebastian hadn't meant to open his mouth, but he was so intrigued.

"No. I only disguised myself after the meeting—I was plenty suspicious afterward. They questioned me about the Watchmen—our hideouts, meeting places, numbers, shifts . . . every possible question they could ask about our task force, they did. And, of course, I answered. I had no reason to believe I shouldn't. After all, Marcell is technically our leader."

All the men nodded in understanding, but Haskell gripped the side of the bar. "They're studying you for a reason. I don't like this."

"The last question they asked was if I knew of the activities happening down at the bridge."

Bert clenched his fists. "What did you say?"

"That was the first time I sensed something wasn't right, so I said nothing of what I had seen so far. Of course, he thanked me for leading the Watchmen in my area—you know, keeping Waiz safe, and that's about it. One thing I did overhear, though, is that Marcell plans to bring in a diplomat from Differe. Uh, Langston is his name. He's a pretty high up general for their army, and a Templin as well. His reputation precedes him, but that's all I know."

Corwin's eyes glanced toward the ceiling. "Just as I suspected. Differe will be involved in the war between our cities."

CHAPTER 43

GIDEON, THAT WAS most insightful. Thank you for your help." Corwin bowed his head at him and turned to Mr. Rutherford. "Haskell, what happened with the Templins?"

The man straightened the red glasses on his face. "Well, they started snooping around right before they dropped off the letter for Joel."

Dade leaned between them. "Who's Joel?"

"The redheaded kid who killed Clovis."

"He did not!" Sebastian shot Bert a stern look.

Corwin didn't try to hide that he was annoyed. "Enough. Continue, Haskell. And, please, no more interruptions!"

"Right. Well, I wasn't sure who they were until I saw their emblem on the back of the envelope. I figured Joel was from Differe, but not necessarily the temple. From there it's simple, really. They asked to use my shop as a stakeout to catch him. I left after that . . . they would've taken it over anyway." He shrugged.

Madame Bontecou held her wide hips. "You have some explaining to do about that young man."

"I'll say." Haskell nodded.

Corwin motioned for Sebastian to come around the bar. "Yes, I do. To give you some insight, I'll let my nephew help me. Thaddean Army, I want to properly introduce my nephew, Sebastian Bennett."

257

Sebastian hobbled forward, and murmurs rippled throughout the room.

"Shh. Yes, it's true. I actually did go to Differe long ago. Sebastian's proof of that. We happened to meet Joel at Crossroads Station in Differe. He'd just escaped from The Temple of Differe School."

"What a feat!"

"Yes, he's quite remarkable, as you'll soon discover. Sebastian has some documents Joel brought with him from the temple. I'd like for him to share them with you. I'll go grab them from our bags."

Sebastian felt his heart begin to race as Corwin left the room.

Dade cocked his head and tapped his lips. "Well, why don't you tell us about yourself while we wait on Corwin."

Sebastian swallowed hard. "Uh, well, I grew up in Differe, as most of you already know." He looked into their hard eyes and took a deep breath. "My family's one of the 'unfortunates' . . . or that's what Differian society calls us. My parents work in factories from dawn til dark."

"What kinds?"

"All kinds. Anything we export. They do whatever the government tells them—where, when, and how much to work."

Madame Bontecou sent him an encouraging smile.

"I've been sickly ever since birth, spent my entire life being cared for by my sister, Augustine. She's, uh, she's half-Waizen."

"Your half-sister, then."

He started to protest, but Corwin tapped his shoulder and handed him the scrolls. A surprising authority washed over him as he unraveled the parchment. "All right, listen up. Joel probably stole these from the temple. This is the only one I've figured out so far. The others will take more time. First, these scrolls are old. Looks like the initial settlers brought a bunch of these from Waiz when the regions were being claimed. I'm just gonna assume you all know your history."

He hesitated and looked at Corwin. The man winked, and Sebastian flipped the parchment around to show the group the scroll. Three fourths of the page held writing while the last bit was a drawing. He looked down at the scroll and began to read.

"So was given to the region of Differe, the rhydid. Though in the shape of a sword, it holds many powers besides combat and precision. Unlike the sacred stones, tenehs, and bariques given to the other regions, the North Corner was given a weapon that provokes violence. It seems our object is the only one whose owner has the choice to use it for good or evil. Should men be given such a choice?"

Sebastian paused to look up at the group. He licked his lips then continued.

"Even the councils of Waiz agree that not just any man should have such a choice, as the rhydids have only been passed to noblemen and their generations. We fear evil is spreading across the regions with the black carriers being spotted daily.

Do they mean the black birds, Corwin?" When he got a nod, he went on.

"And the winters lingering—"

"They were never supposed to linger. People were never supposed to survive such climates." Haskell glanced at Sebastian's braces and nodded sadly. "Oh, sorry. Go on."

"Our fear of evil is greater than our trust in the goodness of men. In faith, we choose to remove our allegiance to and alliance with Waiz and the Majestic. Our future rests on man's choices, so we choose to limit ours. Waiz and the other regions respect our decision to withdraw and change our region's name to Differe. Our name change symbolizes that our allegiance is to no one but our people. Even the finest of men can choose evil, so we will destroy all existing rhydids in Differe except for the Holy One's, the leader of the Temple of Differe, who guides and trains our people in goodness and holiness. The last rhydid will be kept safe in the temple chapel where truth will now be worshiped in place of the Majestic. All remembrance of rhydids and Waiz will be forgotten to ensure our people live on in safety. Furthermore, to keep the rhydid protected, we have called on the master of the white bear to cast a spell over the object. A person may only remove the rhydid if he carries the bloodline of the King of Waiz himself. Below is a drawing of the proposed rhydid placement."

Sebastian finished, and Dade pushed a cup of water for him across the bar.

Haskell handed him the cup. "Well, Sebastian, that certainly clears up some questions about Differe's past, but what does it have to do with Waiz now?"

"According to this, Differe has fought for well over a few hundred years to wipe Waiz from their memory. What's causing them to come back . . . send in troops, Templins, and even a diplomat?"

Dade eyed the families. "They want the drug."

Corwin shook his head. "I don't know. There's a spell on that rhydid, and it takes a spell to make the drug. You who've heard my story understand what I'm saying. Both sides are dipped in evil."

Bert stepped forward. "Gideon, I think your Watchmen are in Marcell's way."

Gideon cast him a nervous look. "You might be right, but I thought Differe was here because the New Order asked them to help fight Old Waiz. If that's the case, Marcell needs the Watchmen . . . I'm confused."

Dade waved his hands at them and pointed back to Sebastian. "Okay, Sebastian, get to the point. Why has Differe decided to acknowledge Waiz again? We know it's not out of the goodness of their hearts."

Madame Bontecou spoke before Sebastian could answer. "I think it's the boy, Joel."

"Who is this boy?"

Corwin exchanged a glance with Madame Bontecou then returned his eyes to the crowd. "As I said, Joel is from Differe. He escaped from the temple after being tormented by the faculty as well as the mouthpieces. He came here in faith, hoping Waiz was real and could help him. After being attacked by the black carriers in the Marcell House, he climbed Mount Waiz and found a caychura. When I found him there, he was wrapped in chains. I used my rhydid to cut him loose, and when we left all the poisoned holes had vanished."

The place fell into hushed amazement at Corwin's words.

Madame Bontecou clasped her hands. "Who is he really, then?"

"I sent him with Augustine to retrieve the sacred rhydid."

More gasps followed as her eyes widened. "You—you think he's related to the king?"

Corwin gritted his teeth. "I don't know . . . but I knew the spell was cast in fear. Joel faced his fears in going back . . . perhaps that was powerful enough to break the rhydid spell. I-I can only hope I was right."

Sebastian looked at him in shock.

"If I can meet with the new diplomat . . . he's a Templin, he will know for sure. I want to help Joel in any way I can. After all, he has my niece."

"This can't be true! The king's relative from Differe? It doesn't make sense." Bert wasn't buying it.

Madame Bontecou finally stood. "So, as I said earlier, the boy—Differe didn't want him to escape . . . especially to Waiz."

Gideon rubbed his head. "I still don't understand. Differe joining New Waiz in taking over Old Waiz, Templins wanting drugs, Marcell taking out the Watchmen, Differe wanting this Joel character—which is it? How can we even make a plan?"

Haskell rubbed his bald head. "I agree. There are too many questions. We need a basic strategy until we know more."

"All right, what about the new diplomat? Let's start there. How do we get to him?" Dade looked around the room.

"I could get us into one of the parties."

"I could get into his hotel."

"I could take him on my boat."

Bert waved his hands. "Too risky, all of it. He'll have Green Cloaks and Differian Guards crawling all over him."

Corwin nodded. "I agree with Bert. We need something political or enticing. I want to put him in our favor . . . or better yet, our debt."

"All rings true. My own flesh and blood has succumbed to it." A quiet voice from the staircase grabbed the room's attention.

A woman was standing above them. Her dark hair and pale face made Sebastian think she was a ghost for a moment.

"Lucy!" Corwin rushed to the bottom of the stairs.

"Have you thought about the possibility that it's all true? The boy, the alliance between New Waiz and Differe, the Watchmen—deceit is running rampant between all parties. They're bound to fall. As your young Kendrew warned of secrets, it's best not to hide anything from one another anymore." She took a step toward Corwin. "The darkness has been stirred, Corwin. That's what your Sebastian was trying to say. The alliance on the surface may appear political or perhaps just a military tactic, but beneath the surface the tie is darkness. Evil is brewing . . . just like you saw long ago." She peered out at the crowded room. "The evil is brewing right here in Waiz. A greed for strength and power seeded and gave root here, so Gideon is right—the drug is homegrown. And, Differe would like nothing more than to determine how to plant it among themselves. However, Differe clearly has its own spells. They are very good at control, as you heard from Sebastian. They desire to limit choices. Fear, control, and greed are powerful weapons—when used together some might say . . . unstoppable."

Sebastian could hardly breathe as the woman took another step.

"But the truth has been revealed, and you all know what that means . . . ." She cocked an eyebrow at the group, but none responded. "Hm. Never mind, then."

Sebastian heard a touch of disappointment in her voice. She had almost reached Corwin but turned her gaze to the Kendrews.

"Gideon, I have news for you and your Watchmen. And, Corwin, I know how you can get to Langston." She slowly pulled an arrow quiver from behind her back.

It was empty so no one made a fuss.

Corwin instantly understood her gesture. "Andropolis. Yes . . . it's the best way."

This was followed by a roomful of cries about the young's man treachery and involvement in the New Order.

"Stop! He's Thad's son. He's had no choice but to believe what he's been told." He reached toward Lucy.

She smiled and held the quiver out to him. "He's ready. He's seeing. And, oh how he needs you."

Corwin took the quiver but kept one hand on hers. Sebastian barely made out his next words. "I do know what you mean . . . truth has been revealed. It brings a freedom that no amount of darkness can shut out."

She touched his face. "And what is truth, dear Corwin?"

"Truth is a person."

CHAPTER 44

JOEL GROGGILY PEERED around the white sterile hospital room. "Was there a woman here earlier?"

The doctor writing on his clipboard nodded. "She hasn't left your side. She's waiting out on the lunch terrace."

Joel rubbed his head as he slowly sat up. "How long have I been here?"

"About a week. Whatever was in that smoke nearly killed your senses."

He was starting to remember now. The black smoke, the villages, Dillon. "My men!" He startled, then winced in pain.

"Easy. Your insides are still healing from the toxins." He placed a hand on Joel's shoulder. "Your men . . . all of them are fine. They've been pretty worried about you. You had the worst of it."

Joel gripped the side of the bed to steady himself. "Dillon?"

"Yes, he had a bad case. Not as bad as yours, but he's recovering well. They've all been alert for several days."

"Differe?"

The man shrugged and scribbled more notes on Joel's record. "Well, there's lots to say there, but they weren't as lucky as you and your comrades—lost several units of men. I think they've all headed back to Differe."

"To prepare their revenge."

"Perhaps, but you shouldn't worry yourself with that now. The city has agreed to protect you."

Joel sighed, greatly relieved at this and the news of his men.

"Why don't you try some clear liquids for today? Water and soup."

Joel nodded. He felt hungry enough to try anything.

The doctor put his clipboard down and lowered the railing on Joel's bed. "Want to try to get on your feet?"

Joel nodded again. He stood with the doctor's help, glad to find the floor was steady under his feet.

"Very good." The man grabbed his papers and crossed his arms. "Some fresh air would do you good. The smoke isn't inside the city. I'll have your lunch sent to the terrace."

"Sounds good."

"I'll send a nurse to help you get ready."

Joel fussed at the nurse who helped him dress but soon realized how weak he was. "Thank you," he finally muttered when she was done.

Joel squinted as the sunlight hit his eyes. He stepped onto the terrace and looked around for the woman who was to be his lunch date. He gazed over to the far right and saw a dark-haired beauty standing next to the wall. The dark tresses cascading over her shoulders held a white flower with leaves the color of her long pale green dress. As he studied her further, elation spread deep within him. *Augustine! She's safe!* His heart beat faster as he moved closer, and all the weakness he'd felt a moment earlier was replaced with vigor. His hospital slipper scuffed just as he was within her reach.

"Oh, you're up!"

He smiled as her eyes widened in delight then looked him over in concern.

"How do you feel?"

"Pretty good. Hungry." He moved closer and grabbed her shoulder.

She threw her hand onto his forearm. "Well, leave me again, and I'll kill you myself."

Joel grinned and nodded. "Fair enough."

The two stared at one another in silence as the moment passed between them.

Augustine eventually looked down and slid her hand from his arm up to his neck. When he felt her other arm reach up to embrace him, he wrapped his arms around her and pulled her gently toward him. He closed his eyes as he took in her embrace. He felt her warmth, her soft skin, her petite curves, and her arms tighten in a squeeze around him. He softly squeezed back, and she laid her head on his chest. Afraid she would hear his furious heartbeat, he quickly pushed her away. "Don't crush the little flower in your hair."

Augustine lifted her head and laughed. She reached her hand back to touch the little bud. "I'm sure it's fine. We little flowers are stronger than we look."

Joel reached up to touch the flower and moved his face in front of hers. She was close enough to kiss. *And, I want to.* As he stroked her face, she smiled up at him, and he suddenly remembered. *It was her! She was the woman calling my name! I did kiss her. I kissed her the day I got here.* The revelation suddenly made him feel exposed. Though she didn't seem to mind his actions, uncertainty overtook him and he pulled away. He looked down at his hands to avoid seeing her reaction.

The awkward silence that followed wasn't something he expected. *I need to sit down. I need to see my men. What's going on with me?*

"Have you seen the city? Here, take a look." Augustine moved out of his way so he could peer over the terrace wall.

Joel was glad for the view but was more interested in food at the moment. He took a quick look then moved to a nearby table. "It's beautiful. Almost like a sunny green Differe. The buildings are magnificent."

Augustine sat down across from him. "I thought that too. Suppose the place is a haven for us."

"Feels like a prison to me. I'm stuck here." His head was beginning to throb.

"I think that'd be the case wherever we are. The mouthpieces, the Templins—they're everywhere. From now on, freedom will be what we make it."

Joel rubbed his head. "Yeah."

She reached across the table and took his hand. "Are you all right? Can I get you anything?"

He didn't return her sweet smile. He avoided her gaze altogether, confused about his emotions and the signals she was sending. She was not the bratty teenage girl he had met at Crossroads Station anymore. "Augustine, I'm glad you're safe, but I'm not happy to see you . . . not in Facilis." He could tell his words stung as a scowl crossed her face. "Why aren't you in Waiz?"

"Lunch is here!"

Augustine secretly rejoiced at the nurse's interruption. She didn't want to answer Joel's question . . . not with the truth. She could've gotten to Waiz by way of the Southern Regions just days before he had arrived. Earl had told her it was the only way with Differe blocking the trains through the rest of the regions. *But I didn't go.* Corwin and Sebastian were probably camping out in the cave by now and seriously worried about them. *I chose to stay.* She looked at the redhead in front of her. *And it's your fault.* She had even risked staying after Earl told her he thought the smoke had subsided enough for her to get into the Southern Regions if she used her rhydid. Joel had just arrived two days before, and most of Differe's Army had retreated. And she'd almost been brave enough to leave—that is, until Dillon recognized her.

"Yous—yous are the one! Joel's Augustine!" The young man grabbed the hand that was gently sponging sweat off his forehead.

"Shh. Lay back now."

"I see yous with Joel!"

Augustine put the sponge back in the cool water and bit her lip. *Saw me? He couldn't have seen the kiss . . . could he?*

"Hungry."

"Yes, I'm getting your dinner." Augustine prepared to feed the young man just as she had done for the rest of Joel's comrades. "Here's some soup. I'll help you eat it."

"Yous Augustine."

She held up a spoonful of soup and nodded. "Yes, how do you know that?"

"Yous are beautiful."

She slightly rolled her eyes at his flattery. "Did Joel mention me?"

He broke into a severe cough before he could answer.

She patted his back. "It's from the smoke, but it should get better. Here, have another spoonful."

The boy waved his hand. "Stop. Wait. Yes, yes, he mention yous several times."

Augustine froze. "Oh . . . and what did he say?"

"He share his story."

"Oh, I see."

"He shall be glad yous are safe. I-I am sorry he was late. My fault." The young man took her hand.

"Beg your pardon?" She tried to pull her hand away.

"He . . . he did want to come straight here—to be with yous—but we keep him. He was the leader and helping us and the villages."

She sat the bowl down. She ignored any romantic feelings and commanded herself to think logically. "Oh, well, he would've helped either way. He's like that. A magnet for people who need help."

Dillon chuckled through coughs. "I think yous are right, but yous always seem to be on his mind."

"Hmm."

"That is how I know your name."

Augustine shook her head in confusion. "What do you mean?"

"He would call out for yous when he was unconscious. Sometimes he call for yous in his sleep."

Her heart skipped a beat.

"But, Augustine," he paused to look around and leaned toward her, "I saw yous. I saw yous call for him at the gate. Yous are the voice that led him to safety."

Now, as she sat across from a brooding Joel, the memory of the conversation with Dillon, paired with Joel asking why she wasn't in Waiz, created confusion in her mind. She wondered how to answer Joel's question. *What have I stayed to find out? If Joel needs me?* She knew he had his men, an entire hospital staff, and a whole city willing to hide him. She had discovered he was a genius, thanks to his temple file. And whether or not she believed all the hoopla behind the rhydid's history, Joel probably had broken the spell. *He doesn't need me.* But even as she entertained this thought, she knew it wasn't entirely true. She had been the one who had pronounced him "the rainmaker." She had told the guards he was coming. She had gotten him to the hospital. *That's it then. I just stayed to help him. But . . . the lightning, all the people he's saved . . .*

She knew all the arguments flying around in her head were a cover for the real reason. The kiss, Dillon's words . . . she had fallen in love with him. And, she had stayed back to see if he felt the same.

CHAPTER 45

JOEL MOTIONED TO the nurse to set the lunch tray on the table.

"Uh, yummy." Augustine sweetly eyed Joel's soup and unraveled his napkin for him.

"Answer me. You were supposed to get to Sebastian."

Her usual fiery self did something then that he didn't expect. She shrunk back in silence.

"I left you to keep you safe. There was nothing stopping you from what we set out to do for him. I can't believe you're still here."

She swallowed hard and avoided his stare. "So—so you're . . . disappointed in me?"

He raised his eyebrows and slurped a spoonful of soup. "Let's just say leaving you was a bit of a sacrifice, and, well, Augustine, I thought you'd steward it a little better."

Her eyes locked back onto his. "Oh, really? A sacrifice? I didn't ask you to leave me."

Though not thrilled at where things were headed, he was glad to see her come back to life. *There's my girl.* "Listen, sorry. Let's talk about this later. I've been through a lot."

"Oh, yes, and I've just been sitting on my hands since you left me! Judge my actions all you want, but how dare you question my motives!"

"I didn't question your motives. I asked you a question that you still haven't answered." Her face was red with fury, and he knew something was brewing below the surface—something that was about to explode.

"I couldn't have left, Joel. Once I got here, all the trains were stopped to Waiz. I'd have had to go through the Southern Regions. And maybe you didn't notice, but with the refugees, starvation, political upheaval, and let's not forget that lovely black smoke, there weren't the best circumstances to possibly end up traveling on foot. I didn't think it was safe enough for me to leave." She took a breath and stood up. "And rather than sit here and do nothing, I have studied Mr. Rutherford's book—"

"Oh, I've been meaning to ask you about that—"

"Shut up! I had to navigate this city, find a place to stay, and figure out who to trust all by myself. Then whose face do I see plastered on Differe's wanted banners? Yours! I befriended the Facilis guards in order to steal them, repaint them, and reveal to this whole city that you were 'the rainmaker.' The city isn't too keen on hiding fugitives right now, so I was hoping the truth would win the people over. And it did." She threw the napkin at him. "Or did you see how you were welcomed—the guards pulling you inside the gate, protecting you, and placing you and your men in the best medical care? But now, I see, you're right. I shouldn't be here any longer. I can probably find my way into the Southern Regions. I'm sorry I stayed to help you. I'm sorry I nursed your entire troop back to health. And you know what, I'm not too arrogant to say I stayed around because I thought I might actually need you, but apparently I don't . . . and—and—"

Tears crept into her eyes, but Joel was too unnerved to do anything.

"You—you don't want me. I suppose you left never intending to see me again. I'm happy to fulfill the conditions of your precious sacrifice. Goodbye."

Joel stood, but he was too weak to chase after her. "Wait, Augustine, wait! Please don't leave. I'm—I-I . . . I need you!"

"No, you don't. You have your men and," she tossed her hand in the air, "your father's coming for you."

That was the last he had seen of her in several days. In addition to seeing his men again, he had also met a man named Earl. Earl knew nothing of what Augustine had said of his father, but he knew plenty about the rhydid, the rain, and the state of the West End . . . and all Differe had done to it.

"Why do they have the ability to do what they're doing . . . the black smoke, the taxes?"

"We let them in, Joel. We handed them power in return for our greed."

"The exports and imports? Differe was using your greed against you."

Earl scratched his gray head. "Enemies don't play fair. They'll use any weakness their opponents have to take them down."

Joel threw back the covers of his hospital bed. "What's Facilis saying about me?"

"Well, after your cyclone spectacle I think most are convinced you hold some power . . . maybe to make it rain, maybe not. But they know you have something. Some think that's marvelous while others find it dangerous."

Joel sighed. "Division. Of course. It seems to follow me around."

"I doubt that. You probably just force what's already underlying out into the open. You're not to blame. But the tricky thing about you being here is Facilis has been in the process of changing some of its political laws—in particular the ones that include safety for another region's fugitive."

"Great timing on my part."

Earl's eyes narrowed. "It's sinister in my opinion. I think some council members have been swayed by Differe to side with them."

Joel sat back and crossed his arms. "You mean Differe bribed them. How can they agree to such treachery when it's affecting their lands? People have been taken hostage while others are dying of starvation."

"They just believe what they're told, Joel. Thankfully you brought proof of what has been going on. Because of the villagers you saved, I think Facilis is inclined to hide you."

"Where are the villagers now?"

"Much to their dismay, sleeping in various venues—mostly chapels."

Joel grimaced. "Ugh. Why not inns or hotel rooms?"

"The city is full, Joel. It's full of refugees from the West End or those like Augustine who got stuck here. It's at maximum capacity."

Joel watched a dark shadow cross the man's face. *The siege.* "The smoke . . . it wasn't just to find me . . . was it?"

The man shook his head. "I don't know. The smoked seemed to die down as Differe retreated . . . but it swiftly returned—with a vengeance. It's surrounding the walls of the city now. We're being held captive, it seems."

"Just like I told Augustine. I've jumped from one prison to the next."

"Have you spoken to her lately?"

"She's still here?" He was surprised at the way his heart leapt.

Earl smiled. "Of course. There's no way out now."

CHAPTER 46

JOEL HAD TOO much pride to ask for Augustine directly, so during his last meal he had decided to casually ask the Galanneans if they'd seen her.

Dillon shook his head at him. "Yous have not gone off and been stupid now have yous—lost the girl—the one yous cry for since leaving her?"

Joel shrugged. "I haven't cried for her."

The entire group shot him unconvinced glances.

"Whatever. She's just mad. Just needs to cool off is all."

It had been several days since then, and Joel was beginning to question his theory. He stood at the window in his hospital room, peering into the darkness. It would be morning soon. Now eating regularly and having performed a few rounds of physical therapy, he was beginning to feel like himself again—not quite as strong as before, but he knew he was on his way. He turned to sit on the edge of the hospital bed and thought of Dillon's words again. *Maybe I was stupid.* He knew he had spoken out of turn with Augustine. He especially hated the way she had shrunk back from him that day. *After all, she took care of all my men and me . . . and the first thing I did was scold her.*

He removed the hospital monitoring cuffs from his body and carefully silenced the alarms. His experiences at Trompè and the Temple Infirmary had made him quite a pro at slipping out of medical facilities unnoticed. He reached for his bag to get dressed.

"She scares you."

Joel froze, then realized it was the voice in his head. "Who?"

"You know who."

He did his best to ignore the thought and finished getting dressed. He had to get out of there by morning. He didn't want to face what Earl had warned him about earlier that day. He emptied the pillowcase that contained a surgical mask, hat, and white lab coat. Hopefully he would appear unassuming. He gently cracked open his door, then slipped into the hallway and made for the stairwell.

Though Dillon and the others had been discharged, they were acutely aware of being watched by the city officials. They had decided to meet at the park during lunch later that day, hoping to blend in with the hundreds of refugees eating there. Joel had plenty of time to kill before then and knew exactly what he wanted to do. He opened the door to the street and headed to a dark corner. He removed his disguise and threw it into the yellow laundry bin outside. He turned to walk away, delighted at how easy escaping had been.

"Decided you didn't want to meet with the city council in the morning?"

He turned to see Augustine step out from behind the laundry bin. He wasn't sure what to say. Her hair was pulled back under a black barrette while the rest of her was cloaked in a short black and white trench coat. Her legs were wrapped in black tights, and Joel thought the coat clenched around her waist accented her curves just right. *Stop looking at her like that! She's just your friend. You only like her because of Sebastian. What should I say? Why am I so nervous? She's the most beautiful person I've ever seen.* He couldn't make thoughts like the latter one stop. *Say something. Quick!* "I was an idiot. Spoke out of turn." He pulled his lips in then blew them apart. "Forgive me?"

She pursed her lips then nodded. "Only because you called yourself an 'idiot'."

He nodded, knowing he deserved the words. She was close enough to touch now, and he longed to take her in his arms yet punch her in the shoulder at the same time. He stepped back to refrain from doing either. "You ready?"

"I suppose you'll explain on the way? I wore my flats expecting we'd be walking a bit."

"Good thinking. Uh, Madame Bontecou dress you tonight? With all that black you kind of look like you're up to no good."

"No, I sold most of those loud clothes. This is more my style and mostly what the women wear here. I love it." She looked down at her coat then sent him a mischievous grin. "Aren't we always up to 'something' . . . good or bad?"

Joel shrugged. "I suppose. Speaking of being up to something, I met your Earl."

"A wonderful human being."

"Yes, and he's very knowledgeable. He gave me this." Joel showed her Mr. Rutherford's book.

"Oh, I forgot he had it."

"So, he told you about the council wanting to meet with me?"

"Yes. Apparently they think you've recovered enough to attend the meeting."

"Yeah, but you know how much I love meeting with city authorities. I'm not interested in them deciding my fate. I like your idea better."

She leaned toward his face. "My idea was better? Okay, I'm listening."

He felt the urge to kiss her cheek. *This is torture.* He moved away from her, attempting to regain his composure. "Uh, yeah. You know, letting the masses decide, like you did with the banners."

She crossed her arms and looked apprehensive. "Oh dear, this sounds like a revolt."

"Well, I don't think I want to take my chances with a bunch of bribed councilmen, Augie."

She lifted her index finger in agreement. "Good point."

He gave her his signature bow. "Why, thank you. So, who told you about me sneaking out tonight?"

"Dillon."

He smiled to himself. *Good man.* "Yeah, well, your Earl also told me something interesting about this book. He said all the regions are mapped and marked with historical sites of the Majestic."

Augustine went silent.

Joel opened the book to the West End map. "Okay, so you're obviously still not convinced, but in any case I want to check out one of the places in the West End that happens to be right here in Facilis."

She sighed and shook her head. "What good will it do? The smoke is surrounding the city walls."

Joel shrugged. "I have no idea. Honestly, I have a few hours of free time and thought it would be interesting. I mean, come on, so far things have been pretty interesting when searching out the Majestic stuff. The birds—"

"Terrible!"

"Yes, but also interesting. The cave, the rhydid, sacred stones, rain—"

"I want to hear about that."

"Yes, and I want to tell you. So, back to my question . . . are you ready?"

She looked down at the arm he was offering to her. "All right, ready."

She took his arm, and they started up a steep incline toward the oldest part of the city. Along the way, Joel told her everything that had occurred since they'd parted.

"I can't believe that all happened! It's amazing what we've both learned about how Differe became Differe . . . or the history of our world. I'm concerned though, Joel. You were right the whole time about Differe's control. I mean, the headmaster is referring to himself as 'His Majesty' like he's trying to be Waiz's 'Majestic'—some sort of deity almost. They say they're hiding the truth to keep the peace, but I think fear is their real motive. They're using their fear to control us."

Joel nodded in agreement. "I don't know what they're so afraid of." He was glad to still have her arm tucked under his. "So, sounds like you believe me?"

"Well, you have to remember I did see the cyclone and the lightning. Believing it rained isn't so hard to imagine."

Joel scratched his head as they started up a grassy hillside. "I wonder how you met Earl. Seems almost too good to be true that he happened to be the one you asked for help."

"You know, I thought about that. Wasn't even sure I should trust him. But, the more I thought about it, I realized over the past few months when we've needed help . . . it's been there."

Joel cocked his head at her.

"Think about it. At Crossroads Station, there was Corwin and you. In Waiz there was Mr. Rutherford, the Hallie farm . . . Sarah at the temple, and Hubert on the train with me . . . ."

"What do you think it means?"

"It means fate wants us to win."

Joel stopped walking and removed her arm. "Fate? Augie—"

"Look, my rhydid has worked just fine without me believing in anything but myself. Which is more than I could say when I tried to believe or whatever the first time, but never mind that. I'm just saying what if the real power is simply within us? I just figure I don't have to believe. It's my choice."

Joel couldn't argue with her on that. He didn't know why her object had demonstrated power without any faith in the one who'd supposedly made it. "Well, I have to believe. First, because of my experiences—the cave, the rain, and I think I keep hearing his voice in my head . . . this voice seems to have taken the place of the mouthpieces. And, secondly, because I need hope. Hope that good's gonna win over evil. And, you know I want to know what happened with you and your 'whatever' deal, but I'm not gonna press the issue."

She shrugged and looked down the lonely hillside behind him. "Well, while we're on the topic of 'issues,' why haven't you asked me about your father? I have a whole letter from the Templin's office. It's really—"

"Probably because I don't have a father as far as I'm concerned."

Joel studied the map again then glanced at the top of the hill where an old building sat. According to the red dot on the map, the building was the site of a Majestic sighting or encounter. *Looks abandoned.* He put a finger to his lips, and the two moved forward to go inside. It was still dark, but the massive windows allowed enough moonlight inside to illuminate the interior of the warehouse. The two looked around the place in shock. Instead of being old and empty, it was full of surplus items. *This place is a stockpile.* There was produce, grain, cotton, metals, wood, and more. He started forward to explore and felt Augustine grab his hand. He led her around the piles of lumber, metal, and bricks that were stacked over twenty feet high.

Augustine suddenly jerked his arm. He froze and looked at her then heard a shuffling sound. Glancing up, he saw movement in the shadows ahead. He pulled Augustine behind him and tried to remain calm. It made sense to him that a guard would be overlooking all of the goods. The shadow moved again toward the back of the room. He wondered if they should call out and identify themselves. Joel jumped as the door behind them burst open. A strong wind whooshed inside, taking Augustine's hat with it. She started after it, but

Joel kept a firm grip on her hand. He felt her stare as he stood motionless, every sense piqued. He knew he'd felt this way before. Both listened to the windows rattle as the wind blew inside, yet none of the surrounding piles moved. Joel made for the back of the room. Bam! He turned to find Augustine had shut the door. His eyes bulged at her in question.

She shrugged and mouthed, "What?"

He pressed forward, peering around the corner of every pile then quietly slid the rhydid from his belt as he drew near to where the shadow had disappeared. Hope leapt in his heart. He knew Augustine was wrong. Fate wasn't behind him. *I don't want fate. Fate doesn't have any power.* Heart racing and adrenaline flowing, he reached the end of the building hoping to find the shadowy figure. He crept around the last pile and gasped. A tall figure illuminated by the moonlight and seemingly aglow stood before him. Cloaked in an iridescent shimmering white garment, head adorned by glistening white hair, the being was breathtaking. Joel hesitated to move forward when he realized he was looking at a man. He blinked furiously to be sure he wasn't imagining things as the man's long beard came into view. He barely noticed Augustine come up behind him. He heard her suck in a breath just before she bolted forward.

Chapter 47

V ICAR! SIR! SORRY to disturb you. Can we . . . do you need anything, Your Honor?" Joel watched Augustine perform a slight curtsy.

"Ha!" The angelic being chuckled as he walked forward out of the mesmerizing light.

Joel shrank back. "It's just an old man."

"An odd question, My Dear, considering I'm surrounded by plenty of supplies. I could live here the rest of my life and be cared for." He passed between them and gave Joel a knowing glance. "Come. My watch is almost up. Let's have a chat before I leave."

Augustine followed him toward the middle of the room where the moonlight shone brightly. The man pulled some sturdy boxes together and gestured for Augustine to sit down.

Puzzled, Joel stayed back and crossed his arms. The door . . . the wind . . . the light . . . *Who is this man? What had Augustine called him? Vicar?* The title sounded familiar to him, but he couldn't remember what it meant. Joel became suspicious when the man motioned for him to sit down next to Augustine. He had yet to meet a man in that kind of getup he could trust. He squinted at the man as he thought of all the greedy and controlling leaders he'd met or heard of the last few months. He took a step forward and saw the man look at Augustine then reach for something hidden deep within his robe. Joel dodged in front of her and thrust his rhydid out.

"Joel!"

He didn't flinch when Augustine grabbed the back of his shirt. His sword's tip was pointed right at the man's chest.

The old man stared calmly at Joel then down at the metal. "My, that's bigger than when you first retrieved it. Oh, I have something for you both . . . well, actually two things." He backed away from Joel's sword and sat down across from him.

Joel, heart pumping, swallowed hard and lowered his sword a bit.

"Joel, please. This is the Vicar of Facilis. He's—he's the one—"

"I know who he is. He's in league with the Headmaster of Differe. You answer to him don't you?" Joel looked around the room and shook his head, now remembering why the office had sounded familiar to him. Vicars were appointed representatives of the headmaster, to oversee the chapels in each land. "It's you. You've been hoarding all of this, leaving your villages to starve . . . or . . . are you the one who's led them here to fall into Differe's trap? Piling all your people into the city to become the Templins' slaves?"

"Joel!" Augustine pulled on his shoulder.

Joel jerked away from her. "Well? What say you?"

The man thoughtfully stroked his beard. "Hmm. Assumptions. All assumptions. Do you know what's said of people who assume too much?"

Rage surged through Joel's veins, and the rhydid shook in his hand. "You think this is funny? I'm not assuming. What's in your hand?

The man finally pulled his hand out of his robe and revealed a tightly wrapped piece of cloth. "However, when I helped Earl get this, he told me I was also making assumptions. Difference is, I knew then, and most certainly now, that my assumptions were correct. Young man, you are brash, controlling, and disrespectful. You push everyone away before they can get near you."

"Wh-what are you talking about?" Joel felt sweat running down his temple.

"Mother dead. Abandoned by your father. You're so afraid now that you've found people to love and who love you back, that you insist on leaving them before they leave you . . . or you control them."

"You don't know me!" He lifted the sword again, but Augustine dashed between them this time.

She gripped the forearm that held the rhydid. "Joel! Joel, put that down! Listen to me. He helped Earl get the banners. He's the one who instructed the guards to get you inside the gate. He made sure you were put in the hospital and kept away from the council until you were well enough. Now, stop! Put that away."

The shocking information settled into his brain, and he slowly dropped the sword.

"Good job. Now, sit down and hush." She pointed to the box next to hers.

Still feeling the heat of anger, Joel begrudgingly obeyed.

"Augustine, here. They've taken the banners down, but . . . I thought you'd like a souvenir. Being reminded of such a brave act may be helpful to you someday." The Vicar handed her the piece of cloth.

Augustine unraveled the cloth, and Joel saw the square only held the word "rainmaker" and Augustine's initials.

"Oh, thank you." She smiled at the man then turned back to sit beside Joel. "Can you tell us how to get out of here, Vicar . . . back to Waiz? The longer we stay the more dangerous it becomes for your region."

Joel started to open his mouth, but Augustine's hand firmly pushed against it.

"Yes, I know you need to get to someone in your family. Who is it?"

"My brother."

The Vicar closed his eyes and pressed a finger to his temple. "He's . . . he's doing well, for now . . . yes, his health will hold until the next season. He's creating something with your other family member—"

"My uncle."

"Yes. You and Joel will both have something to do when you get back to Waiz. It's . . . hmm . . . it's reviving something that's been dormant for many years. It will gather many to become like-minded . . . again."

Joel looked at the man with skepticism. "Have you talked to Corwin?"

The man opened his eyes and shrugged. "Who's Corwin?"

Joel shot Augustine a confused glance.

"Now, as for you, young man, your gift from me is words."

"I don't want—"

"I'd be careful not to accept a gift."

Joel sighed and waited for the man to continue.

"Why did you stay in Baithe?"

"To empower the people." Joel hadn't expected the words to pour out of his mouth, and it seemed the man hadn't either.

The Vicar cocked his head at him. "Impressive. Noble."

Joel didn't respond. He'd felt numb to everyone's praise since waking up. It was as if Differe's black cloud had also infected his soul.

"What is this darkness you feel?

Joel stared at the man in astonishment. "How . . . ." The weight of his dark feelings flooded his being and he began to shake. "No, stop. Th-th-this is over. Stop shaking. What's going on with me? I don't hear anything! N-n-no mouthpieces . . . stop! Pl-please, can you help me? Can you-can you make it stop?"

The Vicar stood up and walked toward him. "Come now, this is different for you. Your mouthpieces are usually voices, not feelings . . . but these feelings are just as powerful, sabotaging your thoughts."

Joel gasped for breath as his shaking body fell forward off the box.

Augustine was instantly at his side, lifting his head off the ground.

"Please." He looked up earnestly at the man. "P-p-please, let me sp-sp-speak to you alone."

"Of course, but I will not be the one to send Augustine away."

"But I-I don't want her to see this. I don't w-want you to s-see me like this." He searched her face.

She was calm and tightly wrapped her arms around him. "I'm not going to leave you."

Joel lifted his gaze to the Vicar and motioned for him to move closer. "The darkness, it's—it's like I breathed it in. W-with the mouthpieces it's always like the darkness . . . it's—it's outside of me, but the s-smoke . . . when I breathed it in . . . I-I felt it flow inside me. When I think of the black smoke . . . the—the black cyclone . . . all I can see is the men . . . the men—"

"Your enemies, Joel." Augustine shook her head at him.

Tears crept to his eyes. "Men, fathers, sons, brothers, dying . . . breathing in the darkness and dying."

Augustine got right in his face. "They brought it upon themselves. They're serving someone evil."

"But the s-s-smoke came because of me. Th-they were killed because of me." Tears began streaming down his cheeks. "And—and the villagers, th-they would have hidden me. Risked their lives. The whole city here . . . I-I want to leave because they're in danger . . . the—the headmaster will siege this place because of me. Everywhere I go, I bring harm. Th-that's the real curse. As much as I try, I-I can't keep anyone safe. Th-that's why I p-push them away."

"I don't want to be safe anymore. I want to be with you." Augustine released her grip on him and sank back on her knees, holding his gaze.

The Vicar knelt down between them. "Joel, you must quit assuming. Good leaders communicate. Even feelings. Feelings that you don't understand."

Joel wiped his eyes. "I've always been told that feelings are weak."

"And how does it feel to cry?"

He sighed. He had to admit he felt better. "Not as bad as I expected."

"Hmm. How does it feel to cry in front of a woman?"

Augustine wasn't just any woman; she was one of his closest friends. He could still feel the warmth of her arms around him and marveled at her firm embrace in the midst of the scene he'd just caused. He'd cried in front of Isabelle plenty of times as children and was obliged by her pity, but crying in front of Augustine was . . . he searched for a word.

"S-s-scary." It was true. He felt quite exposed.

"Well, here are my words for you. Yes, you're right; I do report to the headmaster. He's head of all the Chapel Vicars."

Joel tried to control the instant suspicion that rose in him again.

"Before you make an assumption, hear me out. It's true; I do answer to him, but I do not always obey him. There are plenty of us . . . even a few inside the temple who are very good at playing two sides. The curse of no rain happened because Differe wanted the West End to be indebted to them. First it was for greed or monetary reasons, but I knew it would soon become political. I feel that was the real reason all along. You see, Facilis has pardoned several key figures over the past few decades . . . figures Differe would have liked to see returned to them for justice. The taxes, of course, moved things to a more political arena, yet something more was needed if Differe was to succeed in overtaking the Facilis government. Even bribing the councilmen was not working as planned—many had family in the villages being ravaged.

No rain certainly weakened our people, but we were still too scattered, too powerful . . . or, that's what the headmaster told me. Yes, he said it would be much easier for Differe to take the West End by force if the citizens were all in one place, starving or not. So, a more threatening tactic was devised."

"The smoke."

"Yes. And though you were a grand excuse for it, you were not the sole purpose. This is my stockpile, Joel, but it is for the city. I brought the taxes upon us— let the Templins in by hoarding this. Those arrogant fools thought we weren't producing because there was no rain, but that curse came a little too late for it to be completely effective. I've been ready for this. I foresaw the siege. I'm ready to empower the city just like you empowered the villages. We will fight Differe."

"Wait. You mean, they're—they're not just after me?" Joel felt his burdensome feelings begin to lift.

The Vicar propped a hand under his chin. "Now, they want you— that's just a fact—but they planned the siege long before you decided to go back and retrieve your rhydid. So, Joel, as I said, my gift to you is words—the truth. The Templins died at their own hands, so guilt be gone and rest be released to you." The man rubbed his chin then raised his eyebrows. "However, if indeed you were the cause of death, do not focus on it, but instead enjoy the lives you saved. You, Rainmaker, have reminded the people of Facilis that Differe is not as powerful as it seems. You have reignited their sense of independence and freedom. So, guilt and dread be gone. Be thankful and hopeful for what you bring, my friend."

Joel felt light flood his soul again.

"And, as to you bringing harm to everyone . . . to my knowledge, no one who has chosen to follow you is blind to the danger that lingers, but, Joel, they choose not to focus on that either." The man turned to Augustine. "What do you see in him?"

Augustine seemed taken aback but bravely turned to face Joel. "I-I see a leader who's kind, sacrificial, and only wants good for others . . . and most importantly, freedom. You're also goofy and childish—you give value to every generation, from the smallest child to the oldest adult, and you can laugh in the worst of situations. I see someone who's risky and took leadership when no one else would. The people who follow you do it because they see it too, and they *feel* it. If you'd only see yourself as others do, truly believe in yourself . . . nothing could stop you."

Joel stared at her in disbelief. She had changed dramatically since the day they'd met. It was evident much had also changed between the two of them.

"You seemed surprised at her words."

Joel slowly nodded. "Yes, I don't see how . . . I don't see what she does."

"It's clear then that you've misread how the rest of your followers view you as well—the ones you keep trying to leave. Your dear friend here hit on something most important, Joel. The accolades of your men or friends won't matter much until you see yourself as you truly are. You are not your past. You see yourself as the weak tormented soul who escaped on the train to Waiz . . . something you'd been afraid of doing since your mother died. You see yourself as the comatose soul in Trompè or the bullied schoolboy at the Temple School. But your past does not define you, Joel."

Joel gritted his teeth in frustration. "I just . . . I just think I now realize things could have been different for me a long time ago."

"Maybe, but you would've changed that if you'd known what you know now. You didn't though, so remain thankful you received any revelation at all. Always remain thankful, Joel, and hopeful. You can save others from the life you experienced."

"Do you believe I'm all those things you said about me earlier—you know, brash, disrespectful?"

The Vicar folded his hands and sat down again. "To a degree, yes. You see yourself the way you do because you're carrying around your past . . . and, unfortunately, you see others through the same grid—your past. I'm a Vicar and, through your past's eyes, evil."

Joel's body had relaxed, and he finally smiled at the man. "Assumptions."

"Yes. You're wiser, smarter, and better off not relying on those. Assumptions create false expectations, and vice versa."

Joel leaned forward, longing to receive more of the gift the man had offered. "Tell me who I am."

The man closed his eyes again. "I will say who you are, but it's more of who you are becoming—what is already there and being pulled to the surface. Ah, yes, your leadership will bring many into their own destiny—destinies they cannot perform without you carving a path for them. You will see in your lifetime all you desire. Freedom for others—"

Trompè.

"Healing for the sick—"

Sebastian.

"And peace with your father."

I don't want anything to do with my father.

"There is something . . . something he gave you that you will need soon. You will be a force of empowerment. The weak will be made strong by you."

Joel's heart resounded at the latter remarks, looking past what the man had said about his father. He pushed himself off the ground. "Those were a gift. Thank you. I'm—please forgive me for assuming the worst of you." Joel stuck out his hand.

The man seemed amused but took it nonetheless. "So, I know you want to get to Waiz, a city looking much like Facilis underneath."

"How do you mean?"

"We are divided."

"Politics?"

The man nodded. "Yes. We have young zealous men and old reserved folks like myself."

Joel raised his eyebrows in recognition. "Old Waiz and New Waiz."

He stood up to face Joel. "I do have a request for you both, but it is just that. Say the word, and I'll show you the way out."

It was tempting. They could leave right now. Joel thought about Sebastian, his men, and the people. "Go on, let's hear it."

"Because of your favor with the villages and Facilis at this point, I believe the people will listen to you. Both sides."

"Listen to me tell them what?"

"What you know about Differe."

"But—but that will mean—"

"That will mean I am now your hostage or the headmaster's spy—however it plays out."

The group stared at one another in silence.

"You know Differe will come, Joel, and I believe Facilis will fall more quickly if we are divided."

"You want me to unite the people . . . against Differe?" It was almost laughable to him.

The man put a hand on his shoulder. "Just unite them. Then let them decide for themselves what they want."

Joel looked at Augustine. "Sebastian."

She nodded and lowered her head. "I know, but . . . you heard the Vicar. He's doing okay right now."

He grabbed her hand. "You could go on without me."

"I'm not leaving you."

The man cleared his throat and starting putting the boxes away. "I'll leave the two of you to decide. Today the council will meet at Ryder Square across from the north end of the park. It's in front of my cathedral and the only place with the proper acoustics. I believe all the refugees and inhabitants will attend. Speak up, and I'll make sure you get the floor."

The two nodded as he approached the door.

"Oh." He stopped and turned around. "I almost forgot these." He reached inside the robe again and pulled out two new rhydid sheaths. "These should work better than the tattered ones you're wearing around."

Augustine curtsied again. "Oh, thank you."

The Vicar opened the door, and Joel was shocked to see he looked aglow again. "Uh, Sir . . . who are you? How did you know all that stuff about me?"

The man smiled back at him. "I hear voices too. And, Joel, you are scared. Fearful people control others . . . remember that." His eyes moved to Augustine. "Love, however, lets the other be free."

CHAPTER 48

UGUSTINE, JOEL, AND the Galanneans were scattered among the huge crowd gathered in Ryder Square in front of the cathedral. All tried to appear unassuming, waiting for Joel to make his move. There had been little discussion among the group when they met in the park. After Joel and Augustine shared about their encounter with the Vicar, the young men understood what had to be done. All decided to stay, and now they were doing their best to blend in with the people of the West End.

Joel glanced around at the audience. It was as large as the crowd that had gathered around the Bridge of Miren when he got entangled in the murder. The city folk and villagers were standing in separate groups, so it had been harder than he'd imagined for his troop to scatter and remain unnoticed. And, just as the Vicar said, the older generation was distinctly detached from the younger. The groups of villagers were the only ones that held mixed ages.

As he stood listening to the bribed political councilmen claim that he was the cause of Differe's curse on their land, Joel longed to hear from the voice. *What should I say? Are you there?* His heart pounded as he imagined defending himself in front of the crowd. His palms became sweaty when he noticed the Differian Flag waving above the ivory cathedral. *What's that doing there?* He could only figure it was because the Vicar and his parish answered to the headmaster. It didn't settle well with him, and he instantly heard the Vicar's words again.

"And, Joel, you are scared."

What is it? He shuddered inside, knowing the words resonated with him somehow. He looked again at the council in disgust. He wanted to expose the temple for what it was—a complete counterfeit. As he felt the rhydid hanging in its new sheath, he realized Differe had no real power. In fact, Differe's only supposed power was simply controlling others.

"Control stems from fear."

Yes, that's what the Vicar said. He relaxed some, relieved to hear the good voice enter his thoughts. He lowered his head as he recalled the Vicar telling him the mouthpieces had used his feelings against him.

"It's all right, Joel. There's no shame in revelation. There's no guilt in learning. Only freedom."

A warmth coursed through him as the voice spoke his name. *I don't know how I let them get the best of me . . . again. I guess—I guess I didn't know they worked that way.*

"Well, you've now discovered another key to defeating them."

I know I don't have to listen to them anymore, but . . .

"Right, so they're not talking to you anymore. Instead, they tried another tactic."

Using my feelings against me? It was almost too easy for them . . . they didn't have to speak this time. I created my own crazy thoughts without them. Joel was amazed at unearthing his enemy's new ploy. *But, what do I do now . . . now that I know?* He glanced over at Augustine. *I'm not sure I want to shut off my feelings. The temple never allowed them—kind of makes me want to keep them.*

"You don't shut down all thoughts or feelings just because they can be skewed. You bring them in line with what you know, which means you must remember."

Joel shrugged. *What did I forget?*

"You forgot who you are. You forgot about those you led, about how far you've come. You forgot I am with you. And what's this talk of Differe's power? Are you powerful?"

As he pondered these questions, the real reason he was standing in the shadows about to crash the council meeting suddenly became clear. *That's it! Differe knows power resides even in these small villages. That's why—that's why they've fought so hard to overtake them . . . weaken them. If these villagers could understand how powerful they are on the inside, they could overpower Differe!* A cold sweat broke out on his forehead. *It's . . . it's just like me . . . you know, forgetting who I am, wondering if I'm worth it. Uh, right?*

Joel heard nothing, but it didn't matter this time. He marched forward, pushing his way through the crowd, until he stood in the clearing in front of the cathedral steps below the council's stage. The crowd's murmuring soon distracted the councilmen from their presentation. Joel removed his hat and turned to the West End, triggering a myriad of shouts from the people.

"Rainmaker!"

"Joel!"

"Our leader!"

"The fugitive!"

A councilman banged his gavel several times attempting to hush the crowd. When this didn't work, Joel motioned for the crowd to quiet down, and they immediately obeyed. He turned to face the council and cleared his throat.

"I would like the floor."

"How dare you!" Several stood to their feet, but the cries from the crowd soon overpowered their protests.

"Yes, let him speak!"

"Give him the floor!"

"We want to hear from him!"

Joel waited for the council to reply and soon felt a hand on his shoulder. He was pleased to find the Vicar standing behind him. The man led him to the top of the cathedral's steps. He held his hand out toward the crowd and nodded to Joel. This gesture obviously trumped the council's opinion.

Heart in his throat, Joel took a deep breath. *Come on, you can do it. At least you know what to say.* He cupped his hands around his mouth. "A lot of you want to know who I am—the rainmaker or the fugitive?" He shrugged at the crowd. "I must confess I'm both. I *have* escaped from the Temple of Differe . . . actually, twice now—the first time going to Waiz and the second time to retrieve this." He stopped and removed his sword, holding it up for all to see. "This is my rhydid . . . I brought it into the West End. This is what I used to make it rain, along with a sacred stone from the Northern Regions and a barique from the West End."

The crowd stared at him in amazement.

He focused his eyes on the silver blade. "You see, Differe's been afraid. They're still afraid—afraid that if they release such a weapon, one that is rightfully mine, it will be used for evil. And, maybe it could be, but . . . what if the opposite were true? What if it was used for good? Never given the choice, how will they ever know what good could be done with this . . . or by me . . . us? Differe is afraid of freedom because it empowers people. I did not bring the curse to your land. If that were so, why would I bring the rain?"

Joel walked down a few steps then pointed the sword behind him. "Look! Their flag—Differe's flag—is flying above this meeting. That army wasn't waiting outside the gates just for me. They're holding you hostage in this city, just as they've taken many of your loved ones hostage to Trompè. But I tell you this, the real reason Differe is afraid is because they know . . . they know who you are." He extended his rhydid toward them. "You are powerful. I believe you can choose to do good over evil. Allowing choice is a risk. I believe freedom is worth the risk, but Differe will not allow it. They will return to take this city, *your* region. Blame me if you want, but it seems you owe them a debt. You've chosen peace too many times—this peace and grace that sets you apart from all other regions for fugitives such as me." Joel smiled at the beaming faces looking back at him. "West End, your power is to empower. Differe will send curses, but you can break them. They will send armies, but you can fight them."

He quickly eyed both sides of the audience. "But, there is no use trying if you're not united." He moved forward again, looking back and forth between the disjointed crowds. "Listen to me! Differe's afraid of losing its power by setting you free, but what they don't realize is . . . they've already lost. The temple's leader will die one day, going away with everything he's fought for to keep himself in power. But you . . . you can choose to live and pass on all you know to those around you. You, your legacy, will live on forever." He clasped both hands around the rhydid and lifted the sword above his head. "Unite, Facilis! Unite, West End! Don't hold onto the baggage of your past, but unite in hope of a better future! Make the choice! Choose goodness! Choose freedom!" Joel looked at the sword and only heard himself panting for breath. He finally glanced out at the speechless crowd, wondering what would happen next. Soon the shouts began.

"It's true!"

"It's Differe!"

"We are Facilis!"

"Differe's to blame!"

"We are the West End!"

"I believe him!"

"We will fight!"

"I will fight for my children!"

"I will fight for my grandchildren!"

"I will not stay silent!"

"Unite!"

The crowd began to chant the word "unite" over and over as a group. Joel raised his eyebrows in relief and turned back to the Vicar. He had accomplished what the man had asked. He was finished and sighed in satisfaction. The crowd suddenly went silent as he began walking down the rest of the steps. A clicking sound caught his attention, and Joel turned to find the Vicar slowly approaching him. His grand scepter clunked against the ivory stone every time he took a step. Joel stopped and searched his face, hoping for some direction. He met the breathless man near the top of the steps. He eyed Joel up and down as all waited to hear his words.

"Young man, I have counted the costs as well, or 'risks' as you mentioned." He turned to the crowd. "Freedom will be costly, citizens, mark my words, but . . . I believe as this one—the price is worth it. It is time." He put a hand on Joel's shoulder. "It is time for all generations to band together. Put aside your differences! Let the young ones rise up and take their place. I will not be like those of Differe, afraid of empowerment. We will empower! We are the West End, and I purpose to see the young ones succeed, to go beyond where I have." He turned and stared into Joel's eyes. "And, I believe you will . . . farther, faster, deeper, wider. I will give my last days to help get you as far as you can."

Joel was overcome with emotion, but he knew it was okay this time. Tears crept into the corners of his eyes as he choked out his response to the very man who had called him "brash, controlling, and disrespectful" a few hours earlier. "Thank you, Sir."

"Let us seal these words with an act of declaration. Come." He motioned to Joel with his scepter.

Joel followed the man to the archway under the bell tower.

The man presented him with the Facilis flag. "Take this, and put it where it belongs."

Joel stared up at the tower and heard the commotion from the crowd below. He took the flag and looked at the Vicar in question. "How do I get up there?" The man pointed to a nearby ladder, yet Joel saw the bottom rungs had been sawed off, making the ladder impossible to climb.

"Differe removed those."

Joel nodded in understanding. He startled when the man stabbed his scepter onto the marble floor. The crowd instantly went silent again.

"Joel!"

Bewildered, Joel faced the man.

"Stand on my shoulders!"

Augustine watched in wonder as Joel climbed onto the shoulders of the most powerful man in Facilis. Tears streamed down the cheeks of the people around her. *They've been waiting for this.* She was proud of her friend and his speech, no doubt, but it was no match for this act. She knew this moment of humility, honor, and empowerment would be the true catalyst causing Facilis to unite. She smirked as the council tried to flee the scene.

As Joel disappeared up the ladder, Augustine realized that this was only the beginning. He had led a group of no name bandits from Galanne to empower an army of villages, and now an entire metropolis was about to follow him. *Perhaps even a whole region.* If what the Vicar had said hours before was true, about there being something for them to do in Waiz, the place was sure to be Joel's next target. *Not because he is looking, but because they need him. And he will go.*

Joel stopped midway up and looked over the crowd through one of the windows, searching the faces below. *What's he . . . oh!* Augustine's heart fluttered when she realized in his moment of glory he was looking for her. She slowly lifted her hand and waved. He didn't see her, so she started jumping and waving both hands, not caring how silly she looked. When he spotted her she stopped and grinned up at him. He beamed back at her then continued climbing.

The moment he switched out the flags, the crowd broke into cheers at the sight of the Facilis's blue emblem waving above them. Joel raised his rhydid again. "For the king!"

The crowd burst into shouts of praise until the Vicar hushed them again as Joel climbed back down. "All right, every older man choose a younger one, and women do the same. Find more than one if you can. The next three days work together and share all your meals. Come up with a plan to defeat Differe's impending siege. Each group will report to their village or city borough leader. The leaders will convene here again after three days to compare strategies and to make our plans."

As the council was taken into custody by the Facilis Guards, the crowd began to merge. People began shaking hands, hugging, and smiling at one another. The generational barrier had been disarmed. Augustine made her way toward Joel until a voice called out to her just as she reached the cathedral steps.

"Miss? Miss, can I help you?"

Augustine found a gray-haired woman humbly staring at her. She gritted her teeth, grateful at the offer but not wanting to be separated from Joel. "Oh, I thank you so much, but . . . I-I—"

"Jonell, I'll be taking both Joel *and* his companion under my wing, but you may join us if you like."

Augustine was grateful to hear the Vicar's voice. She turned to find Joel's outstretched hand.

"Well?" The old man looked at the three of them. "Shall we? Jonell, how about your apartment?"

Jonell smiled and nodded.

Joel winked at the woman. "Joel and Jonell. Won't be hard to remember your name."

"This way then."

Joel nodded for Augustine to take his arm.

She playfully hesitated as they followed Jonell. "I thought you might try to leave me again."

"Me leave you again after clearly receiving a death threat about doing so? I don't think so."

She squinted her nose at his smirk until he looked away from her.

"Quit worrying, Augie. If anyone leaves, it won't be me."

She looked at him, trying to decide if he was serious.

"It'll be you."

Augustine followed Joel onto Jonell's balcony. The group had just finished their first meal together.

"So . . . how was today for you?"

"Hmm . . . ." She searched for the right word as he closed the door behind her. "The Vicar and Jonell aren't joining us?"

He shook his head. "They're cleaning up. Vicar said we should watch the sunset." He walked over and settled onto a railing snugly held between two large columns. He propped his hand under his chin and gazed out toward the falling sun.

Augustine studied his perched silhouette before sliding next to him. *Typical Joel. So much going on in that head.* She bumped his shoulder to get his attention. "Move over."

He didn't budge. "There's plenty of balcony to my right."

"Yeah, but it's not the best view. You're hogging the best spot." She nudged him again.

"Fine, I'll share." He leaned over the rail and barely moved an inch.

"You're mean."

"I am not!"

"I'll tell you my word for today if you move over."

He was clearly amused at her bribe. "Like you've never seen a sunset. Come on, this is my spot."

Her lips formed a small pout.

Joel rolled his eyes. "Good grief. Okay, if I like your word I'll move over."

"Oh, you'll like it. I'm good with words, remember?"

He rolled his eyes. "How could I forget? Just don't make it too big for me."

"Don't worry it's only four letters."

"I'm listening."

She drew in a deep breath. "Epic. Today was . . . epic."

His face softened as he glowed at the compliment. He slid over for her to join him.

"Thank goodness you approve." She pointed to the sunset. "It's hard to see through the smoke."

Joel nodded in agreement.

"You . . . you were amazing up there today. I hardly recognize the old Joel I first met at Crossroads. Whatever is left of him has only improved."

He turned to her with a furrowed brow.

"What? I like you way better now. There were . . . well, there were a few things that *needed* to improve."

His eyes widened as he dramatically placed a hand over his chest. "Me? Need to improve? In what way?"

Augustine laughed. "It's hard for us to stay serious too long, isn't it?"

He chuckled and dropped his hand to the rhydid. "I don't think there's anything wrong with that. There's enough serious stuff going on around us. 'Serious' is inevitable. But," he shook his head and pointed to the sunset, "these moments, these are the ones I think about when I'm climbing a bell tower. I'm not going to fight for some humdrum, boring life, Augie."

"Well said."

He cleared his throat. "Now, what were you referring to about me needing to improve?"

"You have already. You're much stronger than you used to be. Nicer too."

He didn't respond but took the opportunity to spit across the square below.

"Uh, your manners obviously haven't improved."

He turned to her with a puzzled glance. "What do you mean about being stronger? Stronger how?"

"Well, your build. Oh, I mean—I mean your character." Embarrassment overcame her, and she knew Joel saw it.

"My build, huh? You've been noticing the ole physique?" He took the opportunity to flex for her. "You'd have muscles like these too if you had to haul women and their luggage around, well, you know . . . everywhere."

His smile, the way the dim light hit his face . . . it was intoxicating to her. She cut her eyes away from his and turned back from the ledge.

"I'm—I'm just kidding you, Augie." He caught her arm, but she didn't look up. He turned to face her. "Hey. Augustine?"

She knew he was searching for her eyes, but she feared they would give away the feelings of her heart.

He slid his hand off her arm and reached for the small of her back. "I'm sorry. I didn't mean to . . . Augie, look at me." He tried to position his face down in front of hers.

She waited until she couldn't avoid him anymore. She felt terrified at giving herself away but bravely tilted her head up and gazed into his eyes—the eyes of her very best friend.

The look of concern on his face slowly faded, but neither moved. He stood frozen before her with her in his arm. Finally, he swallowed hard. He drew his lips in and steadied himself on the railing with his free hand as he leaned toward her.

She lifted her face as she felt his arm draw her slightly inward. When he was within inches of her face his eyes left hers, drifting to her lips. She smiled slightly then closed her eyes. Her heart raced as his lips brushed against hers. His kiss was light and left her hoping for another. She moved closer and put her hands on his arms as he wrapped them around her. Suddenly she giggled.

"What?"

She squeezed one of his biceps. "These *are* nice muscles."

Joel laughed hesitantly with a disheartening expression. In an instant the magical moment was over. She knew the look in his eyes. *Doubt.* He was uncertain as to how he felt about her.

Her heart sank as she looked away from him. "Oh, we missed the sunset."

She felt his arms release her. "Nah, I didn't miss a thing."

CHAPTER 49

ISABELLE LAY IN bed with all her allies' words rolling around in her head. Dr. Pryderi's fake prescription had read, "The answer lies on paper," and Professor Louis had made it clear in his extra credit tutorial on "Discovering Your Legacy" that discovering was best done by "fleshing out your own secrets." But Sarah's voice and her admonishment, "You must hurry; get caught if you must!" was the loudest of all. The woman had not been able to offer her any explanation as to her urgency. She looked around at her empty dark room. What was even left for her to take if she escaped? The locket was long gone, and that was the only thing of value she'd ever owned besides the music room key. She had tied the key onto a long string around her neck. Thankfully, it had yet to be noticed.

She pondered for what seemed like the millionth time whether or not to risk getting caught, when a loud chirping started. She sat straight up in bed when the sound grew into a whistle alarm.

"Evacuate! Evacuate!" Down the halls, she heard the dorm wardens' yells accompany their fists pounding on doors.

"Hallelujah!" It was the middle of the night, much like the time before, as she filed into the line of girls throwing on long johns, coats, scarves, and other warm clothing as they staggered down the hallway. Instead of being forced outside like last time, most of the girls gathered under the arched foyer with a few spilling into the common room. Isabelle stood in the doorway to the common room as she watched dozens of armed guards march through the place. They weren't all Templins this time. *Differian Guards. What is going on?*

A Templin rushed into the common room, almost knocking Isabelle over as he motioned to the troop of officers behind him. "In here!"

The sea of girls parted to let them inside the room. The Templins faced the army soldiers then looked up at the glass dome ceiling. The leader traced the side of the wall with his fingers in the air. "Here. Now, get these girls out of here."

She smiled to herself. *Probably the first and last time in my life I'd like to thank a Templin.* Slipping away from the group to the boundary gate was easy amidst the overall chaos of leading a whole dorm of girls into the freezing cold. *Plus, I'm invisible now. No one cares that I even exist.* She realized there was a hint of sadness in her tone, but also gratitude. *Being excluded isn't always bad.* She sighed when she spotted the sight where she'd last seen someone who would certainly disagree with her. *Poor Augustine.* She hadn't thought much about her since that night until this moment; however, she'd thought of Joel plenty. She wanted to find him and be wherever he was, but she wasn't sure if she and Augustine would ever be able to adjust to being together . . . *again.* She'd certainly been surprised at how beautiful her half-sister had become. *And Joel had changed, too.* She wasn't sure how she felt about either of those things, especially since the two were traveling alone together. She gazed at the darkened snowy doorframe at the front of Moonstruck, yet made for the back door.

She was surprised to find the limestone lion heads staring at her uncovered. The snow had been knocked off. Someone had been there recently . . . or someone was still there. Breathing deeply, she pulled one of the heads forward to unlock the door. She pressed the door open and was relieved to find darkness on the other side. She closed the door and felt her way down the stairs.

Once inside her old quarters, she cautiously made her way through the dark into the old school room. She felt for the iron bars that encased the room and darted inside. Only when she had made it to her locker and waited several minutes did she pull out a light. Sarah's desk lamp still had enough oil to be used, so she lit it and retrieved her file as well as the maps Joel had left behind.

The maps were of the Temple grounds and Crossroads Train Station. She rolled them up and put them into her left sleeve then opened her file and flipped through the record of her quarterly grades. "There has to be something in here I need to find." She found the "Operation Flight" plan again, in which she had discovered she was the bait to get Joel back to the temple. A glaring red tab marked "Operation Flight" and several other papers within the file. *Let's start with these.* The first thing in the file was her acceptance contract. She searched for her grandfather's signature, the man who had both the name and financial means for her to attend The Temple of Differe School. She was shocked to find her father's name staring back at her on the paper and quickly searched the rest of the contract. A few pages later she finally found her grandfather's signature. *William Chanton.* Her mother's signature was there also. *Sylvia Chanton.* The few pages they'd signed indicated her grandfather had adopted her to change her last name, with her mother signing over full parental privileges. She squinted at the next clause.

> Because of the potential student's family name and the ability to complete all financial requirements, Isabelle Chanton is now eligible for acceptance.

She looked further down.

> The family is in agreement with the school's plan to restore the student's physical appearance, even if isolation at Trompè is necessary.

"What?!" Her angry cry echoed around the room, and she willed herself to calm down. She stared at the signatures again. "You—you signed it. It was you . . . you gave them permission to take me there?" She could hardly breathe. She wanted to rip the paper to shreds but thought better of it as she tore it from the file. *Yes, I'd like proof of this.*

She was now all too curious about her father's signature and the attached tests on his signed page. She gasped when she saw Augustine's name on one of the assessments. Her fingers felt numb as she saw both girls' entry test forms staring her in the face. Her nose crinkled when she saw the scores. *She beat me.* Not only had Augustine surpassed Isabelle's scores; she was in the top fifteen percent of test takers for the past several decades. She flipped back to her father's signature.

> I, Alexander Bennet, as Augustine Bennet's guardian, hereby forfeit her rights to attend The Temple of Differe School and, instead, give her acceptance to my daughter Isabelle Chanton.

Isabelle's ears pounded with blood as she spied writing on the backside. She flipped the paper over. It was a handwritten note from her father to the headmaster. She didn't even know he could write. Her eyes zoomed down the page.

> I realized initially that Augustine's racial issues did not comply with the temple's code. I do, however, thank Your Grace for allowing her the opportunity to take the test with Isabelle. It undoubtedly has made explaining certain issues easier for Sylvia and me. My superior and I also greatly appreciate your silence about our arrangement. We are humbled by Your Grace for remembering our bargain and honored you would offer this as a solution. I am pleased to see he has excelled. His father would be proud, and we are forever in your debt.
>
> Yours,
> Alex Bennet

She couldn't move. She felt paralyzed with questions and overtaken with emotions. Anger, rage, sadness, jealousy, betrayal—all were running rampant. She studied her father's words again. Suddenly she sensed someone's presence in the room with her and felt her insides quiver. She shrunk back into the chair and let out a piercing scream as a shadowy face leaned across the desk.

"Well, well, well. What do we have here?"

Isabelle let out a sigh of relief when the nasty face of head Templin, Hertz Marlis, came into view.

"Oh, pleased to see me? That'll be short-lived. You're wanted at the headmaster's."

Isabelle's eyes widened in surprise. "His quarters?"

Hertz slammed the file shut. "Correct. He's quite angry. You know how he enjoys a good night's rest." He motioned for her to stand up. "What were you thinking, leaving the group during the raid like that? He'll probably lock you up down here again." He gazed around the room and picked up the file. "Where did you find this?"

"In my locker."

"We've been searching all over for it. How long has it been in your locker?"

Isabelle shrugged. "Probably since it's been missing."

"Right. Let's go." He put the file under his arm and wrapped a chain around her wrists.

He was ruthless as he dragged her through knee-deep snow to the headmaster's quarters. With no way of catching herself, most of Hertz's jerks sent her sprawling face first into the snow. She was sopping wet and freezing by the time they arrived at the front door.

An older butler opened the door and bid them to come inside. Isabelle attempted to stomp the remaining snow from her boots as she looked around. She was amazed at the foyer's golden chandelier hanging over the largest bouquet of flowers she'd ever laid eyes upon, especially in the cold climate of Differe. A double staircase stood behind the table of flowers, and large portraits of the Headmaster and his game hung on both sides of the place. A jerk from Hertz moved her toward him.

"Through here." The butler commanded them forward.

The two moved past the staircase into a large living area where they were met by a dozen soldiers and half a dozen Templins. All were encircling the headmaster's large leather chair.

"Let her go, Hertz." The man seemed irritated by her wet appearance and even more so at the chains around her wrists.

"But, headmaster, I found her—"

"I didn't ask, Hertz. That's enough."

The room was silent as Hertz quietly undid her chains.

"Isabelle, please come have a seat." He motioned to the ottoman in front of him and the other men. "I have some sad news, I'm afraid."

Isabelle sat down, wondering what could be wrong. She thought she was here to be reprimanded for leaving her dorm. She was still reeling from the information in the file but tried to brace herself. *What now?*

He reached over and patted her hand.

She fought the urge to make a fist.

"My Dear, we have just received word that your grandfather has passed away. He went quickly and peacefully."

Isabelle looked down, unsure of what this would mean for her. She wondered why her family hadn't sent for her to say goodbye to the man, but then she remembered her file. *Seems there's a lot about my family I don't understand right now.* She lifted her head when the headmaster held out a tissue. "Will I be able to stay here?"

He seemed surprised at her lack of tears as he rubbed the tissue between his fingers. "Well, as soon as we received the news, his last will and testament was thoroughly examined. He does wish you to remain with us; however . . . it's clever." He stopped and nodded to a Templin. "His payment to ensure your completion here at the temple, he actually hid in your dormitory."

"The night raids . . . ."

"Yes, My Dear. We were finally able to discover the object this evening, but we can't seem to open it. I thought you might have an idea as to how to do that."

His phony smile disgusted her as she felt a Templin come up behind her. The man placed a small egg-shaped case into the headmaster's hands.

She raised her eyebrows at the object. "Can you break it?"

He shook his head. "Then I would risk breaking what's inside."
He carefully gave her the hand painted porcelain case. "See, on the bottom, there's a lock code with numbers and also a spot for a key."

Isabelle took the turquoise egg and looked for another opening. Thin lines of gold trimmed the side portions, but there were no visible cracks or hinges that she could find. She turned the egg over and studied the bottom portion with the lock code. She instantly sat back in recognition, and she knew the others saw the expression register on her face as well. *There's no use in hiding it.* "Yes. I do know how to open this."

The man clasped his hands in delight. "Splendid. I'm glad you'll be able to stay with us."

She narrowed her eyes at the man's manipulation. "I said I *know* how to open it, not that I *can* open it. You have what I need."

"I? What do I have of yours?"

The eagerness in the quiet room was palpable.

She held it back out to him. "My locket. My locket contains the code *and* the key to open this."

His smile faded into a dark frown. "You're sure?"

"Positive. Besides, I'm sure you searched my room and didn't find any codes or keys. Hertz also has my school file now. You can look for a code in there, but it'll be useless without the key."

The headmaster rubbed his dark mustache then rose and looked around the room. "Proceed, then, with your plans." The surrounding men sprang into action at these words, separating in all directions. When it was just the two of them, he looked down at her again and stuck his hands inside the pockets of his silk robe. "Isabelle, it seems we've located your old friend again. I know the rumor is that he magically made his way to Waiz, but we both know his handicap would make him incapable of such a feat. Though, we do know for certain it was him who came back and broke into the chapel."

Isabelle didn't move.

"No, it seems he only got as far as the West End. He's caused quite a bit of trouble there, but the imbeciles of that place are hiding him in Facilis. They don't know what a danger Joel is, to them or their region. He must be contained. We need something to draw him out . . . or someone." He leered over her.

"Bait," she whispered.

"The stakes are higher this time, My Dear. We have joined forces with New Waiz, and they need a menial task to try out a new operative force. Catching Joel in Facilis is part of the plan. That way, I win and they win."

She drew her eyes away and wondered what she'd be asked to do this time.

"He didn't take you with him either time. I believe that was because he knew you'd be all right. We can't provide that as an option this time. He will come to your rescue and be captured, or you will be killed. Those are the terms. He won't have a choice not to take the bait."

Her eyes blazed with fury as she stood to face the man. "Yes. Yes, he will."

Startled, he backed away from her. "Fine. For your sake then, I hope he makes the right choice." He waved a hand in the air. "Officers, come! You may take her."

"Wait!"

He held up his hand to the officers clutching her arms.

"Sir, please. Please may I—may I write a note to my family . . . to my brother?"

He folded his hands. "You could, Miss Isabelle, if that were possible. You see, your brother was taken to Waiz according to your parents report. They were hoping to improve his health, but . . . their efforts are in vain. He's dying, with little time left, and no amount of fresh air or warm weather can change that."

Isabelle was escorted back toward campus by a Templin and a Differian guard. As they moved through the snowy night, the guard stopped when the group heard a rustling noise in the trees beside the trail. "What was that?"

An owl hooting drew the three over to the edge of the trail. The woods seemed silent until suddenly the guard vanished into the thick brush. She and the Templin stared at one another just before the man was snatched before her very eyes. She stood wide-eyed in panic until a voice called to her, "Isabelle! Run!"

She dashed up the trail.

"Faster! Keep going!"

Someone in the woods was moving alongside her. She finally stopped at the boundary gate and searched for her rescuer in the clearing.

A junior Templin rushed toward her. "You've got to run. You've got to get out of here!"

"Holt!"

"Come on! What can I do to help you leave?"

She tugged at his coat. "Holt, stop. I can't." She shook her head at him. "I can't run. Not this time. It's no use."

He stopped pacing and grabbed her hands. "Isabelle, no. No, you have to run."

She drew them away. "To stay here is a lie. To run is impossible. You saw the army, all those Templins."

"Isabelle, please! They . . . they really will kill you. It's not a game this time. Not some junior Templin training exercise. Isabelle?" He tried to block the gate.

"No, Holt." She squeezed his shoulder and pushed past him to open the gate. "But, thank you for buying me some time to go see Sarah."

Isabelle flew to the music room. She was desperate to see Sarah before they took her. She fumbled with the key in the dark but was soon locking herself inside, hopefully buying a few precious minutes. She raced to Sarah's quarters and pounded her fists on the door. "Sarah! Sarah, wake up!"

The door opened, and Sarah's eyes squinted at Isabelle in the light as she awakened from her sleep. She widened the door and urged the girl inside. "Come in. Come in. Tell me what's happened."

Isabelle didn't sit in the chair Sarah motioned to. She shook her head as Sarah sat on her bed.

"I don't have much time. They'll find me here any minute."

"Who? What's going on?"

"The Templins . . . my grandfather died."

She nodded for her to go on.

"They found Joel. He's in Facilis, and it seems the people are hiding him. It's terrible, but that's not the worst of it."

Sarah rubbed her face as she digested all the information.

"New Waiz and Differe have joined forces. I'm not sure what it means, but as a preliminary move to celebrate their alliance they're going to Facilis. 'Just a menial task,' Dark said." Isabelle jumped when she heard banging on the door downstairs.

"To catch Joel?"

"Yes, and just him . . . but it seems they couldn't come up with a new plan. 'They lack creativity' as Dr. Pryderi would say." Isabelle stopped when they heard the door open downstairs.

Sarah rushed to her side and grabbed her arms.

"I'm not afraid, Sarah. I only ran away so it would look good . . . so I could tell you goodbye."

"Oh, Isabelle." Both hearts pounded as loud footsteps marched across the floor downstairs. Sarah pulled her into an embrace.

"With my grandfather gone, they have no use for me here. Please, Sarah." Tears choked her speech as the footsteps marched up the stairs. "P-p-please, contact him for me. Don't let him come for me. Please."

Sarah reached out and held her face one last time. "You are so brave. Much braver than I ever was." Then she quickly pushed Isabelle away. "Here she is, officer. I've been waiting for you."

"What did she tell you, Ms. Harte?"

She crossed her arms. "Goodbye."

The man nodded. "It's time."

CHAPTER 50

ANDI TOOK NOTHING with him. He didn't want what he'd just discovered about his father to fall into the wrong hands, and by that he meant be buried. As he traveled in the dim light of dusk, he felt unafraid about turning himself in. However, he did fear for Arianna and what might happen to her.

"She's a grown woman, Andropolis. Whether you want to admit it or not, she is, and she has the right to choose her own life."

"Yes, but, Mother, she's making the wrong decisions. Will you do nothing to intervene?"

"Would it have done any good in your case when you joined the Order?"

Andi shook his head as he recalled his mother's words and crossed over the river. Though her words were the truth, they didn't remove the nagging feeling deep inside him. He still desperately wanted to do something to stop his sister.

He crept to the edge of downtown and made his way through the streets stealthily even with his slight limp. He wasn't going to get caught. *I won't give them that pleasure.* He stopped at one of the Order's hideouts to retrieve a brand new green cloak and thought hard about taking the bow in the corner of the room. He knew Marcell wanted a grand scene, especially one with him exposing the murder weapon. Though Arianna said the man's orders were simply for Andi to turn himself in, the orders in the man's letter had read differently. He'd been instructed to get caught during one of the higher class parties to impress the new diplomat from Differe. *He intends to make a spectacle of me . . . there and at the trial.*

Andi searched the room for a clock. It was Friday, and he knew full well where Marcell would be tonight. *He'll be dining at the Amerus Mansion along with other members of the Order.* Many of Andi's first assignments were to simply stand guard at these elaborate parties. The top business owners of New Waiz usually spared no expense, and, though watching the richest of the rich mingle was hardly a job, the food was always delectable. He pulled the green hood over his head and realized he was more than happy to give the people a party no one would soon forget.

Once the mansion was in sight he stopped to determine the best entry point. *The roof? Up from the basement? Just walk up the front steps?* He gazed at the security checkpoints and eyed all the Green Cloaks standing by. *Should be easy to blend in among them.*

"Hey, you there."

Startled by the whisper and angry he'd been spotted, Andi slowly turned around to find a young man in uniform. *A Differian?*

"Headed to the mansion?"

Andi nodded from underneath his hood, suspicious as to why the soldier was still whispering.

"I know I'm not with your party, but might I accompany you? My general's inside. I know he'd be most obliged, as would the Headmaster of Differe."

Andi knew the soldier dropped the headmaster's name to show some weight, which only served to pique his curiosity further. "You may . . . in exchange for information. What business does your general have with New Waiz?"

"Well, Sir, you've probably already heard. It's General Langston, the new diplomat between Differe and Waiz. He's helping your head council, Master Marcell, implement some new government policies."

"Ah, so you're with Langston. You're welcome to accompany me." Andi started moving down the darkened street, his heart racing as he thought of what to do next. *Langston? What's he doing here?* "Do you think I could have an audience with your general?"

The young man shrugged. "I'm not sure his duties would permit him time."

"Well, I met him in Differe not too long ago. He told me to contact him once I was done delivering letters."

The soldier chuckled and seemed to relax a bit. "He meant you joining the army, didn't he?"

Andi nodded again.

"Well, he's going to meet me outside in half an hour. Why don't you tell him yourself?"

"Perfect."

The two guarded the right rear of the house in silence, which made the half hour seem tortuous. Andi was relieved when he finally saw a glamorous individual head from the mansion in their direction. *It's Langston all right.* The man was out of his uniform and decked out in a double-breasted suit. His hair was combed straight but had just enough curl to perfectly frame the handsome features of his face.

Langston looked behind him then faced the hedge Andi was standing beside. "Howell?"

"Over here, General Langston. I have an acquaintance of yours with me." The soldier pointed to Andi as Langston came around the hedge.

Langston raised an eyebrow at Andi's hood. "Oh, and who's that?"

"Says he's ready to join your army, Sir."

The general studied Andi's frame and fiercely marched toward him. "Is that so?"

Andi didn't budge. "Big or small—I can work with either."

Langston stopped as his eyes narrowed in recollection. "Hm. Yes, you proved that in our sword match at the temple. Done delivering letters, Andropolis?"

"I've been doing a little more than that these days, Sir. You may have heard."

The man nodded and crossed his arms over his chest. "I have, and I must say I'm impressed."

Andi removed his hood, and the general reached out to shake his hand.

"What can I do for you, Andropolis? You must know, due to my new title, I can't hide you with my men."

"I understand, General, but I didn't come here to join your ranks."

Langston didn't try to hide his surprise. "Oh?"

"No, I came to turn myself in."

"What? Why would you do such a thing?"

"It would give the Order great pleasure to find and capture me themselves." Andi took a step forward and held the palms of his hands out to Langston.

The man looked down then searched Andi's face. "And . . . you intend to make them look bad, is that it?"

"I intend to pay them back for using me."

The general looked down at Andi's surrendered hands again. "And, that's where I come in."

Andi waited silently as the general rubbed his knuckles back and forth over his lips. The man finally turned back to Officer Howell.

"Get the others. We'll be fine until you get back." The soldier hurried off, leaving the two alone in the darkness. "Tell you what, Andropolis, I'll go along with your plan. I like it—makes Differe look good—but . . . I'd still like for you to consider my original offer. I need some information that you might know. In exchange for it and your allegiance, I'll sway the trial and get you out of here."

Stunned by the offer, Andi didn't know quite what to say.

"Just think about it. I'll expect your decision before the trial."

Andi nodded, and soon Howell returned with three more soldiers.

The general began unbuttoning his coat. "Well, I'm sorry to say, we'll need to roughen you up a bit before we drag you inside."

CHAPTER 51

"Vᴇʀʏ ɢᴏᴏᴅ." JOEL patted Erin's father on the back.

"Who says you can't teach an old man something new?" Harding's leathered face drew into a smile as he pulled another arrow from the stack.

"It's 'teach an old dog new tricks,' Father." Erin approached with Dillon at her side. The two had been inseparable since being reunited in Facilis, and thankfully Harding had softened quite a bit. He actually seemed pleased about the romance.

The man steadied his bow again. "I'd prefer to let Jack be in his own category."

The group chuckled as they spied Earl's dog nearby.

"Drat, you made me miss the target again."

"It's our fault, huh?" Erin laughed as she threw her arms around her father's neck.

"Yes, it is." He squinted his eyes at her then kissed her cheek.

Joel searched over the archery training ground. There were over a hundred and fifty people practicing, with fifty more folks like himself overseeing. *Except . . . I suppose I'm a bit different than the rest of them.*

Joel had become "master overseer" of the West End Regime. The surrounding villages and cities were quick to voice their agreement when the Vicar had initially endorsed Joel for the role. The matter was then settled among the leaders after the council was reorganized. The week had flown by since he'd put up the Facilis Flag, and community had sprung up everywhere. The Vicar had gathered groups inside the chapel, teaching them about the sacred stones, bariques, and rhydids. Joel desperately wanted to sit in on one of the classes not only to learn more himself, but also because he figured the Vicar would explain how to read people. The man had somehow known all about him—his past *and* his future. *And I want to know how to do that.* But being master overseer didn't allow him the luxury of much free time, so he could only duck into the Vicar's classes from time to time as he oversaw the other leaders and their groups. Some groups he tended to supervise more than others. Simon led the archery ground, Dillon led the guards in hand-to-hand combat, and Earl worked with the city engineers. Even Violet was leading agriculture groups in the park. Joel was pleased each time he visited a different spot to find two things: the groups were not only diverse in age and social class ranking, but also being equally led by Facilis inhabitants and those once considered outsiders. Everyone was working hard to prepare for Differe's attack, but being the overseer meant he didn't quite belong to any group. Though he felt lonely at times, he always reminded himself to look at the people's faces. *It's okay. We're all where we're supposed to be.*

One group he tried to visit more often was the hospital workers. Augustine was the leader there, collaborating with the specialists on using medicine and herbs to protect the people from more smoke and other elements Differe might try to use. He glanced at his watch and decided a visit was in order today. He darted through the city streets he'd come to know well and made his way toward the hospital. After he'd kissed Augustine, the two had been swept away in meetings then separated into their positions, never getting a chance to talk about . . . *well, we haven't been alone together since then.* Though both were now staying in rooms in the Vicar's tower, he had yet to see her. He figured she was coming in late and waited every night on the Midway Terrace for her, but she never came. He wanted to speak to the Vicar about their situation, but they too had yet to have a private meeting since he'd taken leadership. It seemed he was either never alone or always alone. He told himself they had made the right choice in staying here, and only felt unsure of this when Sebastian's face haunted his dreams in the night.

He ran up the back staircase, secretly hoping he'd get a private audience with the group's leader today. He very much enjoyed entering the way he'd escaped, always surprising the floors by coming from the stairs versus the elevator. The response was generally the same, and today was no exception.

"Oh, hello, Master Joel." The charge nurse grabbed at the white lab coat hanging on the back of her chair, and suddenly the whole floor stood in attention. Rarely did anyone move from his or her position until he spoke.

He nodded and offered them a salute of sorts. "Hello, just checking in. Everything going all right?"

Everyone always smiled and nodded politely, but today he sensed an uneasy tension in the room. He looked around the floor at the hardworking bunch and noticed someone was missing. "Where's your leader?"

The group responded with silent glances to one another until one of the young doctors at the back of group stepped forward. "She's—she's on the terrace, Sir. Needed some air."

Joel sighed, knowing the temper of his dear friend. "I'm sorry if she was too harsh on any of you."

Several glanced down at the tile floor while the young man shook his head. "No, Sir. Not at all. She's much harder on herself."

Joel nodded and made a few more observations before heading out to the lunch terrace. He found the dark beauty tucked in a corner chair with her knees pulled to her chest. She jumped when he pulled a chair beside her, but then immediately went back to her pensive posture.

"Uh, hi." When she ignored him, he tried again. "Bad day?"

She buried her face into her knees.

"Want to talk about it?"

She shook her head back and forth.

"Okay." He shrugged as a sigh escaped from his lips. He sat back to stare at the sky, and, without meaning to, fell into a light sleep. When he awoke from his nap the chair beside him was empty. *Great. Good job, Joel.* He sat up and found Augustine looking over the terrace wall with her shoulders slightly shaking. He frowned, wanting to know what would make her feel better, yet enjoying the view of her standing in front of him. Her dark hair flowed wildly down her back as a long black dress peaked out from under her lab coat. As he studied her though, he soon discovered something wasn't right. Worry crept over him as he quickly stood up and moved toward her. "Augie?"

Her head turned toward him. Her eyes red from crying didn't concern him nearly as much as the dark circles outlining them.

"Augie!" Alarmed, he rounded in front of her and gripped both of her arms. "When was the last time you slept? Have you been eating?" He looked down and shook the baggy dress.

"The file . . . ." Her voice sounded distant, almost comatose. "I lost the file . . . a whole week's worth gone."

Her pale face made him want to shake her. "Good grief, you're exhausted. You haven't been coming home at all, have you? Augustine!" He tried to get her attention, but it was like she was looking past him. "I've—I've been waiting for you every night on the Midway Terrace. I just thought you'd been going on to bed. I knew you were coming in late but—"

"Why were you waiting for me?"

He was glad to see a sign of life in her puzzled stare but felt a lump in his throat when he attempted to answer her question. "Well, uh, I-I wanted to see you."

"To talk about the hospital?"

He shook his head and smiled. "No. Not at all." He gently moved a piece of hair from her face. He reached out to take her in his arms, but she didn't budge. "Because I-I . . . I'm ready to not be afraid of losing you anymore."

Her stiffness seemed to melt at his words, and soon the two were in a full embrace. She sighed as he rested his chin on the top of her head.

"You need a day off."

"I can't. No one else is taking one."

"I'm ordering you to take a day, or a few days, off." To his surprise, he felt her nod in agreement. "I'm taking you back with me right now."

She drew her head back, forcing Joel to look down at her. Her eyes filled with tears, yet he saw beyond the sheer physical exhaustion into her very soul. With every wall crumbling down, he saw Augustine raising her white flag in surrender to him. "Please take care of me."

He was sure it was the first time she'd ever uttered those words in her life. He held her face and nodded. "That's exactly what I plan to do."

CHAPTER 52

SUNLIGHT SPILLED INTO Andi's cell from the window high above him. He held his tin plate up to the bright beams to catch his reflection. His curly raven black hair was matted down from sweat and dirt after a fitful night's sleep on the grimy prison floor. Dried blood was caked around his mouth and under his nose. Langston had only hit him twice, but the man had made them count. All of his teeth looked intact, but he wondered if his nose might be broken. He rubbed his head and attempted to loosen the hair plastered to his forehead.

The prison was located close to the Bridge of Miren, with its architecture mirroring the two towers. The medieval gray stone surrounding Andi made for less than comfortable seating on the uneven floor. His cell had three walls of this stone with an entrance comprised of wrought iron bars. "So we can keep an eye on you," the guard had told him.

As he studied his beat up face, he couldn't help but contemplate Langston's offer again. He hadn't been able to stop thinking about it. He had the opportunity to be acquitted and removed from the clutches of the Order. *The Order.* He wanted to give Marcell a piece of his mind. Why had no one told him the truth about his father? He already felt used by his boss, but Marcell stealing his sister's innocence and controlling his mother's health fueled Andi's hate with feelings of betrayal, manipulation, and even persecution. It was as if all his rights were gone. *But they're not.* Seeing the guests' faces at the Amerus

Mansion when he was dragged in by someone other than the Order was most satisfying. He'd helped secure Langston's favor with the most influential New Waizens outside of the Order.

Though pleased at the turn of events, he couldn't help but feel suspicious of his new ally. After all, hadn't Langston used him too? Something about the man seemed amiss. His title wasn't befitting. The man certainly had diplomatic charm, but Andi knew he was truly a general at heart. *What's he really doing here?* He hated the thought of dishing out the Order's secrets even if they had wronged him. If he betrayed them, he would sink to their level in a way. He also wasn't sure he wanted to jump into another army right away. *Especially in such a cold place.* He despised the notion of living in Differe. *But . . . at least I'd be free.* Arianna and his mother soon came to the forefront of his mind. He'd be leaving Waiz, but more importantly he'd be leaving them.

For the first time in years, now knowing the truth, he longed for his father. *If only I had his book to search through right now, maybe I'd have some direction.* He heard a shuffling down the hallway then a slamming door. He faced the back wall and tried to catch a glimpse of the blue sky far above his head. When the shuffling feet stopped outside his cell, he tossed his plate across the floor.

"I didn't come to eat."

Puzzled, Andi turned around. He found a man dressed in white and khaki linen standing in front of his cell. The large, burly man had a long brown beard and seemed strangely familiar to him. He looked to see if the man held his cell keys.

"Andropolis, I came to talk. Well, that is to say I've been appointed to defend you in the trial."

Andi took a step closer. "Who are you?"

"My name is Corwin Audrey Atticus."

Andi took another cautious step as he thought about the name. "I recognize your name. You! I remember you now—you're a spy from the Old Order."

"Am I? And how do you know such particulars, Andropolis . . . have any ties to the New Order?"

Andi was annoyed by the man's playful tone. "What do you want?"

"I need you to talk to me. No one from New Waiz signed up to defend you, so now your defense is me—"

"Old Waiz is defending me? Might as well have a death sentence." Andi gritted his teeth angrily until the pain from his sore jaw stopped him.

"Easy now. Don't get all worked up. I'm more of a diplomat for the Old Order . . . much like Langston is for Differe." The man stopped there and cocked his head. "Have you considered his offer, Andropolis?"

Andi's eyes widened in surprise. "What do you know of it?"

"Let's just say we diplomats stick together. We both need information, which means we both share a little with the other. Now, back to my question. Do you want to join Langston?"

Andi sighed as a door slammed overhead. "I don't know."

The man nodded. "Very good. I'm glad you're not being impulsive. You've got some time to think on it. The trial is set in two days."

"Does that mean I have to listen to you the next two days?"

"Polite chap, aren't you? No, today is our only meeting." Corwin went silent as a guard approached the floor. He quickly moved out of the man's way so he could retrieve Andi's plate.

"Mr. Fancy Attorney, did you bring me the fortis? I need some to make it through my next shift. Working overtime." The man hacked into a cloth and looked at Corwin eagerly.

Andi watched Corwin pull a vial from his shirt pocket. "Here. They have you working this whole place alone?"

The man pulled the cork stopper out with his teeth. "Yeah. Short-handed. Seems odd, though. Think something's brewing around here." The man nodded at Corwin then took the shot of fortis.

The whole scene disgusted Andi. This Corwin character was no better than Marcell. They were all dabbling in the drug system. The thought of this man defending him suddenly made him feel sick. A loud thud outside the bars distracted him, and he rushed forward to find the guard passed out on the floor.

"He'll be fine, Andi. I gave him a sleeping drug. I need to speak with you alone. I worked with your father in the New Order many years ago—"

"You knew my father?"

"Yes, he . . . he was a mentor of sorts to me. I guess you could say I was once his apprentice."

Andi stared at the man, dumbfounded and breathless.

"I knew you too once . . . when you were young."

"What happened?"

"Too long of a story for now, but I promise when we have time I'll tell you everything. Until then, I need to tell you what's going on right now."

Andi gripped the iron bars separating the two.

"First of all, I want you to know your mother contacted me. Lucy's much more involved than you give her credit for."

Andi shook his head in disbelief.

"She told me about Arianna and the Ferox. You do realize your sister is one of the biggest chess pieces in Differe's game, don't you?"

Sudden heat rose into his chest. "What do you mean?"

"She discovered and concocted the drugs. She also discovered Differe's army in your woods . . . ."

"I don't understand . . . ."

"I don't fully either yet, but I think that troop was sent here to scout out Waiz for Differe, not to help New Waiz. Getting their hands on that drug will ensure they have an invincible army."

The pieces started coming together in his mind. "Oh no. Arianna . . . oh, Arianna. It's bigger than I realized."

"Yes. Arianna helped create the Black Ferox, but what she doesn't know is she's helping create a world power—an army of Ferox—more powerful than she realizes."

"Can you get me out of here? I have to get to her!"

"I can . . . but I need you to go to the trial. We need Langston on our side . . . we need to see what we're dealing with—the Ferox."

"And the Watchmen. They're sure to side with you after they are attacked."

Corwin nodded.

"But Corwin, Arianna—"

"She's a key player, Andi."

He ran his fingers through his hair. "Why?"

"Because she gets her instructions from something supernatural. The old woman who first gave her the salus venom . . . what did Arianna say happened to her?"

Andi paused, trying to remember what Arianna had told him. "I . . . oh yeah! She refused to say. Corwin, she was terrified."

The man crossed his arms and nodded. "Right. I'm not sure what that's about, but your father's book will help, I think."

"Right." Andi nodded then covered his face with his hands. "Oh no. I-I left it with my mother. I—"

"Andi, I've seen your mother. I've got the book, more than one in fact."

Andi nodded as he wiped beads of sweat from his brow. "Thank you."

"All right, now that you understand about Arianna, you can understand the plans."

"What plans?"

"Marcell's, Differe's, and Old Waiz's. This is where it gets even more interesting. They're after a certain acquaintance of yours."

"Who?"

"His name is Joel. You met him in my room at the inn in Adams."

Andi wasn't sure what Corwin was talking about. He had searched loads of rooms in Old Waiz.

"Then you met him again in the hotel room following the murder. In fact, some think he's the one who murdered Clovis."

"The redheaded kid!"

"Right. That's the one."

"What on earth do they want him for?"

"I haven't quite figured that one out except for the fact that Joel escaped from the Temple of Differe, and I don't think that's allowed."

"That's Differe's fight then. What does that have to do with Marcell?"

"That's the part I haven't figured out yet." Corwin looked down then back into Andi's eyes. "But they want him . . . badly . . . which means something. I know you don't know me, Andi, but if they catch him whatever is valuable about him will be in their hands—"

"The wrong hands in your mind."

"Exactly."

Andi thought about the kid for a minute. He still vividly recalled his sword clashing against Joel's iron poker in Corwin's room. Andi had seen something about him change, something he still didn't quite understand. *But Corwin's right. There's something valuable about him.* He crossed his arms and smirked at Corwin. "So, you want him too? Is that it? For Old Waiz . . . bargaining power?" His expression faded when he saw a sadness overcome Corwin's face.

"He has my niece."

"Where is he?"

"The West End in Facilis. As you know, the place is neutral, so neither side can go in and get him . . . yet. He has her with him, and they have something her dying brother needs."

"What do you want from me, Corwin?"

"I want my niece safe. They're going after him, so she doesn't mean anything to them, and I'm not confident in her safety." The man closed his eyes and let out a big sigh. He took a step forward and grabbed one of the bars. "Langston's given you until the trial to decide about joining his army and sharing the secrets of the New Order. I'm giving you until you return my niece to decide if you want to join Old Waiz."

Andi threw his head back. "What? Are you kidding? Join Old Waiz? Why would I want to do that? They hate me. I killed Clovis! Uh, I mean—"

"That stays between me and you for now. Andi, I know I can convince Old Waiz to forgive you. I—"

"There's no way. I don't believe that for a second! And, why would I want to join another Order? All you're going to do is use me."

"I'm just saying think about it. Wait to see how things play out. Above all, read your father's book."

"And how will I get my hands on it again?"

"Arianna. She's your ticket out of this mess. She's going to save your life."

CHAPTER 53

ANDI WAS PARADED onto the Bridge of Miren with his wrists shackled, flanked on either side by Watchmen. Because the murder concerned both the North and the South, the trial was being held in Neutral Waiz. It was the exact same spot as the murder leading Andi to believe the Order had probably planned this on purpose so the people would remember. They were making sure he would be found guilty.

His head bobbed underneath the hood as he was moved along. He was grateful he'd at least been allowed to keep his green cloak. As soon as he reached the middle of the bridge, angry shouts rose up from Old Waiz, and New Waiz called out nasty jeers in his direction. The Order had succeeded in turning both sides against him. His Watchman guard led him to a bench facing the Old Waiz crowd. After a few minutes, Andi felt a shift on the bench and noticed Corwin had joined him. He glanced past the man, finding an identical bench next to theirs holding two men from Old Waiz. *Clovis's representatives.* Beyond the podium a few feet in front of them, rows of chairs had begun filling up with the Old Waiz Council. Andi guessed the New Waiz Council was settling in behind them.

"Good day, Andropolis."

Andi nodded but didn't look at the man. "Corwin."

"It's a big day . . . pay close attention."

Confused by his sharp tone, Andi's head swiveled to see the man's face.

"*Watch,* and be on *guard.*"

Andi raised his eyebrows at Corwin's coded words then searched around the bridge. He noted the entrances were guarded by Watchmen, and many of them were managing the crowds on either side. The surrounding hotel balconies were even full of spectators, and he soon spotted the one he'd shot from. *They're everywhere. Do they know about the Ferox?* He sucked in a short breath. "Why are there so many Watchmen?"

"Be on your guard, Andi, then get out."

"Corwin, I—"

"Ready, Corwin? Let's get this thing going." A man from the adjoining bench strutted toward the podium and motioned to Andi's counselor.

Corwin stood to his feet and smoothed his shirt. "Proceed. My defendant and I are ready."

By the time the man reached the podium both sides had grown quiet. "Good morning citizens of Waiz. Because this offense was against Old Waiz the trial will be directed toward the west side. We welcome our friends from the North but remind you that you are in neutral territory." The man turned around to face the audience on the east side. "New Waiz citizens, you are also welcome here as this trial involves one of your own. Thank you all for attending. I will now give each representative the floor to disclose his opening statements." The man moved aside and motioned Clovis Macon's representative to come forward.

"Waizens, we have suffered an enormous loss in leadership. The taking of Clovis Macon's life, or any man's life for that matter, is unacceptable in this region. The taking of one's life devalues mankind. Andropolis Fidel has not only taken a man's life; he has devalued his own as well as those around him. His actions suggest that he does not value life, so I propose his be taken as restitution for Old Waiz and for the safety of New Waiz. In my opinion, there is only one verdict that will satisfy both sides—guilty." The man backed away, and to Andi's dismay both sides seemed to nod in agreement.

A knot formed in his stomach as Corwin approached the podium. His heart raced as he waited for his father's old apprentice to defend him. His eyes combed the crowd for General Langston. Where was the man who'd promised to spare him, to meet with him before the trial so Andi could give him his answer? He dared not look behind him but searched the surrounding entrances and balconies. With no luck, he directed his gaze back to Corwin.

"Old and New Waiz citizens, I volunteered to represent Andropolis Fidel in this matter. Though a citizen of Old Waiz, I have deep-rooted ties with the young man's late father, Thaddeus Fidel." Gasps escaped from both sides, and Corwin waited for the crowd to quiet again before he continued. "I had a clear view of the event that took Clovis Macon's life and believe I have evidence that will prove Andropolis Fidel is innocent in this matter, or, at least, not entirely guilty . . . particularly, in that he was not alone. If you recall, there was a redheaded young man stumbling onto the balcony from where the shot was fired. So, I ask you, Waizens, before you pronounce Andropolis guilty . . . take his life . . . where is the redhead? What happened to *him*?" Not one in the crowd responded. Corwin gripped the podium and leaned forward. "Old Waiz, in addition to these questions, I ask you to consider, or perhaps remember, the sacrifices his father made for you before the New Order condemned him to death. His father's death was more than enough retribution for this action." The man licked his lips and turned to the east side. "And, New Waiz, why are you so quick to judge one of your own? One who chose to give his life for you? His cloak symbolizes his ranking as a member of your Order. He took an oath of duty. So, I have a question for you to ponder as well. Was this murder done by the redhead or by one of your members in the name of duty?"

Andi stared at the man in awe. Corwin had just given himself a death sentence. The grim expression on Corwin's face as he returned to the bench led Andi to believe he knew this as well. *Why? Why would this man defend me like that . . . give up his life? And what did my father do for Old Waiz?*

The silence lasted only a moment before shouts from Old Waiz erupted. "I say we kill him!"

"Yeah, kill him!"

"Hear, hear!"

A cold sweat came over Andi as the shouts grew louder and New Waiz joined.

"Wait! Give him to us!"

"Let us deal with our own!"

"Yes, we'll kill him!"

Panic festered in his soul, but he soon felt Corwin's large hand on his shoulder.

"Andi, get ready." He nodded toward the towers.

Andi squinted through the morning sun at the tower window and suddenly saw movement. *The Ferox!* He looked down at the chains binding his hands then to Corwin. The man's eyes were locked on the Watchmen who were beginning to block the angry mobs from the bridge's entrance. As the crowds grew louder and the commotion escalated, suddenly dozens of black cords draped down from the tower window. Andi turned to find the same sight on the other tower, where individuals clad in black leather army suits were already zipping down the cords. He turned back just in time to see the black suits take out several of the Watchmen guarding the bridge's entrance. More cords were expelled from the towers, some even shooting onto the nearby buildings. Black suits continued pouring out of the tower, flying over the crowd and onto the buildings to attack the Watchmen. The crowd was in a frenzy, with people screaming and running in every direction. *This is it! This is what Corwin meant about Arianna saving my life!* The Ferox overtaking the Watchmen was the perfect diversion needed for him to break free.

His racing thoughts were interrupted by Corwin pulling him to his feet. The man lifted a radiant sword from under his robe and motioned for Andi to extend his hands. Though puzzled, Andi obeyed and watched in wonder as Corwin sliced the chains in half and opened the clasps. "How did you—"

"Andi, find Arianna, and get out of here!"

"They'll—they'll kill you—"

"Your bag's in the barn behind the hotel. It has everything you need. Take this." Corwin tossed him a small sword.

"I-I, Corwin—"

"Go! And remember, when you decide which side you're on, come find me. I'll make a path for you." Corwin started forward, waving his sword at the approaching black suits, but Andi rushed forward to pull him back.

"No! I'm not choosing a side, and I'm not losing you—not until I find out about my father."

Corwin seemed astounded by his strength. "Andi, what are you doing? Get out of here! We can't both escape."

"Yes . . . yes, we can, but I'm taking you another way." Andi looked away from the Old Waiz crowd and finally spotted Marcell, Langston, and the New Waiz Council scrambling toward them. "Follow my lead." Andi jumped behind Corwin onto the bridge wall and grabbed the man's sword. He brought it to Corwin's neck just as the councilmen from either side encroached upon the scene. Both sides stopped at his threatening gesture.

"We can't let him get away!"

"I think we have bigger problems than him." Corwin nodded in the direction of the Watchmen, who appeared to be losing their fight against the Black Ferox.

"Get up!" To the other's horror, Andi forced Corwin onto the wall with him.

"He's going to force Corwin to jump!"

"Stop! Get down!"

Marcell finally moved to the front. "Andropolis, drop the sword. There's nowhere for you to go. This is foolishness!"

Andi ignored him. "Langston!"

The general made eye contact with him.

"You didn't think I'd actually get caught for good, did you? I'm done carrying letters." And with that he forced himself and Corwin over the side of the bridge.

Corwin broke their fall, knocking him out cold on the stone floor. As Andi caught his breath, he couldn't believe what he'd just done. He only hoped what the crowd saw was a disappearing act—that he and Corwin had simply vanished into thin air. *And, I hope Langston saw something more.* He had just exposed one of the Order's greatest secrets. Right in the middle of the bridge, on either side, was a small landing jutting out several feet from underneath the bridge. The structures were enclosed by refracting mirrors, making them literally nonexistent to the naked eye. The mirror covering the top of the landing was a swinging trap door, allowing for an impressive escape or a remarkable spying spot. The landings themselves led to tunnels in the underside of the bridge. Andi dragged Corwin off the landing and into the tunnel. Though he believed most of the New Order wouldn't dare follow him and risk more suspicion, he also knew no one had seen a splash in the river below. Hopefully the councils had enough on their hands with the Watchmen-Ferox chaos. He grimaced, knowing full well he had provided the perfect opportunity to launch them. *Both sides at the bridge, the Watchmen all gathered . . . pretty strategic in gaining the upper hand. Yes, "surround Old Waiz, demonstrate power, and draw out fear." Reads just like the Headmaster's letter I brought back to Marcell.*

Andi struggled to heave a limp Corwin over his shoulder. The large man was heavy, but Andi's surging adrenaline provided the edge he needed to start down the tunnel. He headed right when the tunnel forked at the end of the bridge, knowing it would lead him all the way to the train station. He had to get out of Waiz, but he stopped suddenly when he felt Corwin's sword at his side. *Arrows. I have to get arrows. And those books. The barn. Corwin said, "It will have everything you need."* He sighed as he considered taking a detour to get the bag. *How will I not be seen? If I keep going, where will I leave Corwin? He has to be left someplace safe. I guess—I guess I can leave him in the barn.* Andi figured if the man thought it was safe enough to stash the bag there, he'd be fine there as well.

Andi switched directions and tried to calculate how far away the barn was from the bridge. He couldn't remember the exact exit, so he began counting his steps. Sweat poured down his body as he walked through the dark tunnel with the heavy load. He wiped his eyes when he realized he might be close and looked above for a way out. Corwin moaned as Andi set him down to light one of the torches hanging next to the wall. With his exit spotted, he loosened Corwin's leather sheath from his waist and secured it around the man's left shoulder then removed the jury robe and tied it around his other shoulder. After blowing out the lantern, he climbed up the skinny metal ladder to force open the exit.

To his dismay, he popped up in an empty street. His eyes darted around the area and spotted the barn in the distance. He clamored back down the ladder and heaved Corwin upward using his makeshift ropes. They both groaned in pain as Andi lifted the man onto the street. He hurried to remove the sheath and robe from Corwin then hefted the man over his shoulder again. He shuddered as something whizzed by his head. *The Ferox!* A black figure zooming down the building across the street from him sent Andi running. *Get to the barn. Just get to the barn.* As he rushed forward, he wrestled with whether or not to lose Corwin. The unconscious man was an easy target. Andi scrambled up the street in a zigzag pattern trying to confuse his pursuer. When he heard the boots speed up then stop, he knew what was coming. Just a few feet shy of the barn door, he threw Corwin onto the ground and grabbed the metal top of a trashcan to shield both of them from a flying arrow. The black guard instantly moved forward again to take another shot. The blows felt unlike any Andi had ever experienced. His arm soon ached from holding the lid and deflecting the steady stream of arrows.

The frustrated Ferox shot a cord from his gear into a tree hovering over the barn and zipped out of sight. Andi panicked as he searched the tree, now not knowing which direction to protect. An arrow nearly grazed his left arm, then his right. He was shielding back and forth until the uneven cobblestones under his feet sent him sprawling backwards. With his back on the ground and his gaze upward, he finally spotted the black guard again. His enemy was drawing an arrow, but this time it was aimed at the lifeless Corwin. Andi jerked himself upward and rolled onto Corwin's body, bracing himself for the hit. He was surprised when he felt nothing and heard a loud thud in front of him. He glanced up to find the Black Ferox in a pool of blood under the tree.

"Psst. In here."

Andi looked up to find a man leaning out from the barn loft. The barn door slid open, and several men came out to help bring Corwin inside. Andi slid the door shut then turned to face around seventy men and women. His eyes were suddenly drawn to a little boy hoisted up on crutches. "I recognize you."

The little boy nodded and pulled Andi's quiver from around his back.

Andi slowly took the object from him. "You were with that redhead and the girl . . . and Corwin."

"That's right."

"You're the one who's dying." Andi immediately regretted saying the words, but the little boy remained calm.

"I need Joel, and I need *that girl.*"

"Who are all of you?" Andi searched the group's faces.

"The Thaddean Army."

He scratched his head. "Never heard of it."

An older man stepped forward and handed Andi a bag and his bow. "You will. Your father started it long ago."

Blood rushed to his head. "Why . . . why after all these years do I know nothing? And, why aren't you killing me—taking me prisoner? I killed Clovis." He was unafraid to look them in the eye.

A large woman shook her head. "You were just doing your duty. You're not a murderer."

The man handed him a stack of arrows. "Corwin believes in you . . . and, when I saw you lay across him to sacrifice your life, I saw your father."

Andi stuffed the quiver full of arrows. "Corwin told me nothing about you. He told me to find Arianna—to get out of here."

"Then go." The man gestured to the door.

Andi gritted his teeth as he looked at Corwin then the little boy.

"I'm Sebastian, and I *know* Corwin. He told you to go, but he also gave you something to think about—that something is us."

Andi knew the little boy wasn't referring to Corwin asking him to return his niece or to deliver Joel; the boy meant joining them. He leaned toward Sebastian and shook his head. "You don't want me on your side."

"It's not my choice. You—you're the one with the decision. The Ferox, the Watchmen, New Waiz, Old Waiz, New Order, Old Order, Differe's Army . . . the choice is up to you."

A cough from Corwin startled everyone in the room. The man opened his eyes in a daze. "Andi—Andi, where are you?"

He strode over to the man. "I'm here. In the barn . . . with your army."

"Never mind that! I overheard from Langston that Arianna will be on assignment to Facilis. Get to the train station now!"

Andi blended in beautifully with the surrounding Green Cloaks around and inside the New Waiz train station. He concealed his quiver under the cloak, along with the small sword Corwin had given him. He was alarmed to find a huddled group of Watchmen entrenched in the middle of the station. Two Green Cloaks guarded them with a Black Ferox nearby. He searched the station for more Ferox and Watchmen, but most importantly the train to Facilis. He spotted the departure listings and saw the train was leaving in twenty minutes.

Andi passed by the ticket counter and headed straight to the platform. He would stowaway if necessary.

Much to Andi's aid, the platform was extremely busy. Steam was pouring from the engine car up front while engineers tinkered with and inspected it. The rest of the train was being loaded with passengers or parcels carried by Green Cloaks and station employees. *Perfect.* He gave his hood another tug as he got in line alongside his former comrades to help load the train. He knew most would recognize him in an instant. Andi marched behind the others into the loading car, set down his box, yet instead of turning around with the others he walked through to the other side of the car. Just as he hoped, there was no one on the other side of the train as he made his way toward the back cars. Hiding in the back made the most sense at this point.

Andi cautiously crept beside the train, then searched for a way to climb one of the last cars on the train. *The ladder's too obvious.* He looked at the lever on the sliding door and thought it might be high enough to secure a grasp on the roof. He placed his foot on the lever to hoist himself up, but a black flash caught his eye. In one quick motion he placed an arrow in his bow and spun around.

CHAPTER 54

A NDI!" A FAMILIAR shape dressed in a leathery black suit rushed toward him. "What are you doing here? Are you all right? Oh, I'm so glad you're all right!" Arianna reached out and hugged him tightly.

Though relieved to see she was well, Andi found it hard to embrace her as his fingers met the slick black fabric. He pushed her away, unsure of what to make of his feelings. "Look at you."

"I heard it was quite a spectacle . . . taking over the Watchmen."

"Uh, yeah. So nice of me to provide the perfect scene for your black tyrants."

"Andi!"

"They'll use you, Arianna. Marcell . . . he'll use you to get what he wants. He has little regard for your well-being. I—"

"We've had this conversation, and I've made my decision."

"Arianna, I just want to see you—"

"You're not my father."

He put the arrow back into the quiver. "I hope I'm closer than I realized."

"You're talking madness."

Though she'd already broken his heart with her choices, it filled with grief as he made the decision to choose against her. *If she's to save me . . . I'll have to lie to her.* He drew in a deep breath and crossed his arms. "I-I, Arianna, no,

332

I've always wanted to care for you, but even a good father eventually let's go. Sorry, seeing you like this is new for me. I mean, look at you." He circled around her, and she seemed a bit startled. "You're no longer a girl. You're a warrior, Arianna. I'm proud of you. It took me being in prison to realize that. You've made your choice, and I support your right to choose your own way."

She straightened slightly and narrowed her eyes at him. "What are you really doing here?"

"Uh, if you think long enough, I'm pretty sure the answer will be obvious."

"Oh, it wasn't just to make up with me?"

"Well, you missed the trial, but let's just say I have a death sentence if I stay in Waiz. Both sides want my life."

She pulled her hood back and tousled her black hair. "Yes, hence the disappearing act. Marcell won't take kindly to you taking such a risk in exposing the underground tunnels, Andi."

"I'm done with Marcell, Arianna, and that was for his benefit. General Langston cut me a deal."

Her eyes narrowed in confusion.

"I met him in Differe on duty, and he invited me to join his army before the murder. As far as I know the offer still stands."

She crossed her arms. "We'll see about that. He's near the front of the passenger cars. Come on. I'll take you to him."

Andi found Langston exactly as he expected—dressed in the best uniform money could buy and sitting down to a meal served on fine china.

Due to her new position, Arianna appeared to have complete clearance to the man's car. "General Langston, may I interrupt your meal with an official matter?"

He dabbed his mouth with the linen napkin on his lap and welcomed her inside. "Of course. Work always trumps food."

"I found this man attempting to sneak into a car near the back of the train." She motioned to Andi behind her.

"A Green Cloak? Why the need to hide, Sir?"

With only the three of them inside the car, Andi removed his hood.

Langston sat back in his chair and clasped his hands. "Ah, that would explain it. Andi, I must say I'm impressed again. I'm glad I was right about you—there's much more to you than meets the eye." He stood up and held out his hand. Andi took it and noted Arianna's look of confusion.

Langston nodded to her. "That will be all, Arianna. Thank you."

She shot Andi a timid glance.

"Thank you, Arianna." Andi smiled at her reassuringly and followed her out with his eyes.

"I hear she's one of the best they have."

"The Ferox?"

"Yes, Marcell's lovely super humans."

Andi took a seat across from the man. "You disapprove, Sir?"

The man poured himself a cup of coffee. "Of the Ferox? Not necessarily. Or if you're referring to Marcell, well, I'd be more inclined to disapprove there. Would you care for a cup?"

"No, Sir."

Langston poured a bit of cream into the mug. "Did Corwin survive the fall?"

"Yes, but I left him unconscious."

Langston finally looked up and smiled at him. "Thank you for that little tip. Refracting mirrors. Clever. Very clever."

"Just letting you know I was serious about taking your offer."

"Ah, and where would you like to go, Andropolis? What would you like to do?"

"Well, Differe's a bit cold for me, so I'd like to stay south or . . . in the West End perhaps."

The man nodded as he pulled some forms together. "Yes, Differe wouldn't suit you. Too boring anyway for a talent such as yourself. Is there anything else you would like for me to consider in your placement?"

"Sorry, is that your son?" Andi pointed to a picture of a brown-haired boy sitting on the man's desk.

"Yes, that's my only child, Holt. He's just a little bit older than Arianna."

"I recognize him. I think I met him in Differe . . . yes, he took me to get the letter from Isabelle the day I met you."

The man rubbed his hands across his face. "Huh, funny you should mention her."

"Why?"

"She's the Ferox's first assignment."

Andi didn't understand. "What about taking over the Watchmen? That didn't count?"

"That was in Waiz, Andi. No, this is Marcell's opportunity to show them off to the other regions, to breed fear and gain power." Andi could tell Langston wasn't in favor of this plan.

"What does Differe think about this?"

The man waved his hands at him. "Well, you know Differe. Oh, I forget you really don't." The man sighed and looked back at his son's photo. "Andi, Differe is all about rules, principles, and regulations. We don't believe in manipulating power for power's sake. What Marcell is doing with these Ferox must be stopped, or, well, given boundaries. He's already running wild with his power in Waiz, taking out the Watchmen like that."

"What does he want with Isabelle?"

"He doesn't." Langston went silent and took a sip from his mug.

"All right, then why does Differe want her?"

"Because she will lead us to someone."

"The redhead."

The general appeared amused at his guess. "Ah, you know about him? Oh, that's right, you've encountered him already—the murder. Anyway, Marcell is sending out his Ferox to show them off."

Andi's eyes narrowed. "To who?"

"The Headmaster. If all goes well, they have plans to work together on something more important and much more political. This is simply a test run for Marcell and the Ferox."

"How about me being involved in the more important political scheme? Sounds interesting."

Langston seemed surprised at his request, but a coy, almost wicked smile soon crossed his face. "Hmm . . . I think you need a test drive too. I like to test my men's loyalty."

"The coup at the trial wasn't enough evidence for you, or the fact that I face a death sentence here?"

"I like your directness, Andi, but you're a bit different than most of my men. I'm taking a spy and making him my spy. Pretty precarious for me. A big win or big slip up."

Andi stood up. "Name your task."

Langston pursed his lips then looked toward the door. "Accompany the Ferox, or rather, follow your sister on this assignment. No doubt you want to keep an eye on her."

"Fine." He was grateful he'd be with Arianna.

"Family is important to me too, Andropolis." His eyes rested on the picture of Holt again. "Your assignment on this team is to ensure the Ferox fail."

"Sir?"

Langston's eyes glowed as he turned them to Andi. "You heard me."

Andi didn't flinch, but simply signed himself over. "I'm in."

CHAPTER 55

BEING IN THE same car with Arianna and the two Ferox was near torture for Andi. He mentally reviewed Langston's assignment for him several times. The man wasn't convinced this Joel kid would show. This freed Andi from having to make a decision just yet. If this boy, whom all the regions wanted, didn't come for Isabelle, then Andi wouldn't be forced to choose a side. His head was swimming with all the information. *It's either betray Arianna, pay back Marcell, and secure my future in Langston's army or rescue Corwin's niece and Joel then return to the Thaddean Regime. And there's almost too many options with this Joel kid—save him for Corwin, kill him for Marcell, or wound him for Langston.*

"You're lucky, you know." Arianna slid into a chair across from him.

"Am I? I don't feel it."

"Just think, the Order led you to Langston, Marcell brought Langston to Waiz, your trial brought in the Ferox, and now you have a future under one of the most powerful generals of our time. Yes, I'd call that lucky."

"But now we're no longer on the same side."

"Close enough. Both have amazing leaders."

He sighed. "Arianna, I'm not lucky. I'm not even free. I'm being forced into choosing the Differian Army. And do you know why? Do you know *who* forced me out of my region?

"Ugh, Andi. Quit being so ungrateful at the turn of good events."

"I don't forget that quickly, Arianna. I performed actions for the Order, and this is how I was repaid. They'd have let me die."

"You don't know that. Besides, don't you take a member oath that states you're willing to die anyway?"

Andi paused to remember the oath. Though his member robe had been waiting for him in the tower, he hadn't had the opportunity to take it upon his return. "Maybe. I wouldn't know."

She shrugged and smiled at him. "Well, in any case, I'm glad you'll be with me. You can see me in action for the first time."

Her smile reminded him of who she used to be, and he smiled back. "I'm glad too, and I've been meaning to ask you something."

Her eyes danced with excitement. "What?"

"You never could beat me before . . . but by the looks of your arms, well, I'd say I'm a little nervous to ask for a match."

She smirked and let out a little laugh. "Yes, Dear Brother, I do think I'd bet on myself this time around. An arm wrestling match it is."

"You're on."

The two gripped hands and were about to count down when one of Arianna's comrades interrupted them. "Arianna, time for your fortis and a few others."

She kept her grip. "It can wait."

"No, come now. Marcell's orders."

She sighed and pulled back from Andi in defeat. Her eyes drifted across the room as she stood up and strode over to the guard.

Andi sighed as he weighed the idea of betraying her, realizing how much she trusted him now. It made his stomach churn almost as much as the memory of a man he barely knew being willing to give up his life for him today. Corwin's trusting spirit somewhat disgusted Andi. *Fool. Why would he have any faith in me? I can still betray him—I could tell the Ferox or Green Cloaks all about his barn full of traitors, yet he seems confident somehow . . . maybe even certain . . . that I'll do what he asked.* Andi had an idea as to his certainty, but even he wasn't willing to admit Corwin's option was the "right way" just yet. *For now, it's just "Corwin's way."* He couldn't argue that the man had challenged his thinking, or morals rather, in the past few days. *But haven't I been searching for answers? For meaning? For something else . . . something to make sense?*

As he recalled the events of the trial, he realized the most terrifying moment of the day hadn't been seeing the Ferox taking out his region's Watchmen. Not even Corwin's self-sacrifice had impacted him the deepest. He knew what had wrecked him most was the faces of the people in the barn. They, this regime apparently named after his father, had every right to despise him, accuse him, and pity him, but they didn't. He closed his eyes. *Bunch of soft lunatics. What was it about them? It made me feel . . . feel . . . I don't know.* Corwin said Old Waiz would forgive him. Was it forgiveness he'd felt? He'd forgiven others, though, and it hadn't ever had this effect on them. The faces in the barn had showed him esteem, hope, and like Corwin—*faith in me.* He straightened his cloak as he watched his baby sister pull up the sleeve of her uniform. He reminded himself one more time that he was still in control, yet was overcome by a deep pain in his soul as he watched Arianna inject herself with the powerful drug. He grimaced and finally looked away, knowing right then his decision regarding Langston's assignment was made. As he looked out the window he heard the man's last words to him, "Above all else, the girl must live."

Isabelle was thankful the Templins didn't bind her hands as she rode on the train. The windows were blacked out with dark panels, so she had no way of knowing the time or the terrain, but at least she knew where she was heading. *Somewhere near Facilis.* No one had spoken to her except the kitchen chef, and then she was only asked, "Fish or chicken?" Usually there were two Templins in the car with her except during shift changes, then there would be four in the room for a few minutes. She tried to listen for any information that would be helpful to her, but so far she'd heard none. After several shift changes she was finally left with just one guard. As she eyed the man, she realized he was nearly her father's age. She was surprised when he returned her stare.

"Um, am I allowed to ask questions?"

The man shrugged. "Sure, just understand I may not be allowed to answer them."

"How much longer on the train?"

"Not much. This is the last shift."

Isabelle nodded. "How many days until action?"

"Two."

"So, what will you do with me for two days?"

"About like today."

"Right." She was glad his tone wasn't unkind as he simply relayed the facts. Even so, she looked up at the ceiling feeling hopeless. *There's no way out.* She closed her eyes. "What will happen to him . . . if he comes?"

"Those aren't our orders."

She turned her gaze back toward him. "What will happen to me if he comes?"

He drummed his fingers across the chair. "Well, you, uh, you'll be set free in Facilis. You can do whatever you like after we have him."

The twitch at the corner of his mouth led her to believe he wasn't being entirely truthful. *No one is ever truly free from Differe.* She sighed and swallowed hard. "And if he doesn't come . . . what then?"

He finally dropped his gaze from hers. "I was told you knew the orders."

She suddenly found herself wanting to force the Templin to say what he obviously knew was wrong. She narrowed her eyes at him as he continued avoiding her gaze. "I forget, what did they say?"

"You will die."

"Oh, that's right. I remember now."

He finally turned back toward her. "I'm sure he will come." She knew he meant to bring her comfort, but in the end neither result would do that.

"Who will catch one of us?"

"We're not supposed to say, Miss."

"I'm going to find out in two days whether you tell me now or I meet them myself."

His mouth twitched again. "It's some new division. It's not ours . . . but our ally's."

"Yes, New Waiz. I'm surprised they'd waste their time on such a task." *Come on, tell me something! Why is New Waiz involved? Who's the new operative?*

"No task the headmaster desires is ever seen as small."

Their conversation ended there, with Isabelle being thankful Sarah had two days left to contact Joel. If there was any way she could, she knew the woman would find it. The hours ticked by, and eventually the lone guard fell asleep. This shift seemed longer than normal, yet Isabelle was thrilled to have the opportunity to move about the train car without anyone watching her. She peeked underneath the black panels and saw nothing but the dark night sky outside. Her stomach growled, and she remembered the chef hadn't brought her dinner yet, so she headed to the small kitchen near the back of the car directly across from the washroom.

The chef dropped a pile of ingredients on the floor when he noticed her in the doorway. "Goodness me!" He wiped some sweat from his forehead with a dirty dishtowel. "Sorry, Miss, you startled me. Hungry?"

She nodded then began helping him pick up the items off the floor. "Yes, very. I'm sorry about scaring you."

"How about the Templin? Does he want anything?"

"No, he's fast asleep."

He shot her a sly smile as he put a spice box onto the shelf next to her. "More for you then. What can I get you?"

She sighed then grimaced as tears suddenly filled her eyes. "I'm sorry. It's just—" She waved her hand at him and took a deep breath to compose herself. "Make me one of your favorites . . . y-yes, that's what I want."

He patted her hand. "I'll do just that. Here, this seems to help all the prisoners we take aboard." He stuck a small electronic contraption into her hand.

"What is it?" She held it up and studied the buttons on the small device.

"It's a voice recorder. You can, well . . . put your last words or your last will and testament on there if you like."

"How about . . . how about a message to someone?"

He nodded with a sympathetic smile. "Perhaps. Whatever will do you the most good. Just let it all out."

Isabelle pursed her lips then looked to see if the Templin was still sleeping. "What will you do with it when I'm finished?"

"I'll get it to Joel, of course."

CHAPTER 56

A DAY AND a half later Augustine had slept nearly twenty hours and spent the remaining hours taking three bubble baths and eating generous amounts. Joel had somehow managed to make sure she had everything she needed and more. In fact, she hadn't left her room since the day he'd practically carried her from the hospital. She was feeling revived but wasn't ready to go back to work just yet. During her down time she realized how little rest she'd had since leaving Waiz. *Joel and I are due for a vacation.*

After finishing her supper, she decided it was time to put on something other than pajamas. She hoped Joel would be waiting for her on the Midway Terrace and decided on the short blue dress she wore the first time she visited Mr. Rutherford's shop. Though she'd been so mean to him that day, she could tell he liked the dress when he'd mentioned it later as they were talking in the barn. She was glad Corwin had suggested she stuff one dress in her backpack. The dress had been a little snug then, so with a few extra pounds gone it fit just right. One final look in the mirror and she headed to find Joel.

She smiled to herself when she spied him just outside her door. "Joel!"

He sprung to his feet and broke into a huge smile as he rushed toward her. "Now, this girl looks familiar to me."

"Yes, I'm much better."

"Yeah, you had me a little concerned there. You look great."

Suddenly it felt surprisingly awkward for them to be alone, and neither knew what to say next. Augustine shifted in her dress and twisted her ring around her finger while Joel fidgeted with his hands.

"Thank you. I mean, thanks for all the food and rest—"

"Come on." He suddenly grabbed her hand and pulled her outside toward the massive terrace.

"Where are we going?"

"Really, Augustine?" He looked at her then to the narrow walkway.

"Be nice! I'm recovering from exhaustion."

"Yeah, I just didn't know it affected your brain."

"Uh . . . ." She tried to remove her hand, but his grip tightened. "Slow down!" They were practically skipping along the narrow walkway of the Midway Terrace.

"We've got to hurry! I don't want to miss another chance to do this."

"Do what?" She scurried behind him until they reached the end where the Vicar usually stood.

Joel turned to face her and tilted his head. "Look out there."

"Okay." She turned her head slowly. "Wow, I . . . this is what the Vicar sees." She gazed down into the square below.

"Not down, Augie. Look out."

She sucked in a breath. "I . . . I see the sunset. The smoke's nearly gone." She leaned forward and squinted. "Looks like a few riders coming up."

"What?" Joel looked out to find she was right. He pursed his lips then shrugged. "Well, at the least the Vicar's down there. Look." He pointed below. "See him? He's right by the gate."

She nodded, as his brow furrowed in concern.

"I'm sure . . . I guess it's nothing."

She could tell he was clearly distracted by whatever he was wanting to do. "All right then, out with it. What's the rush? What are we doing out here?"

"Well . . . the sunset. I wanted to give you the best view. As I recall, the last time you complained about me taking the best spot."

"You did, but there's lots of room here."

"Oh, I don't think so. I think there's less room on this one." He slowly reached out for her.

"Oh?" Her heart fluttered as she drifted into his arms. *What's happening?* She tried to calm herself down.

"I want to kiss you."

She heard the nervousness in his voice but saw a blazing new confidence in his eyes. She marveled again at the change in him. "What do you hear in your head right now?"

Joel looked down and shuffled his feet. "Don't be afraid, Joel . . . don't be afraid."

She raised his chin with her hands and looked into the eyes that seemed to pierce her soul. "Well, then. Don't. Be. Afraid." She closed her eyes as he moved in but only felt him graze her lips before he knocked her onto the concrete.

"Wha?" Her eyes fluttered open just in time to see a string of arrows fly above them. Joel hurried her into the corner while shielding her body. She covered her mouth in fear. "The riders! Joel, the Vicar!"

He nodded then grimaced. "I'm a fool, so careless."

"It's my fault. I-I distracted you. I—"

"No. You're not a distraction. It was a mistake."

He looked away from her, and the words, however he meant them, stung her deeply.

"All right, let's crawl forward. I think they've stopped. Augustine, come on!"

She quickly shook off her pain. "What? Right, I'm coming."

The two made their way quickly across the terrace on their hands and knees. "Get inside, Augustine."

"Joel!"

"Shush! Don't say my name!"

She cringed at his scolding then dashed inside the building. Guards were inside to meet them.

Joel threw his hands up in the air. "What's happened?"

"Templin riders, Master Joel. You were in full view."

Dread overwhelmed Augustine. "The Vicar?"

"He's negotiating with them now."

Joel started forward. "I have to go to him."

"Wait a minute!"

"They'll kill you!"

The Facilis Guards attempted to block his way.

"Wait." Joel stopped pushing the officers. "Why are the Templins here . . . or why are there only a few of them? Our numbers clearly exceed theirs."

"I believe that's my fault, Sir." A short man covered in ashes stepped forward.

"Hubert!" Augustine broke through the officers into the arms of her chef and fashion consultant from the train to Waiz.

"Hello, again. You look lovely, as usual."

She hugged him then brought him over to Joel. "Joel, this is Hubert, the one who hid me and helped me get off the Waiz train."

Recollection flooded Joel's face. He stretched out his hand to the man.

Hubert became solemn as he shook Joel's hand. "I've recently helped another one of your female friends." He pulled a small rectangular object from his pocket and handed it to Joel. "It's a voice recorder, and it has a message for you. I-I had to escape the Templins to get it to you in time." The man let out a horrible cough and staggered backwards.

"Oh, Hubert!" Augustine saw blood seeping through his trousers near his left thigh. "Guards, get me some bandages!"

"The Templins were after *me*, Joel, but . . . I'm sure they were delighted to see you as well."

Joel eyed the guards angrily. "How did you get inside the gate?"

"I let him in."

Joel bit his tongue and gave Simon a curt nod before turning his attention to the voice recorder. "How do I use this?"

"Just—just hit the button to hear the message."

"He needs water." Augustine began trying to stop the bleeding.

The room went silent as someone from both Joel and Augustine's past spoke from the little black box. "Joel? Joel, it's me. It's Bella. I've—I don't have much time, but the Templins . . . the headmaster is going to try to convince you to—to rescue me. You can't come, Joel. It's a trap just like last time . . . except . . . this one is worse. They're sending a new operative. I'm—I'm not sure what that means, but it's not Differe. It's Differe's ally—New Waiz, I think. They're going to tell you it's an exchange—your life for mine—but they're lying. Do you hear me? They're lying, Joel! You can't come. Don't come for me. Go to Sebastian! Oh, please take care of my brother. The headmaster—I don't know how he knows . . . but he knows Sebastian's in Waiz. Oh, Joel, he says he's horribly ill . . . doesn't have much time. Oh, please hurry to him! Tell him—tell him I love him . . . and take care of Augustine. And, I want you to know that you—you were right . . . about everything. Don't forget to tell Sebastian I love him."

Every fire that could be ignited in Joel's spirit was lit as he rushed down the stairs. Blood pumping, rhydid drawn, he was ready to cut the Templins' heads off. The shouts from the guards chasing him were drowned out by Isabelle's voice in his head. It was the first time in his life he was actually ready to kill someone. *And I am. I'm going to kill them.* He was nearly out of breath by the time he reached the door at the bottom of the capitol building. He forced it open only to be met by four more guards.

"Master Joel, put the sword down."

"Let the Vicar handle it for now."

As the guards tried to reason with him, Joel seethed inside but knew he couldn't fight his own men. With guards blocking him behind and in front, they led him out of the stairwell and under the building's stone awnings. From there he could make out the Templins and the Vicar talking near the gate.

"Why are you all here? Go guard the gate! No one's at the gate with the Vicar!"

"Master Joel, he's negotiating. The guards can't interfere."

He couldn't believe they were all standing by watching the meeting from afar. *I have to do something.* He cupped his hands and drew in a deep breath. "LET HER GO! DO YOU HEAR ME? LET HER GO!" He was pleased to see the Vicar turn around. He had the gate's attention.

"Joel, is that you? Come out here! As soon as we have you, we will let Isabelle go!" The Templin slammed his hands against the gate.

"Lies! You bring her here!"

"You think us mad? Bring her here with your whole army inside?"

"Joel, quit talking! Get back inside!"

The guards finally let him step forward when the Vicar started marching toward them. He ignored the Vicar but kept his eyes on the Templins gripping the gate. "No! Our orders are for you to meet her in Baithe."

Joel stepped out from under the awning. "I'm not a fool! Your proposal is madness!"

"Stop!" The Vicar held his hands out between the opposing parties. He looked at Joel with obvious disappointment then turned back to the Templins. "He will not come."

"Then we will kill her!"

"NO!" Joel bolted forward on a wild rampage. The Facilis Guards swarmed behind him, but he kept his focus on the Templin cloaks, his sword out and aimed to kill. The Vicar darted into his line of vision and caused Joel to stop short of the gate. Joel tried to resist him until the man froze and let out a shout of pain. He fell forward taking Joel with him.

"Vicar! Vicar!" Joel heard the guards shouting as he pushed the man upward.

Blood spilled from his mouth as he tried to speak. "Juh-juh—"

"Oh no." Joel craned his neck over the man's shoulder and found an arrow piercing his thick robe. The white fabric was turning a deep red. "Vicar!" He pushed the man onto his side. "I'm sorry. Oh, Vicar—"

The man gasped for air. "Joel . . . Joel, focus on who you can save. The time for you to leave Facilis is soon. Leave before Differe comes. L-l-leave soon . . . ." He gasped again, his eyes fluttering. "The underground . . . the pipes . . . to the Southern Regions . . . hi-hi-h . . . ."

Joel couldn't make out the man's last word. The Vicar of Facilis was dead.

CHAPTER 57

ANDI KEPT HIS eyes focused on the area he knew his target would enter. Langston assured him this Joel character wouldn't show, so instead of stationing himself among the Ferox inside Baithe's square he climbed a high tree right outside the stone wall to wait for Isabelle. *She'll be coming from the north train.* It was late afternoon, and Joel's bait was to arrive in five minutes. She'd be alone and was to head to the village square for the exchange, yet his plan was to make sure she never made it beyond the tall grassy field in front of him. Andi steadied his breath when he saw movement across the field. A small, cloaked individual scurried around the brush and made for the woods in the opposite direction of Baithe. "What in the world—"

"Odd thing for him to do if he's hoping to be found."

Andi jumped when Arianna skillfully slid toward him from a nearby tree on one of her black cords.

She let out a low whistle and another Ferox instantly appeared behind her. "Seems our bait is loose. Looks like he's trying to hide."

He? They think Isabelle is a "he?" Andi nodded. "Who's in the square?"

"You worry too much, Andi. We left one of us there . . . we knew the redhead's showing up was a bit of a long shot."

"Apparently, so did his bait." He fumbled with his bow and wondered what Isabelle knew.

"Hm. Well, I suppose we'll still wait our twenty minutes to see if this Joel guy comes, but after that . . . ." She lifted a knife from her belt.

Andi tried not to grimace at his sister's gesture. He glanced back across the field. *Oh, Arianna. No guilt at the prospect of killing . . . just like me with Clovis.* He wished he could tell her the action wasn't worth facing the aftermath of emotions and torment. "I've lost sight of her—uh, him."

"Hunting such a small radius shouldn't be a problem. I'm more concerned about the weapon he has. You know, the one he and Joel stole from the temple?"

"Hunting an unfamiliar area in the dark . . . that might be a challenge, Arianna." *Weapon? What's she talking about?* Then he understood. *Langston! He lied to the Ferox to help me out and to keep her safe.*

She nodded to Andi then the other Ferox. "Well, let's move then to get a head start in 'rescuing' the bait."

Andi sighed as he made his way down the tree. He tugged at the strap on his quiver and questioned whether or not he'd be successful in completing his mission. *Does Isabelle know she's as good as dead?*

Hoping the gray cloak the Templins had given her would provide a bit of camouflage, Isabelle huddled and faced the inside of an old hollow tree. Her heart pounded as she awaited her pursuers' next move. The whistle, a few calls . . . her enemy was here. *And Joel's not.* She fought off tears, thankful he'd obeyed her request. He'd laid down himself—his desires, his love, his heart—for her his whole life. *And now it's my turn.* She fidgeted with trembling hands, knowing this game of hide and seek wouldn't last forever.

"The stakes are higher this time, My Dear. If he does not come, you will die." She cringed, recalling the headmaster's casual tone in delivering her death sentence. Joel was needed alive. She somehow knew that she was always meant to be a casualty. The sound of footsteps sent her heart racing. She cowered as the steps drew nearer to her hiding spot. *Should I run? But then what?* She shuddered as the footsteps grew closer and closer. Then, to her amazement, they kept going. Hope surged through her. *Maybe they won't find me. Maybe that's the only one. Maybe*

. . . maybe I could run . . . . She slowly turned around, and a quick peak revealed a heavily armed man and woman only a few yards away.

"All clear! East?"

Isabelle jumped at the sound of the woman's voice and heard someone coming from another direction.

"Clear."

"Clear on the west. And he would've had to pass us to go south."

Isabelle waited as the footsteps moved past her again, but she heard only silence. *Four. One woman and three men.*

"Well, I say we make camp for the night and wait the bait out."

A shiver went up Isabelle's spine as the woman walked up right behind her.

"Hear that? We aren't leaving! We have orders to kill you!"

"Arianna, shut your mouth!"

"I'll say what I want, Andi. We Ferox will pair up here. You can do whatever you want. Seems you like hiding out by yourself anyway."

"Fine. I'll stay south, and I do hope those slick black suits of yours can get wet. There's going to be a downpour tonight."

"Oh, what on earth are you going on about?"

"The drought's over in the West End. Didn't you tell me rumor has it this Joel kid is the cause?"

"So what? He's obviously not going to come. His magic won't work on—wait! Andi, where are you going? What are you saying about the rain coming? I command you to stop." Isabelle heard her run after the guard.

"South, Arianna. I'll leave you three to your duties."

Isabelle remained huddled in her tree, desperately hoping the one called "Andi" was right about the rain, but there was no evidence seen in the sky above. She was parched by nightfall, and her legs were cramping from being stuck in her position. The group behind her sat in the dark divulging all sorts of information about something called the "New Order" and its plans.

Surprised the team didn't build a fire, she finally stood up to stretch her legs. The group instantly went silent, and Isabelle feared she'd blown her cover. She turned her head just in time for a swift breeze to hit her face. The hairs on her neck stiffened as a blazing flash of light whizzed past her.

BOOM!

Isabelle went sprawling from the tree. Lightning, thunder, and a harrowing wind descended on the group, sending each person scrambling for cover. One man made for Isabelle's hollow tree but was thrown back by a flash of lightning. The other man yelled for the group to move out of the woods and ran for the clearing. The woman, however, who Isabelle discovered was near her own age, spotted her and screamed as she covered her ears to mute the thunder claps. The two stared at one another amidst the chaos, and the young woman lunged toward her.

Buckets of rain began pouring from the sky as Isabelle made a run for it. She dashed out of the woods into the field in front of Baithe. The girl was right on her heels. Lightning revealed the entrance to the village, and Isabelle sprinted toward the stone wall in search of a hiding place. She felt the young woman slow her pace as she tore across the field. *Why's she slowing down?* Isabelle suddenly became frightened she was headed into a trap. *Andi! He was headed south. What if he's waiting for me behind the wall?* She glanced back to find one of the men had joined the girl in pursuit.

It's no use. Just keep going! It was nearly impossible to find her bearings in the downpour, but she hoped this meant the two behind were also having trouble. She was grateful for the lightning revealing her path. *Almost there!* She screamed as lightning shot from every direction near the wall. The flashing bolts soon seemed to block the entrance. *Just go, Isabelle. Just run into the light!* She hurried into the flashing lights and pushed inside the gate. She turned around to find her attackers were not so brave. They were close but slipping and sliding in the muddied field as lightning crashed around them. She was relieved to see them backtracking. She started up the hill and was horrified to see a dark individual standing directly in front of her. She shrieked, then noted the hooded cloak. "Joel! Joel! Is that you?" She stood frozen until another crash of lightning sent her sprawling against the stone wall, knocking her out cold.

CHAPTER 58

AUGUSTINE AWOKE WITH a start. She felt sweat trickle down her face. *Another nightmare.* She wiped her face and shivered. *It's just a dream, Augie. It's just a dream. Sebastian's not dead. The Vicar said you had until the end of the season.* A calendar flashed through her mind, and she knew time was running out. *Oh, please, I've got to get to him!* She heard the rumble of faraway thunder and looked at the clock. *Midnight.* She'd hoped it was near dawn. *Anything to get through this night more quickly.* She rubbed her eyes and knew there was no sense in trying to go back to sleep. *Isabelle's probably been released into Baithe by now and . . . .* She stopped herself, unable to bear the thought any more than Joel could. *Joel. I wonder how he's faring?* She knew if he could he'd be in Baithe this very moment. *But that's impossible now.*

The two had been put on lockdown in the cathedral. The Facilis guards wanted them safe in the middle of the city, yet being on the top floors near the bell tower served only as a horrible reminder of the Vicar's death. She was unsure if they were being kept there because the people of Facilis may try to harm them or if Differe's Templins were on their way to get them. She hadn't even been allowed to see Joel at first. Tonight was the first time since the Vicar's death that they'd been permitted to share a meal together. Joel had refused his dinner and remained silent at the table. Augustine knew what he was thinking. *The headmaster would surely keep his word.*

She shuddered as she rose to put on her robe. The only good thing that had come from that awful day was the information in the documents given to the Vicar regarding Differe's terms. Apparently Joel was still guilty of escaping from the temple and very much wanted by Differe, but he'd been acquitted of the murder charges in Waiz. *How does Differe know such a thing? Why even acknowledge Waiz and that Joel was ever there in the first place?* It didn't make sense to her, and she wasn't convinced Differe was telling the truth. She pondered what it all meant. And then there was the kiss. She wondered what would've happened if the riders had never come, never interrupting their moment in the sunset and giving Joel time to express his feelings to her. *I suppose I'll never know the answer.*

The guard outside her room stood to attention when she pushed open the door. "Just getting a glass of water . . . please."

He nodded and let her by.

She passed several more down the narrow hallway, having to gesture each time that she was thirsty and simply headed to the kitchenette to get a drink. None seemed too upset at her wandering about, as most of the men were perched outside a particular doorway in the large circular space that separated the hallways on the floor. She noted the curtains blowing about and figured the group was standing around a lookout spot. She got her cup of water and returned to the common area just in time to see the breeze from the open doorway blowing some army hats around. She tiptoed toward the opening and was barely able to make out Joel's head over the guards. He was leaning heavily on the railing, of what she now realized was a tower lookout, with his hand propped under his chin. She immediately went back into the kitchenette to grab him a glass of something other than water.

She took a deep breath and gestured at her two glasses as she approached the guards. They parted to let her onto the small lookout with Joel. Obviously deep in thought, he didn't seem to notice her. She finally cleared her throat. He slowly turned around, and she answered his look of surprise. "I was thirsty."

He said nothing and looked back out over the stone railing. She tapped his shoulder and gestured with the glass.

"Milk?"

She shrugged. "Well, it's not goat's milk, but . . . I thought it might bring back a few good memories."

He nodded and took the glass. "Waiz. Feels so long since we've been there. I wonder what's going on." He took a sip and grimaced. "Can't be great."

"It can't be altogether bad either. At least you're not wanted for murder anymore."

He bit his thumb and finished his glass. "Agreed. Also, two of our favorite people are there."

Augustine nodded, grateful he was at least talking to her. She kept herself from voicing her concerns about Sebastian just yet. *It's too much for tonight, and he heard Isabelle's message. He knows . . . he knows we need to get to him.*

He walked over and put the glass on a small table then moved back to his spot. He suddenly buried his face in his hands.

Augustine cringed when his shoulders shook. She felt paralyzed at the sight of his being undone.

"I should've gone to her. No matter what she said. No matter what they did to stop me. Why didn't I go?" He raked his fingers through his hair and turned his bloodshot eyes toward Augustine. "I should've just given myself to the Templins at the gate. Then the Vicar . . . and Isabelle . . . would still be alive."

"Joel, you don't know that. They may have killed all three of you. Differe can't be trusted!"

"But, Augustine, she risked her life . . . and so did the Vicar." He moaned in defeat. "If she . . . when they . . . ."

She knew he couldn't bring himself to say it.

"I won't be able to live with myself."

Oh, just let this night end . . . but what is that truly gonna solve? The reality of Isabelle's foreseen death combined with his words instantly shattered something inside her. She bit her lip and closed her eyes tight. *Don't cry, Augie. Hold it together for him.* Joel's last statement launched a series of questions to which she was dying to know the answers. She wanted to know about Isabelle and Joel, probably as much as Joel wanted to know about her and Isabelle, but she knew better than to ask anything at this moment. *And . . . part of me doesn't want to know.* The way he looked upon hearing her voice on the recording, the way he fought through the guards . . . it made her afraid his heart had been taken long ago.

Another loud sigh escaped his lips.

"Can—can I do anything?"

He cracked his knuckles and straightened slowly, his face serious and taut. "Get back to Corwin."

She felt stunned and jerked up when a clap of thunder sounded. Rain was coming in. "Did you—did you do that?"

He turned away from her. "I had to do something."

Augustine wandered back to her room like a walking zombie. Her soul was lifeless, her demeanor hopeless. As she rounded the corner she saw a familiar face standing outside her room. "Simon!"

"Hello, Love."

Augustine clasped her hands around his. "I'm so glad to see you. You can tell me what's happening, I hope?"

"Well, it's a bit of a mess really. The West End is still preparing for Differe's siege, but some think Differe won't actually come . . . meaning some believe that the terms Differe gave the Vicar are true—that all Differe wants is Joel."

"It's not safe for him in Facilis anymore . . . is it?" She searched his face.

"I'm afraid not. Opinions are varied."

Augustine shook her head, realizing it had taken less than a month for the people to become divided again. She sighed. "Will the people ever get along?"

"Well, what I came to tell you, Love, is that you're free to go."

She drew back from him in shock. "I am?"

"Yes, we've just been keeping you here for Joel. As long as he knows you're safe, he'll comply with us."

She narrowed her eyes in suspicion. "What do you mean 'comply'?"

The Facilis Guard hung his head.

She covered her mouth. "I can't believe it. Simon!"

He raised his head again. "Sh! The guards, our service . . . we have to listen to the majority, Augustine."

"You should do what's right! That's what the Vicar would want you to do. He'd—he'd find a way to convince the people of Joel's innocence, not use him as a scapegoat."

Simon stood silent.

"You do realize even if you give him up Differe may still try to overtake the West End."

"I do."

Augustine clenched her fists. "Don't tell him I'm free. Not yet."

"Fine."

She reached for the doorknob and twisted it.

"Augustine?"

She didn't turn around. "What?"

"We can only give him up . . . if he's still here."

Augustine pushed forward and slammed the door shut. She threw herself on the bed in the darkness and sobbed into a pillow. She cried throughout the night, envisioning Isabelle giving up her life and Joel's heart dying with her. The hours ticked by slowly, and when the sun finally started to rise she wondered if he was still on the lookout.

"Get back to Corwin," she heard him say in her head. *Yes, but how?* With Sebastian weighing heavily on her mind there was nothing more that she wanted than to get back to her uncle at this point. The black smoke was mostly gone now, but she wasn't sure there was even a way she could get back to Waiz. *The train station is closed, guards are at the gate, and I'm sure the roads are blocked. I don't know of another way out.* She instantly thought of Simon's words. *"We can only give him up . . . if he's still here." There's a way . . . there's got to be another way out!* She sat up and began to pack her things. *I'm free, so I can at least start trying to figure something out. Earl? Dillon? Maybe they'll know something.*

She reached under the bed for her pink bag and winced at the sight of it. She carefully opened the small pouch and dumped its contents onto the floor, fishing through the mess until her fingers reached several old photographs. *There.* She held the one up of her and Isabelle. Isabelle's blue eyes gazed back at her. Augustine's heart pounded as she stared at the two of them. Then, from the corner of her eye she spotted a rectangular piece of paper. Her heart lifted as she saw the name and title on the card. She knew it was worth a shot. *Talan Langston. He'll know the way out.*

Professor Louis shook Headmaster Dark awake. "Delano—"

"Drat, how long have I been asleep? I told you to wake me when—wait! You found them!"

The Professor shoved the headmaster's morning cocktail toward the excited man and sighed. "It's after ten, and you fell asleep about the time lightning took out all our communication systems."

The headmaster stared back at him with contempt and set his glass down.

"Seems there was a horrendous thunderstorm last night. We don't know the status of the Ferox or Isabelle."

The man growled and shook a fist in the air. "Or Joel."

"No, uh, there have been some new developments . . . ."

The headmaster clasped his jewel-adorned fingers together. "Oh? Yes?"

Talan Langston had been watching from behind the door and decided now would be the best time to make his grand entrance. He pried open the creaky door and strode across the room with his cloak flapping behind him. He knelt before the headmaster and kissed his ruby ring. "Your Grace." He bowed his head then stood.

The man clasped Talan's hand in delight. "Langston!"

"I have good news."

The headmaster patted his hand in admiration and motioned for him to sit down. "I'd expect nothing less from you. Such a fine follower."

Talan's insides revolted at the old man's petty compliment. "I've had a lead for some time." He paused and drummed his fingers on the armrest of his chair. "Just been patiently waiting for *her* to come to me."

The headmaster shot him a puzzled glance.

"Joel's had a companion all right. *She's* a Waizen."

"The girl who stole the rhydid with him! He did get there then. It's true. Old Waiz did send him back for the rhydid. They sent him back with that girl!"

Talan pursed his lips. "I'm not convinced it was Old Waiz itself, but someone from the old place, yes. I haven't gotten the girl's real name yet—seems she's known by two names in Facilis—but I'll find the source behind their mischief soon enough." He was pleased to see the headmaster's astonishment.

"Where are they? Is Facilis still hiding him?"

"Oh, they're still in Facilis, but his little friend wants my help. Seems the bait wasn't enough to snare Joel, but the guilt that followed is. He's ready to get back to Waiz. From what you've told me, he's been quite impulsive in the past. I have every indication that he wants to leave Facilis or . . . *escape* so to speak." The scowl on the headmaster's face let Talan know his play on words was recognized. He stood up and motioned to the Templin standing by the liquor caddy.

"You are aware they seem to understand how to use the weapon?"

"I know it has rained if that's what you mean. But, Your Grace, I don't intend to use force. No, I'll offer my services, gain a little more trust, and then we'll catch him."

"Just like that? After all we've been through? Impossible!"

Talan nodded his thanks to the young man, took a sip of his drink, then cocked his head at the exasperated old man across the desk. "Next time, perhaps, you'll contact me *first* in such a matter."

Suddenly the headmaster was on his feet. "I did! Diplomacy with New Waiz and the other regions was vital to our position. No one has the tact or social skills you possess. Wait . . . how long have you known about this situation?"

Talan slammed his glass on the desk and leaned forward. "I met her the day Joel escaped the second time! The entire army was alerted. Of course I knew about it. You even sent Magnus to ask me about any leads. Your Grace, how dare you send me away with such a delicate situation going on."

Professor Louis rounded in front of him, and his look of warning caused Talan to calm down and collect himself.

"I'm . . . I'm sorry, Your Grace. As your head general, I suppose I just feel that I should've been informed about this situation, no matter the entanglements of the past."

"So you can act like this? Defiant? Arrogant?"

Talan bit his tongue, knowing he'd learned these exact traits from the man himself.

"I was trying to protect you, Langston!"

"You lied to me!"

"I most certainly did not. I told you what you needed to know to do your work—keep your head focused on your duties. Emotions cloud your ability to act. You, of all people, should understand that. Besides, we didn't know it was him at first. Who else knows about your plan?"

A searing heat settled over him as he took in these words. "I'm alone."

The headmaster threw his hands up in the air. "I see. Seems you're convinced you can just go behind my back and do whatever you wish."

"I'm only honoring you with the same respect you showed me in this matter."

"Always speak your mind, Langston. I like and dislike that about you . . . far too much like your father."

"I'll take that as a compliment."

The headmaster rubbed his brow and crossed his arms. "Fine then. You have achieved diplomacy, so I want to reward your earnest efforts. I will allow you to retrieve Joel. You may have what you wish, Talan . . . but if you're so intent in bringing your emotions into this matter I have one request."

A rush of relief overcame him. "Thank you, Headmaster. What do you desire of me?"

"This is a father-son fight, so take Holt on the mission. Let him finish his first assignment. Unfortunately for you, James Reagan won't be there, but the girl will have to make up for that."

Talan nodded and rose to leave.

"And, Talan?"

"Yes, Headmaster?"

"I want Joel alive. Don't let the hate you hold for his father sway you to act otherwise."

CHAPTER 59

ISABELLE TRIED TO shake off her hazy stupor when her eyes met the sunlight. Her body convulsed as she tried to move, and when she finally propped up on her side she vomited whatever was left inside her. She wiped her mouth and looked into the nearby woods. *Where am I?* She felt disoriented, and terror overwhelmed her. A low whistle escalated her fear and prompted her to move. Energized by fright, she jumped up and ran like mad for the thickest part of the woods. She heard the guards calling to each other as branches scratched her skin in the thick brush. Looking for a place to hide, her eyes scanned the surroundings for low tree limbs, but it was no use. Unable to get up a tree fast enough and entering a clearing, the little blonde stumbled upon Baithe's old drainage system and quickly hid in one of the pipes. She bit her tongue to keep from whimpering as a pair of boots stepped into her line of vision. They climbed atop her metal cocoon and clomped along the pipe. Minutes later the footsteps were gone and Isabelle sighed in relief. *That's twice—*

A pair of large hands interrupted her thoughts, pinching her shoulders and roughly dragging her out of the pipe. Shaking and crying were only natural now as she stood before her killer, a man in his thirties who seemed surprised at his find. Eventually his puzzled expression faded.

"Of course, a girl for bait . . . but why you?"

Over his shoulder, Isabelle spotted the other man, the young woman, and the cloaked one she'd seen the night before approaching.

"Got her. It's a girl." He nodded in their direction.

The young woman ran toward them. "She's shaking like a leaf."

Isabelle wiped her tears and cleared her throat. "He loved me once."

"But not enough to rescue you, huh?"

Isabelle shook her head as the man pulled a knife from his pocket.

"I'm sorry. I have orders to kill you."

Isabelle looked into his face and saw true remorse. "I-I know." She knelt before him and bowed her head. Closing her eyes, she whispered a prayer for Joel. She wanted him to be her last thought. She braced herself for the blow but was flattened to the ground when something heavy fell on top of her. She shoved off her limp executioner and saw an arrow stuck between his eyes. She gasped and realized the cloaked guard was now standing between her and the two other guards.

"Have you gone mad, Andi?" The young woman clenched her fists but kept her distance.

The cloaked one put another arrow on his bow. "I'm taking the bait."

"No! Besides, there's only one of you and two of us." The girl started toward him but was forced to retreat when he pulled the string back.

Isabelle quickly grabbed the dead man's knife and thrust it out from behind Andi.

The young woman's eyes narrowed at her then Andi. "Traitor! You knew about this all along, didn't you? DIDN'T YOU!" She spat on the ground. "Just like him . . . YOU'RE JUST LIKE HIM!"

Isabelle couldn't believe Andi didn't flinch, but she knew the words had gotten his attention. She worried he wouldn't notice the other guard inching toward him. The other man reached into his pocket, but before he could withdraw his hand Andi put an arrow in his thigh. A dagger fell from the guard's hand as he hit the ground in pain. Andi walked over to him and jerked the arrow out of his leg. Isabelle watched in horror as the man hollered in agony. Andi wiped the bloodied tip on the grass and returned it to his waist. The young woman seized the moment and lunged at them.

"Look out!" Isabelle watched in shock as Andi clutched the girl around the throat cutting off her air supply.

"Enough, Arianna! He needs you in one piece to help get him back to the others." He released her to the ground, and the young woman gasped for air.

"Y-y-y-you'll p-pay for this. Why didn't you just take her last night?

Andi turned to Isabelle. "I couldn't. The lightning protected her."

Fear ran through her veins as she watched her ally treat these people with such force. She was suddenly terrified of her mysterious savior. She startled when he jerked her arm and dragged her a few steps. "Let's go."

Isabelle looked back at the other two but soon hurried after him. She followed him through the horribly thick terrain in silence for nearly two hours. Sweat, fear, and suspicion overwhelmed her every step until she lost focus of the cloak in front of her. The world went black for a few moments, but she heard his voice.

"You need water."

When her eyes regained focus she was lying on the ground with her head propped up in his lap. He was holding a bottle to her lips. She took a quick gulp and choked on the liquid.

"Slowly now." He waited for her to quit coughing and nodded for her to try again. With him bent over her head, she could finally gaze under the hood of his cloak.

Wait . . . his face is familiar. Who is he? She lifted her fingers to the top of his hood just before slipping out of consciousness. "Andi? I know you . . . ."

CHAPTER 60

AUGUSTINE SHARED THE information on Talan's business card with someone she could trust—Earl. He said he recognized the name, but that was all. He still had access to the government offices where he once worked and promised to send an urgent telegram to the man right away. Both knew time was running out for Sebastian and Joel. The season change was nearly upon them, and the city council was meeting in two days to make a final decision on whether or not to release Joel to Differe.

Though Augustine was technically free to leave the tower, Simon didn't like the idea of her roaming the streets alone during such upheaval and suggested she have an escort. She chose one of the Galanneans and hurried to discover if Earl had received a reply. With her hair tucked beneath a plaid driver hat, she and the Galannean waited outside Earl's old government building.

"Meet in the park at three."

Relief flooded over Augustine as Earl hurried down the steps toward them. "Oh thank goodness! What else did he say?"

"That was all it said in the reply."

"Really? How will we know what part of the park to meet him in? It spans most of the city."

Earl smirked at her. "Augustine, if he's a smuggler or some sort of spy I'd imagine we won't have to look for him. He'll find us."

She nodded and turned to the Galannean. "Thank you for your help. Earl can escort me from here, but please tell Dillon we need to meet with him as soon as we return. We'll need all of you to get Joel out of the tower."

The young man nodded. "Yes, we shall make a plan while yous meet."

With only an hour to spare, Augustine and Earl headed toward the park.

"Earl, thank you for sending the telegram. And, thank you for coming with me . . . I mean, really just thank you for being my friend. What would I have done without you since I got here?"

He smiled and took her hand. "Oh, *Honey*, you would've done just fine."

"Ha! Oh, you did use that name instead of Augustine in the telegram didn't you?"

"Yes, I remembered he didn't know you by your real name. Come on." The two rushed across the street to the most northern part of the park.

"Right. Well, if he's spent any time in Facilis lately, I'm sure he knows me by something different. Oh, Earl, how could the council give him up after all we—I mean, Joel—did for the city, for the West End? He made it rain!"

"Augustine, you must realize the West End is known for being a place of peace, remember? It's in the people's very nature to strive for it, so naturally its leaders will do the same. If they feel giving up Joel offers the greatest chance of peace, it's what they'll choose. And, Augustine?"

"Yes?"

"They also hold him responsible for the Vicar's death."

"That was an accident! And clearly if anyone's at fault there it's Differe. The council is deceived if they think Differe will keep their word. They'll take Joel and the West End with them."

Earl sighed. "I can't say I don't fear you are completely correct, which is why I hope this Talan person can help more than just the two of you escape."

"That would depend partly on where you want to escape to."

Augustine and Earl turned around and found a man strolling out of the brush behind them. The collar of his black trench coat was flipped up around his neck, and a white cashmere scarf was wrapped around the bottom part of his face. A pair of large black sunglasses hid his best feature. The man approached the bench separating the group, stopped, and stuck his hands in his pockets.

"Uh, Talan?"

The man pulled his scarf down and smiled. "Hello, Honey. Who have you brought with you today?"

His velvety voice was so calm and reassuring that Augustine felt sure she had made the right decision in contacting him. "Oh, this is Earl. He's, well, he's taken care of me in a way since I arrived here. He helped me get the telegram to you."

Talan stuck out his hand. "Pleased to meet you, Sir."

Earl took his hand and nodded. "A pleasure."

The three stood in awkward silence for a moment until Augustine gestured to the surrounding benches. "Have you—have you been around the city lately?"

He flashed a broad smile at her again. "Are you really asking if I know what you've been up to? It seems you put your fashion skills to work in the hospital."

Her cheeks reddened. "Yes, that's right."

"I also hear you're quite close to the rainmaker."

She nodded. "To Joel, yes."

"I suppose he's the other person you mentioned in the telegram needing help getting out of the city?"

Earl leaned forward. "Augustine, if this was a test, Mr. Talan here would certainly receive high marks."

Talan chuckled. "Has he been able to keep his weapon?"

"I believe so." Augustine bit her lip. "I know he used it two nights ago."

Talan rubbed his chin. "Ah, very good. And have you been able to keep yours?"

"Yes, thankfully, but I'm still not really sure how to use it. Anyway, the soldiers, well, I'm sure you heard of the Vicar's death. They know I need my rhydid. I-I have a family member—"

"The one who's dying?"

"Yes, how did you—"

"I put it in the telegram, Dear."

Augustine felt Earl put his hand on her shoulder. "Oh, right. Thank you, Earl."

Talan sat back against the bench and put his hands on his knees. "So, you need to leave before the season change, and Joel needs to leave before the council meets? That leaves little time."

"Exactly. Oh please, do you—can you help us?"

The man unbuttoned his coat and pulled out a map. "Well, I mostly help Differians receive a fair trial in the city, but in this case I think any attempt there would be futile." He stroked his chin again. "Yes, I can get you both out of the city, but you'll have to get him out of the tower. Can you do that?"

Augustine glanced at Earl.

"Dillon and the others will see to it. I'm sure of it, Dear."

She turned back to Talan. "Yes, we can get him out."

"Right then. Are you familiar with Vicar's Hill on the edge of town?"

"Where the warehouse is? It's called Vicar's Hill?"

He handed her the map. "Yes, in the warehouse is an entrance to the city's old underground tunnels. It's where the trains used to run. They will lead you out."

She clutched the map in triumph. "I knew it! I knew there had to be a way out. Oh, Talan, thank you! Will you meet us there? When can we leave?"

"You can leave tomorrow at dawn. I'll have my apprentice light the way for you. Only take the lit tunnels. It's a maze down there. The tunnels will lead you into the Southern Regions, and I will have my contacts meet you once you exit the tunnels to take you safely to the Waiz train."

Her heart burst with hope. She wanted to give the man a huge hug. "Oh, you'd do that? Oh, Talan, what can we do to thank you—to pay you?"

He glanced toward her waist. "Keep the rhydids safe."

"Oh yes, yes, we will."

She was surprised when he suddenly stood up.

She jumped to her feet. "My family is indebted to you. I'm so glad to have met you . . . I suppose this is goodbye. I won't be seeing you again?"

He smiled sadly and slowly shook his head. "I cannot accompany you in the tunnels . . . or really go anywhere near them. As Earl suggested earlier, many others will need my help. I must keep my identity safe as long as possible for the sake of the others."

Earl stretched out his hand toward the man again. "Yes, we understand. Thank you for the risk you're taking with us. We promise not to tell anyone about the tunnels unless absolutely necessary. We will keep them safe by keeping them a secret."

Augustine nodded in agreement.

Talan turned to leave. "Good luck, then."

Augustine looked down at the map then up at Earl. "Let's hope Dillon has a plan."

CHAPTER 61

"NOW WHO'S THIS guy helping us?" Joel pulled on a clean undershirt, and Augustine tossed him the rest of his uniform.

"I told you. That diplomat guy who picked me up on the road after I got off the Waiz train."

The two were stuffed in the bell tower, mostly due to the help of Dillon's men creating chaos in the Facilis Guards' shifts. Though the group didn't say, she was certain they'd also received a bit of help from Simon. The Galanneans had confused enough officers that they were now the ones guarding Joel, or at this point an empty room. Since the group had succeeded in getting in as fake guards, they felt certain Joel and Augustine could get out the same way.

"And you're sure about the tunnels? Who else knows about them?"

Her eyes met his uncertain expression, and she tried to reassure him. "Well, Earl's an expert on the city—the government's fact specialist and tour guide—and though he's never seen them, he'd at least heard of them. He seems pretty sure the city jail is still connected to them somehow."

"So he thinks they're under the whole city, not just a track out to the Southern Regions?"

She hated how disoriented he still seemed. His hazel eyes were still bloodshot, and his hands trembled as he pulled on the uniform. "I'm not sure, but in any case the map indicates such. Looks like a tangled mess of tunnels, so I'm glad they'll light the correct way."

"Augustine, I'm glad for you to go . . . to get to Sebastian." He suddenly stopped getting dressed.

"Joel, come on. We need to hurry if we're going to make it out of here by dawn. Dillon, can you give him a hand?" Augustine shot the Galannean leader a knowing look.

Joel held his hand up when Dillon moved toward him. "Just give me a minute. I-I just—it's been a long two days. I don't like leaving so soon . . . after Isabelle."

Augustine cringed at the mention of the blonde's name. "We don't have a minute. Sebastian needs us—that's the whole reason we left Waiz. Get him the rhydids and go back. And, we already told you the council will give you to Differe. Joel, that's only a day away!"

He shook his head, trying to think of another solution. "I know. I just . . . I guess I'm tired of running. Maybe I should just stay and face my fate."

Dillon shook his finger in Joel's face. "Yous are not being wise. Joel, do not talk like this."

Joel's eyes widened, and he grabbed Augustine's shoulders. "Augie, you go. You go on to Waiz."

She instantly pulled away from him. "No. Dillon's right. You of all people should already know it's a trick, just like Isabelle said. They'd have taken you then and still—and still—never mind. But you can't think for one moment they won't take you and then siege the city anyway."

"I-I just—"

"Listen, when we get back—get you out of here—there will be plenty of time to think things through. There will be time for you to heal." *Time for all of us to heal.*

He hung his head. "It was okay, you know, the men killed at the gate. The Vicar said to focus on the ones I saved. But with him, with Isabelle . . . it—there's no silver lining. No one benefits. The city will be taken. The only one who survives is me."

"And that is exactly what they would want!"

"She died in vain."

"She died so you could live. And, Joel, Sebastian is her brother too. Her dying request was for you to get to him and care for him." She was pleased to finally have his full attention, yet it broke her heart to see the change in his demeanor. Her asking him to go hadn't been enough, but mentioning Isabelle had.

He slowly nodded then looked at Dillon. "All right. Let's move. When's the next shift change?"

Joel looked down Vicar's Hill at the sleeping city then took a backpack from Dillon's outstretched hands. "So much for having time to think through a plan for the rest of you."

"Yous and I do better on impulses anyway."

Joel barely made out Dillon's weak smile in the faint morning light. The Vicar's murder flashed through his mind as he remembered how impulsive he'd been that day.

"Sorry, I-I did not mean like yous think. Joel?" The young man grabbed his shoulders before he could walk into the warehouse. "I mean what I say from the beginning. I trust yous. I shall follow yous and any of yous orders."

"As long as I give *yous* a choice." The two shook hands. "Listen, now you know where the tunnels are in case you need to get out . . . but I need you to stay. You're a good leader, Dillon. Facilis, the West End, they need you."

Dillon nodded.

"Also, the tunnels . . . this old place houses the entrance, but it's more than that. It's a secret storage room. It'll supply you for months if you need it."

Dillon nodded again. "I hope we shall meet again."

"You know, I just realized I don't even know your first name?"

"It is just Dillon. The Templins make me keep my first name because of my father. They did not want others to know who I was."

"Right. Well, if you ever bring Erin to Waiz come find me." Joel finally smiled, and the two hugged.

As Joel followed Augustine into the old warehouse, he still found the whole idea of the tunnels bizarre. *They were here the whole time, and no one mentioned it. Or . . . wait? The Vicar did offer us a way out the last time we were here. Guess we just didn't realize how close we were that night.*

Another reason for Augustine's discovery also came to his mind, but he wasn't sure how he felt about it. *The King. Maybe he did this.* Joel had been on silent terms with the voice since the recent events. *Where was he?* He'd suddenly felt abandoned. With no direction, Joel feared he was walking right into the plans of the so-called "Mouth." The deaths of the Vicar and Isabelle seemed more in line with the mouthpieces' schemes. Oddly enough, through all his wondering and pain his head had remained silent.

He sighed as he closed the warehouse door behind them and watched Augustine march past the stockpiles. He remembered the reason for her urgency. *Sebastian. Perhaps he's the one paving the way to Waiz. Maybe he's pulling us . . . "home."*

Joel found that word strange. He'd never really felt much at home anywhere. He was just glad to have a place to lay his head without being screamed at. Augustine began moving a pile of goods to reveal the tunnel entrance. He supposed Sarah and Isabelle had somewhat been his family at the temple. Odd as that seemed, now he was paired with two people from a legendary place and the most intuitive little boy he'd ever known. As his hand turned the knob of the door that had been hidden beneath the piles, he knew he'd have to let Isabelle go. He'd have to let the past go before he could settle into his new life in Waiz.

He felt Augustine press against him forcing him inside the door. He finally turned to her and smiled. "We're going home."

Augustine grinned too. She was delighted to see Joel smile again. They closed the door behind them and bounded down the concrete stairs. The two easily walked side by side in the old broad train tunnel. She relaxed upon seeing the lit torches along the walls to guide them. *Thank you, Talan.*

They walked in silence for half an hour before coming to an open area that led in two different directions. Joel stopped and peered into the two tunnels. One was pitch dark while the other was lit just like one they'd been walking through.

He looked over to Augustine and shrugged. "Guess we keep heading toward the light?" Suddenly a loud echo filled the tunnels. Joel held a finger to his lips and pressed Augustine against the wall. He bent toward her ear. "Someone's here."

She tried to whisper back, but he clamped a hand over her mouth. She resisted wiggling free and waited for another sound. A surge of anxiety settled over Augustine as a minute ticked by in silence. *What if it's a guard? What if we're close to the prison?* Joel tugged her forward and immediately moved her into the darkened tunnel. She looked at him in confusion, yet conceded to being hid in the shadows of the tunnel entrance. She saw the determined look on his face when he dropped his bag at her feet, but yanked on his arm anyway in order to keep him from leaving her. He crouched by the lit entrance of the adjoining tunnel. He stopped just short of the opening and waited.

We've got to hurry! We should just run down the other tunnel. She was about to move from her spot when the shuffling echo filled the tunnels again. Joel motioned for her to stay back and ducked inside the tunnel they'd just walked down. A shrill whistle sent a shiver up Augustine's spine. Panic coursed through her veins as a large individual ran past her from the lit tunnel next to hers.

"Argh!" The person charged toward Joel as he scrambled and took off down the tunnel they'd just come through. Terrified and knowing Joel would want her to stay put, she grabbed their bags and moved deeper into the darkness. She cringed as she heard the commotion further down the tunnel. Not being able to see what was happening terrified her, but it was obvious from the sounds there was a fight. From the yells and the size of Joel's attacker, she knew her friend was losing. She agonized as cries from the redhead echoed throughout the place. Suddenly the clamoring stopped. A burst of bright light followed by the sound of jingling metal chains let her know the fight was over.

CHAPTER 62

"YOU ALONE THIS time? Answer me!"

Augustine clutched the side of the brick wall as a deep voice reverberated off the tunnel walls. Chains rattled again then silence filled the air.

"Where's the girl?"

Augustine shivered when she heard running footsteps pounding down the lit tunnel beside hers. She stepped back further. Joel and his attacker arrived in view first. Joel had been stripped of his Facilis uniform, chained, and was being dragged along by someone she recognized. There stood the very boy she'd chained to the wall in Moonstruck.

The young man nodded at the approaching footsteps. "No one else is here."

That's what you think. She freed her rhydid from its sheath.

"Did you get it?"

The young man shook his head at the voice in front of him. "Yeah, I got it . . . but this is all that's left of it."

Augustine held back a gasp when he lifted the hilt of Joel's rhydid. All but the blade was intact.

"You fool! Give me that, and bring him down here. He's just in time for his old morning routine. You can do the honors."

The young man turned toward Augustine's tunnel and stared hard before lifting a leather strap from his belt. He threw Joel to the ground and gave him a firm lash.

"Stop that! I said down here!"

Blood pounded in her ears as she watched the boy from the temple drag Joel away. She slipped further into the darkness and fell to her knees. She was horrified at what she heard next. Though Augustine was no longer an eyewitness to Joel's pain, she could hear his torment. She covered her mouth to keep from screaming. She braced herself for every blow, every yell, every gasp of breath she heard her friend take. She cried, staying in the shadows and wondering what she should do. Her friend was being beaten just a few yards away. She gripped her rhydid tightly wondering if she could be brave enough to save him. She worried that the voice who had taken Joel's rhydid had weapons too. *And then what? But I have to do something, and I've got to hurry.* She was about to make her move into the light when she heard someone else coming from the other direction. *Oh no! Another one.* Augustine held her rhydid out, but this time the footsteps became quieter as the person moved closer. Soon a man emerged into the opening between the two tunnels. *Talan!* She watched him slowly scan the area and suddenly start whispering her name.

"Honey! Honey! Are you here? Are you all right?"

She emerged from the dark tunnel. "Here! Oh, Talan, thank goodness you're here!"

"Yes. I became worried when my comrades in the Southern Regions let me know they hadn't made contact with you yet. What's going on? Where's Joel?"

She started trembling as she rehashed the situation.

"It's all right now. Don't worry we—"

"Who's there? Who's down there? Another traitor of His Majesty?"

Joel's attacker was louder with each question. When the two heard him heading their direction, Talan motioned for them to go back into the darkened tunnel entrance.

The footsteps came running down the way and stopped just in front of the tunnel they were hiding in.

"Father! Father, are you here? I have Joel in the stocks and started his beating. I-I, well, I did get his weapon. B-but the blade, well, I'm not sure what happened. It just sort of shattered."

Augustine and Talan didn't move.

"Um, Father? Is that all for now? Are you there?"

Talan suddenly walked into the light towards the young man then turned around.

"Seems your friend has lost his weapon."

Augustine stayed back, feeling confused.

"Uh, hardly a friend. Would you like to see it, Father?"

His tall, thick stature, his wavy brown locks, the way he was earnestly looking at Talan suddenly clicked in Augustine's brain. *It . . . he really is his son.*

Talan shook his head. "No, I don't need to see it. The headmaster requested Hertz keep them both. Seems he's the man's new secretary." He moved back towards the tunnel entrance. "Now . . . we just need the other one."

"But the girl—"

"Quiet, Holt."

Talan looked through the darkness in Augustine's direction. "My Dear, you have two options. Run further into the darkness behind you, which will lead you straight into the Facilis prison where a host of Facilis soldiers await you. After all, you did take their prisoner. Or, you can surrender your weapon to me, and I'll let you go free. I'll get you to Waiz as promised."

Augustine couldn't move; she was frozen with shock. *What is happening? Who is this man? Why is his son here?*

"Um, sorry, Dear, but I don't have all day. I'm quite, quite busy helping people like yourself."

She finally forced herself to step into the light. "You mean using people like me."

He smirked. "If that definition suits you better."

She thrust her rhydid forward. "No, deceiver, liar, scoundrel, abominable is far more appropriate."

Talan lifted his hands in surrender and nodded to the young man who quickly did the same.

"Who are you?"

"General Langston. I oversee all of Differe's army, and this is my son, Holt. The one I told you about in the car. I didn't lie about everything . . . *Honey.*"

"You don't scare me. My lies were to protect others." She only hoped he couldn't see the truth—that she was terrified.

"Well, Dear, what will it be—surrender to me or Facilis?"

"Haven't you noticed I'm the one holding the rhydid?"

"Oh, yes, the weapon you claimed you really don't know how to use?" He lowered his hands slightly.

"I-I—Holt knows I can use it. How do you think I escaped from him before? In fact, I intend to—"

A cry down the tunnel interrupted her. Augustine jumped and raced around Talan and Holt to catch a glimpse of Joel. He was hunched over with his head and wrists held in some sort of wooden block.

"This is barbaric!"

A short man rounded in front of Joel with something heavy. From her distance she couldn't make out what it was.

"Don't you touch him!" She started down the tunnel with her rhydid out.

"I'd move slowly if I were you."

She heard Talan just a few steps behind her. He raised his arms again when she turned to him.

"I forgot to tell you the rest of our exchange . . . it's your rhydid or Joel's life."

She turned back to Joel in horror and saw that the terrible little man was holding the ends of a thick chain wrapped around Joel's neck. All he had to do was pull and Joel would choke to death.

"No, Augie, no! It's a trap! They need me alive! St—"

A jerk from the chain cut him off. "Quiet, you!"

Talan took a step nearer, held his hand up as a signal to the man holding the chains, and cocked an eyebrow. "What's it going to be, the rhydid or his life?"

Augustine thought of Sebastian. Either way it was taking a life.

"Come now. You can't let him die. Especially since it was you who led him into this situation."

Sweat trickled down her back as she stared at the rhydid. Was this just like the rest of Differe's bargains? Would they kill him anyway?

"Are you sure you want to keep it then? Blood on those pretty hands doesn't seem like you . . . ."

Tears filled her eyes as she heard Talan's taunts. She turned back to Joel whose face was turning purple as he sat defenseless against the chains. "Oh, stop! Stop! Please, stop!" She threw the rhydid at Talan's feet.

He slowly dropped his hand, and Joel was released though the lack of air seemed to have made him unconscious. Talan bent down and carefully picked up the weapon. He seemed pleased when the object remained intact. After looking it over he snapped his fingers at Holt. "Throw her in the cell next to Joel's. It will be good for her to watch the outcome of her marvelous escape plan."

Holt moved forward and grabbed Augustine's wrist before she had a chance to think. "Wait! What? But, you—you promised. You said if I gave you the rhydid, I could go on to Waiz."

"Oh, you will. I am a man of my word; however, I have a feeling the headmaster would like an audience with you before I let you go."

"You should be ashamed of yourself. You're taking the life of a helpless little boy."

Talan held the rhydid up. "Joel, helpless? I don't think so."

"That's not who I meant."

"Enough of this. I need to prepare my men inside these tunnels for the siege. With Facilis's prisoner in our hands the city doesn't have much bargaining power anymore. Don't worry your pretty little head, Honey. It shouldn't take long to gain control of the city and welcome its new leader. The headmaster should see you within the week."

Holt started dragging her away from him. "I-I trusted you. I—"

"Save it. It's simple really. I have orders, and I perform them. No need to take it so personally. I'll get you to Waiz."

"I don't believe you." She was almost to the entrance of what appeared to be a small dungeon before Holt paused.

"Wait, Father, how many lashes?"

Talan rubbed his chin. "He's humiliated you twice now, so whatever you see fit without killing him."

CHAPTER 63

THE UGLIEST MAN Augustine had ever laid eyes upon was running his fingers along the blade of her rhydid.

"Not so sharp."

"Neither are you."

The short man marched over to her cell. "What did you say?"

Augustine crossed her arms in silence.

He pointed the tip of the blade at her. "Don't you know who you're talking to? I work for His Majesty! I'm Hertz Marlis, the headmaster's right hand man."

"Hertz, can you give me a hand with this?" Holt was attempting to move the wooden stock block from the center of the room.

Augustine hugged her knees as she sat on the stony ground of her prison cell somewhere underneath Facilis. It had been traumatizing watching Joel receive the rest of his beating. He lay motionless in a bloodied heap in the cell next to hers. She couldn't believe she had been fooled by Talan. *I lost the rhydid.* It was the one thing she'd come this far to get, and now she feared she'd lose Joel as well. He seemed to have been beaten within an inch of his life. *What are they keeping him alive for?* She finally knew the painful emotions he'd been struggling with the past few weeks. *This is my fault. He might die . . . Sebastian might die . . . because of me.* She had tried everything to get them to open the cell, even asking to go to the bathroom, but it was no use.

"Go in your cell for all I care you nasty Waizen."

The Hertz fellow was a piece of work, complaining about everything he had to do and bossing around Holt, who was more than twice his size. Holt on the other hand had barely said a word. He even seemed a bit remorseful when having to resume Joel's beating. When the two heaved the stocks into a corner cell, the commotion caused Joel to stir.

Augustine rushed to his side and focused on the one thing she could reach. She slid her hand through the bars and stroked the back of Joel's hand. She gripped his fingers in hers and watched him open his eyes. She winced at the sight of his ripped flesh and swollen face. *Oh Joel, this is why. This. This is why you were so afraid of being found. You knew all along what they'd do to you . . . what they've done to you.* But as he pushed up from the ground she realized he'd really never been afraid. *He's always been ready to give himself up for Isabelle . . . and for me.*

He looked around his cell then at her through the bars. "No . . . no, how did this happen? Sebastian."

"No talking." Hertz held Augustine's rhydid in the air.

Joel gripped her hand tighter, and his breathing was labored as he tried to speak. "I'm . . . going to get you . . . out of here. Do you . . . trust me?"

"Joel, no. Please, I can't . . . I can't watch them hurt you again."

"Augie?" His eyes pressed her for an answer.

She finally nodded.

"Listen to me. You've got to . . . to tell Holt about Sebastian. You've got to tell him about Isabelle."

"What? Why?"

"Just do it. It's going . . . to get you out of here." He gave her hand a tight squeeze and let go. "Now."

She took a deep breath and moved to the front of her cell. "Holt! Holt, I have some news you might find interesting."

The young man didn't budge.

"Hush, you!" Hertz's face threatened her as he darted for her cell.

"I-I know about Isabelle."

Holt sat upright, but Hertz quickly intervened.

"Don't listen to them. Don't fraternize with the enemy!"

"It's her brother. Holt you know about Sebastian—I'm sure she told you about him. He's dying. He's the one we were taking the rhydid to."

Augustine was pleased to see Holt make a move towards her, but Hertz intercepted him with the rhydid.

"Stop this! Stop this I say. I'll use this if I have to!"

Holt looked over the top of Hertz's head into Augustine's cell. "Why should I believe you?"

Joel piped in before Augustine could respond. "It's true. Please . . . please let her go. Please . . . he'll only survive another week. We were warned . . . he'd die . . . before the next season began."

Holt eyed the rhydid. "Why's he need that?"

Furious, Hertz stomped his feet and waved the rhydid again. "Stop talking!"

Joel shook his head. "We don't know."

Holt's shoulders dropped, and he backed away from Hertz. "Forget it. There's no reason . . . there's no way I can believe you."

"Wait! Yes! Yes, Holt, you can. In that bag there—Joel's bag—there's a small contraption with her voice on it. She recorded it on the train before . . . well, she tells of Sebastian's illness." Augustine shook the bars with her grip. "Please, at least—"

"No, I'm in charge of the bag. Don't you touch it! Stop talking with these fools, Holt." Hertz grabbed the bag before Holt could and charged Augustine's cell with the rhydid. "I'm in charge! See? I have this, and I command you to—" The man's eyes suddenly rolled back into his head, and he fell to the ground.

Holt stood behind him with a brick in his hand. "I don't think I could stand to listen to him anymore. If anyone asks, you did it."

Augustine nodded. "I appreciate you thinking I'd be capable of such a thing. Now, please, Holt. Listen to the message."

He slowly went through Joel's bag. She watched his face go white upon hearing Isabelle's voice. At one point he even turned his face away.

"Holt? Do you believe me now?"

His eyes were saddened when they met hers again.

"Please, please let me go."

He picked the rhydid up and sighed. "But I can't . . . I can't just let you go, can I? You have to have this."

"Please. It's the only reason we went to the temple—to save Sebastian."

Joel pressed his body off the floor with his hands again. "Holt . . . you know . . . she'd want you to let her go."

He ran his fingers over his lips, nodded at Joel, and then looked in Augustine's direction. "All right. I . . . I-I can let you go, but Joel has to stay. I'll lead you out, but not by the passages lit by my father. His men are stationed outside that opening just in case you got past us. I-I don't think they'd harm you though. My father, well, everyone still thinks Joel's companion is a boy. I'll get you into the Southern Regions. Uh, my word is better than my father's."

Augustine bit her lip and moved toward Joel again. *Should I tell him . . . should I tell him it was me who got us locked up?*

Joel tried to sit up. "He'll do it, Augie. You can . . . trust him."

"I . . . no. No! I'm not going without you!"

He wiped his face and grimaced in pain. "Augustine . . . you have to leave."

She shook her head, knowing it hurt his jaw to speak. "Sh. It's okay, I—"

"They're not looking for you . . . they don't know . . . you're the other boy." His gasping pauses were intensifying. "Please . . . you've got to get . . . to Sebastian." Even through swollen eyes and iron bars he seemed to read the expression on her face. "Come on, Augie . . . we both knew . . . they'd eventually . . . find me."

Tears pooled in her eyes. "They're going to kill you." She buried her face in her hands. *It's all my fault.*

"I don't know. I think . . . I-I think . . . they would've already done that." He closed his eyes and struggled to take another breath. "I have a feeling they're saving me . . . for something."

"I-I can't . . . I can't leave you." *Not after what I've done.* Tears streamed down her cheeks.

Joel raised his head and took a stronger breath. She was shocked as he cocked his eyebrow at her. "Sure you can. Just remember all the rude, reprehensible, and atrocious things I've done to you." He grimaced again, and Augustine didn't know whether it was out of pain or because his joke only made her weep harder.

"Oh, Joel, why? Why does it keep ending up this way?"

"The Mouth . . . we're at war . . . there are . . . there are casualties in every war." His body shivered then he straightened again. He moved across the floor and reached for her hand.

"Joel, stop. Don't try to move. Oh, I just can't. I can't leave you."

His fingers grabbed hers again. "Yes, you can. You have to. Please. Do it for me. I promised myself . . . I promised myself and the king . . . the only way I'd ever be parted with you again . . . was you choosing to leave me."

She shook her head in confusion. "What? What are you talking about?"

"I'm sorry, Augie . . . I'm sorry about leaving you . . . on the train. I should've given you a choice."

"Shh. Stop that. It's okay."

"No, I was trying . . . to keep you safe . . . too safe."

She squeezed his hand. "I would've stayed with you."

"I know. I was trying . . . trying to control what happened . . . trying to keep my heart safe. But . . . ." He shook his head and rubbed his thumbs over her hands. "I'd never want you to stay . . . with me out of force. I'd—I'd want you . . . to choose me."

She leaned her head against the bars. "I do choose you . . . if only we could go back to the terrace . . . to the sunset . . . before the riders."

He lifted his head off the floor to look her in the eyes. He tried to swing her hand as he'd done before. "Go. Go for Sebastian." He looked around his cell. "And . . . go for me. It'll make this . . . worth it. You can do it."

She hung her head as Holt unlocked her cell. "Yes, I can, but know . . . know, Joel, that I don't *want* to do it without you." She removed her hand from his grasp and reached through the bars to hold his face. She brought it near the iron rods separating them and lightly kissed his bruised cheek then his bleeding forehead. She didn't wait to see his reaction but rushed out of the cell to follow Holt down the tunnel leading to the Southern Regions.

Tears of hate, remorse, and betrayal ran down Augustine's cheeks as she walked in the darkness behind Holt. She found some solace in knowing she was finally on her way to saving her brother, but Joel weighed heavily on her mind.

There's no hope. Differe will kill him. What else could they do to him that he hasn't already endured? She thought of Talan's urgency in contacting the headmaster.

Yes, it'll be his doing. She grimaced as more tears fell, yet recalled the many times he'd escaped before—the temple twice, a murder trial, the mouthpieces. It seemed hope kept pushing against the present reality she felt giving her the urge to do something she hadn't done since a child—ask someone for help. *Maybe I should ask the king for help . . . but where was he . . . when I needed him most? No. Forget it. I'm not going there again.* She'd tried with Corwin's help to seek out this so-called king as a child, but after Corwin went back to Waiz . . . and Sebastian never got better . . . she'd turned her back on the voice and relied only on what she could see. She'd vowed never to talk to the being again.

As she thought of her goodbye kisses to Joel, heat stormed her cheeks. "Stop that," she told herself, yet her heart beat faster as she pondered what she was feeling. *I can't love him. Not really. Not when I know he loves Isabelle.* Unconvinced as she was, the face of Talan immediately sent shivers through her. *It's best I never see Joel again. He'll never forgive me.*

"Ahem." Holt cleared his throat as he removed her blindfold.

She looked down the darkened tunnel behind her then turned to find the rhydid pointed at her. "Well, this scene looks familiar."

"Yes, except it turns out you're quite a pretty boy, and I have the rhydid this time." His eyes flickered, then he moved aside and motioned for her to pass by him. "It was never about you. You're free to go."

Tears started again as she moved past him toward the opening and waited for him to give her the sword.

"Please, wait . . . I need to know something."

Augustine raised her eyebrows at him.

"Is it true? Did they . . . did they kill her? Did they kill Isabelle?"

"W-we—Joel didn't go to Baithe. The headmaster promised there would be repercussions. The Templins killed the Vicar from *outside* the gate for protecting him. I have no doubt they showed the same mercy to my sister."

His gaze became curious at the mention of being Isabelle's sibling. "Sebastian I know . . . but she never mentioned you . . . but wait, so, you're not sure then? She might still be alive . . . ."

"I'm *sure* we were both used to get who you wanted."

He looked down then scratched the concrete wall with her rhydid.

"Holt, you're letting me go, which means that somehow the temple hasn't managed to control you completely. You and Joel loved the same girl. I, uh, I'm guessing this isn't something the temple or your father wanted."

He remained silent.

"Her parents work in a factory. Not a great match with your family ranking and status."

"How do you—"

"Whether you realize it or not, you're rebelling against them by letting me go. Something inside you doesn't want to be controlled, Holt. It wants to be free. Listen to it."

He seemed unnerved by what she was saying. "How do you know all this?"

"Never mind how I know. Just try to listen."

"To who?"

She frowned. "Not your father."

Holt didn't reply but handed her the rhydid sheath.

"He used your past with Joel to get you to beat him—to do the headmaster's dirty work. He used your emotions. Don't listen to him."

He sighed in frustration. "If not my father then who?"

She pondered his question and let out a small laugh, startling him and even herself. She shrugged. "To the voices. There's a good one apparently. Listen to the one who makes you feel free." She walked a few feet outside the tunnel. The sunlight felt good on her skin.

"Goodbye . . . Augustine."

"Goodbye. Oh, and Holt?"

They faced each other again.

"Please don't tell him it was me who gave him up to your father. If he lives, I should be the one to tell him."

Holt nodded then threw the rhydid as far outside of the tunnel as he could. She chased after it and turned back only to find a pitch-black opening. Holt was gone. It was time for her to finally go home.

CHAPTER 64

ARIANNA HAD BEEN at a Templin base just outside of Baithe in the medical tent with her injured comrade when she starting hearing more about this Joel person they were hunting. It was then she realized he was more than just some escapee from the temple.

"He made it rain."

"He can make tornados."

"His secret weapon calls lightning."

"He knows the king who disappeared in the caves of Old Waiz."

"He's got all the king's weapons."

It was strange hearing things she knew her father had been known for believing—things about some king and light. Her curiosity was more than piqued not only in regard to her father but also to someone else who dabbled in the supernatural. Once she heard Joel's impending capture was certain, she felt desperate to find him. *This boy has power . . . probably greater than mine.* When the group of Templins accompanying them in Baithe began to move toward Facilis, she made herself invisible and followed them. Apparently Differe was going to invade Facilis, and the group she was trailing planned to storm the gate and a few weak places of the city's walls.

She was crouched in the shadows of early morning when the news came that Joel had been caught in some underground tunnels near Facilis. Knowing the city would be under siege soon, she parted with the group to go on ahead and search for a tunnel, or at least a clue to where one might be. She hunted for Templins, Differian Guards, Facilis Guards, caves, stakeouts— anything that would lead her to this boy. She finally stole a map from a Templin camp and discovered some of the tunnels exited just shy of the Southern Regions. *Perfect! Facilis will be too crowded to get inside to see him . . . better chance of sneaking in this way.* She traveled in the direction of the Southern Regions, taking every possible shortcut in hope of making it to the tunnels before Differe took the city. The heavily wooded terrain eventually ran her in circles and she was forced back onto the main road. She had nearly given up on getting there in time when she caught sight of the first human she'd seen since being on the road.

Curious, she hid in a tree and peered at the horse and rider coming down the road. She noted the rider's hat and uniform but was most interested in the satchel hanging near his leg. *A postman? A spy?* The abandoned roads made her lean toward the latter, and the man was heading in the direction of Facilis. She suddenly wanted whatever was in the satchel.

She began climbing over branches until she wrapped her body around a limb hanging directly over the road. The horse and rider plodded along at a trot, giving her enough time to position herself. Her heartbeat quickened as the rider approached. Clenching her ankles together around the limb, she swung down head first into the rider's chest. The horse reared as Arianna unhooked her ankles from the tree, wrapped her body around the rider, and ripped him off the saddle. The horse fled the scene, taking the satchel with it. Arianna found the rider on the ground, knocked unconscious by the blow, so she took off running after the horse.

After some coaching she eventually won the animal over. Once she was close enough she cautiously lifted the satchel from the saddle. She walked a few feet away from the horse and hurried to search the bag. Inside was one letter marked with a red wax seal that displayed the letter "R." She paused, wondering what she should do and turned the envelope over. She gasped when she read whom the letter was addressed to—Delano Dark. *Oh my! I think that's Differe's Majestic!* She tore open the letter and felt both shocked and pleased with herself as she scanned its contents.

What a goldmine! She grinned as she stuck the letter back into the envelope. Though she was tempted to continue her search for Joel, she knew

Waiz would be desperate for the information she held in her hands. The document would give Marcell all the leverage he needed to control Differe's ruler. The letter could also provide her personal bargaining power with her superiors. *I bet I could secure a meeting with Joel.* She looked over the horizon and nodded. *I need to get back to Waiz. Marcell needs to know about Master James Reagan.*

"Enjoying your peach, gorgeous?"

Augustine straightened and dropped the fruit. She frantically looked around for the source of the voice. She lifted the rhydid from her belt loop and held it steady behind her back.

She was somewhere in the Southern Regions and didn't know how long she'd been walking. The only thing she knew for certain was that she was hungry. She hadn't eaten since she and Joel had left the cathedral, so when she had caught site of a vast fruit orchard she immediately headed that direction. She'd marveled at the lush fruit, ripe for picking. When she'd seen the faint outline of a large mansion in the distance but no one else in sight, she helped herself.

"Seosh? Turan dey qui borshay?"

Augustine didn't understand a word of the southern dialect but thought the voice sounded friendly. *Where is he?*

"For a female you sure are quiet."

She saw the branches rustle in the tree in front of her and took off running. She weaved through the rows of trees, stopping every so often to catch her breath, hoping she'd lost the stranger. *Keep going! Who cares if he sounded nice! Don't trust anyone until you get back to Corwin! Listen to yourself, Augustine! Get back to Sebastian.* She nodded to herself and kept the rhydid out as she ran. The maze of trees engulfed her, making her feel even more disoriented than she already was. She soon lost all sense of direction and wandered into a row of trees, spotting not only one but two young men chasing after her. She darted into the next row and hoisted herself onto a low branch of an apple tree. She climbed until the two chasing her stopped at the row where she was hiding.

After looking up and down the row one tugged on the other. "Come on."

"Philip, wait! She's on this row." She recognized this voice as the one who'd spoken earlier. "It's all right. You can come out!" The young man, just barely twenty she guessed, walked along her row. "Our master is very kind. You don't have to steal from his land. He's happy to share." His sun-kissed skin, jovial expression, and carefree gestures may have convinced some but not Augustine.

She crossed her arms and thought of Talan. *I've just been conned by a handsome face. You'll have to do better than that. I'm not falling for it again.* Still, neither man was armed, and they looked more like rugged farmers than manipulating tyrants. The one speaking had big brown eyes and a smile that lit up his entire face. The other seemed more reserved with his eyes hidden behind strands of dark brown hair. *Brothers?*

"She's gone, Paul. Come on, we should go tell the master."

Paul shook his head and stared directly at her tree. "No, she's here. She's afraid."

She saw the compassion in his dark eyes. *Ugh, go away. I'm not trusting anyone . . . not until I get back to Corwin.*

The two finally started walking away. "Did you see her?"

Philip chuckled. "Only the flash that ran past me."

"She's beautiful . . . dark and beautiful. I've never seen any girl like her before. She can't be from around here."

She almost laughed when Philip whacked Paul on the back of his head. "Beautifully stealing fruit! Paul, keep your wits about you. You're acting like you've never seen a girl."

"Ouch! Well, I haven't. Not like her, I mean. You just wait and see." He turned back toward her row of trees. "Please come out and prove my cousin wrong, Princess!"

Augustine rolled her eyes and shook her head.

Philip grabbed his arm. "Come on, Romeo."

"I'll be waiting for you at the manor house, Heavenly Being!"

"Paul! Enough! Let's go find Master."

Augustine sighed and leaned her head against the tree. "What a day." She supposed she'd rest here until nightfall then travel on in darkness in search of a train. She was certain she'd heard one not too far off a few hours before. As daylight faded, her perch offered a perfect view of the brilliant sunset beyond the orchard. She searched the sky of scant clouds, pink hues, and twinkling stars. *This time of day will haunt me for the rest of my life.*

She slowly climbed down from the tree, knowing Paul and Philip were long gone by now. *The only person waiting for me at this point is Sebastian. I have to get to him. And soon.* She grabbed a few more pieces of forbidden fruit and followed in Paul and Philip's direction just to ensure she was headed out of the place. Unfortunately for Augustine, the orchard backed right up to the manor. She could go back to the river she'd been following, but it was clear to her now that the cypress trees she'd seen lining the way farther down were part of the manor's private drive. She looked at the top of the hill. *If I could just cross over to the other side of the house. Looks like there are some woods I could duck inside. I'll just have to make a run for it.*

The manor was magnificent in size and style. Flickering torches lit the terrace, and its walls were draped in green ivy. Limestone fountains on either side of the arched patio guarded the steps that led to the orchard. Lanterns hanging from shepherd's crooks surrounded the courtyard off the patio, and lightning bugs filled the air. She slowed her pace, mesmerized by the place's beauty. A warm southern breeze set off several strands of wind chimes, and the sound instantly reminded Augustine of the Majestic's room in the Old Waiz museum. The memory of being there with Joel quickly flashed through her mind. *Will everything always remind me of him?* With Joel lost, she ached even more to be back with Sebastian. *Okay, go on now—for Sebastian.*

The place seemed quiet, but she held her rhydid out as she zigzagged through the trees right behind the manor. She zipped near the left side of the house, hopeful she could pass into the woods unnoticed. As she thought about how to cross the large courtyard undetected, a creaking sound alarmed her.

The orchard trees blocked her view, so she crept forward and found an old wooden swing gently swaying back and forth. Its creaks were followed by the sound of the breeze, then a heavy sigh. Augustine shrank back when she realized a figure sat on the swing. She dodged behind the trees again until she was sure the person hadn't seen her. The creaking stopped, and she held her breath. A new sound began, and she gripped the tree in front of her. The man was . . . *weeping.* The cries were soft and low. He coughed and began weeping more loudly.

"My son . . . ." The words escaped through the man's sobs.

She was surprised how her heart hurt at hearing his anguish. *I don't even know him, but . . . to be sad in a place like this . . . he must be devastated.* She wiped a tear from her own eye and turned to leave. As she made for the edge of the woods she heard the man call out a name, one that froze her like stone.

CHAPTER 65

ARIANNA SAT NERVOUSLY staring at the closed door of the New Waiz Council's office. She was the only one from her mission whom the council had requested a meeting with. *I know it's because of Andi. How could he do this to me?* She hoped the letter could smooth things over if need be.

She stood up and hung over the bannister staring down at the spiral staircase below. She frowned then reached into her pocket and leaned away from the railing. Her mother had disappeared since her return home, and having been betrayed by her brother made her feel a bit like an orphan. Not that she wasn't used to fending for herself. *I may be alone, but I'm certainly not defenseless.* She grappled with a new gadget the leader of her division had just given her. The marble-sized ball held enough toxic fumes to smoke out a large tavern. She tossed it up in the air and waited to be called in with the council.

She hummed an old tune her mother used to sing to her at bedtime as she played her game of catch. *Where is she? She's always around. She needs me! I have her medicine.* She rolled the ball between her fingers and sighed. Her mother had more than a month's supply, but Arianna didn't know where she'd be in a few weeks. *And then what? How will I be able to get her what she needs?* As angry as she was at Andi, he entered her thoughts as well. She wondered where he was and if he and the girl were safe. She had been surprised the bait was a girl. *But it didn't make me go all soft, and it certainly didn't deflect my aim.*

The secretary's door suddenly flung open, and a startled Arianna accidently released the ball forward instead of up. She dove after the ball, but it slipped just beyond her grasp over the bannister. She jumped up and dove toward the bannister of the spiral staircase to save the ball from falling beyond her grasp, but it was too late.

"Look out below!"

She cringed at her carelessness and waited for the explosion. To her amazement, an open palm thrust out from the stairs below. The fingers closed around the object as the hand retracted out of sight. She leaned over the bannister attempting to spot her savior. As the footsteps came closer Arianna made out Marcell's salt and pepper hair. He looked up and smirked.

"Drop this?" He made his way up the stairs, eying Arianna with an amused look. He smiled, but it didn't reach his eyes.

"I'm sorry, Sir." She hung her head and removed the weapon from his hand.

"There, now. It's all right. Good to know even you Ferox need a normal human's help every now and then."

Always having been proud of her membership with the elite group, his comment, placing her in a nonhuman category, suddenly made her feel ashamed.

"Go on in and sit down. I'll be there in a moment. We'll just meet in my office today."

The office was quite plain for the likes of New Waiz. Arianna was surprised at the simplicity—just a desk piled with papers, a few plaques on the walls, and a folding chair behind the desk. *He doesn't even have a window.* She sat on a wooden stool across from the man's desk feeling like she was about to be interrogated. She gripped the sides of the wood until her knuckles turned white.

Marcell eventually came in and closed the door behind him. "Now, before you think I'm going to ask all about your mission and get worried— don't. I've talked to your colleagues."

She looked at him in surprise. "You—you talked to them?" *Why didn't they tell me?*

He shuffled some papers then sat behind his desk. "Yes, they told me the whole story. You needn't blame yourself for your brother's actions. I personally blame Langston."

Arianna remained silent.

"Yes, I know all about the little deal he made with your brother to join his army. He used you, Arianna—he and Langston both. Langston wanted a marksman such as Andi for his army—one trained by us—and Andi wanted to be assured of his safety."

Arianna let his words sink in. "Used me . . . they did . . . didn't they?" A fire blazed in her eyes as she stared back at Marcell. Even so, something in her still wondered if the man in front of her was guilty of the same action. Would he have let Andi go to trial and die? *Wouldn't that be using him too?*

"I'm told you did well in the situation—Andi's betrayal. It's unfortunate what happened, but we'll leave Andi and the girl to Differe now."

In some ways these words made Arianna feel at ease. *Maybe Langston will let him live. Maybe we'll fight alongside each other someday.*

The man drummed his fingers across the desk. "Arianna, I'm more interested in finding out what happened after the fiasco with Andi. I hear you left the Ferox after you got your fellow officer to medical care. In fact, they came back a few days earlier . . . without you. Where did you go?"

Arianna sat back and turned red. She hadn't thought about how to explain why she had left before she discovered the letter. "I-I . . . I went to find him."

"Who?"

"Joel."

The man raised his eyebrows in question. "So, was it worth it to leave your comrades, your mission, for this special boy?"

Arianna sat up straight, no longer agreeing to slink down in front of him or his disapproving tone. "Yes, I believe you'll find it worth my efforts." She untucked her shirt and pulled an envelope from her waistline.

"What is it?"

"Open it and see."

His eyes flickered at her tone as he opened the letter. The look of utter surprise that crossed his face turned to elation as he unfolded the paper. "His father. You have a letter from the boy's father."

"Yes, one that states his negotiations with the head of Differe's Temple or whatever. Seems Dark might have a pretty powerful enemy as well as a debt he owes this man."

Marcell licked his lips and smiled. "Arianna, you are a gem. I think it's time I paid a visit to the West End."

She crossed her arms and pursed her lips. "To Delano Dark and Joel, you mean."

"Yes, and I'd very much like for you to accompany me."

CHAPTER 66

CORWIN CHOSE HIS steps carefully as he made his way up the base of the mountain. Sweat trickled down his neck as he climbed, and his shoulders felt heavy today. *But I must hope.* It was the same thing he told himself every day as he walked this familiar path.

It had been over two months since Augustine and Joel had left Waiz. He and Sebastian had resurrected an army and were in the middle of planning to free the Watchmen from the New Order when they'd gotten the news of Facilis falling to Differe. Corwin also now knew Joel had been captured. He was fairly certain Langston had kept his word in keeping Isabelle safe and that Andi had taken her captive. Yet all this information begged a question in Corwin's mind. *Where is Augustine?*

More anxious than ever, he climbed the base of the mountain to be sure she hadn't returned to the cave where the group had agreed to meet if their journey took longer than a few days. He made the trek every day, and with each passing day he felt his glimmer of hope fading. It was unlike him to lose hope, but the fall of the West End and Joel's capture weighed on him. His heart was heavy as he thought of his dear Augustine. *She's so beautiful, so brave, so caring. Oh please, please, let her be alive.*

He fought back tears every time he arrived at the cave and found it empty. Today was no exception. He went inside, found it empty, and sighed. This time he let the tears fall. He was beginning to question his actions of sending the two to Differe. *Had they been ready? Will Sebastian be able to survive a little longer? Is Joel who I think he is?* He pressed his forehead against the cave then turned to leave. He saw something of a blur in the corner of his eyes and wiped the tears away.

Augustine ran into his arms. Corwin barely had time to catch her face before she thrust herself on him. Her body shook with sobs as she buried her head into his chest. He stroked her back and ran his fingers through her wavy hair. Relief washed over him and quickly turned to joy as his head sunk into her hair.

He couldn't imagine all she had been through, but she'd returned alone and that was evidence enough that things had been difficult. As he held her, he couldn't help feeling proud of his niece. The ever distrusting, suspicious young lady he'd picked up months ago had matured into a woman of pure courage. She finally settled down enough to hear his voice.

"You look older."

She sniffed and shook her head. "It's the makeup."

Corwin chuckled. "So, that's the outside. I was referring to your spirit."

"What do you mean?"

"I can see it in your eyes. You've grown in courage, faced your fears. You've opened your heart to love. I'm . . . I'm so proud of you." He pulled the rhydid from her sheath and pointed to the sword. "See what I mean? You have grown."

Recollection flooded over her. "Oh, right. Sebastian. Is he . . . is he all right? Am I too late?"

"He's just fine. He's been up to quite a bit since you've been gone. He's missed you, that's for certain. He'll . . . well . . . ." Corwin removed her hands from his face and held them. "He'll be surprised to find you alone."

"Are you surprised?"

"No, I'm not. I heard the news just yesterday, but I haven't told him yet."

She looked down, bit her lip, and trembled as more tears fell. "I just . . . I'm so sorry."

"It's okay, Dear. No need to rehash everything right now—you need rest . . . though I have wondered where you've been."

She sighed. "That *will* be a surprise. I can assure you."

"Well, like Sebastian, I've missed you too, Augustine. Thank you for all you endured to come back here." He squeezed her hands. "I want to hear everything . . . when you feel up to it."

She nodded. "I'd like to see Sebastian first."

"Of course."

Sebastian was standing at the window when the two arrived, and Corwin felt slightly apprehensive as to what would take place at this meeting. Augustine had been through a tremendous ordeal, yet she needed to know, or in this case see, that it was worth it in some way. *She needs her brother.*

Corwin watched as recognition registered on Sebastian's face. His mouth dropped open, and he lit up from ear to ear. It soon became obvious he was searching for someone else also, which made Corwin all the more thankful for the lengthy path that led to the house. Sebastian had plenty of time to figure out Joel was not with them. Corwin gritted his teeth at the front door, but Augustine nodded at him.

"I'm okay."

Before he could respond, Sebastian flung the door open.

"You're here!"

Augustine fell to her knees, and Corwin stood back to let the siblings embrace. Sebastian clung to her until she pried him off to look him over, touching his face and hands. Tears streamed down her face as she took him all in and Sebastian smiled back at her.

"Wow! Where'd you get that sword? Can I see it?" Sebastian caught a glimpse of the sheath jutting out from Augustine's side.

She stood up and held it out to him. "Yes. Here. I got it for you. I went all the way to Differe and back to get this . . . just for you."

The boy marveled at the object. "It's amazing, Augie—you're amazing!"

"Um, let's take it inside." Both nodded at Corwin and stepped inside the house.

Sebastian tugged Augustine's hand. "This way. I have something for you too!"

Corwin smiled as Sebastian led Augustine to the kitchen.

"Augustine, look! We've gotten these everyday hoping you'd be back. See? It's your favorites!" Sebastian seemed pleased when Augustine smiled at the dozens of pastries sitting on the counter.

"I'll get some hot water ready." Corwin moved past her to fill the kettle. He hoped this small gesture from the two of them would comfort his niece.

She patted Corwin's arm and sat down in the chair Sebastian pulled out for her. "Thank you. Sebastian, you look well. I can't wait to hear what you've been up to." She rubbed her temples and smoothed back her dark tresses. "I'm sorry it took me so long to get back. We—I, uh, got delayed."

"Corwin told you I've been busy, huh? We knew you'd come back. Don't worry about being late. It's okay. You're here now."

"I am, and I never intend to leave you again. It was horrible being away from you. Even now, looking at you . . . I forgot how much just being with you makes me happy." Tears filled her eyes again.

Sebastian let out a satisfied sigh and pointed to the platters in front of them. "Come on, pick out some. At least three."

"Three, huh?"

Corwin poured their tea and then let them just enjoy each other for a couple hours. Their conversation centered on Sebastian and what he'd been doing in Augustine's absence. He was glad Sebastian resisted the urge to ask questions. Augustine needed time to process, but there was not a lot of time to offer. Not with the news they'd just intercepted from Langston. Corwin wasn't sure what would be safest at this point—to leave them here with the regime or take them with him. It was a mess of sorts, and Corwin thought it only fair to leave the final decision up to Augustine . . . though he secretly hoped to never be parted from her again.

As daylight faded, the three enjoyed their first meal together in months. Though Sebastian seemed determined to stay awake all night, it wasn't long after dinner before Corwin carried him to bed sound asleep. He tucked him in and marveled at how the boy had grown in the past few months. *He has wisdom*

beyond his years. He returned to the main room and found Augustine curled up in an arm chair with her feet tucked under her legs. Her tired eyes met Corwin's.

"You told him not to ask me anything, didn't you?"

Corwin stared at the girl sitting by the fire and nodded quietly. "That and he's pretty intuitive. He knows you'll tell him after you've rested." The wood crackling pierced through their next few minutes of silence.

"He seems well. Thank you for taking such good care of him. I wish I could fall asleep as fast as him."

Corwin smiled. "It was my pleasure, and he's been very much a help to me."

She stared into the fire "Corwin, my tale . . . it's not pleasant. It's doesn't have a happy ending."

"Perhaps it hasn't ended quite yet. But please know, in either case, I still want to hear it. I need to hear it . . . and you need to tell it."

She turned back to him.

"It will suffocate you if you don't."

She nodded. "Yes, I won't deny it. Sometimes I feel like I can't breathe."

"I know it's hard . . . to want to rehash it . . . to relive it, but you must try. That way I can understand."

"I don't want your perspective!"

He leaned forward and lit his pipe. "I just want to listen, Augustine. I promise. I won't say a word."

She took a breath. "This will be the bravest thing I've done yet."

Corwin nodded in agreement. He knew the value in sharing her heart, her story. It would bring freedom not only for her but also for others. He pulled on his pipe and sat back. With Joel's capture taking place several days ago and the siege of Facilis shortly after, he was more than curious to know where she'd been. "Yes, yes it will."

Corwin listened for hours as Augustine recounted her journey with and without Joel. He marveled at their abilities, triumphs, and failures. He kept every ounce of emotion off his face so she'd feel free to share as much as she could. He just listened intently and gave her a nod every now and then. Inside his head, he assimilated all the pieces of information he felt could help the regime, yet his deepest concern was for the girl sitting right in front of him.

Her heart was most important of all. Seeing her retell the story of being betrayed then leaving Joel was painful to watch. The tears, clenched fists, guilt, shame, and trauma he saw gripping her nearly caused him to break his promise of silence, yet he didn't. His only outburst happened when she revealed meeting Joel's father.

"That's where you've been? That's unbelievable! Oh, I'm sorry, Dear. Please continue."

"Oh, Corwin, what will I do? I can't tell Sebastian what I've done. He'd never forgive me."

"Augustine, his forgiveness is the least of your problems."

Eyes wet and forehead sweaty, she shook her head at him.

"You have to forgive yourself. You'll never be able to fully embrace the forgiveness of anyone else if you don't even offer it to yourself."

"I can't. I can't, Corwin. I know what I've done. I can't forget it. I can't make it right."

"Okay then, what would make it right?"

She sighed in frustration. "I don't know. I don't know!"

"Calm down, Dear. Calm down and think about it. What would make this right in your world?"

She shuddered and closed her eyes. "I-I suppose if . . . if Joel was still alive . . . if Isabelle was still alive . . . maybe if his father knew the truth—all impossibilities."

"Well, I'm not sure of all three, but I'm fairly certain one is within reach."

Augustine's eyes flung open. "Who? Master Reagan? You've talked to him?"

Corwin shook his head. "No."

"Isabelle? She's alive? She escaped?"

"I'm more fifty-fifty on that."

The two locked eyes. Augustine got up on all fours and crawled over to his chair. "Joel?"

Corwin slowly nodded. "Yes, your story's not over yet. I have it on very good authority he's still alive."

Augustine froze. "But—but the letter . . . Philip showed me the letter."

Corwin furrowed his brow.

"Corwin, I . . . I can't describe the guilt I felt in being there . . . at his house, so I-I left in the middle of the night. Phillip caught me sneaking out, and I confessed the whole thing about Joel . . . Paul already knew. Then, oh dear, then—" Tears cut her off again.

Corwin handed her a tissue and waited.

"Philip reads Master Reagan's mail—it's deceptive, but he does it to protect the man . . . he's so fragile. Sorry, I know I'm not making sense. Well, after I told Philip about Joel he showed me a letter that came that day. Corwin, it was from the headmaster himself. It was horrible . . . just as I feared. It was horrible to read Joel had died . . . knowing it was my fault. I gave Paul Joel's temple file before I left. You know, I thought Master Reagan should have it . . . but after I confirmed the headmaster's letter was true, Philip and I decided the truth about Joel's time at the temple—the file—would only hurt his father."

Corwin rubbed his face. "So, his father doesn't know . . . ."

"He doesn't know he's . . . dead?"

"He's not dead, Augustine."

She pulled herself up to face him and gripped his arms. "He's . . . he's alive? You're sure?"

Corwin nodded as she burst into sobs. He took her into his arms, but she quickly pulled away.

"I-I could tell him the truth. That . . . that would make it right."

The pain on her face was agonizing to see. Corwin knew telling Joel the truth would be no easy task. It would take every ounce of courage she had.

"Do you love him, Augustine?"

She didn't answer, but there was no hiding it in her eyes.

He gently cupped her face. "Do you want to go get him with me?"

CHAPTER 67

HOLT SLOWED HIS stride as he walked through the Facilis square, glad for a few moments in the sun. Across the street, the Chrysos Prison gleamed in the early morning light, its gold trim reflecting the sun's rays like tiny mirrors. The enormous building had long ago been a palace belonging to the rulers of the West End, and once converted to a prison it had hidden or housed some of the most famous villains in history.

Chrysos was oddly beautiful on the inside as well, with most of the building housing political figures, officers, Facilis guards, and prisoners on house arrest. What many outside Chrysos didn't know was that beneath the foundations of the building lay four floors of prison cells. In Holt's mind, the dark stone dungeons were a perpetual underground labyrinth. Though he'd been sent on the menial task of fetching his father's breakfast, he was glad to get away and at least see the sky again.

He looked up and squinted into the sun's rays. Its warmth made him long never to go back to the cold gray climate of Differe. Nearly finished with his studies and Templin training, he wondered what his future held. *Maybe the headmaster will just pass me.* In any case, he hoped he wouldn't have to stay here. Every street corner in the city was lined with Differian guards or the Facilis Army . . . or what was left of it. Those involved in the revolt, as well as those who'd refused to serve Differe, were now imprisoned with Joel.

Most of the shops along his walk were barred, having been looted shortly after the siege. It was a pitiful scene. The parks were full of homeless scavengers, and throngs of beggars sat outside on the cathedral's steps. What had obviously once been a beautiful, thriving, and even powerful place had become a war-torn disaster. As Holt saw the impact of this day after day, he had finally gotten the nerve to ask his father what good it had done to take over this place.

"Holt, power and glory have to be stripped away in order for another to possess them."

Holt shook his head. "Yes, but what gain is there here . . . even for Differe? It isn't glorious—it's a mess."

"They did it to themselves, Son. Facilis could have quietly conceded— the headmaster even gave them that option—but they instead chose to follow Joel and revolt. This mess you see is the consequence of their poor choice."

"The headmaster's option . . . I wonder what the terms were?" He was certain they weren't fair.

He startled when his father gripped his shoulders and pressed him against the wall. "Holt! Why is Joel here? Why did you come along?"

His eyes darted away from the man, and his father gripped tighter.

"Look at me, and answer."

"Let go of me."

"Holt, Joel is here to make an example of those who cross Headmaster Dark and Differe on both a personal and corporate level. Joel escaped from the temple—"

Personal.

"And people had the audacity to follow him—rise up against Differe. It was sheer madness on their part."

Corporate. Holt dared not speak with his shoulders still in a vice grip.

"The West End, nor any other regions, will dare fight against the headmaster now."

Holt finally met his father's flaming green eyes.

"And, let me remind you why *you* are here. *You* have chosen to serve your region and its leader."

Holt fought the urge to shove the man off him. "Are you done?"

"You have no idea how hard I've fought for my title . . . for you to follow after me. How dare you treat me with such disrespect!"

Holt froze again under his fury.

"The headmaster is coming tomorrow. You've been an embarrassment to me by failing to catch Joel without assistance. And, I know, Holt . . . ."

His heart raced at the man's threatening tone, but he didn't flinch on the outside. "Know what?"

"You were defeated during Joel's second escape by that girl."

Holt grimaced as beads of sweat trickled down his face.

"And just like Joel, you let her escape . . . again. You can say it was Hertz's fault all day long—which is what we'll tell Dark—but I know it was you, Holt."

How does he know? Joel wouldn't have told him. He wants the girl safe. He—

"You forced me into this, Holt. I had to clear the Langston name. So now you will keep your place. You will remember who you serve above all else. Do you understand?"

Holt didn't budge, both terrified and furious at the way he was being treated.

"Do you hear me? Do you understand me, Holt? Don't embarrass me again, or I'll see to it myself that Isabelle is killed."

"Wha-what? Wait . . . what are you talking about?"

His father finally relaxed his grip. "The headmaster didn't tell you? Using her as bait was my idea."

Holt clenched his fists at his father's all too calm tone. *I want to smash his face.*

"Come now, a factory worker's daughter? She lived with Joel too long. She's infected with whatever he's carrying around. And then there's the issue of that scar."

Holt began to shake as he held back the fury boiling inside him. "That's . . . it's not your decision!"

Talan brushed his hands together. "Ah, but you see, Holt, it is. You haven't proved yourself trustworthy to decide your course in life, and I intend for you to go far—farther than I ever dreamed of."

"By controlling me? Is that how I *forced* you into this?" *Augustine was right.*

His father sighed and finally backed away. "I will continue to control you until I see fit not to. That's my job as your father—to protect you." The man looked down at the floor then toward Joel's prison hall. "Holt, in reality I forced myself into this years ago due to a poor decision I made. I intend for you to never be in the same situation." He turned to leave.

"Wait! Father . . . is she alive?"

The man had never answered.

As Holt waited in line, he thought long and hard about the conversation from yesterday. He wasn't sure what his father had meant by the tirade or what poor decision he'd made in the past. He just knew, as Augustine had told him, he had a choice in what his own future could be.

He paid for his father's breakfast and glanced at his watch. The headmaster would be here by noon. *In time for Joel's beating.* His father had put him in charge of this daily regimen, yet he'd only felt pleasure in performing such an act in the tunnel. Joel had a chance to fight back then, and Holt had not only won the fight fairly but also in front of his father. Now, he beat a defenseless Joel who had no chance of escaping or harming anyone. The task really seemed futile in his mind . . . inhumane even. His former classmate was starving, beaten, and seemed to have had his spirit broken. Holt wondered why Differe was saving him. Every time he saw the despondent redhead he had the same thought. *Just kill him.* For at each beating he was reminded of Isabelle, and he knew that, just like him, Joel was half dead anyway.

CHAPTER 68

DUE TO HER valiant efforts Arianna held a prized seat next to Emil Marcell as she entered the city of Facilis. Her heart pounded every time she thought of meeting Joel. She and an entourage of Ferox had travelled by train to the southwest corner of the Northern Regions then via norracs through the West End. Arianna found the West End fairly primitive like Old Waiz, seeing mostly farmland and quaint little villages.

After traveling through the bland countryside Arianna's expectations were greatly exceeded upon reaching the gates of Facilis. *This place is beautiful.* She stared in awe at the capitol building as they entered through the gate. The deeper the group went into the city, the more confused she became. *What happened here?* The siege appeared to have devastated most of the city. The place resembled utter mayhem. Political banners were scorched from flames, garbage was overflowing everywhere, storefronts were in disarray, and the streets were crawling with homeless people alongside Differian officers. *So much for beautiful. This place is destroyed.*

She was asked to exit the norrac in front of a large building she assumed was the prison. Though the way was paved with armed guards, she kept in close step behind Marcell. She felt the stares of the guards and street people yet tried to convince herself it wasn't because of her muscular build or looks, just that she was the only female in the group. She'd argued against wearing a dress, but Marcell had insisted.

"The headmaster will expect a young lady like you to be dressed appropriately."

There's no place to hide my weapons! But, at least it's long enough to cover my feet. She fiddled with the skinny belt wrapped around her waist as her boots clicked together underneath the dress. She felt silly in the long crimson gown. She was strong, not beautiful, like the blonde Andi had taken. *I wonder if Langston will be here.* Though still angry, she hoped he might explain himself or at least tell her where Andi was now.

Marcell walked into the old palace like he owned Facilis, so the rest of them followed suit.

"Counselor Marcell, we are pleased to have you and most grateful for your help." A man in a blue uniform stepped forward and extended his hand. "I'm Officer Simon Fortner."

The two shook hands. "Yes, the leader who convinced most of your army . . . what was left of it . . . to join Differe. Well done, officer."

The man grimaced slightly at Marcell's words.

"These are my Ferox, as well as my interceptor." Marcell gestured to Arianna.

Simon nodded at her. "Miss."

Arianna suddenly felt embarrassed at being singled out and quickly looked away from him. She was relieved to hear the man clear his throat and turn everyone's attention back to the task at hand.

"His Grace only just arrived, but he will see you alone, Counselor. The rest of your group will have to wait here."

"I suppose that's reasonable." Marcell nodded to the group to sit down on the benches and chairs provided in the hallway.

Arianna plopped down in the nearest chair and propped her left ankle over her right knee, exposing her boots for the others to see. Marcell instantly shot her a look of disapproval. She knew she wasn't holding to his ladylike standards, but he was leaving so she didn't budge.

Marcell held his hand up to Simon. "All right, let's go."

"Yes, Sir. Just around the way . . . the old Vicar's office."

Time crept by slowly for the group over the next hour. Arianna dozed, played a rhyming game in her mind, and fought off coarse jokes from her comrades.

"Plan to fight in that long thing? What is that, a dress?"

"Where are you hiding your weapons?"

"Nice touch picking out the color of blood."

"She's just following orders. Leave her alone."

Arianna crossed her arms and turned away from them after the head of their rank defended her. As she looked in the direction Simon had taken Marcell, she saw a very young soldier coming down the hallway. Chin taut and fists clenched, the handsome young man was clearly on a mission. Soon their eyes locked, his blazing full of hate—or passion—she couldn't tell.

"You there, Miss."

Arianna shot up at his commanding tone.

"The headmaster will see you now." He turned back around without giving her a chance to respond, so she hurried to keep up with him. After they rounded the corner to an empty hallway his pace slowed to a stop.

"I like your dress . . . but not as much as I like your boots."

She didn't respond, feeling nervous as to why he'd stopped walking.

He turned to face her and looked down at her hands. "I hear you're kind of powerful."

She immediately crossed her arms yet stayed silent.

"Marcell and Dark have been talking about you the last half hour. They plan to use your power."

Arianna looked up at him in surprise.

"I serve the drinks in such meetings."

She cocked her eyebrow at him. "Why are you talking to me?"

He moved closer, his jaw tightening again. "They'll use you—use you for their own personal gain. Whatever they tell you, I can assure you it's not for the people. Have you seen the city?"

She nodded, remembering how demolished the area looked. "But why should I believe you? Marcell told me himself he doesn't want to *use* my power. He said he wants me to *grow* into it. This Joel person can—"

"They'll use you . . . just like my father used you to get your brother."

Her eyes widened at the mention of Andi. "What! How do you know about my brother? Who's your father?"

"Langston."

"Wait . . . you're Langston's son?"

"Don't let them use you, Arianna. Only use your power for yourself."

"But—but I need guidance. I don't know what to do . . . I don't really know what I want."

"You might want to find a different guide. Come on, they're waiting for you."

The headmaster descended the prison steps one at a time, making him appear more feeble than Arianna expected. Whether he'd been upset about her intercepting the letter from Joel's father she was still unsure.

"The contents of the letter you confiscated have been discussed with your leader, Marcell. The letter has now been burned and will not be remembered . . . by anyone. Do you understand?"

She nodded upon seeing Marcell's urgency for her to do so.

"Now, though only a few pairs of eyes have seen this letter, I think we should take the opportunity to dispel any rumors or misconceptions it may have created in your minds . . . or any other rumors you may have heard about our captive. That will require a trip to the dungeons. Shall we?"

The dungeons below were very much a tangled web of dark corners and turns. The headmaster, Arianna, Marcell, and two Templins walked through the maze, passing cells full of prisoners along the way. The first floor unnerved her as the inmates sent her an array of catcalls and whistles as she walked by; she didn't dare look at them. The second level was quiet, and she gasped when she noticed women and children inside the rows of cells. She quickly focused forward, following the headmaster deeper underground and farther away from any human contact.

They finally stopped at an iron door in the middle of an empty corridor on the lowest level of the prison. *This is it. He's just on the other side of that door.* There was a slat near the top of the door for viewing inside the room and a bottom slat near the floor to serve meals or retrieve waste. A guard opened the top slat and stood back for the headmaster to peer inside. He took a long look then nodded at the lock on the door. Once the door was opened he turned around to the group.

"Just Arianna and me. The rest of you stay outside." He beckoned her forward.

She followed the man into the dank, dark cell and watched him stop to light a torch on the wall. Arianna waited behind him and took in the wall-to-wall stone surrounding them. A set of chains hung on the wall, and there was a jagged stone pedestal near the center of the room. It was bloodied, and Arianna was sure it had been used for Joel's beatings. Slumped over in the corner behind the rock was a filthy heap of rags.

The headmaster strode forward, yet nothing happened until he took a leather strap out and slapped the jagged stone. "Joel."

Arianna shrunk back at the crack lashed upon the block, and the pile of rags moved slightly. She was only able to make out the young man's face amidst the grimy filth due to his hazel eyes slowly opening and closing. At that point she didn't care to see the rest of him.

"Yes, it's me, Joel."

Joel said nothing as the headmaster drummed his fingers across the bloodstains on the pedestal.

"You've been caught . . . and the city you thought would pardon you now belongs to me."

The young man moaned slightly then closed his eyes.

"Your so-called leaders were forced to give their allegiance to Differe, and I've been keeping you here as an example to the people. There is no power greater than truth and tradition. You have thwarted both of these ancient powers by your actions. You have undermined such powers with your false magic."

Arianna raised her eyebrows at his words. *What's he talking about?* Her powers had nothing to do with truth. They had to do with need. Isn't that what Joel had done—given the people rain when they needed it? Trained them for battle? No matter what side she was on, she didn't find his actions dishonest. *Perhaps untraditional, but isn't change good? That's what New Waiz was founded upon.*

"But somehow . . . somewhere, a few still hold to the silly notion that magical objects and lack of true appointed authority will give birth to power. Yes, what did you call it?"

Joel didn't respond.

"Can't remember, Joel? Well, I do. Your father calls your kind of power 'freedom.' A power stemming from some old legend that died a long time ago. But as you will soon see, mankind can create its own supernatural just fine. We do not need your fairytales or a higher power. We are the higher power. None of this nonsense your father has said about light inside you. My power will squelch yours like I've done with many before you."

When the headmaster mentioned Joel's father it was the first time Arianna saw a spark of life in the young man. She shuddered when the headmaster moved back and put his arm around her.

"Now, Joel, I'll let you see what created power, power under guidance and influence from authority, truly looks like."

Joel sat up slightly, finally seeming to notice her. His eyes widened as he frantically searched her over.

"She reminds you of someone, doesn't she?"

The unkindness in his words made Arianna want to bolt out of the room. *"They're going to use your power." Maybe the Langston boy was right.*

"Well, this young lady has no magic weapons on her." He lifted her open hands to Joel. "No, she herself is the weapon. Let's see what she can do . . . and I dare you to stop her."

Arianna drew her hands back and trembled, wondering what the headmaster wanted her to do. She sent him a questioning look.

He patted her shoulder reassuringly. "Arianna, I want you to release your power in this place. Call up your helpers."

Terrified at such a request, she frantically shook her head at him, but he pressed back.

"Yes, that's what Marcell and I want you to do." He stepped away from her until he was outside the room and locked her inside with Joel.

She looked at the door in terror then heard a faint whisper.

"Augustine?"

"No. Arianna."

"No, I know. I mean . . . ." Joel stopped to gasp for breath. "Please, tell Augustine—"

"Do not consort with the enemy, My Dear."

Arianna turned around, and her eyes met the headmaster's through the slat on the door. Marcell's head bobbed behind the older man. "Yes, Arianna, release your power and get out. That's an order."

Joel attempted his request again, but she blocked him out this time, only focusing on Marcell's words, "That's an order." She called up the dark voices the woman had introduced to her at the riverside. These were the ones who had given her the formulas, the ones who had saved her mother's life, had given her a job, and had given her power. She smiled slightly as the darkness enveloped her, and she recalled the headmaster's words. *I am the weapon. A weapon of power . . . power that the most influential men in my world want.*

CHAPTER 69

JOEL SAT ALONE in a damp prison cell. He looked toward the place he'd last seen the headmaster, barely making out the door through his swollen eyes. They soon moved to another object, and his mind drifted back to the man's last words to him.

"This is your last home, Joel, and mark my words you are powerless. Yet, since you've insisted you only want power through freedom, well, here's a kind gesture from me." The man tossed a short sword before him and cackled as he turned to leave. "I know you'll make the right *choice.*"

Joel's eyes widened in hope, but the feeling quickly flickered away when he saw it was not his or any other's rhydid. He squinted back at the iron door and thought he could make out two guards with their backs to him through the top slat. He was wet with perspiration and felt his insides raging against him. He suddenly was desperately fighting nausea, and soon his body began trembling for no reason. He struggled for breath between terrified gasps as the mouthpieces called to him.

"Take the sword, Joel."

"The easiest path is right there."

"Take your life."

The sword was well beyond its prime, and Joel wasn't convinced the object could even perform the deed. He reasoned with himself that he'd been in this place before, the same terror and pain, the same voices. *But you broke free.*

You can do it again. How did I get rid of these before? The last time he hadn't had his sword yet, but someone had come to his aid. *Corwin.* He had come to his rescue. *Won't someone come today?*

"No one's coming, not this time."

Joel sat up. *Whose voice was that?* He thought only the king could read his thoughts. He looked up at the pack of mouthpieces the girl had released upon him and saw no light, only their glowing x-shaped eyes staring back at him. *But . . . the voice . . . it sounded like . . . the king. It couldn't be though.* After Isabelle had died he'd told the king, "I couldn't care less what you have to say anymore," effectively banning the being from speaking to him anymore.

And then there was Augustine. Even though she'd gotten away it hadn't felt like a victory. *Just more loss.* On that day he realized there was no one left he cared about worth saving. He told himself he no longer needed some king to exist.

He looked at the sword again, confused and perhaps even tempted to take it. He lay back down in utter defeat as the wicked mouthless creatures crouched upon him.

"King . . . I need . . . ."

He croaked the words as his lungs burned for air. The mouthpieces pressed in further, smothering his breath, his hope. As they attempted to overtake him, a desperate cry rose from his chest.

"I need something supernatural. I do need your power . . . I need you!"

"Augustine, are you sure this is the way?" Sebastian leaned over Corwin's shoulder. The man was carrying him on his back while Augustine led them through the underground tunnels.

She nodded and pointed to the very spot Joel was taken captive. "One hundred percent. That's where I left him." She gave the empty cell a long look. As far as she knew, only Corwin and the Langstons knew the whole truth about Joel's capture. She didn't want Sebastian to find out until she'd had a chance to tell Joel herself. *He needs to be the next to know.*

The three had traveled just outside the West End by train. She was grateful their stop in the Southern Regions was nowhere near Reagan Manor.

Corwin had even discovered a different entrance into the tunnels from one of the ancient scrolls Joel had given him. Fortunately the map also verified what Talan Langston had said about the tunnels leading straight into the Chrysos Prison. It almost seemed too convenient, but Augustine didn't care. She'd decided on the train she would risk her life in order to get to him. *He did it for me, and I know he and Corwin would take care of Sebastian.* As she glanced back at her sickly brother and outcast uncle, she realized that in some way they were all risking their lives.

Corwin's sources had informed him the headmaster was scheduled to have an audience with Joel over the weekend. It was now mid-week and the group hoped the old man was long gone by now. She was a little nervous Joel might have been taken to Differe, but the letter Phillip intercepted at Reagan Manor had indicated otherwise. Both the letter and Corwin's spies were told Joel would be left in the city to serve as an example to the people. It angered her greatly, and she feared for Facilis. *I wonder how the people are faring?*

"Augustine?"

She shook her head, realizing she was still staring at the place where she'd last seen Joel. "Corwin, you'd better look at the map. I remember which tunnel I was told led to the prison . . . but make sure it's really the right one."

He put Sebastian down. "Okay. You two go ahead and get dressed."

Augustine reprised her role as a boy, but this time she was clothed in something altogether different. She tucked her hair underneath a thick uniform hat. She was to be Corwin's junior Templin in training. Sebastian had been a bit trickier to disguise, but a wounded child found abandoned in the tunnel would have to work.

The little boy walked over to Augustine and put his arm around her. "You're way braver than I thought you were."

She patted his arm and flashed him a smile.

"If I haven't told you yet . . . well, thank you, Augie. Thank you for this." He tugged at her rhydid.

She looked down at his small hand and cleared her throat. "Well, I know it was never a conditional thing—me expecting something in return—but . . . I might *need* something later."

He kissed her cheek. "Anything. You name it."

She turned her face away from his curious eyes. "Forgiveness . . . undeserved forgiveness."

"Uh, isn't that how it works? But anyway, yeah, sure, nothing's unforgivable."

She kept her face hidden while furiously blinking her watery eyes. "Well, I'm afraid . . . I'm afraid something might be to someone."

"Well, not to me. You should—"

"This way." Corwin pointed down a tunnel Augustine hadn't remembered seeing the last time. The three zigzagged in silence as they wound through the passageways. *This is taking too long. It will take us forever to get back out of here.* Just when she thought she couldn't take another step in the dark channel, a loud noise rang out in front of them. They rounded the corner to find the tunnel not only widened but was lit at the end of the next stretch.

Corwin put Sebastian back down and held a hand up. "Everyone remember what we're doing here?"

Sebastian nodded. "Ready."

"Got it." Augustine was first to reach the end of the tunnel's passage. She found herself surrounded by three walls, each gated and opening into larger tunnels. She twisted her lips as she eyed the gates. *Easy enough.* She ran over to the only guarded gate. "Guard! Excuse me, guard!" She hoped her voice sounded low enough.

The guard slowly made his way to the entrance.

Though a small surgical mask covered his face, she could tell he was frowning at her. She stared at the officer's blue jacket. *A Facilis guard.* "I'm Templin Garrett. I was sent to investigate the tunnels leading to the Southern Regions. I've—we've found—"

"Junior Templin, you mean. Officer, we found a straggler—may have escaped from your prison." She heard Corwin's heavy footsteps approach behind her.

The guard raised his eyebrows as he looked upon a limp Sebastian in Corwin's arms.

"Hate to trouble you, but this was the quickest way to get him to our leading officers. They can decide whether or not to give him medical treatment."

The guard stared hard at Corwin then Augustine. He gripped the bars of the gate and bent down to Augustine's height. She swallowed nervously as the man studied every inch of her face. He finally pulled back and crossed his arms.

"Please, we're following orders. You know how thorough our superiors like things."

The man placed his hand on his chin then slowly pulled down the mask. "And, just what are your orders . . . Augustine?"

CHAPTER 70

S IMON!"

"Hello, Love."

"Oh, Simon, I'm so glad to see you. Why the mask?"

"Damp, dirty, unfiltered air down here. Wasn't sure if any of that black smoke got into the tunnels."

"Oh, I hadn't thought of that." She looked back at Sebastian, relieved his breathing appeared unaltered, then turned back to Simon. "I want to know how you are. How are the people? Will you let us in?"

He rubbed his face where the mask had been. "On one condition."

Augustine waited.

"That I get a role in your plot. I want to follow your orders, Love."

Augustine grinned. "Agreed. What are you doing down here anyway?"

"I'm one of the few leaders that didn't revolt. I gave my allegiance to Differe as soon as the siege began—Dillon and I planned it shortly after you left. A few of the leaders would give up their allegiance if it looked like the region would fall. That way most of our army, or the army Differe leaves to lead Facilis, will actually be our own Facilis guards."

"How's the place . . . the people?"

He shook his head sadly. "You wouldn't believe it if you saw it. It's terrible. They've got me and many other old leaders stationed down here, so I haven't been able to connect with the people and figure out a way to get them into the storehouse without Differe knowing. We thought about just smuggling people into the Southern Regions using these tunnels. I'm not sure what we'll do. Either way, Differe didn't want to give an officer of my ranking anything important to do, so they stuck me in the pit of the city the beginning of this week. Here I'm safe and sound—harmless . . . until now."

She was pleased to see the smirk on his face. "Well, I'm glad you're here, and I'm glad you had a plan. This is my uncle, Corwin Atticus, and my brother, Sebastian Bennett."

"Nice to meet you both."

Corwin nodded and put Sebastian down. "Tell us about the prison. What's the layout?"

"Right. As you can see on the map the main building is above ground, while all of the actual prison cells are beneath it. There are quite a few floors and they wind around—much more than this map lets on. As for us, just like with any security position, we work in shifts. Most of the villagers revolted and were captured, Dillon and his men as well. They're in the cells closest to the main floor. The first or second, I'm not sure. It's the most crowded area with guards, cooks, Templins. We could easily sneak among the crowd. And, last I heard, as you might imagine, Joel's somewhere in the lowest level of the prison. It's a complete maze, this underground place . . . but that also means there are several ways to get to him."

"Dillon, Violet . . . where are the bariques, the sacred stones?"

"Safe. We hid them well before they were captured."

"I, uh, suppose they're not anywhere near here are they?"

He shook his head as he opened the gate. "No, Love. We'll have to use different weapons today.

Half an hour later, the four were in the bowels of the prison wandering carefully around every corner. Augustine had no concept of direction except down. Simon proved to be an incredible guide in the darkened silence and eventually led them into a room the size of a closet.

"Augustine, Corwin, there will be several guards on the other side of this room." He put her hand on the door in front of them. "Take out your rhydids, and I'll send you in."

Augustine took a deep breath as she and Corwin pulled the swords out. The objects hummed as they met the air. She felt Corwin's hand on her shoulder but didn't turn around. She crouched with her blade out. "Do a count. I'm ready."

"One, two, three." The door flung open, and she flew inside.

She stumbled into the room and thrust the sword in all directions but straightened in confusion. The place was abandoned. There was no one in sight, and the heavy iron cell door in front of her was open. She stepped forward and peered around the door. Hanging chains, a jagged stone table splattered with blood, and a horrible smell were all that remained. She backed away in frustration and turned to the others. "It's all right. No one's here."

The group entered the room to discover the truth as she sighed in dismay. Suddenly a shuffle behind them caught her attention. A dark shadow emerged, and Augustine raised the rhydid again.

"He's been moved."

"Holt!"

Talan's son raised his hands and opened his coat. "I'm unarmed."

She cautiously lowered her weapon and encouraged the others to do the same. "How did you find us?"

"I followed you. As Simon said . . . there are a lot of ways around this place."

Augustine wasn't sure what to do next. "So . . . now what?"

"You kill me, or I give you up."

She sucked in a deep breath. She'd said she would kill for Joel but now, faced with the decision, she wasn't sure she could do it.

He turned to leave when he noticed the group didn't pick up their weapons again. "I'll give you enough time to get out. Just go back to the Southern Regions."

"But why? Why would you do that?"

He turned around and raised his eyes to hers. "Because . . . you were right."

She wasn't sure what he meant, but she had to stop him. "Holt! Holt, listen to me . . . we—we think Isabelle's alive."

He leaned back inside the room. "A-alive? You're . . . you're sure?"

"Yes. We're pretty sure, but your father would definitely know. You have my word."

He stared at her and gripped the bricks on the wall of the opening. "He's on the first floor—Joel. He's in a cell there. If you get to him before the shift change, well, Simon should be able to get you near him. It's mostly Facilis guards watching him at lunch."

"Holt, I—"

"This isn't over between me and him. You tell him the only reason I want him free is so we can have an even fight. I look forward to killing him . . . on my own terms."

Augustine swallowed hard. "I'll tell him."

He slipped around the doorway, and she ran after him. "Holt! Wait! The key? How do we get the key?"

His dark shadow kept walking. "You don't need one. The cell only opens from the inside. Joel's the only one who can set himself free."

CHAPTER 71

AUGUSTINE SHOOK HER head in disgust as her group of four huddled just outside the third floor dungeon. The guards were hardly taking their job seriously and instead were gorging themselves in front of the rows of starving prisoners.

"Spying on our lunch?"

Augustine jumped as a Templin spotted their hiding spot and strode toward her.

"And who's the child? Is he one of them?" The man motioned to the prisoners behind him.

Corwin stepped in between the two and flashed his Templin badge. "They're all with me. This is my apprentice, and we found this child in the tunnels below. We ordered Officer Fortner from his post to help us bring this child to the Templin Headquarters. We just guard the tunnels, not the dungeons, and were unsure of the way."

The officer shrugged. "Guess that leaves no one down there, but probably doesn't matter much. Fortner. Templin. Junior Templin." The man bid them to come inside and quickly brushed past them.

Corwin pressed Augustine from behind. "Well, for once I'm thankful for their stupidity *and* arrogance."

She smiled and put a hand on Simon's arm. "How many of your men are stationed on the next two floors?"

"Enough to take any who oppose us."

Augustine nodded. "All right. Corwin, get Sebastian to Joel. I think once he sees him or hears his voice—"

"Got it." He nodded.

"Take Simon with you. You'll need him to get his men on your side. His guards don't know you and aren't likely to trust you dressed like that." She waved a hand before he could protest. "I'll free the prisoners. They and the Facilis guards should all recognize me. I'm completely safe. We can imprison the remaining Differian guards in the cells and meet you on the first floor to help get Joel out of the city. If . . . if we need a diversion, we'll split up to get out safely."

The three stared back at her with eyes full of concern.

"You said you'd follow my plan. This is it." The group nodded in unison, and she squeezed Sebastian's hands. "Let's go. For Joel."

The four staggered their departure from the third floor at varying times. As Augustine entered the second floor alone, she held back a horrified gasp as she eyed the rows and rows of cells crammed with people. It was a pitiful scene of men, women, and children clothed in rags and sitting quietly, stuffed in their cages. Augustine willed herself to take breaths without gagging from the stench. Several coughs from the children reminded her of Sebastian, and fury rose in her as she spotted the Differian guards hunched over their lunch plates. *So many people. How will I ever find Dillon?* The peaceful cells only had one guard stationed on each hallway, but she knew she'd be questioned if she tried pass into one of the rows. *What should I—*

"Where have you been?"

Augustine locked onto a pair of black boots next to her feet. "I've, uh, I was, I was just guarding the dungeons with my mentor."

"No, I mean before that . . . before the siege. You didn't say goodbye."

She gazed up into a warm familiar face. *Oh, Earl!* She resisted the urge to hug him. "Yes, well, I'm so sorry. There's no time to explain, but . . . I'm here now, that's what matters most."

"Yes, you are."

"Care to point me in the right direction? I have something for one of your captives . . . the Galanneans."

He quickly shoved two buckets of water at her. "Take these to cell number 147. The officer on the hall will direct you. Don't take too long."

Augustine felt like she was walking through a ghost town as she passed the quiet sad cells. She was glad to finally approach her row. The guard was well beyond earshot when she finally reached the last cell on the back row.

"Time for your water." She searched the cell for familiar faces. She was relieved to see the Galanneans appeared in fairly decent condition. They were dirty, but not sick, bleeding, or dying as she'd seen in some of the other cells.

"Please, please, give it to the women and children. Yous are giving them nothing. They need the water more than us. Do not keep us strong to punish them. Please." Dillon barely looked up at her and his men also began pleading with her.

"No, drink it."

"Give to children."

She held her hand up and dropped her pretense. "They had to put you in the last cell on the last row. Did you cause that much trouble?"

The cell went silent until Augustine lifted her hat and pulled a dark strand around her face.

Recognition instantly registered on Dillon's face. "Augustine! What are yous doing here?"

She slid her hand to the rhydid and smiled.

"To rescue Joel?"

"Simon and two others are doing that very thing right now. I'm here to set you free."

"No! No, Augustine!"

His frantic tone unnerved her, and she checked to make sure the guarding officer didn't seem suspicious. "Sh! What's wrong?"

He shook his head at her. "It has to be yous. Remember?"

"Dillon, we have to hurry. What are you talking about?"

He reached through the bars for her hand. "Yous, Augustine. He is under some sort of spell. Yous are the voice that help Joel to the gate. Yous are the voice that lead him. I see it. I see yous call to him . . . that is when he push through the black smoke and make for the gate. He—he shall not be able to leave his cell without yous. Leave us! Go get him out!"

Augustine drew back in alarm. *Is this true?*

"Do not think, Augustine; just go!"

Her shaky hands spilled water from the buckets onto the floor, and she quickly set them down. She pulled out her rhydid and stuck it into the lock opening. It immediately clicked, but neither she nor Dillon opened the door. She hurried to slide the weapon through the bars. "Take this. We'll need a diversion."

CHAPTER 72

JOEL FELT LIKE he was going in and out of consciousness. He thought he might be dreaming, but opened his eyes only to discover the ghostly screams were real. He shut his eyes tight and realized it didn't feel like he was breathing. He tried to move his body, but he was immobile. His sense of touch had vanished, and he had no idea if he was lying down or standing up. *Am I dead?* He opened his eyes again, remembering the headmaster had left him alone in a new cell. Through the fogginess in his mind and the shrouding mouthpieces, he thought he saw some movement by the door. He thought he heard his name. As he gasped for air again he tried to rouse himself and focus on the sound just outside the door.

"Joel! Joel! It's Corwin. I'm behind the door. I see you. Are you all right?" Corwin cringed as he peered through the top slat to find the dozens of mouthpieces flying around Joel. The young man was choking for air. He kept calling out his name to no avail. At different moments Joel appeared lucid, but it was as if something, maybe even his own body, wouldn't allow him to fully engage with anything beyond the cell. *There are too many of those blasted creatures inside.* He had never seen anyone look so horrid. Joel looked like he was in a terrified trance. *He looks . . . insane. Just like they want him, and everyone else, to believe.*

Sebastian was crouched at the bottom opening. "Corwin, is he . . . is he alone in there?"

Corwin shook his head. "No, it's full of mouthpieces." He sighed as he studied the smooth iron door with no lock or handle in front of him. *Holt was right. The only way to open this door must be on the inside.* He peered through the top slat and made out three latches fastening the door snuggly to the prison wall. "Sebastian, your hands are smaller than mine. Can you reach inside and undo the bottom latch? Perhaps you can even reach the middle one."

"I can try."

"Good, but in the meantime, make sure to keep calling to him. Joel! Joel!"

Sebastian nodded and attempted to fiddle with the latch. "Come on, Joel! Wake up! You can do it! Get up!"

The two continued yelling for several minutes until it looked like Joel was finally stirring.

Sebastian tugged Corwin's pants leg. "Corwin! He's choking!"

Corwin pressed his hands against the door as he watched Joel produce a gagging cough. "Come on, Joel! Oh no! Joel! Joel, stay with us!"

"Corwin, wait! He's not choking . . . he's smelling something."

Sebastian and Corwin turned to find Simon rounding the corner with a bloodied cheek and an ample supply of what appeared to be a prison guard's lunch.

"Here, I thought this might help." He motioned for his men to keep guarding the openings to Joel's corridor and to keep any Differian guards away.

Corwin took the plate and sat it on the ground next to Sebastian by the bottom slat. "How's it going out there?"

"Fine. Everything looks normal."

Corwin raised an eyebrow at his bruised cheek.

"There may have been a brawl or two to keep things quiet."

"Thank you, Simon. Let's hope it was worth your efforts. All right, Sebastian, push the plate through the slat and hold it up. Now listen, we don't want him to get it just yet. We just really want him to want it. Be prepared to snatch it back outside if he comes over."

The three watched Joel through the slats as Sebastian shoved the plate inside. Their friend leaned against the wall continuing to convulse. His hair was standing straight up, and his eyes darted to and fro at the mouthpieces only he and Corwin could see.

Simon covered his mouth in horror. "He looks crazy."

"Shh! Come on, Joel. Come on; take a deep breath." Corwin watched Joel close his mouth to swallow then take a breath through his nose. He breathed again the same way, and hope rose in them as Joel began to blink his eyes. He even began to squint his nose.

"Corwin, he smells it! He's waking up!"

Corwin shared Sebastian's excitement until Joel's head fell into a neutral position again. He grimaced when he realized what was happening. "Come on, Joel. Stop listening to them. Quit looking at the mouthpieces."

"Corwin . . . what are they saying to him?"

Though he hated to do so, Corwin closed his eyes and forced himself to listen. "They're asking him to end his life. Yes, they—"

"Look, you two! He's—he's sniffing!"

Simon was right. It finally seemed the body that had been working desperately against him was now fighting for life.

Corwin gripped Simon's shoulder. "You're right. Joel! Joel, I have a feast over here! It's a Templin's feast! We stole it just for you!"

"I know you're hungry, Joel! Get up!"

"Good job, Sebastian. Keep shouting. We have to be louder than the mouthpieces."

All three began shouting at Joel until the redhead touched his stomach.

"He's hungry! Corwin, Simon, it's working!"

"Yes, Sebastian, keep shouting." Corwin watched Joel try to view the door through the hoard of flying black voices. He growled when a huge one stooped over Joel and blocked his vision. All three started shouting again and banging at the door. Corwin hated being so loud, but he didn't know what else to do. He even clanged his rhydid against the door, causing the mouthpieces to disperse a bit. He rejoiced when Joel finally turned his head toward them. *We've got his attention.* "Joel!"

He seemed to mouth something in their direction.

"Come on, Joel!"

The young man startled a moment later but not due to Corwin's voice.

Joel heard a muffled sound amidst the screams of the mouthpieces. The voice was pure and loud and . . . it was calling to him. *I have to go. I have to go to her.* He looked up and noticed the position of the mouthpieces had changed. They were encircling him, beating themselves, and yelling louder than ever. *They're working hard . . . too hard.* They were so close he could feel their cool breath misting on his skin. As they closed in, he heard something far away shouting, "Joel, the sword! Use the sword!"

But I . . . but I don't have enough strength to walk. I-I can barely breathe. Yet, the voice and something delicious seemed to overpower his senses. His body begged him to go to it, and his spirit pleaded with him to go to the one who was calling to him. He shuddered as he looked at the large creature hovering over him. *Blindly. That's it. I'll have to do it blindly.* Delighted squeals rang out from the mouthpieces as he reached for the blade. He closed his eyes tightly and gave himself a count. "One, two, three!"

CHAPTER 73

AUGUSTINE, CORWIN, SIMON, and Sebastian watched a hair-crazed Joel close his eyes and raise his suicide sword in the air. He ran like a blind maniac toward the door, swinging the sword and yelling.

"Corwin, I see them!"

For the first time, Augustine saw the mouthpieces. Dozens of the dark creatures chased after Joel, spreading and spinning around to regroup and charge toward him at the door. They hovered on top of him, literally pushing him to the ground beside the plate of food. Sebastian snatched it back, and Corwin reached in to grab his face.

Joel jumped at the human contact.

"Joel, Joel! Look at me. Open your eyes! It's Corwin!"

Joel soon recognized the face staring back at him. "Let me out! Open the door! The mouthpieces—help me!" he screamed in terror.

Corwin still had a grip on his face. "Joel, Joel! Look at me! Look!"

His frantic eyes finally fixed on the man.

"I can't open the door. It can only be opened from the inside. See the latch." Corwin pointed to the one on the ground. "Sebastian opened this one and the middle one, but we can't get to the one at the top of the door. Look up quickly to find it then look right back down at me. Understand?"

Augustine winced as the face of a screaming mouthpiece terrorized her friend just as he looked up to search for the latch. "Corwin!"

The man jerked Joel's head back down. "I said 'quickly!' Did you see it?"

Joel nodded "yes" as tears filled his eyes. "But I can't . . . I'll never be able to reach it. I'll never be able to leave."

Augustine's eyes clouded too, knowing she'd put him in there.

"No, you'll have to use this to lift the latch as well as open your eyes." Corwin slid his rhydid under the bottom slat.

Joel looked down at the object in dismay. "This isn't mine."

"Joel, forget your past. You can do it."

"I can't—I can't. There are too many." He knelt further and squinted his eyes shut.

"Joel, open your eyes. Look at this Templin's plate of food. Aren't you hungry?" Sebastian moved the plate as close as possible to Joel's face.

Augustine finally bent down. "Joel, open your eyes."

He obeyed and first saw Sebastian.

"Mhm. Yummy. Come and get some."

She gently pressed her brother aside.

Joel stared at her, and though he still appeared to be in a slight trance, she knew he recognized her.

"You called to me . . . ."

"I came back for you. So, now you know you really did it. Sebastian's fine. He's here. This is real." She stuck her arm inside and put his hand on the rhydid. "Open the latch, Joel. You can do it."

He closed his eyes again and took a breath. When he opened his eyes Corwin let go of his face, and in one small swoop he hit the latch with the rhydid and the door fell open. Joel tumbled out of the cell and into Augustine's arms. She held him while Corwin stood over them with his rhydid, ready to defend his freed prisoner. The world around her disappeared as she held the redhead in her arms. *He's alive, and safe for now. Oh, Joel.*

Only when Corwin began prying the unconscious young man from her arms did she remember the task at hand. *My rhydid. Dillon!* They had to get to the top level to meet the other freed prisoners.

"Hurry!" Simon directed them through the maze of dark corridors. His officers had made a path for them to get to the main floor while avoiding

Differe's guards. As the group neared the prison's top floor, it was obvious a commotion was beginning to break out.

"Simon, how can we get out unseen? Out of Facilis, I mean. Corwin, cover Joel with my coat."

Simon didn't answer as they peered into the hallway that would begin leading them up and out of the building. His men were now in combat with several Templins, and Augustine sucked in a breath as she watched them risk their lives.

"Augie, what about the tunnels?"

"No, Sebastian. They'll have enough time to send their squadrons to most of the exits. We can't use them to get out now, not with only the four of us. I—Simon, we have to go through the gate."

"That's pure suicide, Augustine. They'll never let you out, Love!"

"Don't be so sure. Who's guarding the gate? It's your men, isn't it?" She knew she was right when he looked away from her. "And this hallway is the only way out?"

"I'm afraid so. But, Augustine, my men . . . yes, they're at the gate, but so are Differe's. It's a risky plan."

"It's all we've got, Simon."

She bent down and pulled Sebastian's coat tight. "You stay back here with me until they've cleared the hall. You'll . . . you'll easily slip out. If we get separated just get to the gate. You need to—"

"I've got a map. I know, just head out and to the right. I'll be fine, Augie. No one's looking for me."

"Yes, well, no one should bother you." She gave him a long look then turned to Corwin. "We'll wait here until you come back for Joel . . . whatever you do, make sure to get Joel and Sebastian out. I'll—I'll see you at the gate."

Corwin nodded, gently put Joel on the ground, and hurried after Simon. The two positioned themselves with their swords out and broke into the hallway. Augustine marveled at how they wielded their weapons and took out the enemy. She looked down at her clothes and bit her lip. She took a deep breath and carefully waded through a few dead bodies on the floor behind her. The array of uniform colors made it obvious both sides had been affected in the brawl. She only spotted one Templin's uniform among the bodies, and hurried to rip the cloak off the dead officer. She raced back to Joel, tore off the junior Templin coat, and covered him with the larger cloak. She put her coat back on just before Corwin called back to her.

"It's—it's time. We've cleared enough to almost get him to the door." He was breathless as he lifted Joel off the ground.

She spotted Sebastian already inching up the hall and froze. *My rhydid!*

"Augustine, you don't have to be brave for Joel. You don't have to serve some sort of penance. Don't stay behind."

Tears filled her eyes as she looked back at Corwin. "I know. It's just— I have to find Dillon . . . I've made a mess of things again. I promise I'll meet you at the gate."

"Here. Take my rhydid and lead the way."

She and Simon crept to the corner of the main hallway that led to the exit and were met with a live combat scene from a war book. The entrance to the Differian Army's massive dining hall was open and was being overtaken by a mass of freed prisoners. Augustine smiled as she spotted many of those she'd seen below now eating heartily as Differe's officers were being forced out by the Facilis guards. The combat going on in the hall was mostly a fist brawl until the freed prisoners began collecting the fallen soldiers' weapons.

Simon made sure no one could see Corwin. "Wait, and stay back."

Augustine pressed beside him but felt him push her back as well.

"No, Love. You stay back too. There are plenty without your help. Stay back, and get to the gate."

She wanted to obey him, but seeing Dillon and his men emerge into the fight sent her down the hallway in a sprint. When she reached the action, she suddenly remembered how she was dressed. *I'm a Templin!* She panicked as the blue coats started swiping at her, one slicing into the top of her shoulder. She shrank back and yelped at the sting from the fresh wound. "Wait! I'm not the enemy!" When none held back she thrust the rhydid out and cut the tip off one of her pursuers' sword. The soldier stepped back in awe, and a few others stared at her in confusion. She moved forward and aimed Corwin's rhydid at any and all who dared to mess with her again. "Dillon! Dillon!"

Over the commotion of clanging metal and beating fists, she saw his head pop up. "I hear yous! To the tunnels, everyone! To the tunnels! We are escaping into the Southern Regions! Move out! Let's go!"

The diversion.

"Yes, take Joel to the tunnels!"

"Yes, we take Joel!"

"To Vicar's Hill!"

"Go! Go!"

"Move out!"

She made a futile attempt to get to Dillon before she realized he was gone. She watched as the freed prisoners pushed past her down the hallway in droves, driving the Differian Army back. The people from the dining hall came from the other side and closed in, bursting open the doors of Chrysos Prison. It was quite satisfying to watch the mob flying down the steps into the streets followed by a mass exodus of Facilis Guards from the underground dungeons below. Differe's guards stood back in horror, shouting and pointing to something. Augustine looked up to find their airway system, and soon a loud dispatch echoed throughout the place.

"Differian legions to the tunnels! There has been a mass outbreak at the prison! All exits must be secured! The headmaster's prisoner has been freed! Again, all legions to the tunnels!"

A pit formed in Augustine's stomach as the message was shouted again over the loud speaker. *The prisoners aren't safe . . . but I trust Dillon. He must know what he's doing.* As she held Corwin's rhydid she realized hers, like Joel's, was gone. *Sebastian . . . but perhaps it'll be what they need to win.*

"You're hurt. I brought you this."

She took a blue officer's coat from Simon. "It's all right. I'm fine. Let's get out of here."

Just as they'd hoped, the group easily exited unseen amidst the commotion. Everyone was headed in the direction of the warehouse, leaving the streets to the city gate fairly deserted. With Corwin and Joel dressed as Templins, Sebastian as a prisoner, and Augustine and Simon as Facilis guards, she figured they'd be able to persuade either side at the gate. When the area was within sight, the group exchanged nervous glances. A line of Templins stood outside the gate while a host of blue coats guarded the inside.

She shook her head. "This looks familiar."

Corwin shifted Joel in his arms and sighed. "Now what?"

For the first time that day Augustine was stumped. "I-I don't know. I didn't anticipate this many." She startled when Joel moaned under the cloak.

She gently patted him then grimaced as a sharp pain shot through her bleeding shoulder. She glanced at her wound then to the heap lying under the cloak. "I've got an idea. Come on."

435

CHAPTER 74

THE GROUP APPEARED hesitant to move forward, seeming to lack confidence in Augustine's plan.

"Come on, we've gotten this far. We're going to the medical tents." She motioned for Simon to walk beside her. The blue guards stood to attention when they saw them approaching.

"Hello, men. Quite a commotion up at the prison. Have you heard?"

"It's good to see you, Officer Fortner. And, yes, we heard the dispatch."

"Well, should've quieted down by now. I suppose everyone's underground, which is why they moved me up here today."

They all nodded in understanding.

"Well, as you may have guessed a fair amount are wounded. Many . . . killed. We need medical supplies from the outlying tents."

"What's wrong with the hospital, Sir?"

"Have you been inside since the siege? It's in terrible shape, especially with Miss Augustine gone."

"And, we Templins prefer treatment from our own region."

Augustine smiled to herself as a few smug glances from the Templins outside responded to Corwin's arrogant interruption.

"Well, both sides have orders, Sir. Even the Templins outside. We're not supposed to let anyone pass through the gates, particularly with the high alert today. Uh, who's under the cloak there?"

Augustine's heart beat loudly. "A badly wounded fellow. He, uh, he was the one guarding the headmaster's prisoner. This little fella here was his servant."

The officers seemed impressed.

She balled her fists and took a step forward. "So, you can understand that conventional medicines will be of no use to him."

Simon nodded. "It's true. I'd like to send them on if your troops could come to an agreement on the situation."

His words created a murmur among both groups.

Corwin tried to persuade the groups further. "Please, officers, we must hurry. If he dies, we won't be able to get a full report on how the prisoner escaped. The little boy was knocked out for most of the brawl. The headmaster needs that information if the prisoner is to be captured and contained again."

"I'll accompany them."

"And so will I."

Augustine turned to find a Facilis guard on horseback and a Templin bustling toward them.

"Here, I have clearance." Augustine watched Earl jump off his horse and unfold a document. He handed it to the leading Facilis Officer while the Templin handed his papers to the Templin guards through the gate.

The Facilis guard looked through the gate at the Templins. "Seems in order. It's signed by His Grace, the headmaster himself."

"This one looks fine as well. Signed by Langston."

No one spoke a word until the city gates were out of sight. Earl had provided several horses, and to Augustine's delight, Corwin and Joel were riding on Paz. The group finally came to a crossroad, with one way leading to the medical tents near Baithe and the other to the Southern Regions. The only thing standing in the way of their escape to the West End was the burly Templin riding next to her. His long dark beard covered most of his face, and she could barely see his eyes under his hat. He, like the others, also hadn't said a word.

Augustine stopped at the crossroad and jumped off her horse. "How about a water break?"

The group nodded in agreement, all except one.

"I don't think so. You'd better get going. The dispatch will have a reading on the tunnels in a few hours, and your group should've reached the tents by then. You need as much of a head start as you can get."

All stood speechless at the Templin's words.

"You heard me. Go on. Take this road to the Southern Regions."

Something in his voice was familiar to Augustine. She walked over to the bearded man and slowly patted his horse.

He bent down toward her. "What are you waiting for? Go."

She tugged on the beard and gasped at the face underneath. "Holt!"

"I thought you might want this back." He loosened his cloak and a moment later held out her rhydid.

She looked at him in awe, not sure what to say. "I, yes, you're right . . . thank you."

He nodded and pulled off his disguise. "Well, I'm off to Baithe to find the group who escaped through the gate with Differe's prisoner. Should look pretty good arriving just in time."

"Holt, I should probably head with you. We can come up with a fascinating tale of how they got away from me on the way." Earl clucked his horse over.

"Earl, I—"

"I'm glad we got to say goodbye this time, My Dear."

Augustine smiled at him. "Me too."

"Also, I have something for you." He pulled a coin size bag from the small pocket of his pants. "This is Joel's. I got it from him before they could."

Augustine opened the small bag to find a ruby earring inside. The stone nearly matched the one on her hand from her mother's ring. She felt another object in the bag and saw a hard plastic bead. It was a black cap. She realized then this had been the earring Joel had been wearing all along. She closed the bag and zipped it up in her coat pocket. "Thank you, Earl. When he wakes up I know he'll be very grateful."

He nodded. "Goodbye now, Augustine.

"Goodbye."

Holt grabbed the reins tightly and nodded as well. "Don't forget what I said about telling Joel. I decided I was tired of living by Differe's rulebook, but this isn't over between him and me—just evening up the playing field."

"I won't forget."

As the two rode off in the distance, Augustine wondered what lay ahead for them. Earl would be fine, but she wasn't so sure about Holt. He seemed conflicted about his allegiance, and in a strange way she worried for Joel's old enemy. Though he'd given them a head start she didn't fully trust him. And how could she really? He heard voices just like the rest of them, except his most powerful influence wasn't a mouthpiece. It was his father.

CHAPTER 75

HOLT STARED AT the blood dripping from the throat of the guard who'd just reported his treachery, as Talan Langston cleaned his knife with a handkerchief. "Father, I—"

The man silenced him with an upheld hand.

"But, Father, please let me explain."

"Just don't, Holt. I need a minute." The man slammed his knife into the wooden desk. "Yes, I need a minute to figure out why my son, whose only assignment as a junior Templin was to guard a certain boy, allowed him . . . no, *helped* him escape. AGAIN!" He threw his glass against the wall and turned his bloodshot eyes to Holt. "Do you even know why you were guarding him at the temple—how you even got that position in the first place?"

Holt became perfectly still under his father's rage.

"Because of me, Holt. I asked the headmaster to trust you with such an assignment."

His eyes widened in surprise.

"Yes, son, it was me. Differe has been hiding Joel, keeping him hidden from all other regions. There are things about his past, his lineage, that all other regions would want . . . to use his power. I believed in you—believed you were strong enough to remain unemotionally involved in guarding him. We needed an insider, a peer rather, to keep an eye on him. You were the perfect candidate due to your ongoing feud, but especially . . . because of Isabelle. I recommended you to the headmaster and Templin Guard. I-I thought that's what you wanted. I thought you wanted to be a Templin, to lead a legion of your own one day . . . was I wrong?"

Holt was dumbfounded. He felt duped and stupid at the same time. "Father, I-I didn't know, but I . . . ." He looked down and shrugged.

"Out with it."

He raised his head with a clenched jaw. "I just don't want to be controlled anymore. I want to be the Templin you mentioned . . . like you, but I want to earn it on my own terms. I want to face Joel on my own terms, not be involved in some political message. I want to fight him, but not when he's beaten and chained. I want a fair fight, man to man. Can you—can you understand that?"

His father quietly sat down behind the desk and grabbed a new glass. He poured himself a drink and ran his fingers through his hair. "How did she convince you—the girl? Come now, I know she lured you into what you did. We Langstons have a terrible weakness around women."

Holt looked away from him to the murdered guard then back into his eyes. "She told me something . . . she said you'd know for sure."

"What?"

"That Isabelle's alive."

His father took a sip from his glass then folded his hands under his chin. "Why do you think I killed that man?"

Holt didn't answer.

"Why do you think I sent a rogue soldier on the mission to kill Isabelle, giving him strict instructions to sabotage the mission? I ordered him to make sure the mission failed. Why, Holt? Why did I do that?"

He couldn't believe his ears. *He saved Isabelle?* He was elated at his misjudgment of the man yet was very aware of the dead officer lying behind him. "Oh, Father, I-I . . . is that true? I'm sorry. Please, is she alive?"

"She's safe."

He did his best to please the man and remain unemotional. "Thank you, Father. Thank you for everything."

His father nodded and took off his Templin cloak. "No more control, Holt. Your own terms. You're one of us now." He held the cloak out to Holt.

The young Langston eyed it for a moment then looked into the face of the man who'd thought him worthy of hiding power, had saved his girl, and just now had killed to keep him safe. Without hesitation he made his choice and took the cloak. He was now a Templin.

CHAPTER 76

J OEL SAW HIMSELF on fire. At first he thought the flames were surrounding him until he got a closer look and discovered they were rising up from his own skin. He searched around for a mirror in the inn's room. He slowly walked toward one and found his face aglow. His hair, clothes . . . everything on him was ablaze but not burning up. Curious, Joel touched the mirror, but nothing happened. He tried again, holding the frame longer this time. He removed his hand and was pleased to see golden embers forming on the wood. He spun around when he saw the Green Cloak from the murder standing behind him in the reflection.

As the two locked onto one another, Joel saw his flames in the young man's eyes. The young man suddenly stripped off his cloak and slung a quiver and arrows from around his back. Joel searched for a weapon, but stopped when the young man extended his own to Joel. He bowed his head low as he knelt before Joel. Joel stared at the objects then back at the Green Cloak. *I think he wants me to touch them.* Joel gestured to him, and the young man nodded without looking up. He touched the weapons longer than he had the mirror, and, just as he had hoped, the weapons were consumed yet did not burn up. The Green Cloak humbly nodded his thanks. Joel watched as the flames from the weapons crept up the man's arms. The fire mesmerized him until the archer nodded to the corner of the room where a sleeping Augustine was reclined in a rocking chair.

Joel smiled as he drew near to her. He felt proud of his flames as he eyed the companion who had come back for him. The light radiating from him shone all over her dark skin as she lay there in a peaceful sleep. He reached out to touch her, but his hand found someone else. Isabelle had emerged from the shadows and now stood between them.

A loud ticking sound forced Joel to open his eyes. His skin was wet with perspiration, and he wondered where he was. *I'm burning up.* He pulled a hand out from under the blankets piled on top of him and quickly thrust them off. Sweat dripped down his face as the loud ticking distracted him again. When he rolled over to hit the clock, he saw Augustine sleeping next to him. *Wait . . . what?* He sat up and found the room was the exact same one from his dream, except the Green Cloak wasn't there. There was someone else, though— someone he was much more delighted to see.

Sebastian grinned and waved at him from the foot of the bed.

Joel sighed in relief. *He looks healthy.* When Sebastian pointed to the bed, Joel motioned for him to climb up.

When he was close enough for Joel to touch, Sebastian stopped. He looked over at Augustine then back at Joel. He seemed to be waiting for something.

Joel leaned back on the pillows propped behind him and shook his head. "Well, you just gonna sit there or what?"

Sebastian cocked his head until Joel opened his arms, and the boy tackled him in a fierce hug.

"Oh, careful!" Joel winced. Pain was coming from everywhere. He looked over his hands and arms. "My whole body aches."

"Shh." Sebastian nodded over to Augustine. "You're really hot too. Might have a fever."

He shrugged. "Where's the shower? A cold one might help."

"Just outside the hall, but you tell Augie. She'll freak out if you're not here when she wakes up. And, you *know* it'll be my fault."

He tousled Sebastian's hair then gently stroked Augustine's arm. When she didn't budge he shook the shoulder closest to him. He felt a bandage underneath her sleeve.

She stirred and pulled the shoulder away from him. "That's my hurt shoulder, Sebastian."

"What happened to you?"

Her eyes flew open. "Oh, Joel! Are you all right? Do you need anything?" She rushed to her feet and stumbled forward in her sleepy stance.

Joel jumped up and caught her in his arms. "What happened to your shoulder?"

"Oh, it's fine. Just a scratch. Sorry, didn't mean to be so clumsy. Thanks for catching me."

He raised his eyebrows at her when she shyly turned away from his gaze. "Positive you're okay? And, I'm pretty sure I should be the one thanking *you.*" She still wouldn't look at him, so he bent down and kissed her cheek. Her face went crimson as he let her go.

"Never mind that. What do you need?"

"I'm hot and hurting. I want to go take a cold shower."

"Good. Maybe you'll feel like eating something when you get out."

"Is Corwin here?"

She shrugged and smiled. "He's around here somewhere."

The shower proved to be just what Joel needed. The cool water invigorated his senses and cooled off his body. After he finished he looked at himself in the bathroom mirror. He was no longer the boy who had escaped from Differe. He rubbed his hand over his half-grown beard and thought it suited him for now. His flesh was still deeply sensitive from his floggings, yet, remarkably, all his bones still seemed intact. *The enemy's use of mental attack was far worse, not to mention more effective.*

"But you overcame it."

Joel smiled at the voice inside his head. *That's right. I did.*

Augustine, Corwin, and Sebastian were sitting around a small table in the room when he returned. He gingerly lowered himself into a chair to join them. The three eyed him curiously as he sat down but continued eating in silence. He was confused by their timidity.

"All right, you saw what I've been up to, so now let's hear about all of you."

Sebastian and Corwin exchanged grins while Augustine peered straight down into her bowl.

Something's bothering her. He wanted to get her alone to find out what it was. Was she too embarrassed to display her feelings in front of the other two? Did she not mean what she'd said in the tunnels about not wanting to be without him? He knew how girls could say one thing and it mean something entirely different. *I shouldn't have kissed her on the cheek. I should've waited to see what she's really thinking.* He told his heart to calm down.

Thankfully, Sebastian and Corwin distracted him as they began recounting their adventures of the past few months. Joel was astounded by the turn of events in Waiz. He'd expected New Waiz to join Differe, but Old Waiz would fight against them? He couldn't believe the older generations were taking such a bold risk. It seemed the Southern and Northern Regions were unwilling to pick a side, even refusing to come to the West End's aid when Differe invaded Facilis. He remained fairly calm as he took in all their news until he discovered Talan Langston had played the part of Differe's diplomat.

He slammed his fist on the table. "Who does Differe think they're fooling? They're not siding with New Waiz—they're infecting it. To control it, take it over. That's why the Templins have been pouring in and camping out on the east side of the river. It was the same way with the West End, and it's happening in the Northern Regions too."

"Well, they're certainly fooling New Waiz, if indeed that's their plan. Men and women hungry for power generally aren't guided by wisdom, so in essence they do become fools." The twinkle in Corwin's eye caught his attention.

"You think Differe has a different plan."

"There's much more to tell you. There's a bigger plan behind all this mess, but we'll get to that later. I want you to rest. What we've just told you is enough information for you to take in tonight. You are still recovering from a tremendous struggle."

CHAPTER 77

JOEL FINISHED HIS last bite, thankful none of them had forced him to share the details of his time in Chrysos just yet. *I do feel exhausted.*

After the meal Corwin took Sebastian to the shower, which finally left Joel and Augustine alone.

"Let's go sit on the balcony."

The sun had already disappeared, but there remained some light. The shadows of dusk blanketed the square below. After people watching for a few minutes Augustine sat down, but Joel remained perched over the railing.

"Where are we?"

"In the Southern Regions."

"How long have I been out?"

"A couple of days."

Joel stared at the night sky. *No sunset for us tonight.* "You're awfully quiet."

He heard her sigh. "Yes, I guess that's a bit unlike me."

"A lot on your mind, then?"

"I suppose."

He finally turned to her. "Want to unload on me?"

447

Augustine looked into his kind face and slowly shook her head. She turned away and blinked back tears. *How can I tell him what I've done? How can I explain I'm to blame . . . for everything? He'll want to take back every kiss. But . . . I have to tell him.* That was part of the deal Augustine had made with herself in going back for him. She had to tell him the truth, because she knew if she didn't Corwin would . . . and, more importantly, because his heart was becoming more involved. Hers was also entangled much more than she wanted to admit. She twisted the ring on her finger, knowing the truth was bound to come out, and she couldn't bare his heart being in jeopardy more than it already was. *He's been through enough. He deserves to know the truth . . . I have to break it off . . . or he will.*

However, she couldn't help but wonder how things would play out if the truth was never told. She was no doubt enjoying his admiration. She couldn't deny her desire for him, but she'd closed her heart to the idea after she left him in the tunnel. He could never forgive her, and, if by some remote chance he did, his love would be pity. She couldn't stand for it.

After hearing Corwin say Joel needed to rest, she wasn't sure she should tell him just yet. *I want to give him one more day . . . or perhaps I want to give myself one more day.* She stood up and wrapped her arm around his. He looked at her in a way that made her heart race, so she laid her head against his arm. *No, it has to be now.* Her eyes closed in anguish.

"Joel," her hands shook as she pulled back from him, "there's something I have to tell you . . . something you deserve to know."

He grinned and reached out for her, but she jerked her hand away and stepped back again. His grin faded as he discerned the seriousness in her eyes. "Augie, it's okay. You can tell me anything."

"It . . . it was me."

"What was you?"

"I'm the reason you were captured." She searched his eyes for a response. "I-I trusted Talan Langston. He was the man I met after I got off the Waiz train. I . . . I . . . he lied to me—told me he was some sort of spy that helped people get to Waiz. Earl and I met with him just like I told you, but we didn't see through him. I guess I was so desperate I believed him." Her voice broke when he hung his head. "Oh, Joel, it was me. Everything that happened . . . if only I had known . . . I'm—I'm so sorry . . . I-I-I—"

He put his hand up to silence her.

"Joel, please! I'm so sorry. I came back to make it right—to tell you the tru—"

"It was you? I lost my rhydid because of you—the person I risked my life for to get it? I just endured utter torment *again* because of you? I . . . I can't believe this. Tell me . . . tell me it's not true, Augie."

A cascade of tears rushed down her cheeks as she struggled to get the words out.

"TELL ME!"

"I-I . . . I, um . . . ."

"Forget it." He rubbed his face in his hands and sighed. "This is so like my life for this to happen."

Terrified to tell him the rest, her stomach churned as she cleared her throat.

His hands slowly peeled off his cheeks, and he searched her face. "No way . . . there's more, isn't there?"

"Maybe we should just wait til tommo—"

"You started it. Just go ahead. Finish it."

She hated the seeing irritation on his face before he hung his head again. She didn't think she could go on, but knew she had no choice now. "I . . . I know you probably hate me now, but this . . . . Well, after I left you in the tunnels I traveled into the Southern Regions. It was where Holt led me and the only way to find a train home. I-I stayed someplace there on my way back to Waiz."

He didn't budge from his hunched over position.

"I stayed at Reagan Manor . . . with your father."

The seconds stretched in silence. When at last he raised his head, her heart pounded. His eyes, cold and empty, gazed right through her.

"Get away from me."

CHAPTER 78

JOEL STUDIED THE silver blade in the moonlight, still reeling from its owner's news. He threw Augustine's rhydid into the trunk of the closest tree. The object sliced through the wood with ease. As far as he was concerned, he hoped to never see her again. He knew he'd have to return the rhydid for Sebastian's sake, but after that—*I'm gone.* He crossed his arms and grimaced at the pain he felt in his body. Doubt crept over him as he wondered if he could make it on his own. He stared up at the stars and let out a long, slow breath. "Why did they even come back for me?"

"A number of reasons."

He scowled, feeling enraged as he heard Corwin come up behind him. "Well, I don't care what your reasons are. I'm done with the three of you."

"If you recall, Sebastian and I haven't *done* anything to you, and we certainly aren't through with you."

Joel sighed in frustration. *He's right too much of the time.* He knew he had no qualms with Corwin and Sebastian, but he couldn't help taking his anger out on the man. "Sorry. I'm . . . AH!" He flung his arms up in the air, still absorbing the shock of Augustine's tale.

"Angry, confused, betrayed, hurt?"

"Among other things." He sat down on the ground and hung his head between his knees.

For nearly an hour Corwin stayed by his side, yet neither said a word. Joel finally broke down. "What do you want? You've got your rhydid."

"Well, let me first give you my reasons for coming to get you."

Joel shook his head. "Always such a politician."

"Well, I need every tactic tonight. First, there are the obvious reasons. What kind of person would I be to leave you to your death after you risked your life for my family? I hope my character indicates that planning a rescue is not so surprising. I also wanted you to know you'd been successful—Augustine was safe with her brother—and your sacrifice wasn't in vain. And, well, I thought you should know the truth about your capture . . . and your father. Augustine picked up a fair amount of information while at the manor."

Joel buried his face in his hands. He was physically and emotionally exhausted. "I can't take anymore. I don't want to know the truth."

"Reconciling with your father is your own business, and I choose not to interfere there."

"Good, because it's not going to happen, and I don't want to know what she found out." He stood up and walked over to the rhydid stuck in the tree. "Does Sebastian even need this? He looks the same as when we left . . . was all that a lie too?"

"Joel! How can you even propose such a thing, after you—you used it to make it rain not once but several times. You even used the lightning to protect you and the Galanneans from the Templins. No, your task wasn't a lie."

He turned back to him and shrugged. "Well, mine's gone. It shattered when the Templins took it in the tunnel. All that's left is the hilt."

"Of course it shattered! It's a protective mechanism—part of the magnificent power placed upon the object. Think of how a rhydid replaced the ones you and Augustine took from the temple—it did that to protect you and deceive the headmaster."

"Well, then why hasn't Augustine's shattered? I clearly stole it."

"Were you going to return it?"

Joel stared back at the object dumbfounded. "Wha-how does it know what I'm going to do?"

"It doesn't, but it somehow knows a person's heart."

Joel scratched his head as Corwin came up next to him. "You gotta be kidding me. And, just how is lightning supposed to help Sebastian?"

A smirk crossed the man's face. "It's not."

"Uh . . . this one doesn't do lightning or something?"

"No, it would—but probably just for you."

Corwin had his full attention now. "Okay. So what would it do for you . . . for Augie?"

"What did Augustine do in Facilis when you were in charge?"

"Managed the hospital—you know all the medical stuff." He stared back at the rhydid and a thought hit him. "Wait . . . I get it. Yeah, the lightning for me and something medical . . . healing for her—for Sebastian."

"The rhydid holds many powers, and I for one think we can tap into all of them, but that takes maturity. For now, it will just utilize your strengths."

"Rain and lightning?"

"Freedom, leadership, protection, hope—the rain and lightning are merely tangible examples of the strengths inside you."

Joel stole a glance at Corwin's rhydid hanging from his waist. "Unbelievable."

"Old Waiz is ready to fight, Joel, but not against who you think. They are ready to fight against the mouthpieces, the Mouth."

Joel backed away and narrowed his eyes. "What are you talking about?"

"Augustine told me about Facilis, how the people followed you. Seems so many relate to you."

He shrugged. "Lot of good it did."

"You haven't heard, Joel. Those citizens are the ones who revolted against Differe during the siege."

"What? Is that true? The people tried to fight like we trained them?"

Corwin nodded. "You identified a need and started a movement. Other places in our world are hearing of the revolt and gaining confidence. The fact that you escaped from the temple and Differe, the most threatening region of late . . . well, you're becoming a legend."

Joel ran his fingers through his hair confused. "What are you saying?"

"I'm saying we've been gathering an army for you to lead—the one Sebastian and I told you about. It's yours. You can take out the Mouth—you can stop what happened to you from happening to someone else."

"Ha, what? You're crazy! Why—why would I do that?" He blew his lips apart, yet couldn't deny that the man's words pulled at something deep inside him.

"Me and the Thaddean Army, we're ready. Even the Watchmen are ready to side with us. We want to go straight for the source. It's beyond a human fight."

The latter words made Joel shudder. "Why would they follow me? You saw how well I did in my last supernatural fight. I don't even have a rhydid anymore."

Corwin shook his head. "It's your story. It brings them hope. And, perhaps they have a little faith too. Besides, you can't forget that circumstances are just what happen to you—they don't say who you are. I believe you've known that for quite some time now, and that's why you really left the temple."

"The people . . . Facilis really revolted?" Joel smiled to himself as the Vicar's face came into view. *He was right. It's time now—time for me to lead.*

Corwin cocked an eyebrow and nodded. "So, there are a few more reasons why we came back for you, but only one more for today."

Joel stuffed his hands into his pockets. "Fine, one more."

"Isabelle's alive."

The blood drained from his face. "She's—she's alive?"

"She broke loose with one of her capturers. He appears to have turned rogue. Seems that may have been Langston's doing."

"Langston!"

"She was last seen jumping off the Waiz train in the Northern Regions."

Joel tried to catch his breath. *She's alive? The Waiz train?* "Corwin, she's coming to find me."

The man nodded. "So, will you meet her?"

Joel felt life surge inside him once more. "Yes, I'll go."

"Good."

He waited for the man to give further instructions, but Corwin simply grinned at him and walked over to pull the rhydid from the tree.

"Corwin, how will I get back unnoticed?"

The man tossed him the sword. "Well, it won't be by train."

A Note from the Author

HAPPY TO HAVE you back, my friends. Getting this into your hands was a doozy for me. The overall process of doing so unearthed a bit of darkness I had embraced myself, which made finishing this book quite a fight. If I'm being completely honest, there were times I thought it might kill me due to mental or physical exhaustion. Oddly enough, my characters became sources of strength as I watched them overcome and finish what they set out to do . . . even when it appeared they might not ever see the rewards of their sacrifice. They reminded me of my power to choose—I am in charge of my attitude, and ultimately the only one who can truly will myself to finish, and finish well. This story has gone through more than a dozen rewrites, two different endings, and multiple beginnings. I do hope it has shone light into your heart and onto your path. I am grateful you have chosen to journey with me in this process. Please feel free to connect with me further through **www.mikelynbolden.com**, *The Waiz Chronicles* Facebook page, Twitter (@mikelynbolden), or Instagram (@mikelynhb).

ACKNOWLEDGMENTS

First to my readers, I cannot thank you enough for reaching out to me. Your kind words, emails, phone calls, texts, IG pictures, Facebook posts, tweeting, reviews—you guys are my writing and editing fuel!!!

To my amazing family and friends, I am truly blessed. Thank you for celebrating the wins and hanging in there during the less than glamorous parts of the last two years. I am your biggest fan having benefited from your love . . . and I know that you are mine.

To the Yunis family, thank you for providing the perfect name for my strong, little Noor!

To Heather Johnson, thank you for joining us in the initial editing process—I learned a lot from you.

To Kate Fountain, Clay Dalton, and David Woodham, thank you for taking the time to read the rough draft and provide us with reader feedback! Your insight was so helpful.

To Jason Sharp, oh how it stung . . . but thank you for being honest and helping produce an amazing manuscript. You are a true friend. I hope Lucy will read it one day!

To Josh Martin, PLEASE tell me you want to do Book Three! Your keen eye was extremely helpful in the editing process. Thank you!

To Chad Gibbs, thank you for reassuring me it was okay that I hyperventilated my first time in Babies 'R Us, and that self-publishing was a piece of cake compared to having a baby.

To Blair Thompson, thank you for coming to the rescue! As always, your work was outstanding and just what I envisioned!

To Lorri and my Solletico Team, thank you for being interested in keeping up with and praying for me regularly. Y'all always sent words of encouragement exactly when I needed them.

To SG2, the Circle, Taco Salad Group, and my Bridge Ladies, thank you for providing much needed outlets where I could rest, laugh, cry, and be loved.

To my roomies, who provided amazing support throughout this process as well as the title for my next series, "Fifty Shades of White," through our ongoing hilarious texting rants. I love you girls!

To the Boldens, McCallisters, Sansoms, and Humphreys, for listening to all the highs and lows of my author/mommy life.

To Ann Payne and Lowry Edge, thank you for loving Izzy and having such a heart of generosity.

To my parents, thank you for providing amazing opportunities of inspiration. Many of the places we've traveled are found in this book.

To Jeff Rutherford, Lyndsay Rutherford, and Marshall Bolden, I can never repay you for the year of late nights you gave to this project . . . unless someone figures out how to bottle sleep. If I could, I would give one of you a golf resort, the other free groceries at Whole Foods for life, and the other a villa in the European city of his choice. Seriously, I'm humbled by your ability to give knowing that none of us may see the full return of our investment in this lifetime.

To Jeff, you are truly one of my favorites on the planet. I appreciate all that you have brought to this project—humor, compassion, and above all, patience.

To McDave, we are both people who love to communicate well and some might say we tend to overdo this at times. As I try to describe what you've meant to me in editing this book, in fact both of my books, words fail me. I just cannot express in words what your valuable and precious time has meant to me. Your critiques and writing suggestions shaped this book into its final form. The power of your voice helped tremendously, and your words will impact many!

To my Izzy, you are my joy bundle! The light in your eyes changes atmospheres. You have brought much needed perspective during this journey. Thank you for being so flexible and patient. I am so happy to be your mommy!

To Marby, you are my rebel leader and rescuer. You always help me see the big picture and encourage me to be myself. You have helped me fight against what culture says is "normal"—to rebel and choose a better path. You have rescued me in my writing with your grammar knowledge and ridiculously large vocabulary. You have also rescued me during this season of life that feels so full it might crush me. I know you don't read these kinds of books, so thanks for giving everything simply because you love me.

To My Light in the Darkness, nothing can outshine you. Thank you for showing me I am worth it. Thank you for believing in me and entrusting me with something so precious to share with the world.

Indifference finds dirt
where freedom unearths
gold.

To be continued . . .

9 780990 999300